Praise for *New York Times* bestseller *The Soldier*

"Burrowes's straightforward, sensual love story is intelligent and tender, rising above the crowd with deft dialogue and delightful characters."

—*Publishers Weekly* starred review

"There is a quiet, yet intense power to Burrowes's simple prose and such depth of feeling that it will be difficult to forget this marvelous story."

—*RT Book Reviews* Top Pick of the Month, 4½ stars

"Burrowes continues her winning streak with a delicious, sensual historical romance capturing the spirit of the time."

—*Booklist*

"Flawless; highly recommended for its exceptional storytelling and its unforgettable characters."

—*Library Journal*

"Enthralling... a breathtaking love story that lingers in the mind and heart."

—*Long and Short Reviews*

"Regency romance at its best... With lots of humor and steamy romance, these books are always a delightful read."

—*Night Owl Romance* Top Pick

Also by Grace Burrowes

The Heir

The Soldier

The Virtuoso

Lady Sophie's Christmas Wish

LADY MAGGIE'S
SECRET SCANDAL

GRACE
BURROWES

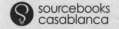

sourcebooks
casablanca

Published by Sourcebooks Casablanca, an imprint of Sourcebooks,
Inc.
P.O. Box 4410, Naperville, Illinois 60567-4410
(630) 961-3900
FAX: (630) 961-2168
www.sourcebooks.com

Printed and bound in the United States of America
QW 10 9 8 7 6 5 4 3 2 1

This book is dedicated to older sisters, and in particular to my oldest sister Gail Cecelia, who is the most tenderhearted, determined, kind, practical, intelligent, lovely person ever to take on impossible tasks and see them through to successful completion. Gaily, you are a gift to all who know you.

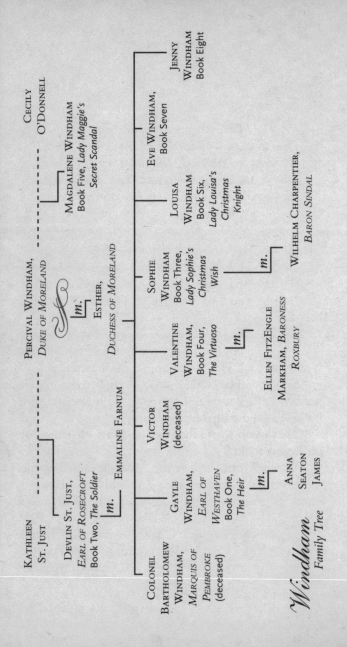

Windham Family Tree

Kathleen St. Just - - - - - Percival Windham, Duke of Moreland — m. — Cecily O'Donnell

Devlin St. Just, Earl of Rosecroft · Book Two, *The Soldier*

Esther, Duchess of Moreland

Emmaline Farnum — m. —

Colonel Bartholomew Windham, Marquis of Pembroke (deceased)

Gayle Windham, Earl of Westhaven Book One, *The Heir*
— m. — Anna Seaton James

Victor Windham (deceased)

Valentine Windham, Book Four, *The Virtuoso*
— m. — Ellen FitzEngle Markham, Baroness Roxbury

Sophie Windham Book Three, *Lady Sophie's Christmas Wish*
— m. — Wilhelm Charpentier, Baron Sindal

Magdalene Windham Book Five, *Lady Maggie's Secret Scandal*

Louisa Windham Book Six, *Lady Louisa's Christmas Knight*

Eve Windham, Book Seven

Jenny Windham Book Eight

One

"THE BLIGHTED, BENIGHTED, BLASTED, PERISHING thing has to be here somewhere." Maggie Windham flopped the bed skirt back down and glared at her wardrobe. "You look in there, Evie, and I'll take the dressing room."

"We've looked in the dressing room," Eve Windham said. "If we don't leave soon, we'll be late for Mama's weekly tea, and Her Grace cannot abide tardiness."

"Except in His Grace," Maggie replied, sitting on her bed. "She'll want to know why we're late and give me one of those oh-Maggie looks."

"They're no worse than her oh-Evie, oh-Jenny, or oh-Louisa looks."

"They're worse, believe me," Maggie said, blowing out a breath. "I am the eldest. I should know better; I should think before I act; I am to set a good example. It's endless."

Eve gave her a smile. "I like the example you set. You do as you please; you come and go as you please; you have your own household and your own funds. You're in charge of your own life."

Maggie did not quite return the smile. "I am a disgrace, but a happy one for the most part. Let's be on our way, and I can turn my rooms upside down when I get home."

Evie took her arm, and as they passed from Maggie's bedroom, they crossed before the full-length mirror.

A study in contrasts, Maggie thought. They were the bookends of the Windham daughters, the eldest and the youngest. No one in his right mind would conclude they had a father in common. Maggie was tall, with flaming red hair and the sturdy proportions of her mother's agrarian Celtic antecedents, while Evie was petite, blonde, and delicate. By happenstance, they both had the green eyes common to every Windham sibling and to Esther, Duchess of Moreland.

"Is this to be a full parade muster?" Maggie asked as she and Evie settled into her town coach.

"A hen party. Our sisters ran out of megrims, sprained ankles, bellyaches, and monthlies, and Mama will be dragging the lot of us off to Almack's directly. Sophie is lucky to be rusticating with her baron."

"I don't envy you Almack's." Maggie did, however, envy Sophie her recently acquired marital bliss. Envied it intensely and silently.

"You had your turn in the ballrooms, Maggie, though how you dodged holy matrimony with both Her Grace and His Grace lining up the Eligibles is beyond me."

"Sheer determination. You refuse the proposals one by one, and honestly, Evie, Papa isn't as anxious to see us wed as Her Grace is. Nobody is good enough for his girls."

"Then Sophie had to go and ruin things by marrying her baron."

Their eyes met, and they broke into giggles. Still, Maggie saw the faint anxiety in Evie's pretty green eyes and knew a moment's gratitude that she herself was so firmly on the shelf. There had been long, fraught years when she'd had to dodge every spotty boy and widowed knight in the realm, and then finally she'd reached the halcyon age of thirty.

By then, even Papa had been willing to concede not defeat—he still occasionally got in his digs—but truce. Maggie had been allowed to set up her own establishment, and the time since had seen significant improvement in her peace of mind.

There were tariffs and tolls, of course. She was expected to show up at Her Grace's weekly teas from time to time. Not every week, not even every other, but often enough. She stood up with her brothers when they deigned to grace the ballrooms, which was thankfully rare of late. She occasionally joined her sisters for a respite at Morelands, the seat of the duchy in Kent.

But mostly, she hid.

They reached the ducal mansion, an imposing edifice set well back from its landscaped square. The place was both family home and the logistical seat of the Duke of Moreland's various parliamentary stratagems. He loved his politics, did His Grace.

And his duchess.

One of his meetings must have been letting out when the hour for Her Grace's tea grew near, because the soaring foyer of the mansion was a beehive of servants, departing gentlemen, and arriving ladies.

Footmen were handing out gloves, hats, and walking sticks to the gentlemen, while taking gloves, bonnets, and wraps from the ladies.

Maggie sidled around to the wall, found a mirror, and unpinned her lace mantilla from her hair. She flipped the lace up and off her shoulders, but it snagged on something.

A tug did nothing to dislodge the lace, though someone behind her let out a muttered curse.

Damn it? Being a lady in company, Maggie decided she'd heard "drat it" and used the mirror to study the situation.

Oh, no.

Of all the men in all the mansions in all of Mayfair, why *him?*

"If you'll hold still," he said, "I'll have us disentangled."

Her beautiful, lacy green shawl had caught on the flower attached to his lapel, a hot pink little damask rose, full of thorns and likely to ruin her mantilla. Maggie half turned, horrified to feel a tug on her hair as she did.

A stray pin came sliding down into her vision, dangling on a fat red curl.

"Gracious." She reached up to extract the pin, but her hand caught in the shawl, now stretched between her and the gentleman's lapel. Another tug, another curl came down.

"Allow me." It wasn't a request. The gentleman's hands were bare and his fingers nimble as he reached up and removed several more pins from Maggie's hair. The entire flaming mass of it listed to the left then slid down over her shoulders in complete disarray.

His dark eyebrows rose, and for one instant, Maggie had the satisfaction of seeing Mr. Benjamin Hazlit at a loss. Then he was handing her several hairpins amid the billows of her mantilla, which were still entangled with the longer skeins of her hair. While Maggie held her mantilla before her, Hazlit got the blasted flower extracted from the lace and held it out to her, as if he'd just plucked it from a bush for her delectation.

"My apologies, my lady. The fault is entirely mine."

And he was laughing at her. The great, dark brute found it amusing that Maggie Windham, illegitimate daughter of the Duke of Moreland, was completely undone before the servants, her sisters, and half her father's cronies from the Lords.

She wanted to smack him.

Maggie instead stepped in closer to Hazlit, took the fragrant little flower, and withdrew the jeweled pin from its stem.

"If you'll just hold still a moment, Mr. Hazlit, I'll have you put to rights in no time." He was tall enough that she had to look up at him—another unforgivable fault, for Maggie liked to look down on men—so she beamed a toothy smile at him when she jabbed the little pin through layers of fabric to prick his arrogant, manly skin.

"Beg pardon," she said, giving his cravat a pat. "The fault is entirely mine."

The humor in his eyes shifted to something not the least funny, though Maggie's spirits were significantly restored.

"Your gloves, sir?" A footman hovered, looking uncertain and very pointedly not noticing Maggie's hair rioting down to her hips. Maggie took the gloves and held them out to Hazlit.

"Can you manage, Mr. Hazlit, or shall I assist you further?" She turned one glove and held it open, as if he were three years old and unable to sort the thing out for himself.

"My thanks." He took the glove and tugged it on, then followed suit with the second.

Except his hand brushed Maggie's while she held out his glove. She didn't think it was intentional, because his expression abruptly shuttered further. He tapped his hat onto his head and was perhaps contemplating a parting bow when Maggie beat him to the exit.

She rose from her curtsy, her hair tumbling forward, and murmured a quiet "Good day," before turning her back on him deliberately. To the casual observer, it wouldn't have been rude.

She hoped Hazlit took it for the slight it was intended to be.

"Oh, Mags." Evie bustled up to her side. "Let's get you upstairs before Mama sees this." She lifted a long, curling hank of hair. "Turn loose of that mantilla before you permanently wrinkle it—and whatever happened to put you in such a state?"

"Not the done thing to stare at a man's daughters under his own roof."

Lucas Denning, Marquis of Deene, kept his voice down, but Benjamin Hazlit heard him nonetheless.

"You're happy enough to be staring," Hazlit said, taking his walking stick from the footman.

Deene glanced around. "Discreetly. Not like I want to leap upon the girl naked. What on earth did you do to that woman? Her hair is quite the most glorious thing I've seen outside a certain brothel in Cairo."

Hazlit felt an abrupt need to plant his fist in Deene's handsome face. "Now who's being rude?"

"We both are." Deene grinned momentarily, turning his severe Nordic features almost boyish. "But Lady Maggie never affords me more than the passing notice due to a family friend, so it matters little. Are you off to your club for a beefsteak?"

"I am for home, and it's a pretty day, so I'll be on foot."

"I could take you up. My tiger is walking my horses as we speak."

"Thanks, but after sitting for two hours and listening to my betters parse the state of the realm, I can use some fresh air."

They parted, Hazlit trailing after the guests who hadn't been detained by a red-haired Amazon bent on mischief.

Except, to be fair, the whole little business had started without anybody intending anything, and it should have ended that way. Lady Maggie hadn't appreciated his nonsense with the flower, so she'd stabbed him with his own pin.

She'd done him a favor, in truth, because his wits had gone begging at the sight of all that silky, warm hair tumbling around her shoulders. He'd caught a whiff of her fragrance, a clean, bracing scent laced with cinnamon, and he'd tangled his fingers in a few long, silky strands of her hair. The feel of it sliding over his skin had momentarily shut down his reasoning powers, something the lady must have sensed.

He didn't often give offense to a lady, but there was something about Moreland's by-blow that threw him off stride and brought out the ungallant side of his nature. They'd met only a handful of times, for Hazlit generally avoided the ballrooms and soirees and Venetian breakfasts. His half brother had recently become the first man to marry into the present generation of Windham daughters, making it even more imperative that Hazlit keep his distance.

Socially, he had to keep a hand in, mostly for business purposes, but nobody was glad to see him arrive at their polite functions, and everybody was relieved to see him leave. The parliamentary matters were little better. On behalf of the Earl of Hazelton, for whom he ostensibly worked, he attended meetings such as Moreland's earlier strategy session. Moreland and a few of the senior titles knew better, but they kept their mouths shut.

Miss Windham's mouth had been open. For just an instant, her jaw had dropped, presumably at the heat in Hazlit's gaze. That was not well done of him. She was a lady, for all her unfortunate origins, and he was a gentleman.

Most of the time.

He made his way to his town house in less than a half hour, which really wasn't long enough to get the mental stench of the duke's meeting out of his mind. Moreland was a staunch Tory, though he had sympathy for the yeoman and could be surprisingly effective garnering votes from the moderates on even the most divisive issues.

Still, Moreland's meetings went on forever and all too often degenerated into grumbling and finger-pointing.

Hazlit handed his hat, walking stick, and gloves to his butler, glanced at the longcase clock in his foyer, and headed for his library. There was still time to plough through several hours' worth of correspondence and reports prior to the evening's obligations.

Before he sat at his desk, though, Hazlit scanned his shelves until he came across a volume of Wordsworth. He unfastened the little rose from his lapel and tucked it carefully between the pages of the book, then forced himself to get down to work.

～

"Valentine!" Maggie flew across her bedroom, throwing her arms around the tall, dark-haired man who'd appeared unannounced in her chambers. "Oh, I have missed you so, you scamp. You scoundrel! When did you get back to Town, and is Ellen with you?"

He hugged her tightly, a good solid hug as only a brother who'd been rusticating with his new wife since Christmas could deliver to his sister, and kept an arm around Maggie's shoulders as he walked her to a window seat.

"Ellen accepted my plea for her to eschew travel," Valentine said. "She gave me a letter for you." Val passed her a single folded piece of paper.

"Ellen is well?" Maggie asked, some of her joy dimming as she glanced at the pretty hand on Ellen's note. Ellen and Val had been married only a short time, and already, they were in anticipation of a joyful event. She was happy for them, truly she was. Also envious.

"Ellen is quite well, though my own nerves are sorely tried to think of her increasing. But, Mags"—he glanced around at the upheaval in her sitting room—"have I come to Town only to find my sister taking fits?"

If Maggie Windham loved any men, it was the men of her family—her father and brothers, Uncle Tony, and her cousins. They were the best of fellows, but they fretted endlessly and called it doting on her, her sisters, and the duchess.

"I've lost track of a favorite frippery. I got a little carried away searching for it."

"I'll buy you another. I'm back in Town to do rehearsals with the Philharmonic Society but expect I've already been spotted by Her Grace's spies. I might as well take you shopping before I face the maternal interrogation."

"You don't have to stay at the mansion. You could stay at Gayle's place, since he and Anna have the room."

"He said as much." Val rose and began to wander the room, putting things to rights. He was sinfully handsome, with emerald green eyes, sable hair just a tad too long, and hands that could conjure from any kind of keyboard the sweetest music ever played.

But he had the Windham gift for fretting over family, probably amplified by impending fatherhood.

"You are not my lady's maid, Val." Maggie rose to straighten the pillows her searching had thrown into disorder.

"I'm your darling baby brother," he replied,

holding up a dancing slipper with little roses embroidered on it. "Lovely, but not very well used. Are you
still impersonating a recluse, Mags?"

"I go out," she said, folding an afghan over her
fainting couch. "Her Grace will not permit me the
privacy I'd choose, were I allowed."

"Neither will I." Val held up another slipper. "I'm
attending the Winterthurs' ball tonight. Say you'll
come with me to be my protection. If I'd known how
sincerely the merry widows considered married men
fair game, I'd likely have declined tonight's invitation."

"You'd best call on your mother before you show
your face in public," Maggie warned. "She could
hardly sip her tea today, so anxious was she to interrogate you in person about your wife's well-being."

"She's your mother, too." Val began draping silk
stockings over the open lid of a cedar chest.

"She is not my mother. Valentine, those are
my unmentionables."

He shrugged. "I like unmentionables. I like pretty
things and pretty ladies. Come dancing with me
tonight, Mags. I won't go without you."

"Very well, but you come by for me after you've
made your bow at the mansion."

"Fair enough." He smiled at her, wrapping a
stocking around his neck and holding it up like a
noose. "If I tell Her Grace you're to come out social-
izing with me, she'll hardly let me finish my tea."

"Stop disrespecting your sister's personal effects."
She snatched the stocking from around his silly neck.
"And how are you, really? You look tired."

"I'm working on a new composition, and it rather

takes over my schedule. Ellen is very understanding, perhaps too much so." As he spoke, he picked up a little music box from Maggie's vanity.

"You gave me that," she said, watching those graceful hands of his lift the lid. "You're going to leave here without playing for me, aren't you?"

"You've heard me play probably more than any other single person on the face of the earth. Just hum a few bars of Beethoven; you'll hardly know it isn't me."

"One doesn't hum Beethoven, for pity's sake." She cocked her head to study him, realizing that in some way, her baby brother had grown up, grown more mature for taking a wife. "Ellen is truly well?"

"She assures you of as much in her letter." Val put the music box down, his signature smile in place. "I got a letter from Dev before I left Bel Canto." He passed Maggie a slim epistle that bore their oldest brother's slashing hand. "He seems to be thriving with his womenfolk."

"Then lucky Devlin."

"But you miss him, don't you?"

"Of course I miss him." Maggie plopped down on the bed, both appreciating and resenting Val's percep- tivity. "We're close in age, and we share…"

"Bastardy." Val crossed the room to sit beside her, taking her left hand in his right. "You've both been legitimated, you're adopted, you're accepted every- where, and yet this haunts you."

"It's different for a woman, Val. I can't buy my colors and guarantee my standing in the world by riding off to whack at Frenchmen. Devlin is a perishing earl."

"He's still our brother." Val tucked a lock of hair

behind Maggie's ear. "And he specifically challenged me to look in on you and get your nose out of your infernal books. Spring is coming, Mags, and it's time to dance."

It sounded not like a lighthearted invitation but rather like a lecture.

Gracious.

She got to her feet. "Shoo. You have a call to pay on your mama, and she won't want to let you out of her sight."

"I'll come by at eight, but let's take your coach," he said, rising as well. "Read Dev's letter. I'm sure he'll expect a prompt reply."

"I'll read it, and I will see you at eight, but I don't intend to stay out all night, Val."

"Nor do I."

He was gone, leaving behind the peculiar sinking of spirit Maggie felt each time a member of her ducal family left her here, alone in her own quarters, just as she'd spent years begging and pleading for them to do.

❧

"Good evening, Mr. Hazlit."

The Winterthurs' butler greeted him, though not in quite the stentorian tones the man might have used for the titled guests. It was the same in the receiving line. Grudging, hesitant, but polite tolerance from those who knew not what to make of the Hon. Benjamin Hazlit.

He preferred it that way, and it was better for business. He didn't pause at the top of the grand staircase when a herald all but muttered his name, but made his way quietly into the crowd milling under the enormous chandeliers.

"Hazlit." Lucas Denning gave him a nod and a grim smile. "I'd hoped the dancing would have started by now."

"I hear the orchestra tuning up, but the first sets always take a while to form. What social cataclysm has wrested you from your club?"

Deene ran a finger around his starched collar and glanced about at the ladies in their finery. "Another lecture from my mother about duty to the succession. One might ask what social cataclysm has provoked *your* attendance. The hostesses never know whether it's a coup when you show up or a reason to fret."

Hazlit took a half step into the shadows under the minstrel's gallery and visually assessed his companion. "We aren't all golden gods such as yourself. Given the title, it truly is a wonder you aren't married."

Deene shuddered, and Hazlit had the impression it wasn't entirely feigned. "Don't say that word. I'm too young to be leg-shackled."

"It's the debutantes who are too young. We marry them off before they've put away their dolls."

"Think that way, and you'll soon be the one married off."

They fell silent as a footman approached, offering champagne from a carefully balanced tray. Deene tossed back his wine then slunk off to the card room, no doubt intent on avoiding the matchmakers.

It was tempting to do likewise, but the evening was young, which meant nobody would be sufficiently inebriated to let slip the kind of information Hazlit came seeking. He made for the refreshment table and helped himself to a second flute of champagne, from which he drank nothing.

Wallflowers and companions were a source of intelligence that often went unnoticed, so Hazlit scanned the ladies seated among the potted ferns and mentally started filling out dance cards.

Abigail Norcross's companion for starters.

Then the companion of Lord Norcross's current discreet interest.

Perhaps Norcross's widowed sister.

That would likely bring him up to the supper waltz, and since there was no telling who might make a late appearance, he left his evening open thereafter.

❧

"Helene, how nice to see you." Maggie gave her friend's hand a squeeze. "Budge over so I can malinger among the ferns with you."

Helene obligingly scooted over. "I saw you dancing with Lord Val. Brave of him to show his face without his new wife."

"He *is* brave." Braver than Maggie, in any event. She settled her skirts around her as she took the half of the padded bench Helene Norcross Anders made available to her. "Growing up the youngest of five brothers, Val is both cannier and more determined than some of his elders. Now, who has made a cake of themselves, and which gentlemen are on the prowl?"

"You aren't a widow yourself, Maggie, to be taking such an approach to an evening of dancing."

"I'm not dancing." Maggie held up a slippered foot

and wiggled her toes. "And you're not spilling. Come, Helene, I'm stuck here until after supper. You might as well entertain me."

"The debutantes are all atwitter because Deene's here, and word is he's looking for a wife."

"I like Deene," Maggie said. "He doesn't dissemble with a lot of flummery and false smiles."

"One hears he's particularly friendly with the fashionable impure," Helene said. "Were I them, I'd be snuggling up to Deene before many of his peers. There he goes now, and God help the twit on his arm. She looks like she went poaching for hares and got a boar in her gun sights."

"Naughty, Helene." Maggie hid her smile by pretending to search in her reticule.

"The truth often is."

They chatted away for the balance of the first set. Helene was a pretty, well-to-do widow, and a few of the more determined fortune hunters tried to get her to stand up. Maggie watched her deftly turn them aside with polite excuses, but Helene adopted a different tactic when Benjamin Hazlit approached.

And oh, didn't he look superb in his evening finery? Against his dark complexion and dark hair, his linen gleamed in the candlelight, and the gold of his stickpin and cuff links winked in coy contrast to his black evening coat. He was as well tricked out as any of the titles in the room, and he had the height and bearing to make evening attire truly magnificent.

No rose, though. On his lapel was a bright red carnation. Maggie caught a whiff of the scent when he bowed over her hand.

The hand he held just a moment too long, the idiot.

"I was hoping Lady Anders might do me the honor of the supper waltz," Hazlit said. The smile he aimed at Helene dazzled, for all it didn't reach his eyes.

"I promised this set to my brother," Lady Helene replied, her show of regret equally superficial. "Perhaps you'd lead Miss Windham out in my stead? She's been sitting here this age, good enough to keep a widow company amid all this gaiety."

Maggie glanced at her friend but saw only devilment in Helene's eyes.

"Lady Magdalene?" Hazlit held out a gloved hand. "May I have this dance?"

The smile dimmed on his handsome face, and his gaze held hers. As much to get away from his inspection as anything, Maggie put her hand in his and rose. "I would be honored."

"Lady Helene, my thanks," he said, holding up his left hand for Maggie to place her fingers over his knuckles.

And it would be a blasted waltz.

"You do not look honored," he said, leading her to a position on the floor. "You look like you're plotting the end of an association with Lady Anders."

"Helene has a peculiar sense of humor, but she knows I will retaliate at some point. I'll make her dance with His Grace or perhaps with Deene."

"That would set tongues wagging." He held out his left hand for Maggie to place her right in it. When she hesitated, he put her left hand on his shoulder, and took her right in his.

"Really, Lady Magdalene, am I so offensive as

all that? Your parents allow me under their roof, and your sister was happy enough to marry my half brother." His hand at her waist was warm, even through her gown and stays.

"You enjoy being difficult," Maggie said as the orchestra began the introduction. "It isn't becoming in a grown man. I'd take offense but I suspect you're like this with most everybody."

"I can be charming."

"When it suits your purpose," she said as the music began. "That isn't charm, Mr. Hazlit. That is guile."

His rejoinder was to dance her around the room, holding her a little more closely than convention allowed, a little more firmly.

She liked it.

She was a good-sized female, and there were few enough partners with the height and presence to lead her on the dance floor. Maggie didn't lead, though it was tempting with the more timid men, but she had to be careful she didn't turn too exuberantly, lean too much, step too far. Partners lacking in assurance could lose their grip on her, stumble, or tangle their feet with hers.

Not Hazlit. He danced well, maybe even better than her brother Val, whom she would have said was her favorite partner.

Before. Before this obnoxious man floated her around the ballroom in his strong arms, his legs moving with hers so smoothly Maggie never once had to look down. It was... disconcerting, to be handled with such confidence and to like it so well.

"Now I know how to still your sharp tongue." He

spoke right into her ear, his cheek almost against her temple. If he moved any closer, they'd become objects of talk. "All I have to do is stand up with you, and your temper falls silent."

"I don't generally dance."

"I know, though I can't fathom why. You move like a sylph."

"Are you teasing me?"

"I am not." He pulled back to study her by the candlelight. "I've partnered many women, and you are an accomplished dancer."

She relaxed a little at his words, because Hazlit might be a wretch, but he was an honest wretch. He'd tell her to her face when he was making fun of her.

"I want you to promise me something," Maggie said. He spun her under his arm and brought her back to waltz position. Perhaps it was her imagination, but he seemed to be holding her just a bit closer.

"I don't make promises lightly, my lady," he said, his expression becoming severe. "Just because I like to dance with you doesn't mean you can trespass on my good nature."

"I wasn't aware you had a good nature. I want you to promise me you won't be spying on any of my family members ever again."

Silence stretched between them while the music played on, and her partner never missed a step.

❧

Benjamin Hazlit was a gentleman when anybody was looking. He did not labor for his living, did not get his hands dirty, did not toil in the creation of something—pots, barrels, corn, ale—such that he'd be denied the status of a gentleman. But because of what he did when others *weren't* looking, weren't watching closely, he was suspect in the eyes of Polite Society.

It would soon be impossible to pursue his livelihood, so interested had his neighbors become in his doings.

"You're bold," he said to his dancing partner, emphasizing his words by holding her a little too closely on a tight turn. "I'll grant you that."

"Not as bold as you," she said, twirling gracefully. "You sneak and snoop and lurk in gardens until nobody has any privacy."

"If I lurk in gardens, I do so to flirt and steal kisses, the same as any other callow swain."

She snorted her disbelief, and Hazlit decided his point was better made in private. As they neared the French doors, he danced her off the floor and out onto the flagstone terrace.

"Mr. Hazlit." She drew back, or tried to. "Whatever are you about?"

"You brought up a subject best aired privately. No doubt you assumed the dance floor was a place where you could upbraid me with impunity. Think again, Lady Magdalene."

"I don't use the title."

The words were shot out of a cannon armed with dignity, but Hazlit heard a little of the hurt also propelling them along.

"Their Graces adopted you. I know that much, since your father thinks my confidence can be trusted."

She glanced up at him sharply in the near darkness. "Adopted perhaps, but *I do not use the title.*"

Her motivations were a little mystery, and Hazlit enjoyed mysteries far more than he should, though unraveling Maggie Windham's motivations wasn't what brought them out into the chilly night air.

"Miss Windham, then." He frowned down at her as she rubbed her hands over her arms. "About my investigations."

"Your snooping."

He draped his evening coat around her shoulders and had the satisfaction of seeing he'd rattled her composure. A notice to the *Times* was in order for that coup. "May I remind you, your family retained me to research the origins of your brother's house-keeper—the very lady now married to him."

"Gayle and Anna's situation was made more perilous by your prying. I will not have it, do you understand me?" She paced away from the house, probably not even realizing she was heading for deeper shadows.

Hazlit fell in step beside her, more than comfortable with poorly lit spaces. "So you will deprive me of my living and deprive your titled peers of the useful services I perform?"

"You brought Lucille Ramboullet back to her papa after she tried to elope. She's now married to Alfred Huxtable, a man twice her age."

Hazlit tucked her hand into the crook of his elbow, as if they were merely chatting, not… bickering. "Which puts the doddering Lord Huxtable at about five-and-thirty years old. The girl ran off with a scoundrel who has pockets to let and was after her money. She's seventeen, Miss Windham, without a brain in her pretty head. Do you claim her judgment on the matter should have carried the day?"

"She ran for reasons. Her circumstances are instructive of the mischief your so-called investigating creates."

"We are not going to agree on this," he said, pausing and frowning. Magdalene Windham was notably retiring, firmly on the shelf—which was a waste of glorious hair, if nothing else—but in her castigation of him, Hazlit detected a genuine note of outrage.

Alarm.

She had secrets. He realized this between one heartbeat and the next, and knew not a little temptation to ferret out those secrets. He did sometimes go secret-hunting without a client's money to show for it. It kept his senses sharp.

"I do not lurk in gardens."

She turned to look over the grounds. "You're lurking in one now."

The moon was coming up, not quite full but spreading illumination as it rose from the horizon.

"I am being chastised for earning my coin providing a needed skill. Come. If we linger near a torch, we'll be seen having our disagreement, and neither one of us wants that."

She took his suggestion, as he knew she would. Magdalene Windham presented at least the appearance of propriety, though he could guess all too easily what kinds of secrets she was hiding. With hair like that…

"Shall we sit?" he asked when they'd gone far enough from the terrace to have privacy. "You're less likely to raise your voice if we're not on our feet."

"I'm less likely to slap you," she rejoined, though

there was little heat in her voice. "You think I'll start begging, but I've done some watching and listening of my own, Mr. Hazlit."

"You're entitled to listen at keyholes, while I am not?" He purposely sat right beside her, body to body, wanting to disconcert her.

Or perhaps keep her warm, or do both.

"I do not listen at keyholes. I listen to my family's table conversation. Just the other night, Her Grace asked how it is that of all the titled lords in Parliament, only the Earl of Hazelton sends a factor to attend confidential meetings. Of all the earls in the land, only Hazelton manages to vote his seat occasionally, but nobody can describe the man's appearance in any detail. His Grace gave her a look and asked for more potatoes. Papa abhors potatoes. He says they're peasant fare but permits them on the table because Evie loves them."

Damnation.

"Hazelton is reclusive," Hazlit said, but a distraction was in order. He tucked a lock of her hair, her warm, glorious, silky hair, over her ear.

"Hands to yourself, Mr. Hazlit. I have brothers, and I can protect myself if need be."

"How would you protect yourself? I'm at least half a foot taller and probably six stone heavier."

"You're a man." She hugged his coat closer. "You have at least one other set of vulnerabilities besides your arrogance and your pride."

"Nasty, Miss Windham." Wonderfully nasty.

She gave him a disparaging glance. "Do you think it's easy being Moreland's bastard?" She turned her face to the rising moon. "There were two schools of thought among the so-called gentlemen. The first believed my unfortunate origins meant my morals would be as corrupt as my mother's—His Grace being completely without blame—and I was fair game."

They would, Hazlit silently conceded. Most men would, that is. They would *hope* she was fair game.

"The second group thought I ought to be grateful for the hand of any cit or baronet's son who offered for me. Thank God for Papa's stickling, or I would have had eight offers my first season."

And now they were on tricky ground indeed.

"Do you still have to fend off these offers, my lady? One hesitates to point out that persistent suitors might be offering from genuine regard."

"Don't think to turn up decent on me now, Mr. Hazlit. I am past thirty, on the shelf, and that is where I shall remain. But we wander from the stated reason for our discussion. You will not spy on my family."

He had a choice. He could offer some vaguely unpleasant rejoinder, because it sat ill with him to ever let anybody have the upper hand, and he enjoyed sparring with her a little too much. He could keep her out here until propriety demanded her return to the ballroom, leaving their discussion unresolved.

Or he could be honest.

"Miss Windham, when I am hired by a party, I do not turn around and gather information on that party without their permission. If I came across something unflattering to the Windham family, I would be honor bound to keep it to myself, lest it reflect poorly on a client."

"But would you tell Her Grace? His Grace?"

This mattered to her, confirming Hazlit's suspicion some lucky and discreet fellow had the regular pleasure of seeing all that hair tumbling down Magdalene Windham's naked back.

"I would not tell them unless I thought the information posed a threat to their physical health or well-being."

She wasn't going to push for more. He saw that in the way she worried her full lower lip, in the frown that had little creases forming between her brows.

"Papa had a heart seizure little more than a year ago."

"Right. Percy Windham, though he reportedly spent two weeks at Melton during hunting season, is on the brink of death."

"Don't be callous. He's Moreland to the world, but to us, he's our papa."

"He's also a tough old boot, Miss Windham. He has years left in him."

She raised her gaze to his, searching his expression.

He did not peer too closely into those troubled eyes. "We need to take this interesting discussion back inside, though I'll teach you a trick if you like."

"I most assuredly do not like."

"That's my girl." He lifted his jacket from around her shoulders and slipped into it. "When we go through the doors, don't sidle along the wall, looking like you've just been stealing kisses in the garden."

"You are fixated on kisses and gardens."

"Walk in the door like a royal princess," he said, buttoning his coat. "And don't go but a few steps into the room before you stop and engage me in conversation."

"Why would I want to do that?"

"So you are not seen coming or going. You are seen standing idly about, the same as a hundred other guests, perhaps nearer the door to get some air, but certainly not skulking around with something to hide."

She didn't look happy, but she nodded.

And shivered.

"Come." He took her hand, wishing they weren't wearing gloves so he might at least offer her fingers a little warmth. She followed his instructions to the letter, stopping just six steps inside the French doors and turning a winsome smile at him.

"The waltz was delightful. You really must allow more ladies the pleasure, Mr. Hazlit."

"Would that more ladies had your grace on the dance floor."

They batted the conversational shuttlecock back and forth a little more before tacitly agreeing neither wanted to endure the other's company at supper. The lady swanned off ostensibly to find her brother, and Hazlit was left to pursue the matter of Abigail Norcross's suspected infidelity.

And as he danced and flirted and chatted up the wallflowers, he wondered what sort of mother would name her by-blow Magdalene. The biblical connotations were not kind. Not kind at all.

❧

"What has you in a swivet?" Evie flounced back against the squabs of her sister's town coach and organized her skirts.

"Nothing." Maggie glanced out the window at the chilly darkness and to the bright façade of the

Winterthur mansion beyond. With every lamp and torch lit, the white marble looked like a ghoulish, openmouthed face, staring at her.

She dropped the curtain and tried to focus her thoughts. "I'm not in a swivet. I still haven't found my reticule."

"It will turn up. I saw you dancing tonight, Maggie dearest, and with the delectable Mr. Hazlit."

"Sometimes, baby sister, your powers of observation border on rudeness."

"It goes with never getting any attention. Val and I have discussed this, each being a youngest. Tagging along is our lot in life, or it was. Don't you think Hazlit is handsome?"

"I suppose."

She should have said yes, for that would have put Evie off the scent. Hazlit was handsome, just not in a typically blond, blue-eyed English way. His looks were wilder than that. More compelling.

"I took my turn dancing with Deene." Evie sighed and sat back. "I rather pity him having to face all the debutantes, and he's not a bad dancing partner."

"Don't be bruiting that about, or Papa will be talking terms. He's a marquis, Evie, and a friend of the family. He'd do."

"He would not do in the least, but he's a marvelous dancer. Jenny says his conversation is amusing."

"His flirting, you mean."

Evie's dreamy smile dimmed. "Mags, when did you become so ungracious toward all save your family? Or are you going to chastise Valentine for tarrying with his friends tonight?"

"I'm just tired." She did not say she was increasingly worried about her reticule.

"Dancing will do that." Evie sat up, and Maggie knew her inquisition wasn't quite over. "You and Mr. Hazlit make a gorgeous couple."

"Nothing I do constitutes a gorgeous anything, Eve Windham. You will cease that talk immediately."

"You sound just like Mama in a taking with one of the boys," Evie said, smiling widely. "You should have seen yourself, Mags. Your eyes sparkled when he held you in his arms."

"Evie!" Though Maggie had to smile. In some ways, Evie was still their baby girl, allowed to hold on to the innocence of childhood well past her come out.

"They did. Mama had already gone on to Almack's with the others, but Val and I saw you."

"I wanted to assure myself the man wasn't up to his spying. Not on us, anyway."

"Mags, he wouldn't be spying at a ball."

"Yes, Evie, he would."

And that was something else she'd be talking to Helene Anders about in the morning.

❧

Hazlit slowed his pace as he made his way home, forcing himself to calm down. He'd made a few more passes among the Winterthurs' guests, had gleaned what information he could, then taken himself off before the dancing had resumed after supper.

Spying, indeed. Spying was for sneaks and voyeurs, not for belted earls.

The hypocrisy of that—his holding a title but

hiding it—slowed his steps even further. He didn't hide his title, exactly, he just didn't trade on it.

He was still trying to sort out his temper when he took a snifter of brandy up to his chambers. He managed without his valet, undressing himself down to his skin, hanging his evening attire on the wardrobe door, then finding his favorite silk dressing gown. The evening was chilly, but his chambers were warm in anticipation of his arrival.

Out of habit, he took his drink to the desk near the blazing hearth in his private sitting room.

What had he seen?

He began to record the evening's harvest of information and concluded he could narrow down the possible paramours for Lady Abigail Norcross to two. Lord Norcross had assured Hazlit he wasn't going to use the information to bring adultery grounds against his wife in a divorcement proceeding.

But he was going to threaten, Hazlit knew. He was going to stomp about, bellow, and strut, when the man himself was no scion of fidelity.

But women could not sue for adultery, as a man's seed was his to spend where he pleased. A wife's womb belonged to her spouse, though, just like the rest of her. Norcross had his heir and two spares; all he wanted was the freedom to live apart from his wife on some sort of terms. The lady was loathe to give up her place at his side but equally given to finding her consolation outside the marriage bed.

It shouldn't matter, of course, since her by-blows were unlikely to inherit, but to Lord Norcross, it did.

The dismal topic brought him back to the matter of Miss Magdalene Windham, a ducal by-blow raised with Moreland's legitimate brood.

Without conscious volition, Hazlit began to sketch her. She had magnificent eyes to go with that hair, and a rather strong nose. The nose suited her, as did the defined jaw and chin. As his pen moved over the paper, he watched the image taking form on the page.

Magdalene Windham was beautiful.

Not in the pale, mousey English mold, but in an earthier, more dramatic way. Her brows and lashes were darker than her hair, and having held her in his arms he could attest to a few freckles across her nose and on her shoulders. Just a few.

They made a man want to kiss...

He tossed the pen down, for he'd drawn the woman not in her ballroom attire but as he'd seen her previously, with her hair tumbling down, her eyes alit with mischief as she prepared to stab him with his lapel pin.

A soft tap on the door interrupted his musings.

"Come in."

"Make way," his visitor said. "It's bloody bleeding cold out for being almost spring, and a man could use a medicinal tot."

"Here." Hazlit passed his untouched drink to his guest. "Shall I ring for food?"

"Please." Archer Portmaine lowered his long bones to the settee facing the fire. "Busy night."

"A fruitful night?" Hazlit gave three tugs on the bellpull in short succession, the signal for a late tray.

"Don't know." Portmaine ran a hand through blond curls, no doubt knowing he was as attractive disheveled as he was dressed to the nines. It was one of the reasons Hazlit was in business with his handsome cousin.

"Lady Abby's coach departed at the close of the dinner hour," Portmaine said. "With her in it. She traveled precisely four blocks before her conveyance stopped and she climbed into Hamway's vehicle. Scurried into it, more like."

"Did you positively identify her?"

"Yes, as she got in at the Winterthurs'. The footmen carried torches so the ladies could watch their step getting into the carriages."

"And Hamway was stupid enough to leave his crest exposed?" Hazlit frowned, because answers this easy were suspect on general principle.

"Later in the evening there was cloud cover over the moon, Benjamin." Portmaine leaned his head back and closed his eyes.

"Then how did you determine it was his?"

"I was riding back with the footman on the boot," he said, "pretending I'd gotten off Lady Norcross's vehicle. I saw the crest for myself by the occasional street lamp."

"Did anybody see your face?"

Portmaine lifted his head and opened his eyes to glare at Hazlit. "I know my job, and you haven't doubted me like this for at least the past two years. I was in disguise, per procedure."

Hazlit frowned, because Archer Portmaine was as good at his job as he was good-looking. The man's instincts were infallible and tonight's job completely routine.

"Last week, she got into Lord Doolish's conveyance in the same manner," Hazlit said.

Portmaine blew out a breath. "You want me to swive her? She apparently likes variety, and she's a pretty little thing. Not her fault if her husband is smitten elsewhere."

Hazlit turned a stern eye on his associate. "There are lines we do not cross, Archer."

"You have lost all sense of fun." Portmaine took a sip of his drink. "It's fortunate you still serve decent brandy, or I'd despair of you entirely."

"You will not get under the lady's skirts now, and you will not offer her consolation when her husband banishes her to their country house."

"Speaking of skirts." Portmaine's eyes began to dance. "I saw you turning down the room with Maggie Windham. Excellent choice, old man. How'd you get her to stand up with you?"

"She was inveigled onto the dance floor by a friend. How is it you know her?" *Much less know her as Maggie?*

"I knew her younger brother in Rome, and we've kept in touch," Portmaine said. "Man can do anything with the keyboard. He's introduced me to his siblings as we've bumped into them. There's an entire gaggle of pretty sisters in addition to the one your half brother married."

"Is this like the old king's problem with his princesses; no one is good enough for his womenfolk?"

"Wouldn't know"—Portmaine got up to answer the tap on the door—"not having made His Majesty's acquaintance." He brought a tray to the desk and pulled up a chair before settling in with his meal. "Lord Val says Maggie's the most retiring of his sisters. She's had to be, given her antecedents. His Grace had her and the other one, the soldier, brought up under his own roof, though. By God, we aren't paying the kitchen enough. This is delicious soup and piping hot."

He slurped delicately, as if to underscore the point.

It was tempting, very, very tempting, to gently pry details from Portmaine. Here in their home, brandy warming his gut, Portmaine would prattle on the same as any other man on familiar turf.

But there were lines Benjamin Hazlit wouldn't cross.

Though it would just be gossip, after all. They gossiped with each other, because really, there wasn't anybody else with whom they could share all the society effluvia they came across in their work.

"So what else had Lord Val to say about his steadiest sister?"

∽

Maggie's head footman rapped on the open door of the breakfast parlor.

"Lord Valentine to see you, madam."

"Thank you, Hobbs," Val said, sauntering in still sporting his evening attire. "But since when do we announce family?"

"Since you've gone for a husband," Maggie said, rising to kiss his cheek. "And your arrival twice in twenty-four hours has to be worth noting. Have some breakfast."

"Don't mind if I do."

"Were you up all night playing?"

He filled a plate at the sideboard, while Maggie noted the signs of fatigue about his eyes. Val had been a gorgeous youth, sensuous, dreamy, and probably more sexually attractive than he knew. Having been parted from her for months though, Maggie saw him with new eyes, realizing he was making the transition from handsome young man to breathtaking maturity. She'd missed him and missed his music, too.

"I played some," he said, taking a seat at her right hand. "I'm bunking in with Viscount Fairly, and I wanted you to have my direction. When was the last time your Broadwood was tuned?" He passed her a calling card with an address on the back. One of the better addresses, actually.

"You sent your fellows over at the first of the year. You always do if you aren't here to see to it yourself."

"Mags, are you happy?" He tucked into his eggs as if he hadn't just asked a very personal, unusual question.

"What makes you ask?"

He looked up from his eggs, green eyes troubled. "That isn't a yes."

"You've been up all night, Valentine. Were you perhaps imbibing for much of the evening?"

"Right." He smiled at her. "I'm knee-crawling drunk and in need of a good old-fashioned scolding. If you're not happy, what would it take to make you happy?"

There was something behind his smile, something Maggie suspected a woman would call concern and a man wouldn't deign to put a label on even under threat of torture.

"It's just that until I married Ellen, there was something missing—a large something. Still, I wasn't unhappy. You're not unhappy, either, unless I miss my guess."

Not unhappy. He was insightful, her baby brother. Inconveniently so.

"I have my charities," she said, rising with the need to put some distance between them. A few beats of silence went by while Maggie stared out the window at her back gardens and Val said nothing.

Then, "You danced with Hazlit."

"Gracious God." Maggie turned and braced her hips on the windowsill. "I danced with Lord Fanshaw and Dudley Parrington, too. What of it?"

"The last two are His Grace's cronies of long standing, and you danced a waltz with Hazlit. I can't recall when you've waltzed with anybody but me or Dev or Gayle."

Or Bart or Victor, their two deceased brothers.

"I waltz with His Grace."

"At your come out, maybe, fifteen years ago."

"It wasn't fifteen years ago." Though it soon would be.

"Mags, bickering won't answer my question. Why Hazlit?"

"I wanted to speak to him, and the dance floor has a kind of privacy."

"About?"

"Valentine." She put as much of the Duchess of Moreland's hauteur in her tone as she could, which was considerable.

"Gayle likes him," Val said, clearly not the least cowed. "And not only because Sophie just married his half brother. I thought you should know."

Which meant Gayle would be coming around to dispense his questions and advice as well. "You may go back to Oxfordshire if all you're going to do is interrogate me about my dancing partners, Valentine."

He studied her for a long moment, green eyes seeing far more than Maggie was comfortable with. "Dev and Emmie? Their Graces?" he said. "Their lives have *meaning*, Maggie, and they have somebody to love them. God willing, that's what I'm building with Ellen, and Gayle with Anna."

"I love you," she said, her concern now for him. "I love all my siblings."

"And we love you," he replied, his smile sad, "but I'm not sure that's enough, Mags. Not for you—it wasn't for me, though I couldn't have said as much to save myself. You'll give Gayle my direction?"

"Of course. You left it with Their Graces?"

"I'm off to the mansion once I change, and yes, I'll pass it along to them."

Val stayed long enough to finish his breakfast, but for the second time, he left without even sitting down at Maggie's piano. When he was gone, Maggie went upstairs, promising herself she would not panic. Methodically, she searched her rooms again—bedroom, sitting room, dressing room.

No reticule.

She searched her back hallway and the closet off the foyer. She traced her usual path from the kitchen to the mews and then wandered every inch of every walkway in her gardens.

No reticule.

She took a break and read the financial pages of the paper, something she'd been doing since the age of twelve, and then repeated her entire search.

Still no reticule.

Her brother Gayle, Earl of Westhaven and the

Moreland heir, chose to stop by and share luncheon with her. All the while she was smiling and nodding at his conversation, Maggie was also trying not to panic.

Where in all of perishing creation could that reticule be?

Two

WILLIAM THE CONQUEROR HAD BEEN A BASTARD.

King Charles II had sired twelve bastards at least, raising three of them to dukedoms with a flourish of the royal pen.

More recently, the Duke of Devonshire had raised two—or was it three bastards?—in the miscellany sharing a roof with him, his duchess, and his mistress.

One of the royal princesses was more than rumored to have a bastard son being raised by the boy's father, and the royal dukes had propagated bastards at a great rate in response to their dear papa's Royal Marriages Act.

These facts and more like them had been imparted to Maggie at her first private tea with Esther, Duchess of Moreland. Maggie had been thirteen, a year into the ordeal of having her courses among a houseful of brothers over whom she towered, a year into the mortification of needing a corset before any of her friends had confessed to same.

With almost two decades of hindsight, Maggie could see Her Grace had been trying to impart reassurance, but what had come across to a young girl floundering for confidence was something on the order of: "Sit up straight, quit feeling sorry for yourself, and stop tapping your spoon on your teacup."

Private teas could still be harrowing to her and her sisters both.

Maggie had only recently begun to suspect private teas were just as harrowing for Her Grace, except that good lady had raised ten children and survived three decades of marriage to Percival Windham. When Esther Windham took a notion to see a thing done, Wellington's determination paled by comparison.

So it was to Esther's example Maggie turned when her reticule remained missing for a third day.

❦

The life of an investigator wasn't easy. Gathering information in the ballrooms kept a man up late of an evening, and meeting clients at breakfast or while riding at dawn had him out of bed before first light.

Hazlit often solved the dilemma by spending the waning hours of the night at his desk, reading reports and getting the bulk of his sleep in the daylight hours. He was no different from many of his peers in this regard, at least during the spring Season.

Lady Norcross had gone to ground, and Hazlit had a sneaking suspicion he knew why. A word whispered in Helene Ander's ear by a certain presuming, statuesque redhead, a little warning between Helene and her sister-in-law, and that would be that. He tried to feel some stirring of regret for Lord Norcross, but taking on the man as a client had been a mistake.

Hazlit made his way back to his chambers, only

to find some servant had pulled back all the drapery, leaving his sitting room flooded with sunlight.

Spring was trying to advance, but it was heavy going. Hazlit considered spending the morning loitering at the coffee shops rather than catching forty winks, and his eyes fell on the jacket he'd worn to Moreland's meeting earlier in the week.

A little glint of fiery gold at the cuff had him examining the sleeve.

And damned if there weren't three long, reddish-gold strands of hair caught on the button. Very long. So long that when he coiled them around and around and around his finger, they made a band as thick as a wedding ring.

A token of a well-fought skirmish. He rummaged in his wardrobe for the sewing kit, bit off a length of silk thread, and tied it around his prize.

"Excuse me, sir."

Hazlit's butler, Morse, stood in the doorway, attired in sufficient dignity to grace the Regent's residence.

"What is it?"

"A lady to see you. I put her in the small parlor and ordered her tea and cakes."

"A lady?" As opposed to a female, since Hazlit employed women as eyes and ears at many levels of society. They generally came in through the mews, after dark, cloaks pulled up over their hair, or they suffered his wrath.

Morse extended a calling card on a silver salver, the salver held in a gloved hand. Hazlit read the card.

Well, well, well.

Another skirmish. His fatigue fell away. He shrugged

into a morning coat, gave his cravat a last-minute inspection, and headed downstairs. His only detour on the way to the small parlor was to tuck his little token into the pages of Wordsworth, several poems away from the drying rose.

"Miss Windham, a pleasure." He bowed over her hand, automatically taking in the details.

She was pretty in the morning sunshine, though that wasn't a detail. He put her age around thirty, which by his lights was the start of a woman's prime or her decline, depending on how she lived her life. Too often late nights, excessive food and drink, and moral laxity aged a lady before her time. She might catch a man's eye by the light of the evening's candles, but morning sun was a brutal mirror of truth.

And the truth was, Maggie Windham was lovely. She had none of the lines of incipient dissipation creeping up around her full mouth. Her eyes were clear and limpid green, the same shade as her beautifully tailored walking dress. Her hair had the healthy luster of a lady who enjoyed fresh air and proper nutrition.

That hair…

She half rose to offer him a little curtsy, then subsided onto the sofa. "Will you be seated, Mr. Hazlit?"

He took a place next to her, just to watch her eyes widen in surprise, though that was her only reaction—no nervous shifting away or popping out of her seat.

"It is a pleasure to see you, Miss Windham, as stated, but an unexpected pleasure. Particularly as you've come calling all on your lonesome, no lady's maid trailing about, no younger sister at your side."

A question dangled on the end of his observation, but his guest was saved responding by the arrival of the tea tray.

"Shall I pour, Mr. Hazlit? And I assure you, my footman is flirting with your scullery maid as we speak."

"Please. It isn't often my tea tray is graced by such a pretty lady."

She drew off her crocheted gloves and set them beside her on the sofa, revealing, of course, *pretty* hands. Not small, but slim, long-fingered, and ringless. Her nails were short and unpainted, which surprised him a little. Practical hands, not ornamental.

"How do you like your tea?"

"Sweet, nearly white."

She served him, prepared a cup for herself, and only then met his gaze. "I need your help."

He nearly sputtered his tea all over them both, so effectively had she surprised him. He took a deliberative sip, letting a silence stretch until he was good and ready to offer return fire.

"You expect me to believe a duke's daughter with no less than three strapping brothers extant requires my assistance?"

"I am a duke's daughter, but having titled antecedents doesn't smooth every bend in the road of life, does it, Mr. Hazlit?"

She let a little silence of her own build, and Hazlit nearly saluted with his teacup.

She was good. By God, she was good.

"I am not enthusiastic about working for a female. Nothing personal."

She didn't even flinch at his brusque tone but

took a delicate sip of fine Darjeeling. "Her Grace has mentioned that you will work for a lady."

"Exceptions, all. I assume you've conferred with her regarding retention of my services?"

"I have not, but I know you are a demanding employee." She grimaced a little at her tea.

"How would you know such a thing?" For it was the truth.

"You will determine the time and place of all meetings. You will not render any reports in writing but will convey them only orally. You demand compensation at the outset in cash and return unused monies in cash only. You're rather like a barrister in that you don't solicit business, but one accounts oneself lucky to have your services."

"I don't believe the analogy flatters me."

"Nor was it intended to."

He might have missed it, because she bent her head to sip her tea. His living depended on noticing the small clues, though, so he saw the first tiny temptation to turn her lips up into a smile. She hid it almost fast enough.

Miss Windham, Miss Windham... She was here in broad daylight but without a companion to ensure the proprieties. He still didn't know what her game was and really did not have time for games in any case.

"Very well." He was gentleman enough to wait until she set down her teacup. "If you're prepared to pay the shot." He named an exorbitant sum and waited to see how she'd regroup without sacrificing her considerable dignity.

"You'd prefer it in cash?"

"I will accept it only in cash." He felt a twinge of pity for her. A very small twinge.

"I'll have the sum delivered to you before the sun sets. More tea?"

"Please." He frowned at her practical, pretty hands while she poured tea he didn't particularly want. Of course, the money would never materialize, and that would be that. While he reasoned himself to this conclusion, she executed the tea ceremony like the daughter of a duke.

No, he corrected himself, like the daughter of a duchess.

"Cakes, Mr. Hazlit?"

"Thank you. My breakfast is becoming a distant memory."

She passed him a plate with two cakes, their hands brushing as she did.

By accident? By design? He was becoming unwittingly curious as to Miss Windham and her stratagems. "You're not having a sweet?"

"One must refrain occasionally for the sake of fitting into one's gowns."

He flicked an eye over her, though did not permit himself to linger at the obvious locations. "Your sacrifice is duly appreciated; but tell me of your circumstances, Miss Windham, and how I might be of service."

She stirred her tea, a slow dragging of the spoon around the bottom of the teacup. A tell, he suspected. A small, personal flag denoting nervousness or impending mendacity.

"I've lost something precious."

"Jewelry? That's easy enough, as it usually turns up

somewhere around Ludgate, kept out of sight for all but particular customers. Was it something that could have been easily broken down and fenced?"

"Why would anyone put a fence around jewels?" She frowned, those little creases appearing between her brows.

"Let me acquaint you with a bit of terminology, Miss Windham. When a thief steals something distinctive, something of value, he can hardly stand on a street corner and wave it about, inviting bids."

"Or she cannot."

"Just so. If the goods are to be liquidated profitably, they are usually transferred to a merchant who traffics in such items, for example, the jewelers over by the City. The thief is given some coin for his wares but nothing like what the thing would be worth if sold openly. The jeweler can recover a great deal for it, though, since he's selling to legitimate customers. The jeweler is the fence."

"And if somebody asks, the jeweler will say it was sold to him as part of some Northumbrian dowager's estate?" The frown smoothed, but her mouth was disapproving.

"You understand the criminal mind."

"I understand not getting caught."

"Have you been caught, then?" He kept his gaze on her face. "Is the missing object a lover's token you shouldn't have?"

"Gracious!" She sat back, looking dismayed but not insulted. "Investigating must call for a vivid imagination, Mr. Hazlit."

"Hardly. Human nature seems to draw most

people into the same predictable peccadilloes over
and over. So which misstep have you taken? Do you
need to locate the child's father? Pay off his wife to
keep her mouth shut? Those aren't strictly investiga-
tory matters, but I can see where the need for discretion... What?"

"I should slap you." The words weren't offered
with any particular animosity, more a tired acceptance. "You are a man, though, and allowances
must be made."

"I beg your pardon."

"And well you should." She sipped her tea then
tipped her head back to regard him. "Despite the
foul implications of your questions, Mr. Hazlit—
questions I doubt you would have put to any of my
sisters—I still need your help, and I still intend to
retain you. I have committed no indiscretion; I have
no ill-conceived child on the way; I need not go for
a tour of the Continent to eschew my dependence
on laudanum."

"So your problem is not that serious," he said,
relieved for her to find it so, and irritated with
himself—for no particular reason.

"It is only serious to me. I will meet with
you to discuss the details when your retainer has
been delivered."

"I'll speak to you tonight at the Livien soiree."

Distaste flitted through her eyes, but he steeled
himself against it. She started this little game; let her
cry forfeit if she couldn't keep up with his rules.

"Until tonight then."

She took her leave, going right out the front door

for all the world to see, and he had to wonder again what exactly Miss Maggie Windham was about.

❦

"So what's your brother up to?" The Duke of Moreland kept his voice down even in his private study, lest his duchess catch him interrogating one sibling about the other. Bad parental form, she claimed, but the children outright told her things they'd never confide in their dear old papa.

Gayle Windham, Earl of Westhaven, shot his father an amused look from his place in the opposite armchair.

"As far as I know, Dev's rusticating in Yorkshire, and Val will soon again be enjoying connubial bliss with Ellen in Oxfordshire."

The duke sat back, smiling broadly. "St. Just is making a go of his earldom, we can say that for him, and he married a good breeder, too. No complaints from this quarter, but I speak of young Mozart. He's departed from his wife's side and is larking about with Fairly here in Town, or with Fairly's piano."

"Why don't you ask him?"

"He never sits still long enough unless his hand-some arse is planted on a piano bench." His Grace's gaze traveled over the paneled ceiling twelve feet above their heads. And this was one of the mansion's cozier rooms.

Westhaven shifted in his chair, crossing his legs with a casual elegance His Grace could only envy. "Last I heard, Val was helping rehearse the Philharmonic Society ensemble and scribbling away on some new composition."

"He's always scribbling away on something these days. I think it agrees with him. How is our Anna?"

"She sends you her regards, and I've sneaked a box of crème cakes to the kitchen for your personal delectation."

"Any of 'em chocolate?"

"At least half. I took all the chocolate ones headed for Maggie and switched them to your box."

"Miss Maggie does enjoy her sweets. Did you know she danced with Ben Hazlit?"

"Keep your ducal paws off, Your Grace," Westhaven said, his tone deceptively mild for the implied rebuke. "Val said it was merely a polite waltz, and they declined to share supper with each other."

"Val said. Do you think he'd hint his sister finally took an interest in a decent man? Thick as thieves, you lot."

"So why are you asking me?"

"Because, dear fellow, when I shuffle off this mortal coil, your unmarried sisters will be your cross to bear."

Westhaven rolled his eyes. "Not the threat-of-death speech. You've never felt better, and you know it."

"Mark me, my boy, a woman left unmarried gets up to tricks. Think of Sophie's little Christmas revel all on her own—or almost on her own but for Sindal's dubious company. Think of your sister Evie and that ghastly footman. Disaster was at hand, and if fate hadn't intervened…"

"Evie would be married to a handsome footman. Maggie isn't Evie, and Hazlit isn't a footman." And the very calm with which his son spoke was a source of pride to His Grace. The boy—the man—was going to make a splendid duke.

"Hazlit is not a commoner, either," the duke said, quietly.

"He told me as much in the course of our dealings. But if I were you, Your Grace, I would not try to push Hazlit on Maggie. She'll balk and head for the barn at a dead gallop, and Her Grace will scold you and hide your stash of cakes." Westhaven rose and went to the sideboard, pouring himself half a glass of… lemonade.

Perhaps the Windham heir was not quite so ducal yet.

"Good heavens, as bad as all that? Has Maggie said something to you?"

"No, she has not." Westhaven eyed the crystal goblet in his hand. "Not that I'd violate her confidences when you've yet to ask her yourself."

"Such a stickler I've raised." But the duke let a little pride infuse his words, for Westhaven was a stickler in the best sense. A detail man who was fast putting the duchy back on sound financial footing.

"Tell Her Grace I'm sorry I missed her." Westhaven drained his glass and set it aside. "And do not let me hear of you meddling in Maggie's affairs, or Hazlit's. And a word of advice?"

"I'm not too arrogant to turn aside a prudent man's advice." Provided the man was his own son.

"Keep an eye on Her Grace," Westhaven said. "She was asking Anna about Maggie's waltz and waited until I was out of earshot to do it."

"My, my, my…" The duke rose, as well, glad once again no twinge of pain flared in his chest as he did.

"You will give Anna my compliments and tell her to keep her ears open."

Westhaven smiled, shook his head, and gave his father a parting hug. The duke saw him out and then made a dash for the kitchen as quickly as stealth and dignity would allow.

❧

Maggie had grown up with five brothers, and she wasn't bothered by a display of male pique. In their frequent tempers, her brothers bellowed and stomped and regularly fell into noisy horseplay that sometimes resulted in broken furniture and those despairing looks from Her Grace.

Her father held one of the most powerful titles short of royalty and wasn't above shouting indoors to get his way or to express his displeasure with the state of his world.

But it was mostly noise, mostly bluster and show. Sound and furying, as Her Grace put it. Nobody was ever going to get hurt in the tantrums and tussles Maggie had seen.

The look in Benjamin Hazlit's eyes communicated lethal intent without a word.

"You want me to find your *reticule*?"

His voice was calm, perfectly civil in fact, as befitted a gentleman on the shadowed terrace outside a genteel soiree, but still Maggie's arms broke out in goose bumps.

"I do. It holds great personal significance for me."

"And about a week's worth of pin money. Come."

He tugged her by the wrist down a dimly lit garden

path. The moon was up, creating some light even on the unlit trails.

"This is not well advised, Mr. Hazlit." She dragged her feet but didn't plant them for fear he'd pull her over onto her face.

"Having this discussion where we could be overheard is less well advised," he said over his shoulder. "There. That bench." He dropped her wrist and waited for her to take a seat. That little civility only made his banked temper more unnerving.

"It's a perfectly reasonable request," she said. "You're an investigator; something of value has gone missing. Investigate."

"For your information, Miss Windham, I find missing people." He dropped down beside her without asking permission. "I find daughters gone haring off to their social ruin; I find embezzlers and arsonists. I track the criminals Bow Street can't touch because of rank and privilege. I do not go chasing after missing hairpins for bored women who have nothing better to do than aggravate a man at his labors."

She was silent, absorbing an aspect of his situation she hadn't appreciated before.

"Cat got your tongue, Miss Windham?"

"This is not a trivial matter to me."

"It is to me," he shot back. "And as you well know, I choose among my potential clients. I serve at my own whim; I do not fetch on command like a handsome young footman trying to cadge his lady's favors."

"That was uncalled for." Particularly when Maggie employed only the plain-faced variety. They worked harder and did not provide fodder for gossip.

Beside her, Hazlit took a deep breath, his broad shoulders heaving up then dropping down. "My apologies, but I am refusing your request."

"I don't believe that's legal."

"Of course it's legal." He turned to frown at her. "You have no hold over me, Miss Windham. I am a free agent. Like a barrister."

She had to smile at him for that. A barrister, indeed. "You are contractually bound to me, sir."

"I'm unbinding myself. I can give you the name of several other investigators who will be happy to work for you at much lower wages than I charge."

"We have a contract," she said, very sure of this point, at least. "You cannot unilaterally renege, or I'll see you sued for breach, and I will win."

"How will you prove such a thing when there's not one word of our dealings in writing and we had no witnesses?"

"Offer, acceptance, consideration, and capacity," she said, drawing the words out for him. "The elements of a contract are in place, and you are equitably estopped from claiming we had no contract just because there is no sealed document."

That got his attention, which wasn't necessarily a good thing in his present mood.

"What are you going on about?"

"My brother Westhaven read law. I consult with him on business matters, as His Grace has no time for ledgers and figures. I've borrowed some of Westhaven's texts and consult with his solicitors when the mood strikes."

"A damned bluestocking spinster. Blackstone is

spinning in his grave." Hazlit sounded amused, which was some relief.

"It isn't complicated, not in theory. Besides, you have a point. There are no witnesses, but I could try you in the court of public opinion, and you would surely not win there."

"You could," he said, his tone thoughtful. "You'd have to go out and about to do that, Miss Windham, and I think you prefer a retiring life."

"I very much do. Which is why I do not relish the idea of quizzing my staff, retracing my steps, quizzing the fellows in the mews, asking my friends and neighbors and family if they've seen my purse, and turning my house upside down to find what is precious to me. I feel like an idiot for losing it."

He gave her another considering look then hunched forward, forearms on his thighs. "You might have started there. You might have tried to gain my sympathy before you bludgeoned me with common law."

"And leave your pride a little fig leaf?"

"Maybe a not too little fig leaf. Maybe a fig bush."

She smiled at his attempt at humor, though it could be interpreted vulgarly, if one had such a turn of mind.

"Mr. Hazlit, won't you please, please help me find my reticule? It is one of my dearest possessions. I feel horrid for having lost track of it, and I'm too embarrassed to prevail upon anybody else but you to aid me in my hour of need." She turned her best swain-slaying gaze on him in the moonlight, the look Val had told her never to use on his friends. For good measure, she let a little sincerity into her eyes, because she'd spoken nothing but the truth.

"God help me." Hazlit scrubbed a hand over his face. "Stick to quoting the law with me, please. I might have a prayer of retaining my wits."

She dropped the pleading expression. "You'll keep our bargain, then?"

"I will make an attempt to find this little purse of yours, but there are no guarantees in my work, Miss Windham. Let's put a limit on the investigation—say, four weeks. If I haven't found the thing by then, I'll refund half your money."

"You needn't." She rose, relieved to have her business concluded. "I can spare it, and this is important to me."

"Where are you going?" He rose, as well, as manners required. But Maggie had the sense he was also just too... primordial to let a woman go off on her own in the moonlight.

"I'm going back to the ballroom. We've been out here quite long enough, unless you're again trying to wiggle out of your obligations?"

"No need to be nasty." He came closer and winged his arm at her. "We've had our bit of air, but you've yet to tell me anything that would aid me in attaining your goal. What does this reticule look like? Who has seen you with it? Where did you acquire it? When did you last have it?"

"All of that?"

"That and more if it's so precious to you," he said, leading her back toward the more-traveled paths. "That is just a start. I will want to establish who had access to the thing, what valuables it contained, and who might have been motivated to steal it."

"*Steal?*" She went still, dropping his arm, for this possibility honestly hadn't occurred to her. She realized, as he replaced her hand on his arm, that she'd held the thought of theft away from her awareness, an unacknowledged fear. "You think somebody would steal a little pin money? People are hung for stealing a few coins, Mr. Hazlit, and transported on those awful ships, and… you think it was a thief?"

"You clearly do not."

She was going to let him know in no uncertain terms that no, she could not have been victimized by a thief. She was too careful, too smart. She'd hired only staff with the best references, she seldom had visitors, and such a thing was utterly…

"I did not reach that conclusion. I don't want to."

Voices came to them from up the path. A woman laughing a little too gaily, drunk, perhaps. Another woman making an equally bright rejoinder, and then a man's voice, or two men's.

"Come." Hazlit drew back into the foliage, his hand around Maggie's wrist. He stepped behind a tree and drew her to stand before him, his legs on either side of hers as he leaned back against the tree.

"Remain still; breathe naturally," he whispered right in her ear, very, very quietly. She did as he suggested, not wanting to be found in the darkness with him by people too inebriated to observe a little discretion.

And while she stood so close to him, the night breeze stirred the air, bringing Hazlit's scent to Maggie's nose. She puzzled over it, because it was faint but alluring.

Complicated, like the man who wore it.

Honeysuckle was the primary note, as sweet a scent as ever graced a bottle—and as intoxicating. She was marveling over that bit of deduction and deciding the undertone was bergamot, when she felt Hazlit's hand in her hair.

Holding her still?

He gathered a few of the locks drifting over her right shoulder and rubbed them silently between his fingers.

When had he taken off his gloves?

Remain still; breathe naturally. It was good advice, when her heart wanted to pound, when she wanted both to run and to stand there forever, his fingers playing with her hair. His hand shifted so he brushed her hair back over her shoulder, just once.

Maggie's heart started to thud in her chest. She wasn't frightened, exactly, but she was rattled. Men never touched her, not if they knew what was good for them, and she ought to abhor being rattled like this. She held still, waiting for him to repeat that simple caress.

"They're gone," he said, still whispering. He took her by the wrist again and led her to the path, offering her his arm with perfect propriety.

They returned to the house without incident, and Maggie thanked every merciful god in the pantheon she and her escort had missed the dancing.

"Will you be going in to supper?" he asked.

"I'd prefer not to."

And what had that business been with her hair? Was he going to pretend he hadn't taken such a liberty?

"I'll fetch your coach. Find your wrap, and if you brought one, your reticule."

He offered her an ironic little bow and went off on his gentlemanly errand. Maggie was home and fighting her way toward sleep before she realized Hazlit hadn't been pretending he'd never touched her hair.

He'd been letting her ignore the fact that she'd allowed it.

⸺

"You were off in the bushes with Maggie Windham," Archer Portmaine said, passing Hazlit a glass with two fingers of brandy in it. "That's two encounters in one week, Benjamin. What's afoot?"

"My ruin." Hazlit nodded his thanks for the drink and settled on the library's leather sofa. "No sign of Lady Norcross this evening, at least not on my territory."

"I picked her up at Lady Bonratty's musicale, but she left in her own carriage and took it all the way home." Portmaine pushed back to sit on Hazlit's desk, his arse on a stack of reports.

"Wee, wee, wee, wee, all the way home," Hazlit quoted the nursery rhyme.

Portmaine paused before sipping his own drink. "Did Maggie Windham strike you on the head?"

"No. She hired me, and it took me half my walk home to figure out what she's truly about."

"She wants to have her way with your tender young flesh," Portmaine suggested. "You're overdue to get your wick dipped, you know."

"Your concern is touching, Archer."

"You always get short-tempered when you've

neglected your romping. Maybe you should go a round or two with Lady Norcross."

"Maybe I should find a partner who can think beyond his next swiving."

"I like swiving." Portmaine pushed off the desk and refilled his drink, then came to rest on the sofa a couple of feet from Hazlit. "It's normal to like swiving. Lady Norcross apparently understands this. You used to understand this. I certainly understand it. More brandy?"

"You're outpacing me," Hazlit said, smiling slightly at Portmaine's predictable simplicity.

"And Lady Maggie's outfoxing you." Portmaine took a substantial swallow of his drink. "You usually avoid the society women, leaving me to console them on your unavailability. What's afoot with Lady Maggie?"

"She doesn't use the title, though she understands business very well, and while I assured her I wouldn't take coin from a client then spy on that client, Maggie Windham is clever enough to recall that her parents retained me, not Maggie herself. If she wants to spike my guns so to speak, to make sure her parents won't ever use me to pry into her life, then she has to hire me herself."

Portmaine nodded in comprehension. "I always say women have the greater natural cunning."

"If they do, it's because men drive them to it."

"You're thinking of your sisters again. I knew something was putting you off your oats."

"It's spring, and for the first time in years, my sisters need not hide from the social pleasures that are their due, but the habit is already ingrained, and the mere acquisition of husbands hasn't affected it. Avis, at least, has the excuse that she's up in Cumbria, where the weather won't moderate for weeks yet." Hazlit eyed the rapidly dropping level of his drink.

"What kind of name is that for a female? Bird. What of the other one, the governess?" Archer tossed back his drink and remained where he was, like some happy, handsome gargoyle sitting on Hazlit's tidy desk.

"Alex says she's too busy being a mother to her stepsons. I suspect she's increasing already."

"So it isn't your sisters plaguing you, specifically," Portmaine said. "We're back to my theory. I'm guessing Maggie Windham has indulged in a discreet liaison or two. You might broach it with her."

"She's a client."

"And what is it you're supposed to do for this client?"

"Find her reticule."

Portmaine's brows rose, and his smile was devilish. "Not very original, finding her reticule. Did she last see it in the vicinity of, say, her spread knees?"

"Your puerile tendencies are showing, Archer."

"I'm tired. My creativity is at low ebb. So why, if you're not going to swive the lady, are you letting yourself be led on this dance?"

"Because I'm contractually obligated."

"Are peers tried in the Lords for breach of contract?"

"We're not going to find out." Hazlit got up and went to the decanter to freshen his drink. "As I handed her up into her coach, she paused and looked around to make sure no one could hear us. When she was assured we had privacy, she gave me one last bit of instruction."

"Say on." Portmaine gestured with his empty glass. "We're not getting younger, and the tale grows interesting."

"She said I must promise not to look inside this reticule. Not even to peek."

Portmaine studied Hazlit by the firelight. "Peeking is what we do best. Well, one of the things we do best... but you promised, didn't you?"

"I did."

"Why?"

"Because in that moment, Archer, the lady's guard dropped just for an instant. She's good, maybe even better than I am, at keeping her reactions under control."

Portmaine shrugged. "She's a duke's by-blow. Maybe she's had to be."

"Maybe, but beneath her pretty looks and sharp wits, Maggie Windham is one very scared lady."

Maggie tossed aside the third gown in a row and stood, hands on hips, in the middle of her dressing room.

"The green velvet looked very nice, mum."

Alice, her lady's maid, had mutiny in her eyes, despite the deferential tone.

"Forgive me, Alice. It's just that for years I've tried to dress so no one would notice me. I wanted to look... forgettable."

"And tonight?"

"I want to make a point." Maggie fingered the

green velvet, which was a recent whim, something she'd had made without being sure she'd ever have a chance to wear it.

"What point would that be?"

"I'm not sure." Maggie put a brown dress trimmed with red piping against her body and considered her image in the mirror. "I don't want to be quite forgettable. This is a pretty dress."

"All your dresses are pretty. It's you the guests should be noticing, not your dresses."

Maggie put down the brown dress and picked up one in aubergine.

"A matron's color," Alice said, taking the dark dress and hanging it up. "If you want to be noticed, mum, you put on the green velvet without a fichu, and you let me do something with that hair."

"My hair?" Maggie's hand went protectively to her hair, twisted back in its usual severe knot. "My hair is impossible, Alice, but I won't let you cut it."

"Trust me a little, Miss Maggie. Cuttin' it is the last thing we'll be doing."

She led Maggie by the hand over to the vanity and Maggie sat, willing for some reason to take risks she'd denied herself for more than a decade.

❧

"Good God Almighty." Lucas Denning's soft, appreciative whistle sounded from beside Hazlit. "Would you look at that?"

Hazlit followed Deene's gaze to the steps leading down to the ballroom.

"Jesus God."

Maggie Windham prowled down the staircase, a shimmery brown silk paisley wrap dangling from her shoulders and soft green velvet clinging to her curves. The dress was decent, though the décolletage was gratifyingly low from a male perspective. What made the whole ensemble so riveting was... that hair.

She'd piled much of it high in a soft coil on her crown, adding to her height, making her even more striking. But the rest of it, oh, the rest of it... It came down around her shoulders in curls and riots, dropped down her back in an ongoing cascade of auburn, and swished around her hips—her curvaceous, womanly hips—to tease against her fundament as she moved.

It was daring, different, and yet, not quite indecent.

Hazlit's hands ached at his sides, though whether he wanted to get a fistful of her hair or spank her, he couldn't say.

"I've taken a sudden notion to appreciate mature females," Deene was saying. "Though if her brothers ask, I'm being protective in their absence. Hold my drink."

And that, the simple fact of Deene's unthinking response to a gorgeous woman, saved Hazlit from making a similar fool of himself. He supposed he'd make a little different fool of himself later in the evening, after Maggie had had her fun and left a trail of broken hearts all over the room.

When the buffet had been served and a violin soloist had performed along with the quartet, Hazlit understood Maggie was waiting for him to come to her. Her glance swept the room occasionally, as if she were merely surveying the attendees, the same as anybody would do on a social evening. When her eyes passed over him, they kept on moving. No telltale nod or widening of the eyes.

Self-possessed, was Maggie Windham.

So he let her stew, made his own plans, then resigned himself to a late evening.

It was a particular pleasure when she climbed into the dark confines of her coach and sat back with a deep sigh, all without realizing he was sitting in the shadows across from her. She rapped on the roof three times, and the coach pulled away with the horses at a sedate walk.

"Did you have fun, Miss Windham?"

She didn't scream, which was a point in her favor, though her hand disappeared into her reticule.

"You might hit me at this range, even in the dark," Hazlit said. "But I really wish you wouldn't. In such a situation, even a gentleman might be forced to take desperate measures."

"Good evening, Mr. Hazlit. Not quite a pleasure to see you."

"You hired me, Miss Windham. Were we to communicate exclusively in notes written in disappearing ink?"

"No." Her ungloved hand emerged from her reticule. "I meant I can't quite see you." She took off her other glove and stuffed them both into her bag. "I suppose it makes sense you'd prefer to meet in private. I wasn't sure whether to approach you, since you insist on determining the time and place you meet with a client. You did not look to be enjoying yourself."

"You did." How could peevishness creep into only two syllables?

In the dark, her teeth gleamed in a smile.

"I did. A little bit, I did. There are advantages to being on the shelf, though I've yet to truly appreciate them."

"One being that you can tease and flirt and carry on like a strumpet all night?"

The peevishness was gone, but Hazlit hardly liked himself for the condescension that had taken its place.

"If I'm flirting and teasing, then the gentlemen are also flirting and teasing, and yet you hardly compare them to streetwalkers. They are being gallant, but you accuse me of being immoral. Hardly fair, Mr. Hazlit."

"They do not have their hair swinging around their backsides like some dollymop working the docks."

She went still, as if he'd slapped her, and Hazlit had to wonder if she wouldn't be justified in shooting him. "That is a gun you have in your purse?"

"A knife."

"Oh, for God's sake." He switched seats and settled directly beside her on the forward-facing seat. "Go ahead, try to stab me."

"You deserve to be deflated, but why attempt a violent felony?"

"So I can show you why you ought not to carry such a thing."

"But my papa…"

"Is a duke, who hasn't been in a hand-to-hand brawl since his duchess got her mitts on him three decades ago. Pull the knife."

"But what if I hurt you?"

"I want you to try to hurt me, try your absolute—"

She got the thing free of her purse, at least, but he had her wrist pinned up against the squabs, his body forcing hers back against the seat so snugly he could feel her breathing.

"I take your point," she said, her breath fanning past his ear.

He wasn't finished. He eased the pressure on her wrist just a hair, and while she perhaps thought the demonstration over, he brought the knifepoint up right under her chin, making further speech for her perilous.

"The gun," he said, "will at least make a hell of a noise and bring help. If both barrels are spent, it's harmless. The knife can be turned on you over and over again, and if you don't bleed to death, then infection will likely carry you off eventually."

"I understand, Mr. Hazlit."

He stayed for a moment, his weight still pressing into hers, lowering the knife only slowly. In the darkness, he couldn't tell if she'd gone pale, but she wasn't crying. Her breathing told him that.

And the scent of her, God in heaven the scent. Cinnamon and mille fleurs, maybe. A little lilac, some hyacinth, even a touch of rose, a whisper of jasmine, and it all twined through a man's senses and made him want to linger near, teasing fragrance from fragrance until he was drunk on an olfactory catalogue of sweetness.

She said nothing. Hazlit felt her hands on his chest, not pushing, but maybe ready to push.

Prey went still like this sometimes when a predator spotted them. It was an attempt to become invisible, a futile attempt. He shifted to sit beside her, fished around for a few moments, then reached in the dark for her hand.

"Get rid of it," he said, settling the hilt of the knife in her palm. "I'll get you a lady's version of a pocket pistol and teach you how to use it, unless you'd rather approach one of your brothers to see to it."

"My brothers?"

"St. Just would be best suited to the task." Devlin St. Just was a decorated cavalry officer, one who'd been awarded an earldom for his exploits in the Peninsular War.

Or for being a duke's firstborn bastard.

"He's gone back North, where he's likely to stay," Miss Windham said. "If you can spare the time, I will take my instruction from you. But I hardly think your purpose in meeting me tonight was to accost me with a knife."

"Of course not. We're to begin your investigation, assuming you still haven't located this reticule?"

"I have not." She sounded tight-lipped about it, though her reply brought Hazlit an odd sense of relief.

"Then let's begin with the obvious. When did you last see it?"

She turned her head to regard him by the light of the occasional porch lamp.

"I could write much of this down for you. When I last saw it, who works for me, what was in it."

"And then there'd be a written record, which could also be stolen, copied, distorted, or lost. We haven't much time, Miss Windham. I suggest you answer the question."

"I last recall having it when I returned from visiting with Anna out in Surrey. That would be four days ago."

"What does it look like?"

"It's beaded, white, brown, and turquoise."

"What shape?"

"Bag-shaped."

"Miss Windham."

"Well, it is. It's a drawstring design and about fifteen inches square."

"Fringed?'

"Yes, fringed at the bottom."

"What all was in it?"

Silence, and Hazlit let his fingers close around the lock of hair he'd been slipping over his knuckles in the dark. Her hair was so long, she hadn't felt him toying with it.

Or she was that distracted by his interrogation.

"Miss Windham, perhaps you didn't hear the question."

"I'm thinking." She was the peevish one now, but he didn't mind if she wanted to keep them trotting around Mayfair all night. "I forget."

"Perhaps you can recall this: You threatened to try me in the court of public opinion, Miss Windham. Did you think I'd find your purse through divination? You're going to have to trust me a little, and if you can't, then I'll return your money to you, and we'll forget this charming interlude over knives in the dark."

"It was only one knife, and you started it."

Did not. She'd started it when she'd come down the stairs to the ballroom looking… *tumbled.* Or worse, willing to be tumbled.

He was certainly willing to be tumbled, by her, anyway. The evidence of same was literally growing in his breeches, and that would never do.

"Do you want my help or not, Miss Windham?" The question cost him, for she'd be smart to cut him loose. He was enjoying their chat in the dark entirely too much.

He let her stew in silence while he offered his unruly parts a stern, silent lecture. He pictured his favorite vistas up at Blessings, recited the Lord's Prayer in Latin, and—most productive of all—dropped the silky coil of hair he'd been tormenting himself with for the past five minutes.

"I can't go to my brothers."

It was an admission; he gathered that much and went carefully as a result. "Over a misplaced reticule?"

"There's more to it," she said, sighing in the dark. Hazlit wasn't sure, but he thought perhaps she leaned a little on him. "I have a half-dozen reticules and could buy a dozen more tomorrow."

"Are you concerned you left it in an incriminating location?"

"You're back to my wicked love life." She sounded amused. "Think what you will about me, Mr. Hazlit, but it will be a waste of time. I don't go places I'm not supposed to be. I don't dally with men who aren't available, and I know better than to deal in the vices that condemn a lady beyond recall."

"What vices would those be?"

"Gambling, opium, cockfights, university boys, the usual list. Given my antecedents, I cannot afford even a whiff of association with any of it."

He sat beside her in the dark, breathing her scent and yet feeling a little ashamed of himself. Her voice rang with truth, underlain with sadness. She was either a consummate liar or she was confessing to a little loneliness.

Maybe a lot of loneliness.

"Would you want to make those associations, Miss Windham?"

It wasn't a fair question, not within the realm of his investigation. It was just him, admitting to a little curiosity about the woman beside him.

"I would want the option to make them," she said, the honesty of her answer surprising him. "The freedom. I have no desire to see two roosters reduce each other to masses of bloody feathers. I have no wish to lose money or even gain it on the turn of a card. I certainly have no wish to lose my wits to opium, but maybe I'd like to think I could if I felt like it."

"You can, but it's risky, as you say." And for reasons that did not bear examining, he would be damned if he'd let her be exposed to such risks.

"I am prudent. My family values this in me; it has been a relief to them."

"They've said as much?"

"Her Grace has." She glanced out the window. "We'll be back to my house soon. Shall I have the coachman drop you off at your own address?"

"We still have much to discuss."

"And yet we've been in constant conversation."

Unfortunate word choice.

"I can call on you tomorrow." But God in heaven, where had that brilliant notion come from? He seldom called on women, and it would be remarked by all and sundry if he started with Maggie Windham.

"I don't generally have callers outside my family."

"None?"

"Helene, a few other women, but not... not gentlemen, and certainly not handsome single gentlemen with polished address."

She thought he was handsome?

"Make an exception for me. We were seen waltzing; a follow-up social call wouldn't be that unusual. I could meet you riding in the park, if you'd rather, but there's less privacy."

"I do not keep a riding horse."

"Then I will call upon you at two of the clock. I will expect you to be a little more forthcoming than you were this evening."

"I will try. You never answered my question: Shall I have John drop you at your home?"

"God, no. You might think he'd keep such a thing to himself, but I've yet to meet the coachman who didn't enjoy his pints at the local watering hole, and that's a situation rife with opportunity for hanging a lady's laundry in the street, so to speak. He'll slow on the turn into the alley, and I'll be off."

"Like a thief in the night."

"Like a gentleman in the night."

He tucked into his pocket the lock of hair he'd surreptitiously cut with her knife, and as soon as the coach slowed, darted out the door without another word.

❧

"You think my wits have gone begging," Maggie said. She didn't blame Alice for a look of exasperation, not in the least. "I just haven't had a caller outside family in ages, and I'm… nervous."

Standing in her corset and stockings, Maggie was undecided.

"Anything in your wardrobe will be above reproach, mum. You'll feel most confident in something you like wearing."

"Good advice. The bronze silk and the cream gloves."

"You're stepping out with your caller?"

"I'm not." Maggie took the dress from Alice and pulled it over her head. "But there's no need for informality."

"A coronet, then?"

"A tidy coronet, one braid, no jewelry." As plain and severe a toilet as she could politely manage for a morning call. Hazlit was coming to talk business, and yet Maggie's insides were jumping around as if she were seventeen and permitted to dine at table for one of Her Grace's formal dinners.

There was no need for this. *None.*

She sat at the vanity and passed a brush back to Alice, who went to work on the thankless task of brushing out Maggie's hair.

"Did you catch your hair on something last night?"

"I did not. Why?"

Alice dangled a coppery skein over Maggie's shoulder. "You must have snagged it. This length is a good three inches shorter."

"I doubt that. The whole business is in need of a good trim, and it's probably just getting uneven."

"Yes, mum."

Alice fell silent, her fingers deftly pinning a fat braid into a circle that coiled one and a half times around Maggie's head. Alice loaded the thing with what felt like several dozen pins, then handed Maggie cream knit gloves.

"Will I do?"

Alice's homely face creased into a smile. "Aye, mum. You'll do. Whoever he is, he's in for a treat."

"How did you know it's a man?"

"Because I've not seen you this flummoxed since your first season," Alice said, hanging a discarded gown back in the wardrobe. "About time, if you ask me."

"Alice..."

"I know." Alice waved a hand and picked up the second dress and the third. "I'm not to be braying your business about should His Grace's footmen get to visiting in the kitchen, or Her Grace's lady's maid, or your sisters or brothers. Your business is yours and yours alone."

"You don't agree?"

Alice had been Maggie's maid since Maggie had turned sixteen—roughly half Maggie's lifetime. She was permitted a certain familiarity, in part because she never took advantage of the privilege.

"I'm thinking a woman with as much decent family as you have, mum, shouldn't be trying so awfully hard to keep her distance from them."

Alice might have said more, might have let Maggie have a rare piece of blunt Irish common sense, but the tweeny rapped on the bedroom doorjamb.

"Beg pardon, mum, there's a gentleman here to see

you." She passed over a silver tray, upon which lay one calling card.

Cream linen, green ink, and all it said was: "The Hon. Benjamin Hazlit."

Honorable? Was he in line for a title, or did he truly have one? Maggie decided to put the question to her papa, who knew as much about the business of the Lords as Her Grace knew about the order of precedence. This would involve a trip to the ducal mansion, but needs must.

"Put him in the family parlor, Millie, and get the teakettle going. Sandwiches and cakes both on the tray."

"Yes, mum." Millie bobbed away toward the servants' stairs, leaving Maggie feeling an odd giddiness.

"Let him wait five minutes," Alice said from the depths of the wardrobe. "You're worth that much of his time."

"But the sooner I greet him, the sooner he'll be gone." Maggie squared her shoulders and prepared to meet her caller. Her first gentleman caller in fourteen years, and all he'd want to talk about was her very sorry personal business.

"You're studying my garden," Miss Windham said. "It isn't very far along yet, but the Holland bulbs are making a good effort."

"I grew up in the North," Hazlit replied. "We appreciate any gestures in the direction of spring, from any quarter. Good day, Miss Windham, a pleasure to see you."

He bowed very correctly over her hand, and she curtsied with equal punctilio.

"Where shall I put…?" A little maid stopped in the doorway, all but hidden behind a large bouquet of bright red carnations.

Alas for my heart. Hazlit knew the sentiment associated with red carnations and had had them delivered anyway. He certainly wasn't going to send the woman roses, for God's sake. Carnations were durable, and they had a fresh, spicy scent that put Hazlit in mind of his hostess. She didn't strike him as the type of lady to waste time decoding bouquets in any case.

"On the sideboard, Millie." Miss Windham's lips turned up in a smile more sweet than any Hazlit had seen on her. "My youngest brother is temporarily returned to Town," she said, taking the card from the bouquet. "Of all my siblings, Valentine is the one most likely to make the gallant gesture…"

She fell silent while she read the card, her smile shifting to something heart-wrenchingly tentative. "This wasn't necessary, Mr. Hazlit."

Regards, Hazlit. Not exactly poetry, but proof he'd upstaged at least her doting brother.

"Perhaps not necessary, but a man can hope his small tokens are appreciated." He glanced pointedly at the maid while he delivered that flummery, because the girl was lingering over the flowers unnecessarily.

"That will be all, Millie. Shall we be seated, Mr. Hazlit?"

Maggie Windham was smart enough to allow him to steer the conversation. While she poured tea and fed him a surprisingly generous cold meal, Hazlit kept the conversation social and inane. If he hadn't been watching her closely, he'd have missed the signs of her growing impatience.

But he was watching her closely, delighting in it, in fact. He saw her steal repeated glances at the flowers, her expression betraying muted strains of longing and bewilderment. He saw her gaze flicker over the chocolates every time he paused to take a bite of his food. He saw her stirring her tea with her spoon, tapping it against the bottom of the cup—plink, plink, plink—as he went on about the weather and the seasonings on the chicken and the previous evening's music.

She was good, never dropping a conversational stitch, never letting the polite interest slip from her eyes.

He was good, too, babbling away, stuffing his maw, and all the while not allowing his attention to linger on the long, graceful line of her throat or the way the sun glossed her hair with brilliant gold highlights.

That hair, spread over a pillow…

"May I offer you another sandwich, Mr. Hazlit?" She lifted the caddy toward him, which meant her décolletage was inclined toward him, as well.

"No, thank you. I've quite disgraced myself. My sisters admonish me regularly about the hazards of neglecting my nutrition. Perhaps if my kitchen were as skilled as yours, I might heed their guidance with more alacrity."

"If you're no longer hungry, shall we take a turn in the garden?" She rose as she spoke, her tone pleasantly causal, though Hazlit acceded her point: It was time to be getting on with business.

"I can walk off the last of those tea cakes." He winged his arm at her. She did not lead him into the corridor, which would have necessitated a trip through her house. She instead took him out a pair of French doors leading directly to her back terrace.

"A pretty afternoon," he said as they moved away from the house. "I'm afraid we're to have a rather unpretty discussion."

"You're going to castigate me again for my coiffure last night." Her tone was mild, teasing almost, and they were still within earshot of the house. His respect for her—a man could respect even his enemies—rose a notch.

"It was daring." He chose the word so as not to offend. Offended women were tedious and endlessly befuddling. "But quite attractive."

"Don't flatter me, Mr. Hazlit. You compared me to a streetwalker."

She spoke very quietly, her expression utterly serene, and he felt... guilty. Guilty for being male and judgmental, and even a little guilty for finding her attractive. The notion was so foreign it took him half the length of the garden to identify it.

"You must be desperate to find this reticule."

"Was your insult a test of my resolve?" She ran her hand up a sprig of lavender a long way from blossoming. "I'm to tolerate your opinion of me, your casual vituperation, in order to see my belongings restored to me?"

"I apologize for calling you a... dollymop." He meant the apologetic words, he just did not enjoy saying them, particularly when they effected not one iota of softening in her serene expression.

"Shall we sit, Mr. Hazlit? We're far enough from the house."

They were. Her back gardens, like those in most of the better neighborhoods', were quite deep and surrounded by walls high enough to ensure privacy. The breeze was blowing toward the mews. If they kept their voices down, they could speak freely.

He led her to a bench in the shade, waiting while she took a seat.

"You can't loom over me if we're to have a proper conversation," she said. "I accept your apology, though I need some assurances, as well."

He took his place beside her, feeling himself brace inside. He'd apologized; it was time to get on to business. "What assurances?"

"You will treat me with the respect due the adopted daughter of a duke and duchess, or no matter how badly I need to find my reticule, I'll seek the assistance of another. If I must, I will, Mr. Hazlit. I'll do so without mention of your disappointing behavior, but I'll do it."

She'd broken off a bit of lavender as they'd strolled along. She was crushing it in her fingers as she spoke, the scent as pungent as her words.

Lavender, for distrust.

"I will treat you with every courtesy due any lady," he said, watching her fingers destroy the little green sprig.

"Not good enough." She continued to torment the remains of the plant. "Courtesy can be a weapon, Mr. Hazlit. Her Grace taught me this before I was out of the schoolroom. She taught me how to wield it and how to defend myself against it."

What was he supposed to say to that?

"We will not have this discussion again." She let her hands settle in her lap. "Their Graces bought me, you know. They'd acquired my brother Devlin the year before, and my mother, inspired by this development, threatened to publish all manner of lurid memoirs regarding His Grace."

Acquired her brother? As if he were a promising yearling colt or an attractive patch of ground?

"You are going to burden me with the details of your family past, I take it?"

"You are the man who glories in details." Without the least rude inflection, she made it sound like a failing. "My point is that my mother sold me. She could just as easily have sold me to a brothel. It's done all the time. Unlike your sisters, Mr. Hazlit, I do not take for granted the propriety with which I was raised. You may ignore it if you please; I will not."

She had such a lovely voice. Light, soft, lilting with a hint of something Gaelic or Celtic... exotic. The sound of her voice was so pretty, it almost disguised the ugliness of her words.

"How old were you?"

"Five, possibly six. It depends on whether I am truly Moreland's by-blow or just a result of my mother's schemes in his direction."

Six years old and sold to a brothel? The food he'd eaten threatened to rebel.

"I'm... sorry." For calling her a dollymop, for making her repeat this miserable tale, for what he was about to suggest.

She turned her head to regard him, the slight sheen in her eyes making him sorrier still. Sorrier than he could recall being about anything in a long, long time. Not just guilty and ashamed, but full of regret—for her.

The way he'd been full of regret for his sisters and powerless to do anything but support them in their solitary struggles. He shoved that thought aside, along with the odd notion that he should take Magdalene Windham's hand in some laughable gesture of comfort.

He passed her his handkerchief instead. "This makes the stated purpose of my call somewhat awkward."

"It makes just about everything somewhat awkward," she said quietly. "Try a few years at finishing school when you're the daughter of not just a courtesan—there are some of those, after all—but a courtesan who sells her offspring. I realized fairly early that my mother's great failing was not a lack of virtue, but rather that she was greedy in her fall from grace."

"She exploited a child," Hazlit said. "That is an order of magnitude different from parlaying with an adult male in a transaction of mutual benefit."

"Do you think so?" She laid his handkerchief out in her lap, her fingers running over his monogrammed initials. "Some might say she was protecting me, providing for me and holding the duke accountable for his youthful indiscretions."

Despite her mild tone, Hazlit didn't think Miss Windham would reach those conclusions. She might long to, but she wouldn't. By the age of six a child usually had the measure of her caretakers.

And to think of Maggie Windham at six... big *innocent* green eyes, masses of red hair, perfect skin... in a brothel.

"I am going to suggest a notion for which you should probably slap me," he said. Hell, he ought to slap himself. Call himself out, more like.

"I gather the topic has been changed." She passed him back his unused hanky. "Say on. I have correspondence to attend to, and you need to be about your snooping."

She did not, he noted, mention having calls to make.

"To facilitate our dealings over the next few weeks, I suggest you allow me to court you. To *appear* to court you."

⤜⤚

Mr. Hazlit had measured his words, neither hurrying through them nor dropping his voice, but making the careful distinction between courting her and *appearing* to court her.

She'd already cried, or nearly had, so Maggie concluded she ought possibly to laugh.

"*Appear* to court me. Explain yourself, Mr. Hazlit."

"What do you know about your maid, Millie?"

She took her time answering, in part because she was mad at him—he'd necessitated that she disclose her origins, something she hadn't felt the need to speak of in years—and in part because she wanted time to study his surprisingly handsome profile.

He was tall and broad-shouldered, like her brothers. He also had dark hair like them, but there the similarity ended. Hazlit's eyes were not the much-vaunted Windham green, but rather a brown so dark as to appear black. Sitting next to him, Maggie could see golden flecks radiating around his pupils, but from across a room, his eyes were merely dark.

And slanted a little under swooping dark brows, giving him a piratical air.

Did she want to be courted—to appearances—by a man with such eyebrows?

His nose was no better recommendation, being on the generous side and a trifle hooked. There was nothing sweet or apologetic about that nose. It was probably a good nose for snooping.

His mouth, however… It was a severe mouth, all grim lines and clipped speech. A perverse part of her wondered if he even knew how to offer a genuine smile. And if he were to kiss her—courting involved kissing, of that she was certain—would his mouth be as cold and stern as it looked?

"Millie has been with me for two years. Her father was wounded on the Peninsula. She's the oldest girl of seven; her family name is Carruthers."

It was more than most employers would know about their tweeny, but as Maggie watched Hazlit's eyebrows twitch down, she realized it wasn't very much at all.

"She likes scones with sultanas," Maggie added, "and she's quite smitten with my head footman, though he's old enough to be her father."

The expression Mr. Hazlit turned on her held lurking I-told-you-so smugness. "She had motive, therefore, to betray you."

"Betray me?"

"To sell your reticule or whatever was inside it that you do not want to discuss with me. To sell it to aid her hungry siblings."

Studying him lost its appeal as Maggie decided it wasn't condescension he was trying to mask, but possibly pity. "Millie is well fed, warm in winter, and given a full day off each week. Her wages are generous, and my housekeeper is a cheerful person to work for. Why should she betray me over a few coins?"

He crossed his legs at the knee like a Continental dandy, except there was nothing fussy about such a posture when he assumed it. "Her father can't work and has what, seven other mouths to feed? They are her family; you are her employer. Her loyalty to you cannot be so great as her loyalty to them."

"You place a great store in family loyalty, Mr. Hazlit."

Though, damn him, he had a point.

"If I am seen to court you, then even before your staff we will have excuses to be whispering in corners and spending a great deal of time together. I make this suggestion to better effect your stated goal of retrieving the reticule, Miss Windham, not to prolong our association or in any way inconvenience you."

That mouth of his was a flat, grim line, which was reassuring in a way. He didn't like this idea any more than she did.

"What is involved in appearing to court me?"

He quirked an eyebrow at her. "You haven't been courted before? What about the climbing cits and baronets' sons? They never came up to scratch?"

"Many of them did." She wondered what he'd look like if somebody were to shave off those piratical eyebrows. "They did not bother much with the other part of the business."

"The wooing?"

"The nonsense."

"We need the nonsense," he said. "We need to drive out at the fashionable hour; we need to be seen arm in arm at the social events. I need to call upon you at the proper times with flowers in hand, to spend time with your menfolk when I creditably can. I'll carry your purchases when you go shopping and be heard begging you to save your waltzes for me."

"There's a problem," she said, curiously disappointed to see the flaw in his clever scheme. He was a wonderful dancer; that was just plain fact.

And she loved flowers, and loved the greenery and fresh air of Hyde Park.

She also liked to shop but generally contented herself with the occasional minor outing with her sisters.

And to hear him begging for her waltzes...

"What sort of problem can there possibly be? Couples are expected to court in spring. It's the whole purpose behind the Season."

"If you court me like that, Their Graces will get wind of it. They very likely already know you've called on me."

"And this is a problem how?"

He wasn't a patient man, or one apparently plagued with meddlesome parents.

"They will *start*, Mr. Hazlit. They will get their hopes up. They will sigh and hint and quiz my siblings, all in hopes that you will take me off their hands."

"Then they will be disappointed. Parents expect to be disappointed. My sister was a governess, and she has explained this to me."

He looked like he was winding up for a lecture before the Royal Society, so she put a hand on his arm. "I do not like to disappoint Their Graces," she said quietly. "They have suffered much at the hands of their children."

He blinked at her, his lips pursing as if her sentiments were incomprehensible.

"I won't declare for you," he said. "If they let their hopes be raised by a few silly gestures, then that is their problem. You have many siblings. Let them fret over the others."

"It isn't like that." She cocked her head to study him. Hadn't he had any parents at all? "I could have seventeen siblings, and Their Graces would still worry about me. You mentioned having sisters. Do you worry less about the one than the other?"

"I do not." He didn't seem at all pleased with this example. "I worry about them both, incessantly. Excessively, to hear them tell it, but they have no regard for my feelings, else they'd write more than just chatty little..."

"Yes?"

"Never mind."

Some imp made her press for details. "What are their names?"

"Avis, who remains near the family seat in Cumbria, and Alexandra, who has recently given up governessing here in the South for the questionable charms of her husband."

His expression had shifted, disgruntlement creasing his brow and banked fraternal frustration lurking in his eyes. He looked like a *brother* then, like a man who wanted to care for his sisters but didn't know quite how to go about it.

Maggie knew that expression, had seen it on all of her brothers, particularly Devlin, the oldest and the only other one to bear the stigma of illegitimacy. Despite her general distaste for Hazlit, she had to approve of brothers who worried.

Within reason.

"You will court me—to appearances—but in a desultory fashion."

"I am not a desultory man, and you are not a woman a sane man could approach in a desultory fashion."

"Is that a compliment?" Because if it wasn't a compliment, then she strongly suspected it was an insult.

"It is a statement of fact." He glanced over at her, his gaze lighting on her hair, which was coiled tidily on her head. He frowned at her hair, then his lips turned up. "And it is a compliment. You are quite pretty, Miss Windham."

"Gracious." She rose, needing distance from him if he was going to spout nonsense and very nearly *smile* at her. "You need not dissemble when we are in private."

"Oh, but I do—though that was the God's honest truth." He was on his feet, strolling along right beside her. "Unless I am absolutely certain we cannot be seen, heard, or detected by others, I will comport myself like a man smitten."

"Smitten?" The notion was laughable. She could conceive of him allowing a discreet, calculated interest in some woman of impeccable breeding and tidy blonde hair, but nobody would believe him smitten with her.

"Smitten." He nodded once, agreeing with his own word choice. "Perhaps cautiously so, but smitten."

"This will require the thespian skills of Mr. Kean." She eyed him curiously. What would it be like if he were smitten with her?

"I shall rise to the challenge easily enough." He glanced around as they approached a greening rose vine winding over an arched trellis. "Allow me to demonstrate."

He turned to face her under the trellis, bent his head, and kissed her.

Three

KISSING MAGDALENE WINDHAM HAD NOT BEEN PART of Hazlit's plan. His plan had been to figure out what was disturbing her otherwise retiring life—he owed the Windham family that much—and to remove the problem in exchange for her coin. *That* was what prompted a need for proximity to her, not some silly reticule.

His plan had been to feign the polite interest of a man looking about for a potential match, a sensible match borne of the motivations of a sensible, reasonably wealthy man when looking to build his dynasty.

His plan had been to keep his senses sharp, not to swamp them with the scent, taste, and feel of a lovely woman on a spring day.

A lovely, somewhat reticent woman, whose height meant she fit him wonderfully, her hips cradling his pelvis, her breasts pressing intimately against his chest. Her mouth was soft and lush and hesitant against his, as if asking him how to go on.

He showed her—which was also not in his plan. He lingered over her jaw and brow, stealing a whiff of the mille fleurs and cinnamon scent of her hair. He nuzzled the curve of her ear and felt a little ripple of shock go through her body. When she curled into him on a sigh, he set his mouth to the corner of her lips, teasing her into turning her face to his.

And then *she* was showing *him*. Showing him how long it had been since a kiss had been more than a mandatory and perfunctory preliminary to equally perfunctory coitus. Showing him the pleasure of eagerness that sought to outmatch shyness, showing him he had something to give, even in such a thing as a feigned kiss.

"Mr. Hazlit…" She wrapped one hand around the back of his neck and used the other to stroke slowly over his chest. "We shouldn't…"

He silenced her by settling his mouth over hers— softly, because as much as her body was indicating his kiss was welcome, Magdalene Windham was possessed of a mind, as well, and a lady's sensibilities, and a past—

The thought was like a trickle of cold water down the back of his neck. When he wanted to thrust his tongue into the plush heat of her mouth, he hesitated. As his hand moved up her rib cage, he stopped maddeningly short of palming her breast. He did not use the arm anchored around her back to pull her into the burgeoning length of his erection.

He instead lifted his mouth a scant inch and rested his forehead against hers.

She didn't move away, which was fortunate, because his unruly male beast of a body needed a few moments to locate its pretensions to civility. He was in a rose arbor, for God's sake, stealing a kiss like a schoolboy chasing the goose girl.

"I am convinced," she said. He leaned closer, the better to catch the sense of her husky whisper, the better to inhale the fragrance of a thousand flowers and one woman.

"Of?" His fingers stroked over the exposed back of her neck, though they itched to uncoil that fat braid so he could bury his face in her unbound hair.

"The desultory approach would sit ill with you."

The desultory...? He should step back, because his mind had gone to mist and fog. Where thoughts, plans, and crisp recollections should be, he had only impulses and impressions.

Her breath against his neck, her fingers toying with the hair at his nape, her hips canted toward his even as their upper bodies were no longer tightly seamed together. He straightened enough to lift his face from hers, but she only leaned against him, her cheek resting on his shoulder.

Maybe she needed a few moments, too? The idea calmed him and sent his hands in a slow caress over her back and neck. She seemed to like it, letting him soothe them both with uncomplicated touch.

"You'll kiss me again?" She put the question to his shoulder, but he made out her words in part because he felt them against his body.

"Very likely." He hadn't meant to growl his response.

"Some warning would be appreciated."

Indeed, it would.

"I'll do better next time." So neither of them was ambushed.

She tipped her face up, and the fool woman was smiling at him. It wasn't quite the smile she'd bestowed on the carnations when she'd thought them a token from her brother. It was more… mischievous, more *female*.

Good God, the lady was dangerous to a man's self-possession, *and she didn't even know it*.

"If you do much better, Mr. Hazlit, I will need my hartshorn and a tisane." She subsided against him, and Benjamin felt his lips quirking up.

She wasn't offended. This was more of a relief than it ought to have been, but he didn't examine it too closely. He'd kissed in the line of duty before, and he probably would again.

In fact, he was rather looking forward to it.

❧

Benjamin Hazlit was a fiend from hell. Maggie became convinced of this when after their third pot of tea—he preferred Darjeeling—he was still grilling her about her household, her habits, her schedule on the day her reticule had gone missing.

And all the while—when she herself ought to have been focused on how to recover the dratted reticule—Maggie had been hard put not to watch his mouth as it formed question after question.

His mouth was neither cold nor stern. It was warm and knowing and even tender… gentle, God help her.

Gracious, gracious, gracious. His mouth was… it was a revelation, a window into a side of the man Maggie would never have guessed existed. With the spotty boys and aging knights, she'd endured some pawing and slobbering. She'd been kissed, groped, and otherwise introduced to the nonsense that went on between men and women.

They'd given her a rare moment of sympathy for her own mother, those suitors who wanted Maggie's settlement despite the fact that it came attached to her hand in marriage.

Until she'd asked her brother Devlin why men felt compelled to behave in such a fashion, and Dev had gotten that tight, lethal look to him. He'd taught her a few moves then, creative uses of the knee, the fist, the fingers, and the suitors had become more respectful as a result.

She wanted to plant her fist in Mr. Hazlit's gut at that moment, though she suspected her fist would be the worse for it.

How could a man kiss so sweetly, so ardently, and yet be so... fiendish?

"Show me your private quarters." He set down his teacup and rose, clearly expecting Maggie to pop up and comply.

"Let me send Millie ahead to see that my rooms are presentable." She remained sitting and took a leisurely sip of her tea for good measure.

"Presentable isn't necessary." He extended a hand down to her. His hands were large, tanned like the rest of him—or perhaps he was simply dark complected—and there was a signet ring on his left little finger.

"Mr. Hazlit?" She took another sip of tea.

"Miss Windham?"

"If you waggle your fingers at me, or—heaven forbid—snap them, I will bite you." She'd bitten one brother, once more than two decades ago, and the other four had all fallen neatly into line.

He dropped his hand. Maggie expected him to launch into a lecture about his trying only to find her reticule and her being contrary and difficult—which she admittedly could be—when he hunkered before her.

"Where?" Something lurked in his eyes, something… playful?

"Where, what?"

"Where would you bite me?"

God help her, he'd dropped his voice to that smoky register she'd heard out in the rose arbor. It did things to her insides when he spoke like that, curious, wonderful, dangerous things.

She met his gaze, sensing it was crucial not to back down. "On your handsome nose."

The mischief in his eyes blossomed into humor, then into a smile of such charm Maggie's insides started Trooping the Colors—full parade bands marching in all directions, cheering crowds, waving banners. *Gracious*.

She realized her mistake. "Your *arrogant*, handsome nose."

"My apologies." He hadn't apologized for kissing her, Maggie realized. That was something. "Will you please allow me to inspect your quarters, Miss Windham, so I might be about finding your reticule sooner rather than later?"

"Of course." She gave him her hand and let him assist her to her feet. Her rooms would be thoroughly in order—her staff wouldn't allow it otherwise—though only as she ushered Hazlit into her sitting room did she realize his presence there could feel quite as intimate as that kiss in the rose arbor.

Or as intimate as his smile.

Two hours later, Maggie sat sipping a nice hearty pekoe—none of that prissy Darjeeling—while she surveyed her personal sitting room.

A room Mr. Hazlit had gone over from the molding to the wainscoting to the carpets and everything in between. She'd forced herself to watch as he'd examined every inch of her most domestic spaces. He'd taken a seat in this chair, then that one, glancing around her room with a frown on his face. He'd sat for several minutes at her desk—a big old relic from Morelands—and fiddled with her pens, ink, sand, and wax.

A bad moment, that. Correspondence was quite, quite personal to any woman.

He'd prowled around, getting the view out of each window, peering up the flue, running his finger over the mantel as if inspecting for dust.

Which he would not find, of course. Maggie's grounding in the domestic arts had come from Esther, Duchess of Moreland, after all.

And then he'd charged off into her bedroom, leaving her to trail behind, relieved that he was done with one room but not at all prepared for the sight of him sitting on her bed.

The bed was another Morelands castoff, but ducal castoffs could be impressive. Maggie was taller than the other women in her family, and she'd appropriated a bed worthy of her stature.

Mr. Hazlit had tugged off his riding boots and scooted back to prop himself against the bank of pillows. He'd crossed his legs at the ankle and started that peering-around business until Maggie was about to scream at him on general principles. For him to just lounge there, amid her shams and pillows and sheets...

But then he'd bounced up, pulled on his boots, and gone to her wardrobe, and that had been far, far worse.

He'd fingered each dress, run his hands over her shawls, knelt to take inventory of her neatly arranged shoes and boots.

"These pale colors do not become you, Miss Windham."

If his inquisitive, frowning silence had been bad, the little pronouncements he made in her bedroom were worse.

"Have you no riding boots, Miss Windham?"

She did, but they were so old, they resided under her bed—which he soon saw, damn him to Hades.

He'd picked up a pamphlet by her bedside and arched one dark eyebrow at her. "The reproductive habits of *swine*, Miss Windham?"

She read everything that particular author wrote because, though he was the youngest son of an earl, his study of the subject was unflinchingly scientific. It wasn't as if she could interview the pigs, for pity's sake.

"No flowers in your bedroom, Miss Windham? Your maids are remiss."

He'd run his hands over her books, making no comment on the Austen novels having pride of place on her mantel, and he'd stood looking at her bed for so long she'd broken her own determined silence.

"What are you doing, Mr. Hazlit? It's only an old and very comfortable bed."

"Counting pillows."

Of course he was counting the pillows. She wanted to smack him with one, or several. "And this will assist you in finding my reticule?"

"The truth would assist me more." He'd spoken quietly, but she heard him.

"What truth?"

He merely stared at her, as if counting unseen pillows in her head, or in her soul.

"Are you quite finished, Mr. Hazlit?"

"No, but I've seen enough for now. Have you plans for the evening?"

"Maybe I'll embroider another pillowcase."

The corners of his mouth flattened. "I'll take you driving tomorrow afternoon, weather permitting."

She folded her arms, not at all prepared to allow his high-handedness. "Perhaps I'm busy tomorrow afternoon. Perhaps I have plans, and perhaps a smitten suitor would patiently wait until his invitation fits in with his lady's plans."

"It wasn't an invitation."

"My point exactly."

She turned on her heel, intent on making a dignified exit, but he stopped her with a hand on her shoulder. When she turned back to him, he did not drop his hand, but rather, drew one finger along her jaw.

"I beg your pardon, Miss Windham. Does it suit your plans to join me for a drive tomorrow afternoon? I'd be ever so grateful for your company."

There was no smile lurking around his mouth, no humor in his eyes, and Maggie's insides started to flutter most inconveniently. He looked for all the world like a man whose every happiness depended on her answer.

Damn him.

"Gracious, Mr. Hazlit. When you ask so prettily, I can but consent." He dropped his hand, which allowed her to start their progress toward the front door. "What did your search of my quarters reveal that could help you find my reticule?"

He blew out a breath and fell in step beside her. "It revealed that you are very careful, that prudence is second nature to you, though probably more a learned skill than a native aspect of your personality. It revealed that you purposely dress to hide your many assets, and you have a lively mind, though not a frivolous one. It revealed that your staff truly does take your welfare to heart."

"You sound disappointed." How had he learned all that by counting her pillows?

"A traitor from within is an easy answer, and for your sake, I was hoping for an easy answer."

For her sake? Whatever did he mean by that?

"I'll come by for you about three," he said as Maggie's head footman handed him gloves and hat then melted back down the hallway. Hazlit tapped the hat onto his head, regarding her out of dark eyes.

"You are not to worry, Miss Windham."

It was the last thing she expected him to say, more insightful than all his previous pronouncements.

"I will worry until my belongings are again in my possession."

"Which they will be shortly." He picked up her

hand and bowed very low over it, so low she felt the heat of his breath on her knuckles.

"Until tomorrow."

And then he left, while all the worry Maggie had held at bay during his lengthy and troubling visit came crashing back to haunt her. The worry only coiled more tightly when Millie told her another note had been delivered to the kitchen during Mr. Hazlit's visit.

❧

"You were making morning calls?"

Archer yawned and scratched his chest as he spoke, but Hazlit wasn't fooled. Despite a display of casual, bored behavior, Archer Portmaine's mind was wide awake and taking in details.

"One morning call." Hazlit rose from the tub and stood dripping until Archer tossed him a bath sheet. Only when he'd toweled off his chest and arms did he climb out to stand on his hearth rug.

Archer settled his long frame into the chair at the escritoire. "One morning call that took all afternoon."

"I'm on a case, Archer." Hazlit finished drying off, then crossed the room to the wardrobe where evening attire had been left waiting for him. "Are you going out tonight?"

"Lady Abby is dining at home, so no. I think I've made some progress with Allard's books, though." He got up and started poking through the tray on the bureau. "Which case has you tooling around Mayfair all afternoon?"

"Not tooling around, making a thorough search of a lady's chambers. I'm on the Windham case." He assembled his evening finery as he spoke, though he'd rather be lounging around the house tonight, letting Archer beat him at cards.

"I thought the housekeeper was innocent." Archer gave him a curious look. "Moreland's cub married her, didn't he?"

"Last year's news, Archer. That was Gayle Windham, Earl of Westhaven, and yes, she's his countess now. Stop being coy. What do you want to know?"

"You don't need all afternoon to search a lady's chambers." Arthur tossed a cuff link in the air, then another and another until he was juggling four. "What are you about, Benjamin?"

"One learns a lot by inspecting a person's habitat." He pulled on smalls, trousers, and stockings while Archer continued to play with the cuff links.

"What did you learn?"

"I'm not sure." The shirt was made for him, which meant it was cut loosely—contrary to current fashion, but comfortable. "I learned that she's a lady."

"You had doubts?" Archer caught each cuff link in succession and dumped two back into the tray.

"I try not to make assumptions." But that hair... that wide, lovely mouth, that generous bosom, and those sweet female curves... And more than all of that, her bewildered smile when she beheld a tame bunch of flowers. "She runs a decent household, takes a genuine interest in her staff, donates both time and coin to charity, and is devoted to her family."

She was also a voracious reader—everything from agricultural pamphlets on the reproductive habits of swine to financial treatises and lurid novels.

Archer approached with a gold cuff link, which Hazlit allowed him to fasten on the right shirt cuff. "You sound puzzled, Benjamin. Her father is a duke. Why wouldn't she behave in accordance with the standards applicable to a duchess?" He slipped the second cuff link through the fabric of the left cuff then peered at Hazlit closely. "Or the standards of a countess?"

"As to that…" Leave it to Archer to anticipate the difficult subjects. "You might hear I'm interested in the lady in a matrimonial sense."

Archer's handsome face creased into a genuine, warmhearted smile. The other kind—the calculating variety—was often in evidence, making this rare sighting all the more unusual. "About time you got your priorities straight."

"I am *not* interested in her."

The smile went out like a snuffed candle. "You have two sisters, Benjamin. Two sisters who prior to their marriages were ill-used by unfeeling brutes, and that ought to…"

He put a hand over Archer's mouth. "I am not toying with a lady's affections, so desist, Sister Mary Portmaine. Magdalene Windham has not been entirely honest with me, and I require a certain proximity to ascertain why that is and what to do as a result."

It sounded so rational, his almighty plan. It did not explain kisses in the rose arbor, or trespassing on the woman's privacy to linger in her boudoir, touching her clothing, learning the exact size of her bed and the number of pillows adorning it.

Or the particular delight he felt upon hearing she thought his somewhat prominent nose handsome.

Archer ambled over to the bureau. "Does she know you're just playacting?"

"She compared me to Mr. Kean." While Archer sorted through the tray on the bureau, Hazlit withdrew a starched cravat from the wardrobe and started tying it into a simple knot.

"For God's sake." Archer marched across the room to bat Hazlit's hands away. "You tie a university boy's knot when what's wanted is a little style."

"A little simple style." Except Archer's sense of fashion was impeccable, so Hazlit held still.

"Simple yet elegant, like me." Archer slipped a jeweled pin into the middle of a deft knot, leaving gold and amber winking out of the creamy linen. "You'll do."

"My thanks."

The mirror suggested Archer was, as usual, correct. The amber was just a hint of style. It picked up on brown eyes and skin a little darker than was fashionable, but did so subtly.

"Really, Benjamin, what would you do without me?"

"Probably retire to Blessings and dandle Avis's offspring on my avuncular knee."

Archer moved around the room, tidying up the bath accessories and folding damp bath sheets. "Would you really? Cumbria can be deuced damp and far from civilization, and something suggests dandling might not be your forte."

"Cumbria can be lovely, which is why all London flocks there of a summer. It's gorgeous, the fells so striking they make Kent look like the most tame garden, the light so pure and the air so bracing… what?" It was quite possible Archer was regarding him with *pity*.

"You're homesick, Benjamin. You worry about your sisters as much now that they're married as you did before they tied their respective knots. You worry about your estate, and you racket around here poking your nose into everybody else's business because it distracts you from your worrying. Find a wife, go home, and leave the snooping to fellows like me who can view it as pure sport."

"I am not homesick." Though he did worry about his sisters.

"My mistake."

"Don't wait up for me."

"I never do." Archer waved him on his way, leaving Hazlit to glance one more time in the mirror: That was the nose Maggie Windham found arrogant, *and handsome.*

"Archer?"

"Dear heart?"

"If you haven't any other plans tonight, do you suppose you could take care of a small errand for me?" It was a whim, a hunch, but cracking a case often turned on such inspirations—and it was for the lady's own good, of course.

"I'm not working tonight, Benjamin. I need my beauty sleep, too."

"It involves keeping an eye on a pretty lady."

A little flicker of interest passed through professionally guileless blue eyes. "Then I'm your man."

⁓

When Old King Hal acquired the papal abbeys and monasteries, he'd simultaneously made a bold statement regarding his opinion of Rome and enriched his own coffers immeasurably.

He had also paved the way for Londoners to enjoy the hundreds of acres of bucolic beauty that came to be known as Hyde Park. As far as Esther, Duchess of Moreland, was concerned, it had been one of Henry's few commendable moves.

A lady could maneuver in the Park, spying out those Eligibles worthy of consideration for addition to the Windham family. For that's how it would be: When the girls married, they would bring a husband into the family.

Not the other way around.

"Each year this place gets more crowded," Evie muttered from her perch beside her mother. The other girls had begged off, leaving their youngest sister pride of place beside Her Grace in the curricle.

"All the more gentlemen from which you might pick your husband," Esther said, smiling serenely. "Chin up, dearest. If Papa gets wind you were acting mopish, he'll fret."

It did the trick, as Esther had known it would. Evie's chin came up, and a smile worthy of her charming papa graced her features.

"Your Grace, Lady Evie."

Lucas Denning—a scamp if ever there was one—rode along beside the carriage. He tipped his hat and flashed them a smile. He might do—he was wealthy enough, newly titled with a marquessate, and Percy approved of his politics, more or less.

"Deene." Esther nodded and returned the smile while Evie held out a gloved hand to the man. He managed to bow over it even while his horse stepped along beside the vehicle.

"The scenery becomes more lovely each time I come here. Lady Evie, my compliments on that bonnet."

"At least you're consistent," Evie said. Esther felt a little sinking inside. "I believe you complimented it, as well, when my cousin wore it last week."

Because she had raised five boys, Esther saw the slight tightening around Lord Deene's mouth. He was freshly out of mourning, but it was no secret his papa had despaired of him. The weight of grief and guilt was telling. To Esther's practiced eye, Deene was a man ready to admit defeat and take a wife.

"True beauty endures over time," Deene said, sending a flirtatious glance in Esther's direction.

"While flattery disappears with the wind," she replied, returning his smile. "Though it offers fleeting amusement. Is that a new horse, my lord?"

As soon as the question was out of her mouth, Esther knew it was quite the wrong thing to say if she wanted to draw Evie to the man's attention. Evie shrank back against the squabs and let Deene prose on about his bay gelding, even going so far as to recite some of the animal's pedigree.

Abruptly, Evie came alert. "I say. That's our Maggie, and she's being driven by the delectable Mr. Hazlit."

Point for the lady. Deene hid it, but referring to Hazlit as delectable had gotten his attention. He sat a little straighter in the saddle. "Where?"

"Under the trees," Evie said. "Mama, drive on. We must not hint we've seen her, or she'll make him take her home directly."

Deene, clever lad, moved his horse a few steps up so
the line of sight between the two vehicles' occupants
would be obstructed.

"You're sure it was Maggie?" Esther asked.

"I'm sure." Evie and Deene spoke at the same
moment then glared at each other.

"And she's with Mr. Hazlit, you say? Benjamin Hazlit?"

"No other gentleman sports such dreamy dark eyes,"
Evie said, "and Dev and Val have both remarked how
closely matched his team of bays is."

Esther could see the horses, two glossy mahogany
bays of equal height, black manes and tails tidily braided,
four perfectly matched white socks on each horse.

"He doesn't drive out often," Deene said, speculation in
his tone. "Perhaps I should give my respects to the lady?"

Esther nodded. "Perhaps you should." Percy would
get the details from the man over steak and kidney pie
at their club. "Good day, my lord."

"Your Grace, Lady Evie." He touched the brim of
his hat with his crop and guided the horse in a neat
pirouette while Esther turned her conveyance down a
side path that would take them off The Ring.

"We're to call on Maggie tomorrow?" Evie asked.

Esther glanced at her youngest child. She worried
about them all—to be a parent was to worry—but this
one had given her particular fits.

"Maybe the day after. One doesn't want to pry."

"One does if she's you and she's just seen Maggie
out with a gentleman for the first time in ten years.
You like Mr. Hazlit, so does Papa."

"His Grace respects Mr. Hazlit," Esther said. When
had her baby girl grown so observant?

"Mama, I love you, but if you push on this, Maggie will drive him away."

"Maggie would not drive away a suitable gentleman."

Though she had, and they both knew it. Time after time, Maggie had driven away suitable gentlemen.

❧

Magdalene Windham came alive in the out of doors. Hazlit had noticed it yesterday in her back gardens and considered this might have been part of the reason he'd kissed her—a small part.

She squirmed beside him on the carriage seat, drawing in a big lungful of air then letting it out on a gusty sigh.

"Spring is such a gift," she said. "I forget each year how much I enjoy it; then the crocuses peek up and the Holland bulbs follow and I can't wait for the trees to leaf out."

"Have you considered living in the country?"

"Morelands is lovely. I spend some time there each summer. What a pair of gentlemen you have in the traces."

"Berlin and Stockholm, or Bear and Stockie." He shifted his wrists over, which meant their arms touched. "Go ahead and take the reins, Miss Windham. You know you want to."

"I couldn't."

He pushed his hands against hers where they rested in her lap. She wasn't wearing driving gloves, so he tucked the ribbons in one hand and used his teeth to pull off his own gloves and drop them in her lap. "Could too."

She glanced down at the gloves, longing in her eyes.

"You do know how?"

"My brother Devlin taught all of us girls, though it's mostly common sense."

He drew the team to a halt near the Cumberland Gate.

"I really shouldn't."

"You really should." He was tempted to point out that if they were truly courting, this is exactly the way an indulgent man—a smitten man—would carry on in public. "You thrive on the fresh air, you look at those horses like they were made of chocolate, and you really do not care if the breeze disturbs your coiffure. Give it a go, Magdalene Windham."

"Maggie." She said it very softly, her eyes glued to the reins. "Nobody calls me Magdalene."

"Take the reins, Maggie, or we'll sit here as all of Polite Society passes by."

She took the reins, not even bothering to put on his gloves. He deftly snatched them back from her lap, taking care to not touch even her skirts as he did. "Do The Ring," he said. "It's the expected thing and early enough we should be able to maneuver."

She nodded, which suggested she knew her way around the park. Had her brothers seen to that, as well, or had the knowledge come from her years on the marriage market? He pondered that mystery while his fool horses preened and trotted along as if they'd been longing for a lady's hands on the reins.

"You don't find it awkward?" she asked. "Being driven by a lady?"

They were in public. Best she get used to their roles. He gave her a heavy-lidded smile. "My lady, no hour spent in your company could ever be awkward."

She grinned at him, a great big devilish smile that reached her wonderful green eyes and had two rows of gleaming white teeth in evidence.

"You are a rascal, Mr. Hazlit. A thoroughgoing rascal. You'll never get the reins back if you don't stifle that nonsense."

Seeing her smile—at him, at the horses, at the day—Hazlit realized how closely confined she'd kept herself with him thus far. Her smiles had been merely pretty, her courtesy ruthlessly correct, her conversation guarded—except for that kiss, of course.

The kiss he'd nipped in the bud because he wasn't a complete fool.

"Is that your mother over there?"

"My moth—?" The smile winked out, replaced by anxiety and… fear? That disappeared from her eyes, too, so quickly Hazlit wasn't sure he'd seen it. "Oh, you mean Her Grace. Gracious. I'd prefer a strategic retreat."

"Do as you please, my lady."

Except she couldn't, because traffic moved only at a crawl, and there were but a few turnings. Hazlit prepared to smile and do the pretty for Her Grace, but a man on a bay horse rode forward the few steps necessary to obscure the occupants of the duchess's carriage from sight.

"Deene is making his bow," Hazlit said, though he had to crane his neck to see around the matched footmen on the back of Lady Dandridge's landau. "I think you've been spared."

"Only for the present. Somebody will say something to Her Grace. Papa will be asking your intentions next." She kept her eyes front, so he had to peek around her bonnet brim to see the downcast expression on her face.

"Must you sound so despondent?" He'd tried to make it a joke, but she only turned her head to look at him with eyes that held a world of unhappiness.

"Miss Windham." Deene tipped his hat from astride his horse. "A rare pleasure to see you out and about. Hazlit."

"Deene. I thought you'd avoid this scene."

"Normally I do." He flashed a grin at Miss Windham. "No reflection on present company. I rose too late today to ride this morning, so I'm letting Beast stretch his legs now."

"What sort of name is that for such a handsome fellow?" Miss Windham switched the ribbons to her right hand and reached out with the left toward the horse. "You'll hurt his feelings." The gelding delicately sniffed at her fingers and then turned its head as if to regard his rider reproachfully.

"He answers to it," Deene said, petting his horse. "Better him than me, right?"

The smile he aimed at Hazlit's companion was dazzling.

"We'd best be off if we're not to hold up traffic," Hazlit said.

Deene—damn his arrogance—nudged his horse forward as Miss Windham signaled the team to walk on.

"If you enjoy driving, my lady, I've a pair of bays you might like to try."

And God bless the woman, she looked faintly

exasperated as she eyed the ribbons. "Mr. Hazlit is indulging me in a rare whim, my lord, but thank you for the offer."

"Perhaps another day." Deene bowed again—how did it *not* look ridiculous when he bowed from the saddle?—and took his aggravating, friendly self off.

"May we go home now?" The sparkle had left her eyes; the roses in her cheeks had faded. The woman looked positively mulish.

"You have the reins. We go where you please."

She turned the horses off the main path, leaving Hazlit to wonder what exactly had blighted their outing. Had it been Deene's flirting? The sight of Her Grace? Or worse, something he himself had said or done?

❦

There was no explaining why, after three decades of raising children, arguing, loving, and arguing some more, His Grace, Percival St. Stephens Tiberius Joachim Windham, should be more dear to his wife than ever. He accepted it as a gift he could only continually try to earn and kissed his duchess on the cheek.

"Damned idiots grow more thickheaded by the day, Esther." He linked his arms around her waist and sighed into her wheat-gold hair. "Prinny must build his fancies while the common soldier starves. I'm tempted to claim senility and hare off to Morelands permanently."

"I take it your meetings were trying?" She started rubbing the back of his neck, and like an old dog who's found his rug before the warm hearth, he felt all the tension and worry of the day draining out of him.

"They're always trying. If the House of Lords doesn't start yielding gracefully on the small issues, we're going to be facing the mob. Mark me on this, Esther."

"Come." She led him by the hand to his favorite chair. "Tell me who's giving you the most trouble, and I'll invite his ladies to tea."

While he prattled on about this and that vote, she tugged off his boots and brought him a glass of wine, then sat embroidering while he parsed each comment made and proposal put forth at his meetings.

"Have you discussed any of this with Westhaven?" she asked an hour later.

It took him a moment to consider the question, because in the candlelight, his wife's profile appeared the same to him then as it had thirty-odd years ago: serene, graceful… peaceful. Thank God he'd had the sense to marry Esther and not one of the other lovelies who'd turned his fool head.

"He's preoccupied with his offspring," His Grace said, peering at his empty wine glass. "And that's as it should be."

"He could use a distraction," Her Grace countered, putting her hoop aside. "And Anna will have a little more room to breathe if her husband is occasionally called to your side for political reasons. He has your knack for building consensus, but he'll need your network of spies and cronies if he's to step into your shoes."

He got up and poured himself another half glass of libation. A year ago—just after his heart seizure—his wife would have frowned at it. Two years ago, he would have gone through half the bottle by now.

"Where did you learn to manage me, my love?" He held the glass to her lips while she took a ladylike sip, then subsided into his chair. "You're telling me I have to be ready to hand the political reins to Gayle, but you're doing it in such a way that I'm flattered and even motivated to author my own retirement."

She looked down and to the right, her lips thinning slightly. It was her How-Do-I-Put-This? look, so he waited.

"I want your opinion on something." She raised her gaze to his—such lovely green eyes his bride had.

He saluted with his drink. "Ask, beloved. You know I can deny you nothing."

"What is your honest assessment of Lucas Denning?"

Ah. Matchmaking again. There was a common misperception among the Windham family members that His Grace was obsessed with building his dynasty and that all manner of mischief had been perpetrated by him to propel his sons to the altar.

He was, and it had, but the rest of the story was that Her Grace was equally if not more invested in the same outcomes. She'd befriended Anna when the woman was only Gayle's housekeeper; she'd made rather pointed remarks to St. Just when he was befuddled over his antecedents; she'd fretted endlessly over Valentine, who'd chosen to spend the previous winter with St. Just—on the Yorkshire dales!— though Valentine had also recently succumbed to the lure of matrimony.

Esther Windham was a force to be reckoned with, and Deene had gotten into her matchmaking gun sights. The man was doomed.

"He's struggling a bit," His Grace said. A neutral answer that applied to most men between toddlerhood and senescence. "Why?"

"Struggling in what sense?" She had her embroidery back in her lap, a tactic to shield her expression from her husband's eyes, of course.

"A title always befalls a man under a cloak of grief and loss. Deene and his papa did not get on well, though I can hardly blame the boy. The old marquis was a brute, despite having wonderful kennels. I think Deene will come right in time—if he finds the right marchioness."

"Do you think he and Evie would suit?"

"Evie?" Their baby, their little girl... the one they'd almost lost track of after Bart and St. Just had joined up? "Might inspire her remaining sisters to get serious about matrimony if she lets the man court her. Sophie can't be the only one to set a good example."

"That doesn't exactly answer my question." She set the blasted hoop aside and turned a frown on her husband. "They strike sparks off each other, but not in a good way. I may be overreacting, but a mother worries."

He patted her hand. "A good mother worries." A mother who'd buried two grown sons was entitled to be slightly mad with worry, come to that.

"But you think he'd do?"

Back to this?

"I have no cause to reject the man, Esther, if that's what you're asking. When he votes, he does so responsibly. He doesn't always toe the party line, but he has sound reasons for breaking ranks, and I've been known to switch allegiance myself sometimes. Keeps the idiots on their toes when a man votes his conscience." He took a sip of his drink while he watched his wife for a reaction.

"I suppose it's up to Evie, then, but you'll make a few inquiries?"

He was being dispatched to send out the scouts, then. Gads… to see his sons married was one thing— their wives were capital additions to the family, and grandchildren were better yet. He'd reconciled himself to seeing Sophie wed to Sindal, whose estate was just a few miles from Morelands—but his baby girl?

Too precious to cast into the arms of any handsome, randy marquis who came along.

"I'll put Hazlit on it. We'll soon know what side of the bed Deene sleeps on and which soap he prefers at his bath. May I offer you the last sip?" He passed her his glass.

"My thanks. I spotted Mr. Hazlit today in the park. Maggie was driving his bays and looking quite smart. I suppose it's time we went down to dinner." She set the glass aside and allowed him to assist her to her feet. "I had a letter from Rose today, too. She specifically asked me if you were available for a visit sometime this summer."

"Rose asked after her old grandpapa? Imagine that!"

He led his duchess into dinner, made all the appropriate noises to his wife and daughters, and presided over a jovial, pleasant family meal as he had countless times before.

Even as he wondered why, exactly, Esther had felt it necessary to use all that flummery about Evie and young Deene to obscure the rather startling news that their dear Maggie had actually driven out with an Eligible.

❧

Archer passed Hazlit a drink and then poured one for himself. "You won't like it."

"I won't like the whiskey?" Hazlit took a whiff of his drink, catching the same subtle, smoky scent it usually bore. The scent of relaxation and comfort. "What are you going on about, Archer?"

"You won't like my report."

The day had been long and busy—so busy Hazlit hadn't had time to speak privately with Archer, much less consider recent developments in the Windham situation. He took a seat on the library's sofa and pulled off his boots.

"I particularly won't like your report if I have to wait what remains of the night to hear it."

Archer took the comfortable chair at a right angle to the sofa and propped his stocking feet on the table. "Abby Norcross has gone to ground. Either she knows we're trailing her, or she's having her menses."

"You aren't on terms with the chambermaid yet?" And for the first time in ages, it occurred to Hazlit to wonder why a man would remain in a line of business where such information had to be gathered. It was distasteful, to pry into a lady's situation to that degree.

"I'm on terms, but I've been a trifle busy. Your Miss Windham had a pair of gentlemen callers."

"A pair? At the same time?" When men called on a pretty woman in pairs, they could either check each other's worst impulses or goad one another into folly.

"At the same time, and they didn't come in the front door. They were admitted to the kitchen by way of the mews after dark."

"The kitchen door, after dark. You're right; I don't like it." Hazlit took a sip of his drink and let the warmth course through his gut. "They weren't just her footmen returning from their evening pint?"

"These were big men, they moved with the well-greased joints of youth, and it's odd…" He fell maddeningly silent.

"I'd beat you, Archer, but I think you'd enjoy it."

"I might." And the bastard smirked while he pretended to consider the notion. "The strange thing was I felt like I was seeing the same man in duplicate. They didn't move nearly alike, Benjamin, they moved *exactly* the same, as if they'd been trained that way."

"The only place I know where a man might train his walk like that is on the stage." Two men? Two big young men? Calling at Maggie's kitchen door? No, he did not like this one bit, but he wouldn't give Archer the satisfaction of being obvious about it.

"They might need that type of training for our line of work," Archer said.

"Bugger that."

Except it made sense. If Maggie were hiding secrets—and she was—then two big fellows skulking about her mews was almost to be expected. "You didn't see their faces?"

"Not enough light. The clothes looked well made but unpretentious. Not a laborer's clothes, perhaps the clothes of men with a skilled trade—a tutor, a jeweler, a secretary, that sort of thing."

"They weren't calling on one of the other servants? There's no law saying domestics can't socialize when their duties are done, at least not in Maggie's household."

"I don't know. You might consider asking the lady if she's aware these fellows are coming around, and if she knows, what their business is."

He might, if he wanted to admit to her he'd been spying. Which he did not.

"How long did they stay?"

"About an hour. They weren't dropping something off, and they didn't appear to be carrying anything with them when they left. I followed them to a tavern between Soho and St. James, but they slipped out while I was... distracted."

Flirting, or worse.

"You will die of a dread disease, Archer. Whom shall I rely on then? Hmm?"

"Whom shall you threaten to beat, you mean?" Archer thrived on the occasional compliment, and he was smiling that sweet, shy smile so few ever saw.

"You didn't see anything else but two curiously similar men of some height and middling sartorial status being admitted to the kitchen door?"

"I saw the little maid—the tweeny—smile at them as they arrived, but then the door was pulled shut. They keep their curtains down after dark, so I couldn't see anything else."

"Well, there you have it: a pair of swains calling on their lady. Even a tweeny is entitled to be courted." Except Maggie had told him the tweeny was enamored of the head footman.

"By two sizable swains at once? After dark? That's not any kind of courting a decent girl should know about."

"Finish your drink, Archer, and then I shall beat you stoutly—at cribbage."

❦

The longer the reticule and its contents stayed missing, the worse Maggie felt about turning to Mr. Hazlit to remedy the situation.

Driving in the park had proven she'd have to at least scotch his idea of courting her. One look from Lady Dandridge, and Maggie's courage had deserted her entirely. One of the biggest gossips in Mayfair, and Maggie had to fret about what the woman knew and to whom she'd tell it.

"Mr. Hazlit to see you, mum." Millie fairly danced with the excitement of announcing the man.

"I'll see him in the front... I'll see him in my sitting room."

On a sunny day like this, it could be remarked that the curtains in her front sitting room were drawn closed—particularly after having driven out with Mr. Hazlit just the day before. Society was that noticing, and Her Grace had seen to it Maggie was that careful.

"I'll escort you up." Hazlit himself stood in the doorway to her office, looking damnably handsome in his riding attire and aiming a genial smile at Millie. "Some refreshments wouldn't go amiss either."

Millie withdrew, and Hazlit's smile dimmed as he focused dark eyes on Maggie.

"You do not look particularly well rested, my dear." He extended a hand down to her where she sat at her desk. "Perhaps dreams of me kept you tossing all night?"

"Or perhaps some bad fish had the same effect." She batted her eyes at him for good measure, not at all pleased when another smile lit his countenance.

"Touché." The idiot man bent and kissed her hand, but he made such a drama out of it. They were both bare-handed, so he not only drew her hand up in his, he used his free hand to brush his fingers slowly over her knuckles and fingers first, pressed his lips firmly to the back of her hand, then held the place he'd kissed against his forehead.

She wanted to snatch her hand back—and she wanted to know how he'd react if she winnowed her fingers through his hair to work out the faint crease left by his hat.

When he straightened, there was just enough challenge in his eyes that she did not satisfy her curiosity.

"This is an interesting room." He let go of her hand as he glanced around.

"It's a mundane room." Maggie's gaze trailed after his: Four white walls, two of them sporting shelves lined with books and pamphlets and treatises, two windows for natural light and fresh air, a desk, a fireplace. Nothing out of the ordinary here.

"Who's this?" Hazlit peered at a portrait of a man in regimentals—tall, blond, with mischievous green eyes. "He has the look of a Windham."

"That is—was—my brother Bartholomew."

He said nothing but studied the picture a little longer before moving on to the frame beside it. "And this?"

"My late brother Victor." Seated. He'd been consumptive even when he'd sat for the painting. "Shall we go upstairs?"

Hazlit frowned at her, then went about peeking and

prying again: pillowcases embroidered by her sisters; a framed manuscript of a little waltz Valentine had written for her when she'd made her come out; the tea service Her Grace had given Maggie as a house-warming present; a shamelessly flattering sketch Victor had done of her as a young girl; Papa's old hunting whip, coiled and hung on the corner of Bart's portrait.

"You have a dog?" He was frowning at Blake's old bed by the hearth.

"When I moved here, my brother Gayle got me a great shaggy mastiff—an older fellow who needed a quiet household for his dotage. They don't typically live very long."

She rose and headed for the door, wanting to drag the man bodily from the room. "I do hope you aren't going to ask me to go driving again?"

"I wasn't going to." And thank the Gods, he fell in step beside her. "We're going shopping instead."

She *adored* shopping. "I'm afraid that won't suit."

"Then we won't go shopping." He waited while she preceded him into her personal sitting room. "We'll instead go on a little sortie to the shops so you can show me where you got the missing reticule and perhaps find one to match it exactly."

He again waited until Maggie took a seat. She chose a rocker by the hearth, a good, safe distance from anywhere he might light.

"I can sketch the thing for you," she said. "You are welcome to take a seat, Mr. Hazlit. Looming over a lady is hardly polite."

He prowled over to the window. "You chose this house for privacy, didn't you? The trees and the fencing and your corner location mean your neighbors can't pry even visually."

"My brother Gayle chose it for me, but yes, I told him what I was looking for."

He turned his back to the window and perched his hips on the sill. Her brothers were tall enough to do that, too. "You're close to Westhaven?"

Peeking and prying again, damn the man. "I love my family, Mr. Hazlit, and yes, I would say I am close to all my siblings."

"No particular favorites?"

When would the perishing damned tray arrive?

"I was close to Bart—there was only a few months' difference in our ages—and Victor was my escort of choice because Valentine had his hands full with the rest of my sisters. Why do you ask?"

He flashed her a saccharine smile. "A man interested in a lady wants to know her every confidence. Would you like to know a few of mine?"

"Have you any worth knowing?" The boredom she was able to inject into the question was supremely satisfying. She more than suspected he was better connected than he let on—perhaps in line for a title. He was an honorable, after all.

"Everybody has secrets, Miss Windham, or am I still to call you Maggie?"

When had he moved? He was perched on the arm of the sofa, not a polite posture at all, and one that put him in proximity to her.

"If you're supposedly courting me, Mr. Hazlit, then you will want to impress me with your manners, not slip into informalities at every turn."

"If I'm courting you, Maggie dear, I will want to appropriate every liberty you don't vociferously object to."

He'd dropped his voice, and now he was letting his gaze tour her person in a manner Maggie could only describe as proprietary. A tap on the almost-closed door—she didn't recall leaving it like that—suggested Millie was at long last appearing with the tray.

"Allow me." Hazlit crossed the room in three strides and held the door for the tweeny, then took the tray from her. "Our thanks."

Our thanks?

"I think you need a wife, in truth, Mr. Hazlit, so convincingly do you take on your role of doting swain."

"Perhaps I do." He set the tray on the table, though Maggie saw something unhappy pass briefly through his eyes. "Shall I pour?" he asked.

There was something significant about his offer, something far less innocent than three prosaic words suggested. Maggie couldn't put her finger on it. "Suit yourself."

Without her instructing him, he fixed her tea exactly as she liked it: plenty of cream, a dash of sugar. He chose a sandwich for her of thick yellow cheese and butter and put that on her plate beside a few ripe strawberries.

"How did you know what I'd choose?" For he'd gotten it exactly right.

"Lucky guess. You don't trust me, do you?"

"I trust you to find my reticule."

He munched on a sandwich of roasted beef and

cheese, consuming the thing in about two bites. "You want me to find your reticule; you don't trust me, though. We're going to have to work on that."

She wrinkled her nose over her tea cup. "I want you to find a lost object, not plight me your troth."

Without an invitation from her, he reached for another sandwich, just as if he were family. "It isn't lost, Maggie Windham. Someone has purloined something of value to you. I don't need to know what exactly has been taken, but it would certainly help."

She bought time by sipping her tea. "Why do you think it was stolen?"

He sighed and sat back, setting his cup and saucer down on the tray very gently. "You live alone, except for a paid companion and your staff, but your papa and your brothers have probably inspected every member of your staff right down to the back teeth, and all with Her Grace's prompting. You aren't a forgetful woman; your staff is loyal to you. When was the last time you really lost something, Maggie?"

She'd lost two brothers, the two people on earth she'd considered her closest friends...

"If I admit the thing is stolen, you'll interrogate me all over again."

He studied her for a long, frowning moment. "I don't kiss and tell, not ever. In my line of work such a failing would be fatal, not to mention dishonorable. Don't view me as a pair of human ears. Consider me like a mechanical toy: wind me up with enough accurate information, and I'll find your reticule—and whatever's inside it. I won't pass judgment on you, regardless of your peccadilloes."

"You say that." She rose and went to the window, putting as much distance between them as possible without leaving the room, the house, the city.

She was tempted, tempted terribly to confide in him. He had a brusque competence about him suggesting he could carry it off—listening to any sordid tale without appearing to pass judgment. He'd probably done it countless times in countless mansions all over Mayfair.

"I'm going to tell you a story," he said, getting up and approaching her. His eyes were absolutely serious—absolutely trustworthy? He took her hand and led her to the sofa, then tugged her down to sit beside him. They'd been this close sitting in his curricle, but it felt different indoors and behind an almost-closed door.

"This is not a happy story," he said, lacing their fingers. Maggie permitted the contact rather than make an issue of it. He meant nothing by the touch—by any of his touches—but it was still human contact.

She told herself she was permitting it, not reveling in it.

"Why tell me an unhappy tale?"

"I'm making a gesture of trust." His lips quirked up, then the smile disappeared. "I have two sisters, both younger than I. They were out riding many years ago on family land and fell in with some bad company. The older sister's engagement was broken as a result; my younger sister was physically injured."

"A scandal." For that's how it would be. Young women came to harm through no fault of their own, and the scandal would still devolve to them. Bad company was a euphemism, Maggie was sure of it. And physically injured could also be a euphemism. *Gracious God.* "Are they all right?"

He pursed his lips. "You don't want to know the details?"

"I want to know if your sisters are managing. That is not a detail." She spoke very sternly to him, while he only continued to study her.

"I don't know." He ran a hand through his hair. "I honestly don't know if they're all right, if they'll ever be all right, but they have married, and now it is no longer my right to see to their welfare."

And this was the real admission. Not the sordid tale itself, but his inability as an older brother to write a decent ending for it. It was a gesture of trust to relay this tale, but probably not in the sense he'd intended it.

"Tell me more about your sisters."

Their hands were still joined. More to distract him than anything else, Maggie started using her index finger to trace his fingers where they laced with hers. "What is your happiest memory of your sisters?"

Four

HOW THE HELL HAD IT COME THIS? HAZLIT'S INSIDES were not calm, his skin felt too tight, and he was on the brink of revealing family history about which he'd stayed silent for twelve years.

He'd wanted to make the point that his family had weathered scandal, too. Whatever indiscretion Maggie Windham had committed, it wasn't going to condemn her in his eyes. Not when his sisters' safety had been jeopardized while he'd been nowhere to be found.

"As I've said, their names are Alexandra and Avis. Avis is the elder and remains near our family seat in Cumbria."

"I'm told it's lovely there."

With her free hand, she poured him more tea, adding the sugar and stirring as if they were discussing whose hem had been torn at last night's ball.

"Cumbria's... indescribable, if you've never been there. There's no place like it in the whole of England. The light is so... clear, the fells so rugged. The forest marches right up to the mountains, and it has a kind of beauty that makes a man glad he has eyes to see it and lungs to breathe it. How Alex found the strength to leave and come south…"

She passed him his teacup when the words trickled into silence.

"You are a good brother," she said, smoothing her fingers over his knuckles, then studying their joined hands while he pretended to sip his tea. "Maybe a short outing to the Strand would make sense. I tend to patronize the same shops, and there are only a few from which I'd purchase a reticule."

She let his hand go and stood. "I'll have my town coach brought around—it might rain yet today—and you'll excuse me while I find a cloak and bonnet."

She was back in a few minutes, before he'd eaten more than a couple of sandwiches. The cloak and bonnet were nondescript to the point of plainness, and the bag she carried more unremarkable still.

Camouflage. Always a good idea when venturing into the jungle.

And there was no way in hell it was going to rain in the next two hours, but he didn't fuss about the closed carriage. It meant her companion would have to go with them. He could only hope that would prevent him from yammering on about clear light and marching forests, for God's sake.

The trip proved to be something of a revelation. Finding a replacement for the missing purse was easy. Maggie Windham did indeed know exactly where she bought what, how much she'd paid for it, which clerk had waited on her, and when the purchase had been made.

The clerks had exchanged a subtle, long-suffering

glance when she'd walked in on Hazlit's arm, the kind of look that signaled the arrival of a customer of exacting standards and meticulous comparisons. All Hazlit had been required to do was stand by, looking harmless and besotted, while Maggie managed the entire store. Watching her in action had been simple and even enjoyable. The difficult part of the outing had been the small talk.

Hazlit knew how to interrogate those of greater, lesser, and middling stations.

He knew how to flirt with women from all walks of life.

He had learned how to flirt with men and was, to his private consternation, fairly good at it.

He knew how to banter with both women and men.

He did not know how to just... talk.

But Maggie Windham did. When they were settled in her coach, she gave the signal for the team to walk on, passed her purchases to the companion, and aimed a perfectly credible smile at Hazlit.

"My brother tells me you're quite a talented artist, Mr. Hazlit. Have you seen the German exhibition at the British Museum?"

He had, and enjoyed it thoroughly. By the time he realized he was babbling about perspective and melancholy themes, she tacked around to a different subject.

"Those gloves look to be particularly well made. May I inquire as to where you purchased them? I've noticed my youngest brother goes through gloves at a great rate."

"That would be Lord Valentine?"

"The musician in the family, though Her Grace

made sure each of us became proficient on at least one instrument. Are you musical?"

He thought of his sister Avis, who had grown so eccentric she'd play her flute along the walking paths and game trails around Blessings. "I'm a fair accompanist, but not solo material. You?"

"I struggled along with the piano for four years then threatened to take up the bagpipes. Her Grace made sure I had two party pieces suitable for social occasions then declared I'd met my obligation at the keyboard."

"Did you take up the bagpipes anyway?"

"I tried, but they're quite difficult. My brothers were forever teasing, and I gave up. Every person and beast on Morelands property was likely grateful for my lack of persistence."

"You didn't just give up, though, did you?" She'd set the bagpipes aside when she'd made her point. She wouldn't give up just because something was difficult. Persistence was part of her character—persistence and stoicism.

And something else, too. It took him a moment to puzzle it out.

When she shopped, she shopped. She did not flirt with the clerks, pass the time of day with this or that chance-met acquaintance, or stand around in her finery, waiting to be seen by the beau monde.

Even in a shop full of people who likely knew her on sight, she was alone.

It was a quality he recognized. His sisters had both acquired it, though as girls, they'd been friendly, garrulous, and amiable. They'd been innocent, oblivious to the worst sorrows that could befall a young woman.

In some indefinable sense, Maggie Windham had lost her innocence, and this left him... hurting for her.

Which was foolish. It didn't do to get emotionally involved with clients, even clients who occasionally required kissing. Protectiveness was one thing—he was a gentleman and she was a female in difficulties—but this other nonsense, this talking and fretting and pondering... it could not be considered in the line of duty. Simply could not.

When the coach brought them back to her house, he bowed to her in the mews—*without* taking her hand—and swung up on his gelding.

There would be no more kissing her hand.

No more bringing up old family troubles.

And for God's sake, no more *talking*.

❧

"Lady Maggie to see you, my lord."

Gayle Windham, Earl of Westhaven and heir to the Moreland duchy, glanced up at his butler. "My sister is here?"

Sterling nodded. "I put her in the family parlor, and the tea tray is on the way."

"I take it my wife is not yet returned from shopping?"

"It's early yet, my lord." Sterling's long face gave away nothing, not humor, not impatience. If anything, there was a faint light of commiseration in the butler's eyes. The right wife was a wonderful addition to any man's life—and Anna was very definitely the right wife—but she was also a source of worry, particularly when she went haring off about Town for hours on end with only staff to attend her.

"Greetings, Brother." Maggie swept into his library, surveying him from head to toe as he rose from his desk. "Westhaven, you need to see the sun occasionally, and your wife has better things to do than drag you out of your cave. Sterling, we will take our tray on the back terrace. Darjeeling will do, and some heartier fare for his lordship."

She kissed Westhaven's cheek before he could get out a word in reply.

"The terrace it is, then. You're looking well, Maggie."

"I do not spend most of each day planted behind a desk, muttering curses and incantations at my profligate sisters and the merchants who continue to indulge them." She grinned at him abruptly, the change in expression having the power to mentally knock him off his pins, though they were merely fraternal pins. "But then, you enjoy muttering and conjuring among the finances. How is dear Anna?"

He let the answer to that question wait until they were outside the house, as platitudes did not serve when Maggie came calling. She looked… quietly magnificent, as always. She dressed to hide her assets—a figure even a brother would have to be dead and buried not to acknowledge as feminine, perfect skin, luminous green eyes, and that hair…

"Anna is well, though motherhood is an adjustment."

He held his sister's chair for her at a wrought iron grouping in the dappled shade. The Holland bulbs were in riot, largely thanks to Anna's efforts, and Maggie had ever been one to appreciate the out-of-doors.

"Fatherhood is an adjustment, too," she said,

studying him as she drew off her gloves. "One can but offer prayers regarding some things. I keep you both in mine."

She fell silent as two footmen appeared, one with the tea tray, one with a second tray bearing sandwiches, sliced fruit, and several pieces of marzipan. Maggie set about pouring for them both.

"Have you been approached about Jamison's canal venture?" She passed him his tea and poured her own.

"I have. It looks quite promising and well capitalized." He sipped his tea. Anna herself could not have prepared it more to his liking.

"Don't be fooled. He's pockets to let, despite that flashy pair of grays and all his lounging about on Brook Street. He went to Worth Kettering in hopes the man could turn his situation around, and Kettering said he was not in a position to take on new business. Jamison has markers out all over Town. Kettering does not suffer fools."

"Maggie, you scare me." Kettering was also legendarily discreet as solicitors and men of business went. "How can you possibly know these things?"

"Men talk to women and around women as if all women were deaf and simple. We're not; though it wasn't a lapse of discretion on Kettering's part we have to thank for this tidbit, merely Jamison's own whining. Have something to eat. Worrying about your wife requires sustenance." She passed him a plate with two sandwiches stacked on it and a couple of pieces of marzipan arranged on one side.

"So I'll steer a course around Jamison. Any other warnings to impart?"

Her lips quirked, as if she hadn't considered it a warning at all. She wouldn't. Maggie had more financial sense than the rest of family put together and was partly responsible for the "luck" Westhaven had had repairing the Windham finances.

"I've heard Prinny has taken a liking to peaches."

"Peaches?"

"They're from China, though the Americans are growing them quite successfully. I'll have some sent over. I intend to find somebody who's importing peach trees and buy an interest. They can tolerate a fairly cold winter but need a mild growing season. Eat your candy. It sweetens your mood."

Knowing Maggie, she'd read everything there was to read about peaches, met with anybody who'd ever seen a peach orchard, sent spies out to learn who was interested in starting peach orchards in the South of England, and started experimenting with peach recipes in her own kitchen.

Westhaven chewed a piece of marzipan. "You look a little tired, Mags."

"Changing seasons makes me restless."

"Go out to Morelands and get in a few good gallops, or even to Willow Bend. You know you're welcome any time."

"And who would listen to Her Grace fret over His Grace and our younger sisters?"

Her Grace spared some concern for her husband and daughters, true, but she fretted over Maggie ceaselessly. Despaired of her, which Westhaven had occasion to hear about often.

"You love the countryside." He passed her a

piece of marzipan. "I can't imagine being in Town during the social whirl has any appeal, so why not go?"

She studied her tea, giving away nothing. She was his older sister, always there, always Maggie, but there were depths to her. Anna fretted over Maggie. *Devlin*, battle-hardened, weary soldier, fretted over Maggie.

But that's all they did—fret. With Maggie, there was nothing really to *do*. The common understanding was likely that Maggie was supported through the ducal finances, but nothing could be further from the truth. With her brothers' help, she'd begun investing upon attaining her majority. By the time she'd turned thirty, she'd been plenty wealthy enough to set up her own grand establishment, and yet she'd chosen a little place on a quiet back street.

"Does Kettering take advice from you, Sister?"

She glanced up from her teacup, her lips turning up in that unexpected, impish smile. "He's a very amiable gentleman, also easy on the eye. We converse occasionally."

"He's also quite eligible, Maggie."

"He's a gadfly. Hasn't the bottom for marriage, though he might acquire it in the company of the right lady. More tea?"

He let her pour him more tea—it truly was a lovely morning to be truant from ledgers and correspondence—and waited to see what topic she'd broach next. He had no doubt his sister loved him, but she wasn't the type to go calling because she'd run out of pin money to shop with.

"I went driving with Mr. Hazlit recently. Lovely team of bays."

This was *news*. "Benjamin Hazlit?" He kept his tone noncommittal with effort.

"The very one. There are rumors about him."

It was a question, but Westhaven was damned if he could parse it out clearly. "What sort of rumors?"

"That he has a title; that he's quite wealthy; that he has Hebrew or gypsy antecedents."

"Would you care if any of that were true?"

She set her teacup on its saucer with more force than a lady ought to show on a polite call. "Gracious, Brother. How shallow do you think I am?"

"Not shallow at all, but you are human. What do you want to know?" It seemed kinder to brace her directly than watch her beating around the bush.

"Do you trust him?"

"Yes. Without exception." He watched as she absorbed the immediacy of his answer.

"Is he a friend?"

A trickier question. "If he had friends, I'd be pleased to be counted among them, but neither he nor I are of a social bent."

She rose, her expression impatient. "Do you *like* him?"

"I like him." Westhaven rose, as well, falling in step beside her. "I suspect he does have a title, or he's in expectation of one, though I know not if it's a nominal barony or a fat marquessate. You might ask His Grace. I suspect Iberian bloodlines myself. And as to wealth, I've wondered."

"What have you wondered?" She bent to sniff a daffodil and came up with pollen on her nose. It was incongruous, the little yellow smudge and her serious green eyes. He passed her his handkerchief and touched the tip of his nose.

She wouldn't want him wiping her face. Probably clock him soundly if he tried.

While Maggie dabbed at the tip of her nose, Westhaven eyed the flowers and chose his words carefully. "I have wondered why, if the man is wealthy, does he take on for coin the missing daughters and misbehaviors of Polite Society? It's a burdensome business, hearing confessions, carrying secrets, and knowing he'll have to deal socially with the same people whose dirty linen he has laundered."

Maggie passed him back his handkerchief. "Unless he likes it. Unless he enjoys knowing everybody's secrets. There are people like that, and some of them are wealthy as a result."

"Hazlit is not of that ilk. Their Graces would not have turned to him if his trustworthiness had been at all in doubt."

This seemed to mollify his sister, but it did not mollify Westhaven. Maggie was in a taking about something, something that might involve Hazlit or might not. It might involve pig farms or peaches, and Maggie in a taking was not something he wanted to contemplate at length.

"If you needed something, Mags, would you tell me?"

"No. Everybody in this family tells you when they need something, when Anna ought to be your chief concern. Would you tell me if you needed something?"

He slipped his arm through hers and kissed her cheek. "Yes. It's part of loving someone. You lean on them occasionally, and they on you. Devlin has abandoned us for the North and the arms of his countess, Valentine is more often than not spinning tunes out in Oxfordshire and admiring his new wife, while Sophie rusticates in matrimonial bliss with her baron in Kent. We who guard the treasury must stick together."

She sighed as he drew in her flowery Maggie-scent. "Marriage does agree with you, Gayle. It agrees with you enormously."

"I do recommend it with the right partner. Their Graces would, as well."

She turned her head to peer at him, her mouth flat. "Hazlit is not marriage material. You will not suffer that rumor to be bruited about, please."

"Wouldn't dream of it." He escorted her back to the table at a leisurely pace. His world had changed radically when he'd married Anna, and it was changing even more radically with the birth of their first child. "You are dear to me, you know."

She dropped his arm and reached for her gloves, merely nodding as if he hadn't offered a sentiment of profound truth.

"What I meant to say, Mags, is I love you. I miss you when you don't come calling, and yet I don't want to make a nuisance of myself on your doorstep, either. Thank you for warning me off the Jamison project—I'd have taken the bait if you hadn't come along."

"Even a wormy apple can look shiny and red from the right angle." She picked up her reticule and faced him. "Don't work too hard."

She would have moved off, but he caught her by

the arm and drew her into a hug. She'd lost weight since last he'd hugged her. "Don't be a stranger, Maggie Windham."

"You could never be a nuisance on my doorstep."

She offered that in a voice slightly above a whisper while hugging him back, a surprisingly fierce embrace from his usually reserved sister. She drew away and headed for the house, clearly not expecting her own brother to escort her to the front door.

Impossible woman, truth be known, but a sister was allowed to be impossible. He looked up a few minutes later to see Anna bustling in the gate from the mews.

"Beloved wife." He rose and held out a hand to her, his eyes traveling over dark hair, gorgeous eyes, and a lush, lovely figure. "Have you bought out the entire Strand?"

"Of course. Are you rebelling against your ledgers, Westhaven? It's a beautiful day, and this generally finds you planted at your desk." She tucked against him as if it were her natural place in the world, which to him, it was.

"Am I really so stuck as all that?"

"You are so dedicated as all that. My guess is Her Grace came calling and blasted you away from your correspondence."

"Maggie. She says marriage agrees with me enormously."

Anna nuzzled his neck. "Perceptive woman, your sister. Shopping has left me a little fatigued. Have you time for a short nap?"

"Of course."

But as he escorted his wife above stairs, Westhaven spared a thought to wonder why Maggie would be investigating the beau monde's most trusted and discreet investigator.

❧

To see the letter sitting among her correspondence was almost a relief.

Almost.

Maggie passed her gloves and bonnet to her house-keeper and felt a familiar icy calm descend—it was never very far from her, welling up from her innards whenever she called upon it. It wasn't ducal. She suspected it was a legacy from a mother who was able to smile and spread her legs repeatedly for men whom she liked not at all.

Drunken men, men who neglected to wash, men with bad teeth and rough hands… Maggie pushed those thoughts to the edge of her mind, where they would lurk until the next time her imagination slipped its leash.

"I'll be at my desk for the balance of the after-noon," she informed Mrs. Danforth. It was the signal to leave her in peace.

Maggie dealt with all her other mail first, from her stewards and solicitors, from a friend she'd met in finishing school who'd married well and happily almost a decade since, from the widower neighbor with whom she kept in touch on farming matters. When her business was in order, she raised her eyes and looked out the window.

She had a small life. A life narrowly circumscribed by the strictures of propriety and by her own love for the family into which she'd been adopted. She had a measure of independence, if she was careful, and she wasn't plying her mother's trade. She'd soon be too old for that fear to have any credence in any case.

Her gut roiling with unease despite the reassuring internal litany, Maggie opened the letter, the page full of flourishes, curlicues, and ink blots to go with all the exclamation points.

Greetings, Maggie!

I adore spring! Spring means kittens in the mews and shopping! Mama says I'm to have a new wardrobe from the skin out, for soon I'm to start going about with her on calls. I'll be fifteen soon, you know, and some girls are married at fifteen. We have gone to the milliner's, too, where Mama ordered me the most cunning little toque, and, Maggie, I have to tell you, when Mama said from the skin out, she meant that very thing.

I never knew lace had such uses! And it comes in colors, too. Pink and even red! Can you imagine!

I have been reading a great deal on rainy days, though Mama says horrid novels are not what wealthy gentlemen are interested in discussing. My French is getting very good since our new lady's maid—Adele is her name, though Mama calls her only Martin—has helped a great deal. I think Mama's French must be quite rusty, for she doesn't seem to understand when I use mine with her.

Or maybe Mama is just preoccupied with the coming season. She goes out sometimes, to the theatre and the opera. Someday soon, I will accompany her, and won't that be exciting!

I miss you. You must write to me. Teddy says

you're in great good looks these days, but Thomas
says you look tired to him. I must go. Mama is
teaching me games of chance, and it's ever so fun.

All my love forever and always,
Bridget

This was much, much worse than another demand
for money, and worse than the last note, which had
been merely chatty. Maggie considered ordering a cup
of tea to steady her nerves, though what if she couldn't
keep it down? It wouldn't do to make such a mess.

But perhaps this was only the warning shot,
fired across the bow of Maggie's finances and her
nerves. Cecily no doubt read every word Bridget
penned, and yet in this note, unlike the previous
one, Bridget had managed to convey a great deal of
information—all of it alarming. A demand for money
would follow, a bigger, bolder demand than any of
the previous springs.

And when that demand came, Maggie would pay
it. She'd spent years of her life learning how to make
money, just so she could always, always pay what
needed to be paid when it needed to be paid. She
was wealthy and getting wealthier by the quarter. The
primary ingredient necessary to becoming wealthier
still was to have coin to invest, and she did.

Thank God, luck, hard work, or the fates, she
had coin.

And there was nothing else she'd rather spend it
on, for no decent girl of almost fifteen wore red lace
anywhere on her person.

∽

"Mr. Hazlit to see you, my lord."

Westhaven caught a smirk from his wife. They were taking tea in the library after a reviving little nap in the middle of the day. The butler had sense enough not to smirk, but Anna showed no such respect.

"I'll just see about sending a fresh tray," she said, rising. "Mr. Hazlit can't possibly have anything to say of interest to me."

"You're abandoning me." It was intended as a statement of fact, not a pout. His wife's smirk became a grin at his peevish tone.

"Shamelessly. Seems even after a nap, I'm quite tired. The effects of getting up and down all night with your son."

He rose and frowned down at her. "You and that baby." Anna was even prettier now than when she'd been carrying, and he'd thought nothing on earth could be more attractive to him than his wife when enceinte. "You are the one getting up and down at night, but I am the one losing the most sleep. Go, then. I'm not fated to get my work done this day."

"Perhaps not." She kissed him on the mouth as Westhaven saw Hazlit looming at the butler's shoulder. "I'll see you in my dreams, husband."

She patted his lapel and swanned off, only to pause before their guest. "Mr. Hazlit, a pleasure."

Hazlit took her hand and bowed over it. "My lady, you're in radiant good looks. His lordship must be attending to more than just his letters if you're blooming so nicely."

"Blooming?" She beamed at the man. "Westhaven,

we must have Mr. Hazlit to dinner. He says I'm blooming." She withdrew her hand. "I'll leave you gentlemen to your business while I go blossoming on my way."

She closed the door quietly, leaving Westhaven to watch the bemused expression fade from Hazlit's face.

"Women in the throes of early motherhood should all be so serene as your lady wife," Hazlit said. "You're to be commended."

"I'm to be pitied." Westhaven came around the desk to shake his guest's hand. "Have a seat, why don't we? And there will be a tea tray the size of Madagascar any minute, but I've whiskey, brandy, and port on the sideboard, as well."

"Why are you to be pitied?" Hazlit shifted to take a chair. There was a prowling quality to the man's gait, a restlessness in his eyes, as if he never stopped inventorying his environment for information.

"If my parents' history is any indication, my wife will be gravid as often as not. It plucks a man's nerves to see the woman he loves blithely managing under such myriad challenges."

Hazlit cocked his head. "You have become quite married, my lord."

"I'm quite pathetically in love with my wife." Westhaven shook his head. He and Hazlit were not friends, but this was a conversation between friends, a conversation he might have had with Valentine or Devlin, or even—surprisingly—with His Grace. "Are you calling upon me in a business capacity today, Hazlit? I confess, my mind does not lend itself easily to business matters of late."

Hazlit pursed his lips and seemed to come to some inner conclusion. "She'll be fine, Westhaven. She's not like many titled ladies, who will sit about on their broad backsides, fainting and sighing and fretting because they're too vain and stupid to discard their stays. She's healthy, happy, and looking forward to many occasions of motherhood. You won't lose her."

Westhaven looked out the window to the gardens profuse with the flowers Anna had brought into his life. "I should not need to hear the words, but thank you."

Hazlit seemed amused. "Every husband needs to hear the words. Ask His Grace how many of his cronies he's had to get roaring drunk during a lying-in. Ask him if the last child was any easier on him than the first one. But there's a lesson for us men in this, too, I think."

Westhaven passed his guest a tot of whiskey, for such a masculine discussion must needs be fortified with masculine drink. "What lesson?"

"The ladies' courage is different from ours," Hazlit said, accepting the drink. "But in some ways, their courage is greater."

Westhaven propped a hip on his desk and peered at the man lounging in his guest chair. "Is there a Mrs. Hazlit who has inspired you to such observations?" A brother was entitled to be sure of these things.

"Not yet. God willing, I'll find such a brave woman before I grow too much older."

"My sister suspects you've a title." Sisters were a safer topic than wives. "I told her to ask His Grace."

"This would be Mag—Miss Windham?"

The slip was telling. Westhaven let it pass. "Maggie,

to her familiars." Among whom, it was just possible Benjamin Hazlit was about to number. Well, well, well. "She adores riding, you know."

Hazlit's gaze narrowed. "She told me she doesn't keep a riding horse."

"She doesn't. Says riding is for young girls seeking to look over the mounted gentlemen in the park. She adores riding nonetheless."

Hazlit seemed to absorb this information, though his expression was unreadable. "You've heard we went driving some days ago, I take it."

"Maggie might have mentioned it. You're to be commended for getting her out."

Hazlit took a sip of this drink, no doubt configuring his reply carefully while he did. "I don't think your sister would appreciate her family making anything of a single outing. She's a skilled driver though, I did notice that. My offside gelding is not the most confident fellow, and he trusted her immediately."

"Children, horses, and dogs..." Westhaven settled himself in the opposite wing chair. "They all love Maggie."

A little considering silence fell, each man sipping his drink in turn.

"So we're not to be getting ideas because Maggie has condescended to drive out with you?"

"I'd appreciate it if you didn't. Not if I dance with her, not if we're seen having ices together or shopping on the Strand. Your sister is not being courted."

Interesting, when two people each insisted there was no courting going on.

"So you wouldn't care to know Maggie's sidesaddle

is out in my mews right now, and Anna's mare—a rather sizable creature with marvelous gaits, if I do say so myself—could use some exercise?"

Hazlit's lips quirked up. "Even if I borrowed the saddle and the mare from time to time over the coming weeks, I would not be courting your sister."

"Pity." Westhaven rose and went to the window. His wife was kneeling before a bed of tulips just starting their decline, her face hidden by a wide-brimmed straw hat. He must ask her what a brother's obligation was in such a circumstance.

He turned to face his guest. "If you were to court Maggie, she'd probably drive you off with her lectures."

"What lectures would those be, my lord?"

When had Hazlit come sauntering over to the window?

"She starts off explaining the percents to you, why they are the most prudent, low-risk investment, and why some of your capital should be in them most of the time. Then she goes on about the financial pages and why this or that article is not as informative or disinterested as it might seem. She can get going on various investment schemes, if you're the determined sort, bore you witless for hours."

"Those are decent topics of conversation, if a trifle unfeminine."

"In Maggie's hands, the financial pages become weapons of destruction. Had you any amorous intent, she could lecture it right out of you. She indirectly owns a sizable portion of the swine industry in the Home Counties, though this is nigh a state secret with His Grace and me."

Hazlit looked intrigued, God help the man. "Swine?"

"Pigs reproduce at a terrific rate, much faster than sheep, and yet they require a great deal less space to raise than sheep, and most do not require grazing, per se. Pork is considered by most preferable to mutton, the hide is valuable, and the meat takes well to preservation. Swine, Mr. Hazlit. Do the math or Maggie will do it for you. She's thinking of investing in peaches next. If she does, you can bet the Moreland resources will be nodding in that direction, as well."

"Fascinating. And yet she lives very modestly."

"She has her charities." Outside, Anna was getting to her feet, a maneuver that made Westhaven impatient to be back at her side. "I suggest you ask Maggie about her causes, as they are near to her heart."

A knock on the door indicated the tea tray was arriving. Westhaven watched while Hazlit's glance went from the tray in the footman's hands to the back terrace to his host's face. Now they must sit and eat polite portions and discuss the coming race meets or some beast lately on the block at Tatt's. Good manners could be such a burden.

"At the risk of ignoring good food, my lord, do you suppose you might introduce me to your wife's mare?"

"Capital notion. Grab a few tea cakes, why don't you? We can go out by way of the garden."

A thought struck him as they headed for the back of the house. "Would you have the time to take on another small project for Their Graces? This one shouldn't involve haring off to the North in search of my wife's antecedents."

Hazlit's eyebrows rose, and he paused inside the door leading to the terrace. "What sort of project?"

Westhaven could see his wife through the door's glass, arching her back with both hands propped at the base of her spine. He spoke quickly, not wanting to belabor an insignificance. "A routine investigation of a potential spouse for one of my sisters. It will probably come to nothing, if you ask me. The gentleman in question doesn't strike me as ready for parson's mousetrap, but then, who among us advertises when he is?"

"The gentleman in question?"

"Lord Deene. Her Grace is hopeful Evie might bring him up to scratch."

"May I consult my calendar before giving you an answer?"

Westhaven swung around to consider Hazlit, but the man's face, as usual, gave away nothing. "Take as long as you like to consult your schedule or conclude whatever bit of sleuthing you're about. The last time I spoke with Evie, she thought she was preserved from the risk of marriage by virtue of being the youngest. Come along. Anna can join us on our visit to the stables."

❧

Three days had passed since Maggie had gotten Bridget's latest letter. Three days of miserable spring weather—cold, wet, windy, and perfectly suited to hiding indoors.

Maggie should never have gone driving in the park. She should never have taken Mr. Hazlit shopping.

She should right this minute be sending him a note excusing him from further obligation to her.

She'd find her own letters. They weren't so very incriminating, not unless they were placed in a larger context...

"Mr. Hazlit to see you, miss." Mrs. Danforth waited in the open door of the office, her plump frame fairly quivering with approval.

"No need to stand on ceremony." Hazlit shouldered past the housekeeper, patting her arm as he did. Maggie could almost see the woman's spine melt when he tossed a toothy smile at her for good measure.

"Mr. Hazlit." Maggie got to her feet, ignoring the very notion she might be pleased to see him, too. "This is a surprise."

"I'll just see about the tea tray." Mrs. Danforth beamed at Hazlit and bustled off.

"Don't blame her." Hazlit advanced into the room, leaving the door only a few inches ajar. "She wants to see you happily wed with babies to love and fuss over."

Maggie crossed her arms, stoutly ignoring the image his words brought to mind. "You and she have been discussing my future?"

"Good intentions on the part of a devoted staff hardly require discussion. How are you?" He picked up her hand, preventing Maggie from turning her back on him.

"I'll be much better when you find my reticule. I'm hoping you disturbed an otherwise peaceful afternoon to report some progress?"

He *petted* her hand. Smoothed his fingers over her knuckles while he regarded her with a frown.

"No, I do not have progress to report, though on the staff's next half day, I'm going to search this place from cellars to attics. I have inquiries out among my contacts, but these things take time to bear fruit. You still look tired. What's amiss, Maggie Windham?"

He was regarding her with some peculiar light in his eyes. Maggie had the sense she wasn't with Mr. Hazlit, the hired investigator, but perhaps with Benjamin Hazlit, the man. His expression wasn't one of clinical inquiry but rather of faint worry.

For her.

A blasted lump rose in her throat, having something to do with that look in his eyes, and something to do with the babies she would never have to fuss over or love.

She snatched her hand back and stalked over to the window. "This is not a convenient time to indulge your notions of a sham connection between us, Mr. Hazlit."

He eyed the door, warning her with one glance she'd broken the rules.

But then, so had he. With that soft, slightly anxious look in his dark eyes he'd broken rules and commandments and the equivalent of papal bulls issued by Maggie's common sense and countersigned by her instinct for self-preservation.

She heard him building up the fire but kept her gaze on the back gardens. The flowers would like the rain, of course—

"Mr. Hazlit!" She kept her voice down with effort, but when a man sneaked up behind a lady and slid his arms around her waist, some exclamation was in order.

"Hush." He turned her in his arms, though part of Maggie was strongly admonishing herself to wrestle free. He'd let her go. She trusted him that far, when a servant was likely to appear any moment with a tea tray. "Something has you in a dither. Tell me."

His embrace was the most beguiling, irresistible mockery of a kindness. Gayle had offered her a hug a few days ago, a brusque, brotherly gesture as careful as it was brief. This was different.

This was… Benjamin Hazlit's warm, strong male body, available for her comfort. No conditions, no awkwardness, no dissembling for the benefit of an audience.

She sighed and tucked her face against his throat, unwilling—or unable—to deny herself what he offered. For a few moments, she was going to pretend she wasn't alone in a sea of trouble. She was going to pretend they were friends—cousins, maybe—and stealing this from him was permitted. She was going to hold on to the fiction that she was as entitled to dream of children and a husband to dote upon as the next woman.

"You are wound as tight as a fiddle string, Maggie Windham." Hazlit's hand settled on her neck, kneading gently. "Are the domestics feuding, or has Her Grace been hounding you?"

"She never hounds or scolds." Maggie rested her forehead on his shoulder, her bones turning to butter at his touch. "She looks at us, disappointment in the prettiest green eyes you've ever seen, and you want to disappear into the ground, never to emerge until you can make her smile again. His Grace says it's the same for him."

When she was held like this, Maggie could detect a unique scent about Hazlit's person: honeysuckle and spice, like an exotic incense. It clung to his clothing, and when she turned her head to rest her cheek on the wool of his coat, she caught the same fragrance rising from the exposed flesh of his neck.

That hand of his went wandering, over her shoulder blades, down her spine.

"You are tired," he said, his voice resonating through her physically. "What is disturbing your sleep, Maggie? And don't think I'll be distracted by more hissing and arching your back."

"I'm not a cat."

"You've cat eyes." He turned her so his arm was around her waist. "Let's sit by the fire, and you can tell me your troubles."

Such a tempting notion! It made her want to laugh—and to cry.

"My troubles are trifling." And as often as she'd told herself the same thing, the words should have sounded far more convincing. "Perhaps you have troubles worth discussing?"

He'd no sooner settled her on the sofa than he went to open the door. A startled footman stood there, a tray in his hands.

"I'll take that." Hazlit appropriated the tray and nudged the door closed with his shoulder. "It's chilly today. We'll keep the heat in, shall we?"

He hadn't used that voice on her before, low, pleasant... confiding. It wound through her senses and left her craving his proximity, which would not do.

He sat right beside her, nonetheless, and began

fussing with the tea tray. "You like it with more cream than sugar, am I right? And my nose tells me the kitchen sent up a pekoe, which I'm guessing is more to your taste than Darjeeling. Here." She watched bemused as he prepared her tea then passed her a cup and saucer.

"Drink up. If I'd thought to bring my pocket pistol, we could be adding a dollop of medicinal courage. That might put the roses back in your cheeks."

He didn't fix himself a cup; instead he studied her, which necessitated that she study her tea.

He didn't chatter; he let her finish her tea in silence. It was the smallest, most mundane pleasure in the world, to sip a cup of tea fixed just for her, but it was a comfort.

"I am not myself today." She set the empty cup and saucer back on the tray. "I apologize for the lack of roses in my cheeks."

"You, my dear, are cranky." He sounded amused. When he reached out and tucked a lock of Maggie's hair behind one ear, she was not amused in the least.

"While I appreciate your solicitude, Mr. Hazlit, it isn't necessary."

And again she felt an urge to cry. To leave the room so she might have proper privacy to indulge inconvenient and unbecoming emotions. Benjamin Hazlit was not a bad man. She was coming to suspect he was at least a decent man, likely even a good man, and to inflict her tears on him wouldn't be sporting.

"Are we always limited to what is necessary, Miss Windham? Is it necessary to visit the park on a pretty day? To add cream and sugar to your tea? Is it necessary to procreate?"

She blinked over at him where he sat beside her, but his tone was still mild.

"What if," he went on, "I tell you a trouble of mine first? Perhaps that will set the proper conspiratorial mood, hmm?"

"Is this another gesture of trust?"

He frowned and reached forward to pour his first cup and her second. "Perhaps it is. Well, no matter. Can't be helped. I've been asked to investigate somebody prior to his suit being considered by a girl's parents."

"Is this in your usual line?" She accepted her teacup from him, their hands brushing as she did. Gracious, even his hands were warm.

"If the client is well placed enough, or the gentleman in question is possessed of a particularly impressive title, I am often called upon. I am discreet, you see." He stirred his tea, and Maggie couldn't tell if he was joking.

"If this is in your usual line, how is this matter a trouble?" Despite herself, she was curious. He looked a bit troubled—around the eyes, the way he held his teacup a few inches above the saucer, as if he forgot he was supposed to drink his beverage.

"I am reluctant to take on the commission." He set the tea down untasted. "More reluctant than I'd realized."

Maggie heard her brother's words from earlier in the week… It couldn't be easy carrying secrets for others… It was hard enough for her to carry her own secrets, come to that.

"Don't take on the job, then," she said. "Unless you desperately need the coin?"

"I do not." Most men would have been offended at the question. His answer was almost absentminded. "I can use money the same as the next person, but I'm no longer destitute."

She returned a small favor he'd extended her earlier and let him consider his trouble in silence. Since he'd built up the fire and closed the door, the room had become a trifle less chilly, but he was sitting close enough that Maggie was also warmed by Hazlit's simple nearness.

She ought to scoot away, though it would be marginally rude. And what did it matter where she sat, when she'd allowed him to close the door?

"I think the gentleman in question would consider it an affront, did I investigate him," he said. "The inquiry would not be regarding just his finances, or else one might dismiss it as purely business."

"What else would it entail?" She took a tea cake from the tray and put it on his saucer.

"My thanks. When the question is matrimony, doting parents will want to know if the potential groom can provide, of course, but they'll also want to know about wagering habits, any tendency to incontinent drinking, bad company, or insanity. They'll want to know how the man treats his mistresses, if any he has. If there's any risk of social diseases… I hope I'm not offending you." He ran a hand through his hair. "It's a delicate business, and this fellow is at least a cordial acquaintance."

"Deene might go so far as argue that he's your friend."

His mouth snapped shut with an audible click. "Has Westhaven taken to gossiping?"

"He has not, but like most men, you assume the only communications of significance pass between the males of the species. Evie is not one for keeping her disgruntlements to herself, not the trivial ones in any case."

"This would be your sister, Lady Eve?"

Maggie felt almost sorry for him. He'd tried hard to make the problem hypothetical, but for him it wasn't a hypothetical at all. He sat in meetings with Deene for hour after hour. She'd seen them together socially, heading off for the card room at some ball, talking near the men's punch bowl at a musicale.

"Eve is the baby of the family. She thinks this keeps her out of Her Grace's matchmaking line of sight, but it does not. Evie and Deene would either drive each other to Bedlam or fall madly in love."

"Or both?" There was rueful humor in his eyes.

"For a time, perhaps. Don't think because my family asks, you must comply."

His brow knit. "I realize as we discuss this that I really don't want to pry into the man's affairs."

"Then don't. There are enough things in this life we must do that are distasteful. Evie does not like Deene except as a flirt and an occasional dancing partner. Let somebody else have the pleasure of learning where the man has secreted his bastards—if any he has."

He gave her a long, searching look. "I wasn't going to mention that."

She rose again, a little stiffly from having sat for so long. The rain had picked up, slapping down in gusts and sheets, while the wind tossed the greening trees this way and that. The weather mirrored her internal landscape: chilly, stormy, bleak.

"Maggie."

He'd warned her this time a moment before he slid his arms around her. After a minute pause to discard the dictates of good sense, she turned to hide her face against his chest. For a long moment, she let him hold her, until words rose up in her aching throat.

"I want to cry." Stupid words. Maybe he hadn't heard them.

"I think it's worse," he said, his hand stroking across her back, "when you want to and you can't. It's an indignity to cry, a worse indignity when you can't even cry."

She nodded against his chest. Why did he know such a thing? Was it because his sisters had been through an ordeal? Because he knew half of the beau monde's sins and mistakes?

"Stop *thinking*, Maggie Windham. Everybody is occasionally blue-deviled."

His voice was very quiet, right near her ear. She liked the sound and feel of it, but he was wrong. Years and years of looking over her shoulder, dreading each day's mail, pinching pennies and carrying secrets was not simply a case of the blue devils. And the worst, hardest, most difficult part was she could see the rest of her life falling into the same dismal pattern, with only death promising her any relief.

Hazlit's hand went from tracing patterns on her back to cradling her jaw. He shifted his hold subtly, turning Maggie's face up to his.

When his lips settled on hers, it was so softly Maggie wanted to groan with the pleasure of it. He tasted of the almond icing on the tea cake, his mouth sweet and warm against hers. She leaned into him, knowing he had the physical strength to support them both.

There was no hurry in his kiss, no fumbling or force. It dawned on her that it was a kiss of invitation, an offer for her to explore him intimately.

A gesture of trust.

She had never been kissed like this, and she found it tantalizing. How could a man's mere mouth—a mouth capable of typical male inanities and profanities—be both soothing and arousing?

Or maybe that was the essence of seduction. The mind was lulled into somnolence while the body and spirit were brought more alive. She burrowed closer, one arm wrapped around his back, the other going higher so she could anchor her hand in his thick, silky hair.

She felt his feet shift, his stance widening to take her weight. And then, so lightly she almost didn't comprehend what it was, his tongue grazed her bottom lip.

Oh, yes... *Yes*.

Somebody groaned softly. Maggie waited for Hazlit to repeat that slight, subtle caress, and when he did, a sinuous, languid hunger began to beat through her veins. It pulsed low in her belly, in her womb, in that place a lady never mentioned and a lonely woman never entirely forgot.

When he did it a third time, she parted her lips and took the same slow, sweet taste of him.

He went still. His hand stopped roving her back; his body stopped shifting even minutely.

Confusion welled up through the wanting singing in Maggie's veins. Was it wrong for her to make such an overture? Did only men kiss in such a manner?

"Again." His voice was a rasping whisper. "Do that again, Maggie."

He bent his head but stopped when their mouths were a half inch apart.

She stretched up almost on her toes and closed the distance. He groaned this time, his mouth parting when she seamed his lips with her tongue.

Ah, so this was kissing. She explored his lips and straight white teeth. She forged into the soft, hot recess between those two. When he touched his tongue to hers, she startled then felt him drawing on her tongue, gently, teasingly.

Gracious God. He was holding her to him, so their bodies were pressed tightly together, and still Maggie felt a frantic need to be closer. To touch more of him, to feel more of him, to taste and gather the scent of more of him. It was unbearable, the wanting and wanting and wanting...

"Maggie..." His voice was hoarse, strained. "Let me hold you."

What was he saying? She felt drunk, like the time she and Bart had consumed the syrup from the brandied pears as children. If Hazlit's arms hadn't been around her, her knees might have buckled.

She sighed against his shoulder, the feel of his hand moving over her hair calming her physically even as she realized exactly the nature of the hard column of male flesh pressed against her belly.

He was aroused. He was aroused, and she was responsible. It ought to feel shameful, but it didn't. She was aroused, too, and she heartily doubted he considered that a shameful thing, though he wasn't crowing and smirking and strutting around. If anything, he seemed as disconcerted as she was. She felt him take a deep breath and let it out slowly, then do it twice more.

"It's no good." He dropped his arms but leaned in and kissed her nose. "As long as I'm holding you, I can think of cold eel pie, my old headmaster at Eton and his mildewed coats, the declension of *hic, haec, hoc*, and I'm still hard as a pikestaff. I consider myself a man of some self-discipline, my dear, but you…"

He cocked his head while Maggie tried to fathom his mood. Was he teasing? Did he regret this? How could he form complete sentences if he was half as rattled as she was?

"How are you, Maggie? And don't poker up on me. I don't think either of us was expecting this."

"I am… I am…" She glanced around the room, anywhere but at his serious dark eyes. "You are very proficient at kissing."

"With you, it seems I am. Enthusiastic, too."

She sensed there was some hidden male meaning to his last comment. She did not like that she couldn't puzzle it out. She felt heat creeping up her neck.

"And now I've made you blush." He slung an arm around her shoulders and kissed her temple. "I didn't intend it to become that kind of kiss, but I'm not sorry it did. If that makes me a cad and a bounder, so be it. That kiss was worth any invective you want to hurl at me."

He stepped away, leaving Maggie only slightly less confused. "You liked it then?"

"Yes, Maggie Windham." He looked her right in the eye. "I liked it. I liked it *a lot*."

∽

"Mama, you are glaring daggers at the Duchess of Moreland." Bridget kept her voice down, even though the park wasn't anywhere near as crowded as it would be later in the afternoon. Remonstrating dear Mama outright, much less in Hyde Park for all to see, could be sufficient folly to earn a girl a sound switching and several days of bread and water.

"When we're abroad, that's Cecily to you, dearest, for no one believes I'm old enough to have a daughter your age."

When Mama spoke through clenched teeth that way, Bridget feared for the horses. They were a boisterous pair, which Mama seemed to enjoy for the most part. At the moment, the horses were twitching their short tails restively, likely in reaction to their driver's ill will toward the lady in the passing landau.

"Esther Windham is too high in the instep for words," Mama said, but she kept her voice down, too. One didn't insult a duchess in public. "She parades around Town with those long-faced, empty-headed daughters of hers as if they weren't every one of them approaching their last prayers."

Bridget cast around desperately for something distracting to say. When Mama got in one of her moods, it could last for days and cost them every piece of Wedgewood in the china cabinet.

"Do you suppose we might see Lady Dandridge out and about today?"

That at least earned her a look.

"That old ape leader, sporting her fancy carriage. Mutton dressed up as lamb."

This was an abiding theme with Mama, and if it was

hypocritical of her, too, well, Bridget had learned the hard way to keep that observation to herself. Mama wasn't old, precisely, and she had been very pretty, but Bridget did not for a moment think her mother was a contented woman.

Mama used to have a number of gentlemen callers. Merry fellows who'd pat Bridget on the head and make comments about her growing up to break hearts. Mama had been happier then, busy with correspondence in the morning, outings in the afternoon, and the theatre and the opera by night, all on the arm of some smiling fellow. They hadn't changed addresses nearly as often then.

And now...

Now Mama made odd comments about Bridget being her revenge, and the high and mighty forgetting who knew what about whom. It was all very worrisome, particularly when Mama got to commenting on how nearly Bridget resembled Maggie. Bridget's letters to Maggie conveyed what information Bridget could manage, but with her mother reading every word, Bridget wasn't at all sure Maggie understood how untenable the situation was becoming.

"Look, over there." Mama nudged Bridget with an elbow. "The Duke of Wellington himself preening at Esther Windham. It isn't to be borne."

"Mrs. Wilson spoke fondly of the Iron Duke, didn't she?"

Mama turned to her with an expression Bridget found hard to read. "She did. She did at that, poor man."

Mrs. Wilson was one of Mama's friends from what she called her "wicked youth." Mama had been truly wicked; that much was clear even to a fourteen-year-old. Cecily had few friends, though there were men who'd smile at her fleetingly when Mama was shopping in Mayfair. The smiles seemed strained to Bridget, and when those smiles were turned on Bridget herself, they felt… dangerous.

As Cecily turned the horses out of the park, Bridget cast around for an innocuous topic—bonnets might do. And while she prattled away, she tried to compose another letter to Maggie that would make clear exactly how worried—how afraid—Bridget was becoming.

❧

Hazlit did not mistake Maggie Windham for a woman without experience. She was too poised, too reserved, for him to think she'd never nudged her dainty toe over the lines drawn in the name of propriety.

But whichever spotty boy or aging knight had encouraged her experiments in lust—or boys and knights plural, given the lady's age and obvious charms—they'd made a damned poor job of it. After a kiss like that—a kiss that left Hazlit's heart galloping around in his chest and lust roaring through his veins—the woman was looking at him as if she needed *reassurances*.

Bugger that. He'd blurted out all the reassurances he was going to. "What about you?" He peered down at her. "Did you like it?"

Which perhaps sounded like *he* needed reassurances, when what he needed was a cold plunge in a deep horse trough.

"I don't know." She sidled over to the sofa and settled gracefully before the tea service. "It was, as you say, a trifle unexpected."

He held his peace and watched as she put a pair of tea cakes on a plate. He was pleased to see her hand trembled slightly as she reached for the cakes. Just to rattle her, or maybe to settle himself, he resumed his place right beside her and stole a cake off her plate. "When is your staff's next half day?"

She munched to every appearance contentedly on her cake with a show of bemusement likely intended to aggravate him. He told himself he wasn't fooled.

"Tomorrow is half day. Even my companion takes off. I usually look forward to it."

"You like being alone?" He put another tiny cake on her plate and took one for himself. The icing was rich with butter underscored with vanilla and something else, something he couldn't quite place, but it reminded him of lunches with Westhaven.

She eyed the cake he'd served her. "I prefer being alone."

"My sisters like to be alone—or they did." He resisted the urge to tuck a lock of hair behind her ear. "It did not make them happy but made their misery more bearable somehow. They think I don't understand, but I do."

She turned to regard him, apparently as willing as he to drift away from the topic of who liked kissing whom. "You think they should go about in a society that will whisper behind their backs and make unkind comments to their faces?"

"Their husbands will be the ones to answer that question, but I think there is more chance of finding some true friendship out among live humans than among the flower gardens at Blessings or the wilds of rural Sussex." He thought to feed her more sweets—she could use some meat on her elegant bones—but the cakes were gone.

She gave him a long, measuring look during which Hazlit could hear her wondering if peeking at windows and skulking around ballrooms could be considered a way to find true friendship.

"I'll be here tomorrow," he said, getting to his feet. "When will the servants leave?"

"By noon. They have their elevenses and then depart." She rose more slowly and paced with him to the closed door.

"That's a rather generous half day."

"They work hard. Some of them are crossing to the East End and back without a conveyance, to see family, and the days are not yet that long."

He pushed her hair behind her ear. She bore it silently, her green eyes giving away nothing. "We will talk about that kiss, Maggie Windham."

Lest she make some dismissive reply, he kissed her again—a swift, claiming kiss—then slipped out the door before they had more than kisses in need of discussion.

Five

ADELE MARTIN HAD TO SUPPRESS A SHUDDER AS SHE watched her charge turning right and left before a full-length mirror.

"Mama says I'm to get used to sleeping in silk."

The child spoke in French as she smoothed a hand down the front of her silk nightgown. The embroidered hem fell nearly to the floor, a parody of modesty when the fabric was so sheer the girl's nipples and pubic hair were all but visible to the naked eye.

"It's not enough to keep a body warm," Adele replied. "Into bed with you."

Bridget took one last look in the mirror. "Mama says I'm to have my hair styled tomorrow. She says we're not to cut it much, because gentlemen adore long hair."

The poor girl sounded worried, which meant she at least had brains enough to know what fate awaited her in the all-too-near future, not that Adele could do a blessed thing for the child.

"You tell the hair dresser what you want." Adele ran a warming pan over the sheets. "Don't give her any room to maneuver, or she'll have your hair swept out with the trash, and despite what others may tell you, red hair is to be envied. I know of what I speak."

"I like my hair." Bridget fingered the long auburn braid resting over one slender shoulder while her gaze traveled over Adele's locks of a brighter shade. "Mama says—"

"Into bed." The girl's mother was a horror, enough to turn the stomach of a maid raised in the East End's worst slums, one who'd honed her French by serving ale in the dockside pubs.

"What do you think of my new things, Adele?" Bridget spun once again before the mirror, as graceful as a ballerina. "I must admit I *adore* silk."

"Miss Bridget…" Adele paused as she folded the bed linens back. What to say? Your mother is unnatural? You are about to be sacrificed to a bitter old woman's wickedness?

But maybe the girl would be lucky and find a wonderful protector. Lady Berwick had been nothing more than her lord's underage mistress before the besotted fool had married her. Her three sisters had remained blithely engaged in the wicked trade even as they'd waved their sister up the church aisle.

"Come to bed, child. I'm sure your new coiffure will be very fetching."

But Bridget was a bright girl, and in her eyes, Adele saw a shadow hover. "You think all this lace and silk is too grown up for me. Lots of girls marry at fifteen."

"You're fourteen, Miss Bridget, and your sheets are getting cold."

Bridget crossed to the bed and sat. "I wish I could talk to Maggie."

Maggie, to whom the child wrote letters. Letters that caused the girl's brow to knit and her tongue to peek out at the corner of her mouth. Maggie, who for all she might care about Bridget, did nothing to rescue the girl from the fate bearing down on her like a runaway mail coach.

Adele was lucky to have the post she did. No proper household would hire a lady's maid who'd worked for a succession of courtesans, and when the last soiled dove had taken ship for Ireland, Adele had been lucky to have even a character to show for three years of devoted service.

She tucked the girl in and started snuffing the candles one by one. Bridget's first protector would likely be an indulgent man. Bridget was stunningly pretty, fresh, and bubbling over with innocence.

But the second man would be a little less kind, the fifth or seventh barely civil. Somewhere down the line, she'd be knocked up and knocked around, and that was if she was lucky enough to avoid death from disease or drink.

"Maybe you should write to Maggie about all the pretty things your Mama gave you today. Tell her about the lace and silk, the visit from the hair dresser tomorrow, the corsets and stockings coming from the modiste next week."

"I've written to Maggie." Bridget drew the covers up to her chin and yawned as Adele knelt to bank the fire. "I do miss her."

Adele straightened and tugged the curtains closed so

they overlapped. "Tell Maggie you miss her, and tell her all about your new wardrobe."

"Mama says this is only the beginning. She says I'm to have new gowns and dresses and night rails and dressing gowns. I suppose I am a lucky girl, Adele…"

The lucky girl—who despite her words did not sound very lucky—yawned again. Adele made sure the screen was snugged right up next to the hearth and wished Bridget sweet dreams. Her mama would be out on the town for hours yet, meaning Adele had a little time to keep an appointment of her own.

❧

The house was like the woman who owned it: Scrupulously maintained, tidy and well secured, at least to initial appearances. Hazlit spent nearly two hours in the understory, examining the servants' parlor, the pantries, the laundry, the still room, the footmen's quarters, the housekeeper's rooms, the cellars, and lastly, the kitchen.

"Mr. Hazlit."

He rose from where he'd perched on the raised hearth. He'd been so lost in thought, he hadn't heard Maggie—she was no longer Miss Windham in his thoughts—come down the stairs.

"My lady." He watched as she perused him from head to toe.

"You have decided to become a gardener or perhaps a stable boy?"

"I have decided to call on you in a manner not likely to be remarked nor to show the effects of poking around in your commendably clean cellars. Do you mind if I help myself to some of that ham?"

"Sit." She took a carving knife from a drawer. "How long have you been here?"

"I waited until your staff departed and then let myself in." He moved to the sink to wash his hands, which allowed him a fine view of his hostess as she started cutting off thin slices of ham.

Ham. "Is that from one of your own farms?"

She glanced at him as the sliced meat piled up on the cutting board. "I thought you didn't snoop about behind a client's back." She hung the ham back on its hook as if it weighed nothing then disappeared into the pantry only to reemerge with a cheese wheel at least a foot across.

"It isn't snooping if you're looking for people with a motive to harm that client. Your finances are the next thing we'll examine."

She set the cheese on the counter with a solid thunk then put both fists on her hips. "I keep my own books, Mr. Hazlit. Nobody is pilfering from the exchequer. Butter or mustard?"

"Both, and your company, if you please. I already know you're quite wealthy."

She looked up sharply, her expression more displeased than surprised. "How did you come to that conclusion?"

She didn't deny it; he noticed that much despite the fact that her hair was in a loose chignon at her nape, and her attire today was an old-fashioned empire day dress in faded green. She looked cozy and approachable, except for the frown creasing her brow and the tension radiating from her.

And the knife in her hand.

He moved toward her. "You hide your wealth,

though it's observable, nonetheless. Your wine cellar is not large, but each bottle is an excellent vintage. Your everyday china is better quality than most of Mayfair trots out on special occasions. The sheets on even the footmen's cots are clean and sturdy. You have a closed range in this kitchen, a luxury half your neighbors are still saving for." He took the knife from her hand and put it on the counter. "Your dresses are beautifully made, even if they're intended to disguise your attributes rather than accentuate them. The furniture in the servants' parlor is new. Only in your own chambers do you resort to castoffs and stringent economies."

He was near enough to get the scent of her, of flowers and cinnamon. This close, he could also see the fatigue around her eyes and mouth, and a mulish determination to the set of her chin. He could kiss that chin...

"Mr. Hazlit, I asked you to find one fairly nondescript reticule, not to make free with my privacy. I really wish you'd let me know you were on the premises."

To keep himself out of trouble, he took the loaf of bread she'd retrieved from the bread box and began to cut slices. "I was making a point."

"The point that I'm not safe in my own house?" Her voice was quiet, but it shook with anger nonetheless. Or fear?

He kept his tone all the more even as he cut the bread. "I came in a cellar window somebody probably cracked for air on a warm day. Your house is safer than most. Whose responsibility is it to make sure the place is locked up each night?"

"Mine."

He stopped slicing to glare at her. "For God's sake, Maggie. That is not a job for the lady of the house."

She snatched up a small bowl and a wooden knife and began to smear a generous dollop of butter on each piece of bread. Her movements were assured, the preparation of at least simple food something she was obviously comfortable with. "I have neither butler nor house steward, Mr. Hazlit. My establishment is modest, despite your accusations to the contrary."

"Your establishment is modest," he said, watching her hands as she worked. "Your fortune is not." He turned to cross the kitchen lest he cover her hands with his own and demand that she tell him what was in the damned reticule.

He put together a tea tray while she fussed with the bread, cheese, ham, and mustard. "We're going to have to talk about your finances, Maggie. Anybody who stole something from you might be laying the groundwork for blackmail if they know the extent of your wealth."

She stopped slapping mustard on their sandwiches and stood, the wooden knife in her hand as she scowled at him. "You are making groundless accusations. You would not be searching this house if you didn't think there was at least some possibility the blasted thing is merely mislaid."

He studied her where she stood some eight feet and three tantrums away from him. Each time he saw her, she was a little more frazzled, a little more tightly wound. Each time he saw her, *he* was a little more frazzled, more tightly stretched between growing desire and an even more intense need to protect her despite her secretiveness and stubbornness.

"You're right." He picked up the tray and lied with smooth professionalism. "I'm eliminating the most obvious possibility first and hoping the reticule is simply lost. Shall we eat at the table?"

She nodded and stacked the sandwiches on a plate. "There are stewed apples in the brown crock in the pantry."

"Perhaps later. Come sit with me, Maggie. I'll tell you what else I learned from your house."

She brought the food to the table, and to his surprise, sat beside him rather than across the table. Perhaps she didn't want him peering directly at her face, and perhaps he didn't want her peering at him. The ensuing discussion was going to be difficult.

Proper English lord that he'd been raised to be, he poured the tea before firing his first broadside. She stirred her tea with that little tapping of the spoon on the bottom of her cup before taking a sip.

"So what did you find in my house?"

He couldn't do it. Couldn't bludgeon her with a truth likely to jar her self-control so badly he'd be able to pry the contents of the reticule loose from her. Not yet.

He passed her a sandwich. "There were children in this house at some point, servants' children, but also children of the master and lady of the house. I suspect they played together when the adults weren't looking, or maybe the previous owners were peculiarly democratic."

"How do you know this?"

Before answering, he watched to make sure she took a bite. "In the cellars, which are the best places to play pirates' cave, there are words and initials carved into the paneling, down at a child's height. Some are simple English, but one motto is in Latin."

"What does it say?"

"It's hard to make out. *Noli desperare*, I think."

Her smile was wan. "Never despair?"

"A good motto for pirates' captives. Finish your sandwich, Maggie."

She glanced at him, her expression curious. "When did you decide to call me Maggie?"

The last time I kissed you. "When did you decide to allow me to?"

Her smile tipped up then spilled over into a grin. "You are a very provoking man, Mr. Hazlit. What else did you find?"

And still, he could not tell her. "Very little dust. Your housekeeper is carrying a torch for a second cousin in the shires. They correspond madly about his sheep and her recipes for tisanes. The underfootman has a lock of the tweeny's hair under his pillow, but you said the tweeny is mooning after someone else. You're forgetting to eat."

She took another bite of her sandwich. There was more he would tell her, but not when she was just beginning to relax and let down her guard.

"It's good ham, Maggie, and you never answered my question about its origins."

"It's from Morelands." She used the back of her wrist to draw a stray lock of hair up over her brow. "We have good stewards in Kent, and there's a neighbor there with whom I correspond on agricultural matters. He gave me the idea of investing in pigs."

A very small disclosure, but he treasured it. His Maggie was a swine nabob.

She lifted the pot. "More tea?"

"Please."

He let her finish the meal in silence, but what he'd found was bouncing around in his brain, making the food sit uneasily in his gut. She'd be upset and scared. Those things would help him get some answers from her, which did not please him in the least.

"Maggie."

She put the pot down, her gaze meeting his. "Just say it, Mr. Hazlit. You've been suspiciously solicitous since I found you in my kitchen. You're trying to spare me something." The warmth in her gaze cooled as she spoke. She was manning the garrison, securing her cannon.

"Is it such a bad thing that I'm trying to respect your sensibilities?"

He wanted to grasp her hand, but she rose, taking the remains of their meal with her to the counter.

"It is tiresome to always be accounted incapable of dealing with life's realities. Bastardy is such a great, defining reality; it provides one a sort of fortitude." She turned to rest her hips against the counter and crossed her arms over her chest. "I would rather know, Mr. Hazlit, than be pampered and cosseted and treated like a child. What did you find?"

He rose, bringing the tea tray back to the counter, and kept advancing on her once he'd set it aside.

"Benjamin." He enunciated clearly and slowly for her. "Benjamin Braithwaite Holloway Portmaine... Hazlit is a name I've assumed to ensure my sisters are never associated with my present profession, but to you I would be myself: Benjamin Portmaine." She swallowed as he came to a halt half a pace before her. "It's my name. I ask you to use it."

"Speak the truth to me, and I will."

Ah, that pleased him. She hadn't dithered or hesitated. She *wanted* to call him by name. He slid his arms around her waist and bent his mouth very near her ear.

"Somebody has been trying to gain surreptitious access to your house, repeatedly, and they have succeeded."

He settled his mouth on the soft, fragrant skin of her neck, gathered her close with one arm, and used his free hand to destroy the tidy bun at her nape.

❧

Damn him, damn him... Maggie could not think, could not form a single sentence in reaction as Hazlit's lips traveled along the column of her throat. Such soft, warm, knowing lips, lips without hurry or hesitation.

"Somebody has broken into my house?"

Lips that settled over hers gently, even as she felt his hand sinking into her hair at the back of her head. He held her still for his kiss, held her steady.

And she wanted him to kiss her. The ugly realities never went away, but sometimes they could be held at arm's length for a few moments. Right now, she needed such moments more than she needed to ponder who had been searching repeatedly for what in her personal domain.

She wrapped her arms around him and tilted her

head, the better to receive his kiss. His mouth left hers, and she was summarily hoisted to sit on the counter.

"Mr. Hazlit?" She was at eye level with him, a novel and pleasing arrangement.

He leaned into her while he said, "Benjamin," against her mouth. His tongue seamed her lips, sweet with the taste of tea and ardent male interest.

"Benjamin." She said it against his mouth, too, proving one could almost talk and kiss at the same time. Sitting on the counter, she could get a proper hold of his silky dark hair and do some exploring of her own.

Somewhere in the mental distance, her common sense was lamenting and hurling questions at her: What was this in aid of? How did kissing address the topic of housebreakers? Where was this leading, for gracious God's sake?

Her body knew where it was leading, for she'd spread her knees to wrap her legs around his flanks, locking her ankles at the small of his back. For the first time in thirty years, Maggie Windham understood the ladies who said they'd been carried away by passion.

"Stop thinking, Maggie mine." He gathered her closer, wedging himself in tightly to her body. His tongue set up a rhythm, slow and naughty, while Maggie's womb leapt and heat poured into her veins.

"I don't want…" She squirmed against him, her body seeking relief or greater arousal, she wasn't sure which.

"You do, too, and God knows I want, as well." His hand was on her knee where it rested above his hip. "You'll let me do this, Maggie Windham, or I'll go mad. We'll both go mad."

Do this? *Do this?*

He shifted his hips away a little, and Maggie moaned in frustration. His tongue in her mouth wasn't enough, and she was about to climb off the counter and knock him out flat on the kitchen floor, so desperately did she crave greater closeness with him.

"Benjamin…"

God help her, she'd just growled at him. She felt him smile at her frustration, and then he took his mouth from hers to cradle her face against his throat. "Let me touch you, Maggie. Just touch you."

While she was trying to locate vocabulary sufficient to form an answer, she felt her skirts being dragged slowly up over her thighs. He *was* touching her, probing against the slit in her silk drawers, when a bolt of lightning shot up Maggie's spine.

"It's only my hand, just a little touch. Let me."

The air left her lungs as she felt the smallest breeze on her damp sex, then he did it again—a delicate brush of his thumb, and all of Maggie's focus riveted on that touch. She wanted to bite something. She opened her mouth on his throat and struggled for breath as her heart kicked against her ribs.

"What are you…?" A little more pressure, this time in a rhythm that sent pleasure cascading through her. Speech having deserted her, she moaned against his neck then slipped her tongue along his jaw.

"Let it happen. Let me give you this." He had one hand under her skirts. Maggie felt the other slide up her rib cage and settle over her breast while she gripped him to her with both arms and legs.

"Give me…" She arched into his hand, shamelessly, greedily. This wasn't coitus; she didn't even have her clothes off.

She wanted them off. She wanted his clothes off of him even more desperately, but that *little touch* of his made it impossible to think or maneuver beyond arching into his hand.

"Benjamin Hazlit…" From where he touched her, heat and wanting were coalescing into some unnameable longing. She was dizzy with it, burning and mad for him to make it better.

And he did. Oh, he did. With a gentle pressure to her breast and a slower, firmer touch against her sex, he sent her off into exquisite, shuddering pleasure. Drenched her in it, held her under until she was making a sound against his throat between a moan and a sigh and a prayer. And when she could no longer stand what was happening in her own body, his touch shifted, gentled, and became soothing and every bit as necessary to her.

He kissed her, and she needed that, too. Needed to cling to his mouth and his broad shoulders, needed to feel the heat and strength of him in her arms.

"Gracious God." She rested her forehead against his collarbone and let her legs slide down his flanks. "Sweet, merciful, gracious…"

Her hair was completely undone, and he swept it back over her shoulders to cascade down her back. She wished again that she were naked so she could enjoy his hands on her skin. Foolish thought. His cheek was against her crown, and though she could also feel his erection rock hard and ready between them, his embrace felt… safe.

It felt *dear*, which was worse.

What had she done?

"Why the sigh, Maggie Windham?"

She shook her head, resenting that he could speak clearly at such a time. She kissed his throat, letting her tongue trace the spot where his pulse beat—rather rapidly, she was pleased to note.

"Tell me you're all right, my dear."

She managed a nod. He kissed her temple, stepped away, and turned his back to her. She saw him withdraw a handkerchief from his pocket then rearrange his clothing, and she knew what he was doing.

She watched anyway, though only from the back of him. As he stroked himself, his spine curved, his head came up and then fell back as bliss claimed him. She wanted to see his face, see *him*, watch as pleasure overcame him, though even this much, just knowing he'd do this in the same room with her, was shockingly intimate.

A gesture of trust?

She scooted back farther on the counter, letting her skirts fall over her knees. When he turned to face her again, she met his gaze squarely. For the first time in her experience, his hair was disheveled, his clothing rumpled, and in his eyes she spied something… flustered. Wary. Vulnerable, maybe.

She smiled at him and held out a hand.

"My hair is a worse fright than yours, *Benjamin*."

His answering smile was crooked and beamish as he helped her down from the counter. "Your hair is gorgeous. I could make love—"

She put two fingers over his lips. "None of that. We strayed from our topic, and while I appreciate that you felt the need to distract me, it was only that: a distraction."

She spoke gently, for she wasn't lecturing him. She was putting as constructive a face on things as she possibly could and reminding herself of their proper agenda. She would castigate herself for this lapse just as soon as her body stopped humming with satisfaction.

And desire.

He held her against his body a moment longer then let her step away.

"We will talk about this, Maggie Windham. This business that draws us to each other isn't simply a distraction. Whether you like it or not, it's more than that."

He ran a hand through his hair, suggesting he might be as rattled as she.

"A very nice distraction, then," she said, a ringing understatement if ever she'd uttered one. "Let's use my office. It has no windows on the street, and I think a change of scene is in order."

He muttered something about a horse trough and followed her up the stairs.

❧

"Abby Norcross is a very confused tramp."

Hazlit made no reply as Archer settled on the sofa beside him, brandy in hand. Confusion seemed to be the order of the day—or night, more accurately—the sort of confusion that could not distinguish between the urge to possess and the urge to protect.

One of Archer's bare, elegant feet appeared on the low table, then the other. "You aren't drinking?"

"Not yet. The night is young."

Archer peered at him. "It's two bloody hours after midnight, Benjamin. I left you sitting, staring at the fire, better than six hours ago, and you're still staring at it, and you're not even drinking. Have a sip of mine."

Archer nudged his elbow, managing to not slosh a drop. Hazlit took a sip lest he be pestered the livelong night.

"Which case is it?" Archer accepted the drink back and slouched lower on the cushions. "It's always a case when you go broody on me like this. For the life of me, I can't figure out what dear Lady Norcross is up to. She did that coach-switching thing again tonight, got into Hammerschmidt's conveyance, but only Mrs. Hammerschmidt was in it."

"That makes no sense." Which was also consistent with his day so far. Like needing to swive Maggie Windham until they were too weak to breathe made no sense.

"Maybe the ladies had a pleasant chat, like we're not having." Archer took another sip, and Hazlit roused himself to take the bait.

"I suspect somebody is blackmailing Maggie Windham, but it's somebody she's trying desperately to protect."

Beside him, Archer perched the drink on his flat stomach. "She's the adopted daughter of a duke. It would have to be somebody in a very high place to have leverage over her."

Archer was a good sounding board, for all he liked to needle and tease, and hours of staring at the fire had yielded no stirring insights—excepting, of course, the stirrings in places low and unmentionable.

"I'm thinking it's one of her brothers," Hazlit said, appropriating another sip of Archer's drink. "The musical one had a left-handed look to him until recently."

"Lord Valentine." Archer smiled at the now-empty glass. He rose and crossed to the decanter. "He had no such tendencies when I knew him in Rome, and what manner of left-handed fellow spends much of his time in a high-class brothel?"

"The kind who's trying to keep his inclinations unknown."

"A dandy does not a nancy boy make. If a duke's spare preferred men, it would be all over Town."

"Maybe. He's out in Oxfordshire now, duly married to the former Baroness Roxbury. By all accounts, it's a love match."

"How unfashionable." Archer passed Hazlit a drink and resumed his spot on the sofa. "You could ask the brothers what dark secrets their sister might be keeping."

"In which case, my will leaves all the unentailed property in a trust for my sisters, to be administered by your sweet self."

"Much obliged. Two comely wenches and a trust fund."

He didn't mention the title, which was typical of Archer's sense of loyalty.

Hazlit blew out a breath and put his better theory into words. "What if Maggie is protecting her father?"

"Percy Windham was a noted hellion in his youth, and he cuts a wide swath in the Lords. You think he's crossed some lines, politically or otherwise?"

"He schemes and plots for pleasure, can't seem to

help himself. I don't know as he'd stoop to outright bullying or bribery, but I'm precluded from investigating too closely."

"Precluded by what?" Archer's eyes closed, giving him a deceptively angelic look.

"Honor, I suppose. Their Graces wouldn't appreciate it if I took their coin and then turned around a year later and went nosing into His Grace's dirty linen."

"Dukes do not have dirty linen. This is an established fact. Look at Devonshire. Bastards and heirs raised under the same merry roof. No dirty linen, though. Not so much as a wrinkled handkerchief. He's a *dewk*."

There was merit in what Archer was saying. The royal dukes, in response to their dear papa's Royal Marriages Act, had at least a dozen illegitimate offspring between them, though some put the estimates closer to twenty. William alone had an entire clutch, and with Princess Charlotte's death, the man might well wear the crown one day.

Archer was right: it was common knowledge dukes were above dirty linen.

"What about duchesses?" Benjamin put the question slowly, because it had the feel of the right, most inconvenient line of inquiry. "Do duchesses have dirty linen?"

Archer was quiet for a moment. "I'm afraid they just might. And Esther Windham wouldn't go running to His Grace to tidy up her messes. Dear Percy would likely skewer someone, and his sons would sharpen the sword for him. At least Rosecroft is rusticating in the North—he's the worst of the lot."

"I normally like puzzles."

"You're very good at them. Why is this one different?"

Uncomfortable question, and the answer likely had to do with what had happened in Maggie's kitchen that very afternoon. Hazlit got up and brought the decanter to the table. "Maggie Windham has hired me to assist her in retrieving a reticule. I don't know how to do that without first gaining her trust, which seems nigh impossible to do."

"You're good with the ladies, Benjamin. They like your broody good looks and broad shoulders."

"They like your golden good looks just as much."

"They do at that. You can't charm your way into Miss Windham's good graces—or her bed?"

"I have the sense if I could charm my way into her bed, once I'd served my purpose there, she'd simply show me the door and ask when I expected to see her reticule again." She'd all but done as much following the incident in the kitchen, at least to appearances.

Archer opened his eyes. "We do so hate it when the ladies treat us the way we treat them. You can't bully her? Rattle some swords, threaten to tattle to Papa?"

"No, I cannot." He was damnably sure he couldn't threaten Maggie Windham. It wouldn't work, and he hadn't the will to do it. "She'd dismiss me without the proverbial character."

"A determined woman. I like determined women."

"You like them so much you try to get under their skirts."

"I like them a very great deal. More brandy?"

Hazlit held out his glass and let Archer pour him two fingers. Archer did like the ladies, liked them practically every chance he got, which was a dangerous propensity, though useful in their line of work.

"Who's the pretty little maid, Archer?"

"Which little maid? There are so many."

"The one who distracted you from following the pair of swains home from Miss Windham's. The one you stopped off to see tonight before you came home."

Archer's expression held a little genuine disgruntlement. "How could you tell?"

"Her scent." Benjamin tapped the side of his own nose. "Floral, with a slight undertone of starch, and notes of cinnamon, lavender, and cedar, as well. A lady's maid who spends hours in the dressing room with her mending and pressing. For good measure, she looks in on the laundresses to see that her ladyship's gowns are getting proper handling." The scent, in fact, bore a striking undertone of Maggie's fragrance.

"Your nose ought to be outlawed. She's just a maid."

"You are my heir, Archer."

This provoked the usual long-suffering sigh. "Lucky me. Shall we get out the cribbage board, or have you more brooding to do?"

Hazlit let Archer beat him several times at cribbage, though he did, indeed, have more brooding to do. He was going to have to do something about Maggie Windham, but he was damned if he knew what.

❧

Maggie sanded the note she'd spent two hours crafting. Three sentences for two hours work, but then, how did a woman politely fire a man for being a delightful… kisser? How did she fire him, when his primary transgression was to be an irresistible source of simple animal comfort?

Or was his primary transgression that he'd been right all along? Maggie glanced at the drawer where she'd stuffed a beaded bag, fringed at the bottom, about fifteen inches square.

The reticule had not been misplaced, nor had it been stolen by a common sneak thief. The thing had fallen into the worst possible pair of hands, hands that would bring down any who attempted to aid Maggie, particularly a man whose family's past included a scandal and whose present was rife with shady undertakings.

She set her note to the Hon. Benjamin Hazlit aside and reached for her tray of correspondence, only to feel the foreboding in her stomach congeal into dread. Another letter from Bridget. Maggie desperately wanted to hear from the girl—needed to—but enclosed with the letter would no doubt be a demand for money.

A great deal of money.

She slit the missive open with a penknife.

Dearest,

You should see my hair! I look at least eighteen now, with curls about my face and the part on the side. We hardly cut it at all, and Mama says I look ever so grown up. Is this how you felt when you first put up your hair? Excited and pleased and just the least little bit anxious?

And my wardrobe! Mama says we need not worry about money, for which I am grateful. I have new unmentionables of the sheerest silk with lace trimming and embroidery all around. My favorite is red silk with black lace, but Mama says that is for a special occasion. Adele does not approve. She says nothing, but I can tell.

When are you going to visit again, Maggie? I would love to show off all my new things. Mama says soon I can go driving with her at the fashionable hour. I cannot wait to be seen all dressed up. I understand now why ladies like to go to balls, though I've asked Mama when we're to have a dancing master in to teach me the dances. My pianoforte is coming along, too, as is my French. You must come speak French with me, Maggie dearest. I miss you so, and it has been ages and ages since I saw you. I will soon be so grown up you won't even recognize me.

All my love,
Your Bridget

Sweet, gracious God... conversing in French, wearing red silk peignoirs, and not yet fifteen. Though Bridget had couched matters in gushing, girlish hyperbole, the threat was clear, and yet Maggie was still at a loss for how to thwart it. Cecily was shrewd. Maggie would bet her entire fortune some demand or other was soon to materialize. The morning's recent discovery guaranteed it.

"Mr. Hazlit to see you, mum."

Mrs. Danforth was again wreathed in smiles, while Maggie felt the dread in her vitals shift to despair. She'd been hoping not to lay eyes on him again. Not

to have to see his dark eyes, his hands, his mouth…
She was going to miss that mouth until her dying day,
and yet she would send Benjamin Hazlit on his way.
For his sake, for hers, for her family's, even for his
family's, she would.

"No need to announce me, Mrs. Danforth." Hazlit
stood behind the much-shorter housekeeper, his top
hat in his hand. "I'm sure on such a pretty day you've
more interesting things to do than keep track of me."

"I'll just see to the tea tray then, shall I?" Maggie's
housekeeper bustled off, smiling like a girl still in
the schoolroom.

Hazlit prowled into the office and closed the door
behind him. "You still aren't getting adequate rest."

"I will be in the near future. My reticule has been
returned to me." She did not report to him that it
had been returned empty of Bridget's previous letters.
Cecily's doing, no doubt, a guarantee to ensure the next
exorbitant demand for funds was met without hesitation.

Hazlit was in the process of putting his hat on the
mantel. Maggie watched him go still, watched the way
his riding jacket pulled across his shoulders, watched
him turn slowly, his eyes giving away nothing. "Has
it, indeed?"

She rose from her desk, intending to literally hand
him his hat. "Just this morning, I found it on the seat of
my traveling coach." And God help her, she was telling
the truth—though certainly not the whole truth.

"I found something this morning, as well. It's
waiting for you out in the mews."

"Mr. Hazlit…"

But he'd already sidled over to her desk, and damn

him to the most vile hog wallow, he didn't even need to turn her letter right way around to read it.

"You are *discharging* me?"

She crossed her arms. "The missing item has been recovered. You may keep the funds I paid you. I'm satisfied, Mr. Hazlit." But gracious, merciful, everlasting God, could she have expressed herself in less fraught terminology?

He was before her, scowling down at her from such close proximity she could catch the spicy, exotic scent of him. "I'm not."

She blinked and pulled her mind away from the study of the amber pin winking out from among the folds of his cravat. "You're not what?"

He leaned in close and spoke right next to her ear. "Satisfied. Come with me."

He took her hand and tugged her toward the French doors, leaving Maggie torn between reveling in the pleasure of his fingers laced with hers and nigh panicked that he wasn't accepting his dismissal.

"Mr. Hazlit, the tea tray—"

"Bugger the tea tray. You and I have both already searched the traveling coach. This only confirms your reticule was stolen, and I would hazard a wild guess it was not returned with all of its contents."

"Not a single penny was stolen." Which ironically confirmed Cecily's grasping hand in the matter.

He stopped so abruptly she almost fetched up against his chest. "And that only makes it worse, doesn't it? Somebody is toying with you, proving they can break into your house, steal something of personal value, and then leave it with you the worse for wear when the whim strikes them. Were you or were you not paying attention when I showed you all the signs of forcible entry about your house?"

When he was impassioned like this—or when he was kissing her—Maggie could see golden flecks radiating around the centers of his irises. His eyes weren't dark so much as they were expressive.

"I saw the scratches around the locks, sir, and yet nothing is missing but my reticule. *You* have seen that the locks have been replaced with newer mechanisms, per your instruction."

He was off again, towing her along behind him in the direction of the mews. "That's only because they haven't found your safe yet."

"How did you know I have a safe?"

"I found it the first night I investigated your domicile."

"You invest—Stop!" She wrenched her hand free and kept her voice down with effort. "*You* broke into my home? While I was sleeping in my own bed you prowled around my house like a thief?"

"Like a man trying to catch a thief." He ran his hand through his hair, and something about his expression led Maggie to believe that while he admitted to sliding in a cellar window in the broad light of day, she wasn't ever to have known about his nocturnal visits. That his composure was fractured allowed her to regain a little of her own.

"Trespassing is a crime, Mr. Hazlit."

"Keeping a lady safe is not. If it's any consolation to you, I found nothing that would incriminate you."

"Gracious God." She paced off, trying to absorb the enormity of his arrogance.

"I am sorry."

She heard him shifting to stand behind her. They were in the back gardens, visible from the house, but only from the house. She turned, arms crossed over her middle.

"What are you sorry for?"

He studied her for a moment before one corner of his mouth kicked up. "For getting caught, if you must know. My partner Archer and I—he's a relation of sorts as well—agreed years ago that standard procedure would include an unannounced inspection of the client's premises. On occasion, our clients aren't completely honest with us, and it can result in us being exposed to needless risk."

"I am not exposing you to any risk. I am discharging you, effective immediately."

He didn't like it. She could tell by the way something calculating came into his gaze. "At least let me show you what I brought you."

He wasn't capitulating, Maggie understood that, as well, but he wasn't going to press the point while standing in the gardens. She fell in step beside him and allowed him to hold the back gate for her.

They did not hold hands, which was a good thing. She'd told herself it was time their paths parted, and the return of the reticule—minus Bridget's letters—took the decision from her, in any case. She would miss him—to herself she could admit that much—but she'd gotten used to missing the people she cared for.

"Steady there." He took her arm when she would have stumbled. "I've actually brought you two things, though one is just a loan." He led her to the mews where Maggie kept the aging team of carriage horses she used for her jaunts around Town.

She dropped Hazlit's arm and stared. "That is my sister-in-law's mare, but whose dog is that?"

The thing was a huge brindle-coated beast with a lot of Scottish deerhound in its ancestry. Its tail began to thump against the legs of the stable boy who held its leash, though the dog neither leapt toward them nor barked.

Hazlit took the leash from the stable boy and passed it to Maggie. "This is Deacon, and he's your newest friend."

"Dogs are messy, Mr. Hazlit." She ran a hand over the animal's head. "They shed and drool and worse. I have no use for a dog."

"He's getting on in years, though he has some good runs in him yet."

Upon closer inspection, Maggie could see the few gray hairs around the dog's muzzle. He was at the wonderful age when the destructive puppy energy had worn off and he was still spry, but could be trusted to lounge before a hearth for hours on end.

"You'll have to take him back from whence you found him, Mr. Hazlit, though I appreciate the gesture."

He knelt by the dog and looked up at her. "You won't even let a dog stay close to you, Maggie? He couldn't violate your confidences if you asked it of him, and he needs a home."

Two pairs of brown eyes turned on her, making an unwelcome lump rise in Maggie's throat. She was sending Hazlit on his way, and what harm was there in taking in a dog who needed a home?

"I do hope he knows to ask when he needs to visit the garden?"

Hazlit rose. "He's a perfect gentleman. Why don't we let him get settled in while we're taking some air?"

"I beg your pardon?"

He glanced around then leaned in a little. "We're going riding, Maggie Windham. I am in a position to know you have all the proper attire. I suggest you get into it. I am willing to serve as lady's maid if you ask it of me."

"Enough nonsense." She paced off a few steps lest that particular lazy tone of voice steal her few remaining wits. "My schedule doesn't permit me to go off frolicking with you, Mr. Hazlit, though I thank you for the invitation and for your efforts thus far on my behalf." She turned to go, but his hand on her arm stopped her.

"That is my coach at the end of the carriage block, Maggie. It is unmarked, and the curtains can be tied closed. Your sidesaddle is in the boot, and we can bring the riding horses behind us as we leave Town. Nobody will see us together, and your brother tells me you love to ride."

Brothers could be such a nuisance—a well-meaning nuisance.

"Westhaven also said his wife's mare could use the exercise."

As he spoke, Hazlit's hand smoothed repeatedly over the dog's head. After today, Maggie might cross paths with the man at the ducal mansion. They'd nod politely at each other and perhaps exchange pleasantries about the weather. She would never again feel that hand caressing her hair, never share another kiss with the first man to reawaken her long-denied wish for a husband and children of her own.

She desired him, which was folly enough, but she also *cared* for him. This inconvenient realization had come to her between one step and the next while she ambled along at his side—contemplating his absence. She wouldn't be sending him away—sending him far from the entire sordid and expensive mess keeping her a prisoner in her own life—if she didn't care for him a great deal.

"If we go riding, we will not be seen?"

"I doubt Richmond is teeming with people today. Lady Davenroy is holding a Venetian breakfast, and Lord Montrose is gathering his forces in preparation for some upcoming votes. We won't be seen by anybody of note."

He couldn't guarantee that, but Papa would be at Lord Montrose's meeting, and Her Grace would likely be at Lady Davenroy's breakfast. It was well Maggie was cutting ties with Benjamin Hazlit—he was entirely too clever and observant for her peace of mind.

"How did you find my safe?"

"The hinges holding the picture in front of it are just a little worn. The painting hangs perhaps a quarter inch off because of it. Nice painting, though."

"My sister Jenny did it a couple of years ago. You'll wait for me to change?"

"My dear, I will always wait for you."

She let that blather pass for the nonsense it was and headed into the house. She loved to ride, and her escort had been clever enough to make it possible for them to do so without being seen.

And he was right: nobody was going to be touring Richmond at this hour, so where was the harm in one final outing with the only man to catch her eye in years?

❦

The enormity of the plan hatching in Hazlit's mind made what should have been simple difficult. His line of work required that he be able to make a convincing show of paying attention to another's words while taking in details of the surroundings, listening to nearby conversations, and otherwise dividing his focus.

Except that taking any part of his attention from the woman beside him was nigh impossible.

Maggie Windham grew prettier the farther he took her from Town. Her speech grew more animated, she laughed occasionally, and when they'd gained the green fields of the countryside, she patted the seat beside her, bidding him to join her on the forward-facing bench.

"Why do you dwell in Town when you're happier in the country?" It wasn't a question he would have attempted even five miles ago.

"Why do you dwell in London when your heart is in Cumbria?" Her eyes held laughter and a little challenge. He'd never seen her looking lovelier or more relaxed, which affirmed the course he was considering—the only course for a man who'd finally found a woman toward whom he felt both protective and possessive.

"I dwell in London because of my sister's situation…" He fell silent. Avis had had twelve years to come to terms with her situation, and she was very happily married now to a decent fellow on the neighboring estate. "Going home would have been difficult previously, and now I have obligations in the Lords."

"You have a title, don't you?"

He didn't hesitate. "An earldom. Earl of Hazelton." She cocked her head, and he waited for her mouth to flatten as she realized he'd been deceptive by omission.

"Papa was a reluctant duke. He didn't want to sell out his commission and man the title, as he put it. I won't tell."

She wouldn't. It came as a small surprise to realize he trusted her to keep his confidences in this.

"I'm running out of time," he said, glancing through a crack in the leather curtains. It was a gorgeous day, so pretty it made a man... homesick. Maggie's fingers laced with his.

"Running out of what sort of time?"

"An earldom is not a simple thing to obscure. Your papa has been complicit in my scheme, because he recalls the ordeal my sisters went through and understands my reasons, but people suspect. There are only so many times I can shuffle into Parliament all but wearing a disguise. Then too, it's one thing to send a mere mister after an errant daughter or missing love token. It's quite another to repose nasty secrets in a belted earl."

She squeezed his hand. "You are telling me this because we've reached a parting of the ways."

No, he was not, but it was as much of an opening as she'd give him, and the weight of his recently hatched scheme was pressing on his chest.

"In truth I do not want to part ways with you, Maggie Windham, and I'd ask you for a fair hearing."

She turned her head to meet his gaze, though her bearing had become positively imperial with a simple lift of her chin. "I'm listening."

"I have an heir, but he's a distant cousin who wants nothing to do with titles, votes, or the obligation my sisters represent. He's a Town man, handy with the ladies, and not given to agricultural matters in the least."

"Is this Archer?"

In for a penny, in for a pound. "Yes. I'd like you to meet him."

She shook her head, but he forged on rather than let her start on her protestations.

"One reluctant heir is not adequate to secure the succession. I am attracted to you, and I think the attraction is mutual. I am asking you to marry me, Maggie Windham. Cry the banns, reserve St. George's, your mama weeping in the first row while your brothers glare at me for my audacity…"

He could not gauge her reaction.

"Her Grace is not my mother, and my brothers would not glare at you, and while I understand the honor you do—"

She tipped her head back, eyes closed. He watched while her throat worked and felt her hand clench in his. "Benjamin, I cannot."

He had expected an uphill battle. He had not expected the single, silver tear that slipped from the corner of her closed eye and trickled down her cheek.

"Why not?"

She shook her head and accepted his handkerchief.

"I'm just a by-blow, and being your countess would only ensure I was the subject of constant gossip. Our children would be ostracized; I'd be the subject of much criticism…"

"Our children would be the grandchildren of a duke and an earl. When one of the Wilson sisters can marry a titled lord and be accepted anywhere, your argument fails. We'd live in Cumbria, where the only ones to pass judgment would be the sheep climbing the fells. I'd give you as many children as you wanted, and we'd suit, Maggie Windham. We'd suit admirably."

He was an educated, resourceful man, but just a man. Words were not winning the fair maid, and while he'd been prepared to work for her capitulation, he was not ready for her to wall herself off in specious arguments and stubborn silence.

He kissed her. He put all of his longing into the kiss, all of his determination to keep her safe and fight her battles for her. When she was sighing into his mouth and her hands were clinging to his biceps, he forced himself to pause, lest he be consummating unspoken vows on the carriage bench.

"You must not…" She drew in a slow, deep breath, their mouths an inch apart. "You cannot ravish my reason, Benjamin. I am discharging you, and we will be cordial acquaintances from this day forward."

She dropped her forehead to his, her fingers circling his wrist where his hand cradled her jaw.

A tactical retreat might be in order, but he was not going to be easily discouraged.

"I will serenade you from the street, Maggie

Windham. I will be so callow, you will marry me to save me from embarrassment."

She smiled at his flummery. "Take me riding, and then let us part on a happier note."

He shifted to bring his arm around her shoulders and urge her against his side. "I brought a picnic as well. Surely a disappointed suitor is entitled to a consolation meal?"

Her head rested on his shoulder, a cozy, comfortable posture that did nothing to still the hammering of his heart in his chest—and that after a single kiss.

She smiled and did not sit up. "If we ride the way I want to, we'll need the sustenance. Tell me some more about your sisters."

He told her. As they saddled up and rode the pretty lanes of Richmond, he babbled. He found himself recalling memories of his siblings from before their lives had been blighted by the assault of one and the physical injury to the other. He described Blessings in all its great, bucolic splendor, and he listened to Maggie wax just as eloquent about the Morelands estate in Kent.

When they handed off the horses to the groom a long hour later, the footmen had already spread the blankets and set out the picnic basket in a secluded copse along a path well away from the lanes.

In all their rambles, Hazlit had seen only one stately old town coach lumbering along, two footmen up behind, a coachman and groom in front. And still the weather held warm and fair, which could only bode well for his next bid to gain Maggie Windham's hand—and to keep her safe.

❧

It was a gorgeous day, the breeze soft and fragrant with the scent of blooming flowers and greening trees.

Maggie glanced around at the park in all its early spring beauty—for the day was genuinely an exponent of early spring—took a lungful of fresh air, and told herself it was the perfect day for a broken heart.

As a girl, she'd dreamed of one day having a husband and children, a home of her own and a family of her own—a real family. It was the same mundane dream every girl from good family felt entitled to have, and it was a wonderful dream.

And then she'd made her come out and shortly thereafter realized that if the family she already had was to be safe from social and financial harm, that simple, solid, mundane dream was not to be hers—not ever.

Benjamin, the Earl of Hazelton, had asked for her hand in marriage, and it hurt with the sweet, piercing ache of a wish that would never come true—a wish so dear she'd been unwilling to admit to herself she still held it in her heart.

A husband she could respect and *care for*, children, a beautiful estate far from gossip and intrigue, passion such as she'd only glimpsed recently, and the illusion of safety and peace.

For it would be only an illusion. When Bridget's first letter found her, the illusion would crack. When Maggie's pin money went missing month after month, the cracks would start radiating through her happiness; when Benjamin put the pieces of the puzzle together, the dream would shatter altogether.

"Chicken or roasted beef?" Benjamin knelt by a huge wicker hamper, rummaging in its depth as he spoke. "This is a momentous decision, as it determines which bottle of wine I open first. And we've forced strawberries." He glanced up at her. "I will wrestle you for the strawberries, be warned."

He went on like that, teasing with a grave face, feeding her all but three of those strawberries, and plying her with a fruity, sweet white wine between every bite of chicken. When the meal was finished, Maggie realized the coach was gone, taking grooms, footmen, and horses with it.

"I'm alone with you, Benjamin, and you've been suspiciously charming for the past hour. What are you about?"

"I'm not sure." He started repacking the hamper. "Enjoying the condemned man's last meal, maybe. Why won't you marry me, Maggie? The real reason, not the polite excuse."

Because he was pretending to be busy with the plates and bottles and glasses, Maggie had a moment to study him. As he efficiently put away the detritus of their meal, she knew he was listening to her, even watching her.

She could not offer him explanations, and after today, gentleman that he was, he'd not ask for them. He'd resume his busy life, one foot in an earldom, another in the shadows of Mayfair, missing his home, fretting over his sisters, and politely *nodding* at Maggie Windham on the street.

The ache in her throat that had started with his proposal threatened to choke her.

"Will you kiss me good-bye, Benjamin?"

He sat back on his heels, the last bottle of wine in

his hand, his shirt sleeves luffing gently in the spring breeze. Without answering, he put the bottle in the hamper and closed the wicker flaps. He met her gaze, his eyes a peculiar amber hue in the dappled shade. "Yes. I will kiss you, Maggie Windham."

He crawled the few feet across the blanket, looking like some dark jungle cat on the scent of prey. Maggie sat, knees drawn to her chest, until Benjamin was nose to nose with her.

And then he was on her, literally and figuratively. She was on her back, his body caging hers, his mouth a force of nature against her own. This wasn't like any kiss they'd shared before; it wasn't like any kiss she might have imagined.

This was a pillaging, plundering kiss. A kiss that drew the passion right up through her body and had her clinging to him without thought. Desire, hot and needy, roared to life in her vitals.

"Benjamin…" She held his head still with her hand fisted in his hair and drew on the tongue he'd sent raiding secrets from her mouth.

"Don't *think*, Maggie. Just kiss me." His hand closed over her breast, and Maggie arched up into the pleasure he gave her. This was wrong, dangerous, stupid… and necessary to the survival of her soul. She kissed him with everything in her, kissed him against years—*more* years—of isolation and despair. Kissed him as if he were her last hope of passion—because he was.

She felt her skirts drifting up against her legs. She was about to whisper at him to hurry when he lifted himself away from her.

"Where are you——?"

He sat back not even a foot from her side and, still holding her gaze, undid the falls of his riding breeches. "I will not take from you what only a husband should accept, but by God, Maggie Windham, I will make you rethink your refusal of me."

He tossed back her skirts and crouched over her. "Stop me now, Maggie, or let me give you the pleasure you deserve."

Her eyes went to the place where his clothing was undone. She wanted to see him, to touch the part of him a wife might touch, to know the intimate scent and feel of him.

She lay on her back, knees drawn up, drawers exposed to the pretty day and to Benjamin Hazlit's hot gaze. "I wouldn't stop you if I could, Benjamin. This once, I want... I want *you*."

"Not all of me." His fingers went to the tapes of her drawers. "I won't ruin you, Maggie, though you have certainly ruined me."

And then with a lift of her hips, her drawers were off. He balled them up and tossed them to a corner of the blanket, and before Maggie could slap her knees closed, his hand was trailing down her thigh.

"I'm going to look, Maggie, and I'm going to touch, and you're going to let me."

He already was looking, staring at flesh Maggie herself had never seen and rarely touched with her own fingers.

"God above, you are gorgeous."

His thumb traced over her mons. She closed her eyes and memorized the sensation. All the frantic need of the previous few minutes drained down into the place he was touching, coalescing into a slow, throbbing ache.

"Your hair is a shade darker here. Do you like this?" The question was almost conversational as he drew his fingers through her curls, slowly, repeatedly. "Or maybe you prefer a more intimate approach."

He shifted his touch, parting folds of flesh in slow caresses. Sensation, hot and shivery at once, rippled up Maggie's body. She arched toward him, need and frustration overcoming any pretense of self-control.

"I wish I could get you naked," he said, staring at her sex. "I want to see your breasts, want to put my hands and mouth on you, want to feel you naked and half mad with passion beneath me."

His voice had dropped to the register of passion, of darkness and pleasure. Maggie shifted on the blanket, the confinement of her clothing a form of torture.

He did something with his hands—used both of them to hold her intimate flesh and stroke over it at the same time. The sensation was exquisite and unbearably arousing.

"You must not." She wrapped her fingers around his wrist, trying to communicate desperation with her grip. "I cannot bear this."

"Shall I kiss you instead?"

For one dumbstruck moment she thought he meant to kiss her *there*, but then he was shifting over her, working one arm beneath her neck as he settled some of his weight on her.

"Gracious, merciful…" His weight was *exactly* what her body had been craving. She lifted her hips against him, feeling the hard column of his erect flesh pressing down against her pelvis. It helped, even as it increased her frustration.

He braced himself on his elbows. "Not like that." With one hand, he rearranged billows of skirts and petticoats, and also his own clothing. "Like this, God help me."

Ah, *God.*

They were flesh against flesh, the hot length of him so close to where Maggie wanted him. He'd said he would not ruin her, but why on earth not? There would be no other lovers, not ever, no one to know, no one to care…

"Please, Benjamin… I want…" There in the bright sunshine and the warm, promising air of spring, she wanted, and wanted, and wanted.

He said nothing, but hitched his body against hers. "Lift your hips. Move with me." His voice was a guttural rasp near her ear. As he spoke, his erection slid over the damp folds of her sex.

"But that's not—"

He shut her up with a kiss then paused, his mouth hovering a half inch away. *"Move with me."*

He did it again, used the hot length of his cock to stroke at her sex. Maggie experimentally tilted her hips, bringing the pressure closer to where she craved him. His pace was maddeningly slow, but it allowed her to find just the angle she needed.

"Better?" He'd gotten his arm under her neck again, supporting the back of her head in his palm as Maggie curled up to him. For her part, she slid a hand down his back, under his breeches to the firm, smooth flesh of his buttocks.

"Not… enough."

He gave her more of his weight, so the drag of flesh against flesh began to drive Maggie toward the dark maelstrom of pleasure he'd shown her once before. She pressed her open mouth to his throat, a low keening emerging as her body grew clamorous for satisfaction.

"Don't rush it." If anything, he slowed down.

Maggie seized the moment. At the precise instant he was shifting the direction of his stroke, she tilted her hips just one inch higher, so he slid home in one sweet, burning thrust of pleasure.

Six

"Jesus God in heaven, Maggie... *We can't...*" He went still then started to withdraw.

"No." Maggie sank her nails into the flesh of his buttocks, more determined on this than on anything previous in her life. "Don't leave me. What's done is done, and I want... I want *so much*..."

She wanted to weep and to draw him so deeply into her body a part of him would always remain with her. She wanted to make wild promises that would only doom him to sharing her unhappiness; she wanted to bear his children and watch them grow up on that distant, beautiful estate in Cumbria.

For long moments, while Maggie mourned the dreams of a girl who'd grown into a lonely, despairing woman, Benjamin did not move. She stroked her hand down his back, desperate to keep him close.

"Please, Benjamin. This is all I will ever ask of you." It was all she would ever dare to ask of him.

His whole body underwent some subtle change, became more supple and somehow closer to her. "It shall be as you wish."

He moved inside her, and the beauty of it robbed Maggie of speech. To be so close, to be held like this, desired, treasured... cherished bodily. Every part of him was attuned to every part of her, listening for her pleasure, listening and straining to please her.

She knew this, felt it physically and emotionally and even spiritually. And now, now when her body was lifting effortlessly toward the pleasure he'd shower on her, she wanted *him* to slow down, to draw out this singular experience for her, for them both.

He wasn't hurrying, but *she* was. With each slow, glorious penetration of her body, she hastened toward fulfillment. Her breath shortened, her hold on him became desperate, and she became frantic until pleasure cascaded over her in convulsions so intense she lost awareness of all save the man in her arms and in her very body.

When the storm subsided, she was pressed so tightly to him her stomach hurt with the effort and tears clogged the back of her throat. She could feel him hilted in her body, still rigid with arousal, a comfort and a source of renewed longing even as she tried to regain control over her breathing.

"Did I hurt you?"

She shook her head and kissed his jaw. He sighed, his body solid and warm above her. Without thinking, she moved her hips in a languid roll, only to blink up at him as he withdrew entirely.

She felt it as a shock, a grief, reverberating from her womb to her mind to her soul.

"Any more of that, my lady, and this will truly be irrevocable." He was braced above her, staring down at her intently. He hadn't spent in her body. Even in her inexperience, she understood that, and he wanted to spend now. She wrapped one hand around the back of his neck, levered up on her elbow, and kissed him.

His return fire was ravenous, though he needed one hand to brace himself above her and used the other to stroke himself. She could feel the slight, rhythmic movement of his hand between them, feel the tension coiling more and more tightly as his moment approached. She wanted to bat his hand aside and impale herself on him, to share his pleasure as he'd shared hers, but then he was groaning softly against her mouth as his hand went still, and a wet warmth struck Maggie's belly.

He hung over her, breathing hard while Maggie subsided to her back. While she heard him fussing with clothing, her own passion ebbed, leaving a hollow ache in its place. She was casting around mentally, wondering what there was to say at such a time when she felt him dabbing at her belly with a handkerchief then rearranging her skirts to some semblance of modesty.

"We are going to talk, Maggie Windham."

His tone was truculent—unhappy—as he shifted to sit next to where she lay. She rolled to her side, giving him her back. When she would have shared with him her dim view of the benefit of conversation, his hand landed on her hair. "You're all undone, my girl. Best sit up and take your medicine."

He sounded a little less unhappy but still brusque. Maggie wrestled skirts and a dragging fatigue to sit cross-legged beside him on the blanket. He produced a pocket comb and had his dark locks put to rights in a thrice, dratted man.

"Say something, my dear, or I will think you have sense enough to regret what just happened on this blanket." He started to work on her hair while she tried to think of an appropriate reply.

"I don't want to fight with you," she said, plucking at the grass beside the blanket. "And I do not regret what happened."

"No." His hands were gentle as he drew her unbound hair over her shoulders. "But you'll regret what will happen now."

She tried to twist around to see him, but he had her by the hair. "What will happen?"

He dropped her hair. "This is my handkerchief, Maggie Windham. My formerly snow-white hand-kerchief." He tossed it over her shoulder so it landed in her lap. At first she didn't see anything except that the thing had been crumpled with recent use, then her eye caught the one faint pink streak cutting across the fabric. She smoothed out the little formerly snow-white square to see a few more streaks of pink.

"This means nothing." She lobbed the offending linen back over her shoulder. "Not one blessed thing. What happened here was of no moment whatsoever."

"I beg to differ. Hold still." He used the comb to restore her part, while Maggie could do nothing but allow him. "When a man has proposed to you and then gains intimate knowledge of your person—and he is the first to have such knowledge, I might add— you are accepting his proposal."

She was glad to be facing away from him, for the

pain his words caused was stunning. "I was doing no such thing."

"Maggie." He bent over her from behind, speaking very softly while he held her by the shoulders. "I did not spend inside you, but you might have conceived nonetheless. Do you want our first child to be a seven-months babe?"

A *baby*. Maggie's hand went to her womb while a pang of nigh unbearable longing shot through her. "Unfair. I am not likely to have conceived."

"You don't know either way." The comb dragging through her hair was applied with a careful touch, systematically working through one skein after another. "And while you're hesitating, waiting to be sure, you're going to give fodder to any gossip ever to take tea with Her Grace."

The idea that Her Grace might find out what Maggie had been up to was disquieting in the extreme. "You don't kiss and tattle." Her voice shook a little, so disconcerted was she.

"I won't have to say a thing when your body is great with our child. We can be married quietly if you prefer, though Their Graces will likely be puzzled by such a choice."

He sounded so damnably sure. Maggie seized on the resentment that engendered and clung to it fiercely. "Stop bleating about marriage. You don't love me, and we're not getting married just because we shared a little pleasure on a blanket behind some secluded bushes."

She could feel him beginning to braid her hair, feel him rearranging arguments like so many longbows poised above a battlefield.

"A *little* pleasure, Maggie?" The pitch of his voice had her insides fluttering in remembrance. "I gave you only *a little* pleasure? Imagine what I could do if we had the privacy of a locked chamber, hours of solitude, no clothes, and a large bed with lots of pillows. Imagine getting your hands on me. You could tie me hand and foot, explore to your heart's content, put your mouth wherever you pleased, and I'd be helpless to stop you."

"Oh, *hush*." She closed her eyes against the weakness his words provoked. "You are naughty, Benjamin Hazlit."

Though she was one to talk about being naughty.

"I am determined." He began to pin her braid in a coil at her nape. He was a more efficient hairdresser than Alice, and Maggie had to drag her mind away from the idea of having him tend her like this for years… much less the idea of that other nonsense.

"Why won't you marry me?"

"Gracious, you are persistent." She patted the bun he'd so expertly fashioned. "Has it occurred to you if I marry you all my wealth and independence would be forfeit?"

"If you don't trust me to leave your fortune in peace, transfer your wealth to your brother's name. He'll steward it as you direct."

Gayle would be more conscientious with her money than she was, which was saying something. "And what of my freedom, my independence?"

How such a big man could move so quickly was beyond her. One moment Maggie was looking around for her boots and stockings, the next she was flat on her back with fifteen stone of determined earl poised above her.

"You call it independence, but you never so much as go for a drive in the park, Maggie Windham. You do not make social calls except on your family members, you do not entertain, and you do not permit yourself even a dog for companionship. As my countess, you'll have the run of the society functions, your invitations will be accepted by all and sundry, and you will have my charming and devoted company at your beck and call, even and especially in your confinements. Plural, God willing. Marry me."

Devoted was a daunting thought, particularly coupled with beck and call and confinements— plural—and most especially when he emphasized his point by lowering his mouth to hers.

This was not a pillaging or plundering kiss, it was a *convincing* kiss. Slow and sweet, mesmerizing in its tenderness. Gracious God, the man was kissing her witless. Maggie raised a hand to cradle his jaw, thinking only of how badly she was going to miss him, when an outraged whiskey baritone cut through the haze of pleasure clouding her mind.

"Magdalene Windham, I cannot believe what my eyes are seeing!"

❧

Benjamin Portmaine's reflexes had stood between him and severe bodily harm on more than one occasion. He was used to the narrowing of vision that came with extreme peril, the electric jump in his system's level of alertness.

"Lady Dandridge." He rose to his feet and extended a hand down to Maggie. Thank God and all His angels they were more-or-less properly attired. "Apologies for my lapse of discretion, but a pretty day and the company of my intended overcame my better sensibilities."

Maggie's head came up, and he could feel a contradiction boiling forth from her, so he leaned over to kiss her cheek.

"*Not now.*" In addition to the warning growled in her ear, he squeezed her hand then turned a fatuous smile on Lady Dandridge. "I'm sure you'll congratulate me on winning Lady Maggie's hand."

"Congratulate you?" A painted eyebrow rose skeptically, and the perfectly matched footmen in their spotless livery and curled wigs looked like they each wanted a turn drawing Ben's cork.

"Lady Maggie has agreed to be my countess. I've yet to conclude discussions with His Grace, so I'm sure we can rely on your discretion."

The hole he was digging yawned wider and deeper with each word coming out of his mouth, but it was a hole he'd be sharing with Maggie, which had been his objective after all.

"Lady Magdalene, is this the truth? If you've been taken advantage of, I can at least inform your mother of Mr. Hazlit's disgraceful conduct."

Without even turning to regard his new fiancée, Ben knew what she was thinking: *Her Grace is not my mother.*

"His lordship has decided to resume the use of his title, Lady Dandridge." Maggie gave him a brilliant smile. "A man contemplating marriage must consider his place in the world."

She would rather have stated a threat to his life, of that he was fairly certain. He smiled at her in return. "My countess is entitled to all that I have, including the privileges of rank."

Lady Dandridge's outrage was visibly giving way to perplexity. "And what rank would that be?"

"He's the Earl of Hazelton," Maggie replied. "The seat is in Cumbria, where I'm sure he'll be repairing as soon as he's spoken with His Grace."

"Or perhaps"—Ben brought her knuckles to his lips—"I will reserve that travel for the wedding journey, my love."

Lady Dandridge thumped her walking stick against the ground. "Enough, you two. I will be touring the grounds here for another hour at least. I expect to see you departing for Town posthaste, and I will also expect an announcement in the *Times* by week's end. Good day."

She turned and moved off in the direction of her coach—the lumbering old vehicle Ben had spotted almost two hours earlier. The footmen glared at him ferociously before falling in step behind their employer.

And with comic timing, Ben's own coach tooled sedately around a bend several hundred yards away, the horses walking along as if God were in His heaven and all were right with the world.

⌘

"Mr. Hazlit to see His Grace, Your Grace." Andover passed a little silver tray with one simple white card on it to the duchess where she sat reading by a window.

Esther Windham glanced at the card. "Show him in here, Andover. The tea tray is fresh, and Mr. Hazlit is a friend of the family."

Andover bowed and silently withdrew, his consternation—he would never presume to disapprove—evident in the angle of his white eyebrows. Andover's view of ducal consequence required that gentlemen be received somewhere besides a cozy little parlor at the back of the ducal mansion.

Leaving Esther to feel some consternation of her own. She liked Benjamin Hazlit and trusted him, but still...

He was an *investigator*. Nobody liked to be investigated. She smoothed the distaste engendered by that thought from her features and uncurled her feet out from under her.

"Your Grace." Hazlit paused inside the door before Esther had slipped on her house mules. He held a particularly low bow for an extra moment, no doubt giving her time to get properly shod.

"Mr. Hazlit. Andover, that will be all." She did not stand but waited until the butler had withdrawn. "This is an unexpected pleasure. You may have a seat, if you prefer."

He quirked one dark eyebrow. "If I prefer?"

"I raised five sons, Mr. Hazlit. Men like to prowl and paw and stalk about, just as little boys must ride down the banisters on rainy days. Would you like some tea?"

"No tea, thank you. Will His Grace be joining us?"

She poured for herself, trying to assess Hazlit's mood. He was utterly unlike dear Percy, whose moods were writ large and loud for the most part.

"His Grace will be at Morelands to oversee plowing and planting this week, or to get away from certain committee obligations. Was it a political matter you needed to discuss with him?"

She sipped her tea, regarding him over the rim of her cup, watching while he ran a hand through his hair. Though his eyes were on the gardens beyond the window, she felt him moving mental chess pieces in the space of a few heartbeats.

"Perhaps it's for the best that His Grace isn't able to join us, though my mission is a trifle urgent."

"A trifle urgent, Mr. Hazlit?" She put her cup down on its saucer. "Is that like being a trifle married?"

She'd meant it as a riposte, nothing more, but his gaze came to rest on her in a particularly considering fashion, and Esther felt her heart speed up.

"Perhaps I'll have a seat after all." He took the chair at right angles to the sofa Esther had appropriated for her reading—a luxury she rarely engaged in during daylight if her husband was underfoot. Hazlit made the delicate little chair look like doll furniture.

"Whatever has brought you here, Mr. Hazlit, you're best advised to just say it and be done with it. We have pigeons in the mews that can get to Morelands in no time."

He gestured to the tea service. "May I?"

"Of course." She shifted to pour him a cup of tea, but he helped himself to a crème cake, chewing with the sort of purpose Esther associated with hungry adult males. Still, she suspected he was strategizing while he put on a display for her benefit.

"I have been considering courting your daughter, Lady Maggie."

Esther heard both the sense of his words and the conditional phrasing: he *had been* considering courting Maggie. Concern for the oldest of the girls she'd raised coursed through her. *Please let there not be any more trouble for dear Maggie. Not now, when it seemed Maggie had finally found some measure of peace.*

"Maggie is a lovely woman, and her path has not been easy, Mr. Hazlit. I would take a dim view of anybody who trifled with her."

"As would I." He sat back and crossed his legs at the knee, when any of Esther's sons would have been up and pacing, and her husband would have been devouring the last of the crème cakes. "I was precipitous in demonstrating my regard for Lady Maggie—precipitous and... ardent—and it has become necessary..."

She cocked her head and waited. Precipitous and ardent meant Maggie and this man had been caught in some breach of propriety. It remained to be seen what Hazlit meant to do about it.

"I would like to marry Lady Maggie, but I'm seeking the approval of her parents before I make a formal declaration."

His voice was perfectly calm, his posture relaxed.

"And yet you mentioned urgency, Mr. Hazlit. I do not apprehend that this is the urgency of a man overcome with tender emotion, but rather some other urgency."

"It is the urgency of a man bent on protecting his lady's peace of mind."

His lady's peace of mind, not *a* lady's peace of mind.

"Do you love Maggie, Mr. Hazlit?" She did not expect him to say he did—men were blockheads when it came to understanding their own feelings—but she was very curious to know what he would say.

He took his time, his gaze roaming the room while he chose his words. It was a pretty little sitting room, Esther's personal retreat. Maggie had a room much like it from whence she ran her private empire.

"I have grown attached to Lady Maggie, and I am protective of her. I think we would suit."

"That is not a bad answer, Mr. Hazlit." Esther got to her feet, which meant he had to, as well. "I expect it's even an honest answer, but Maggie deserves something more than a man who simply thinks she'd suit him. His Grace turned away a good two dozen of those before Maggie's second season." After about the fifth hopeful suitor, he'd stopped even asking Esther for her opinion. He hadn't needed to.

"Two dozen?" Hazlit's brows were pulled together in a scowl, and heaven help poor Maggie, the man was even handsome when he frowned.

"Before the beginning of her second season." Esther crossed her arms and regarded the gardens blooming beyond the window.

Hazlit came up to her side, a large man capable of moving without a sound. "If it makes any difference, I'm fairly sure Lady Maggie is of the same mind as I. She agrees that in significant ways we would suit, though she is not enamored of the idea of marriage in general."

Esther turned to regard him. "Mr. Hazlit, Maggie deserves a man who adores her, who loves her, who would give his life for her. I was fortunate enough to find such a man for myself, and his devotion has been sufficient to allow me to accommodate all manner of otherwise difficult aspects of a long marital union. I cannot possibly speak for His Grace on this matter. Maggie is not my daughter."

It hurt to say the words. It always hurt to say them. It hurt to even think them.

"In many regards, Your Grace, she is nobody's daughter but yours. When will His Grace return from Kent?"

He sounded very sure about his pronouncement, and Esther could not help but hope such a man might win Maggie's hand after all. "His Grace will likely be back on Saturday if the weather holds fair."

"I'm afraid we might not have until Saturday." He spoke carefully, and he'd taken to studying the gardens too.

"You were very ardent, I take it?"

He nodded, a slight flush rising up his neck. It was endearing, that flush. Benjamin Hazlit did the dirty work the good families of Mayfair could not admit they needed done, and he'd undertaken some delicate investigating for the Windhams. He was the approximate age of her grown sons, and he was fond of Maggie.

Also capable of blushing.

"In that case, Mr. Hazlit, I will need to speak with Lady Maggie. In private."

"She's visiting with her sisters in the conservatory. I'll ask her to join you."

He bowed very correctly over her hand and took his leave at a decorous pace, but Esther had seen the relief in his eyes.

Very ardent, indeed.

•—•

"Her Grace wants to speak with you."

Maggie could tell nothing from Benjamin's expression, his tone, or his words. He'd at least waited until they were at the foot of the stairs—far from her sisters' curious glances. "Was Her Grace angry?"

"Concerned, maybe. For you." Benjamin looked concerned, too, which suggested Her Grace had been more than angry. She'd been *disappointed*.

The whole way back from Richmond, Benjamin had said little. He'd taken the seat beside Maggie, put an arm around her shoulders, and after about two miles, spoken five words.

"It will be all right."

She'd given him four in return. "I cannot marry you."

And that had earned her a nod and a comforting squeeze of her hand, but here they were, in the middle of Mayfair, trying to contain a social disaster that would have repercussions far beyond Maggie's private universe.

"Does Her Grace know you're Hazelton?"

"His Grace might have told her as much. She's waiting for you."

Feeling much as she had after that incident with Bart and the brandied pears, Maggie slipped her arm through Benjamin's and let him escort her to the duchess's sanctum sanctorum. In that same pretty little parlor, Her Grace had explained to Maggie how and why women bled and what to do about it. She'd relayed each and every proposal Maggie had garnered, and placidly sipped tea while Maggie had rejected suitor after suitor. Her Grace had explained marital intimacies over another pot of tea, and God only knew what the coming conversation might entail.

"Maggie, my love?"

They were outside the door, Maggie's heart beginning to thump against her ribs.

"I'm nervous." The admission just slipped out.

"You have nothing to apologize for." He held her gaze steadily, more serious than she had ever seen him. "I am responsible for what happened today. You must allow me to do what I can to make reparation to you."

"You are not more responsible than I."

"I was." He spoke very quietly, very sternly. "*I am.* You were innocent, completely without experience, and I took liberties which inspired you to ungovernable passion."

"So this is what you were doing the whole way back into Town? Flagellating yourself for a decision I made?" Except he was right: Her passion had been ungovernable. The thought almost made her smile, despite her pounding heart and queasy stomach.

"Talk to your mother. Be honest with her, Maggie. I think she will guide you out of a true concern for your best interests." He looked like he might say more but held his peace, kissed her lingeringly on the cheek, and took his leave.

A kiss for courage. Who knew there were so many different kinds of kisses?

Maggie tapped on the door and fortified herself against the prospect of dealing with a disappointed duchess.

❧

Esther turned to regard her husband's eldest daughter. Maggie was in a riding habit, looking trim, fit, and composed. If anything, there was a subtle glow to her beauty, a luminance.

"You don't look ruined."

"I don't feel ruined."

"Then come sit with me. We'll determine what's to be done." Esther did not hold out her arms to this woman she'd raised. From the posture of Maggie's spine, a maternal embrace would be politely tolerated, as it had been on the rare occasions Esther had attempted it since the girl had joined the household all those years ago.

Esther resumed her seat on the sofa and lifted the pot. "Shall I pour?"

"I don't think tea and crumpets will put this right, Your Grace." Maggie took the same seat Hazlit had used, but whereas he'd affected a casual posture, Maggie's form was a study in propriety.

"Tea and crumpets won't make it worse either." Esther put a crème cake on a plate, poured Maggie a cup, doctored it, and prayed for something wise and useful to say.

"Could you be carrying?"

"Possibly." Maggie accepted the tea but shook her head at the crème cake.

"Come, Maggie. His Grace will be back soon, and there won't be a crème cake to be had. Your brother Bart was a seven-months baby. Were you aware of this?"

Maggie paused with the teacup halfway to her lips. "Bartholomew came early?"

"He came exactly on time." For pity's sake, did none of her children know this? "His Grace and I could not contain our enthusiasm for each other, though it likely horrifies you to hear of this."

"Times were different." Maggie took a sip of her drink, her expression distracted.

"Maggie, thirty some years ago was not exactly antediluvian. Times might have been a little more tolerant, but young people in certain situations behave with just as much disregard for common sense."

"I'm hardly young."

"You're hardly old, and this might be your last and only worthy chance for a match with a man who esteems you and will give you children. What do you want to do?"

Maggie stared at her tea. "I want to emigrate to Baltimore."

"Or perhaps darkest Peru?"

Maggie looked up, her expression revealing a hopelessness that tore at Esther's heart.

"My dear, your circumstances aren't so unusual as all that. Did Mr. Hazlit take advantage of you?"

Maggie set her teacup down and rose, but she didn't go to the window. She went to the wall opposite Esther's seat, the one where a row of framed sketches hung in a grouping.

"Mr. Hazlit is constitutionally incapable of taking advantage of a woman. His sisters endured some bad treatment years ago, and it haunts him."

"His Grace has alluded to this."

Maggie had paused beside the sketch of her brother Bart. Maggie and Bart had been close, partners in mischief, with Maggie always trying to take the blame for Bart's wild starts.

"If I'm to be honest, I took advantage of Mr. Hazlit, though he does not agree with me."

"Were you trying to trap him into marriage?"

Maggie whirled to face the duchess. "Of course not."

"Was he trying to trap you?"

"Most definitely not."

"This will be a great comfort to your brothers."

The comment had the intended effect of bringing Maggie back to her seat. She collapsed into it, her gaze horror-stricken. "There must not be any duels. You cannot allow it."

"When men take a notion to be honorable, the voice of reason, much less the voice of their mother, has little to say to it. Valentine, in particular, can be deaf to logic, much like his father." That wasn't unfair, though it bordered on ruthless.

"Valentine..." Maggie stared at her hands, probably thinking of Valentine's very talented hands picking up a gun, perhaps never to create beautiful music at the keyboard again.

"My dear, you must decide. As I see it, you have several options. You can weather the scandal. Whoever came upon you and Mr. Hazlit is likely of less consequence than your own family. In a year or two, the impact on your sisters' prospects will be negligible." Esther spoke briskly, despite the color leaving Maggie's cheeks.

Percy, forgive me. He fretted over Maggie, fretted

over her as if she were still seven years old and pining for her doll.

"My sisters don't deserve to suffer over this."

"We are agreed on that, but if you asked it of them, they'd cheerfully stand by you. I hope you know this?"

A nod.

"So you can do nothing, hope you are not with child, and in time, this will blow over. More tea?"

"No, thank you." So polite. While Esther put another crème cake on a plate, Maggie wiped a tear from her cheek.

"You can marry Hazlit, who strikes me as a decent man. He's already privy to some of our less-savory history, having investigated Anna's situation last year. Your father approves of him, if that makes any difference."

"I do not want to marry him. It would not be fair to him." Another tear, while Maggie continued to sit ramrod straight.

"And if you are with child?" Esther spoke as gently as she could, considering she was using logic to blud-geon someone she dearly loved. "Do you want your child to bear the same burden you have?"

Maggie shook her head, but the tears were coursing down her cheeks unchecked. Esther passed her a serviette, when what she wanted to do was hurl her teacup against the wall. "You have another option, Maggie."

Maggie turned her head an inch to meet the duch-ess's eyes. "If I have conceived, I will not do anything to harm our child."

Our child?

"Put such notions from your head. For God's sake, Maggie… to think we'd let you risk yourself, much less… For God's sake."

Boys were difficult to raise into young gentlemen, but girls… girls were the biggest challenge. Especially girls who, despite every effort to the contrary, seemed to have a thorough knowledge of things too sordid and awful to be contemplated.

It was time to conclude this interview and get a pigeon to His Grace.

"Maggie, you can buy yourself a little time and make your choice later, when you know better what your circumstances are."

Maggie blotted her eyes and made no immediate reaction, as if her hearing were slow. She heaved out a sigh and met Esther's gaze. "What do you mean?"

"Put a finger in the dike, so to speak. Announce an engagement; do not set a date. If you are not carrying, then you can cry off quietly next year. If you're expecting, you can marry just as quietly, and when the baby comes, enjoy a long respite in the country, such that dates of birth and other details are not in the forefront of gossip. I will, of course, assist in any and every regard."

Silence, while Maggie contemplated the snow-white serviette balled up in her lap. She stared at the thing as if it held oracular significance, while Esther sent up a prayer for patience.

"I suppose that's the best course." Maggie tossed the napkin onto the tray in the only unladylike gesture Esther had observed in their entire exchange. "We'd best inform Mr. Hazlit." She frowned and blinked. "He's an earl."

"I beg your pardon?"

"Mr. Hazlit is the Earl of Hazelton. He travels under an assumed name in deference to his sisters' past."

Now wasn't this an interesting detail? "And you are not sure you want to be his countess?"

"What I want doesn't matter."

She sounded so forlorn, Esther couldn't hold back a snort. "What you wanted is what got you into this situation, or am I wrong?"

"You are not wrong, Your Grace."

There was so much dignity in that admission, Esther felt momentarily flummoxed. *What, exactly, had transpired between Maggie and Mr. Hazlit?*

"Come along, Maggie. Your intended is likely on tenterhooks awaiting your decision. Buy yourself some time to adjust to this development, and the two of you can sort out where you go from here."

Esther rose and went to the door, Maggie moving more slowly behind her. Hazlit was waiting in the corridor, leaning back against the wall, hands in his pockets. He shoved away from the wall without using his hands, his expression guarded.

"Your Grace."

"Congratulations, your lordship." Esther gave him her best, warmest smile. "It seems you are engaged. I'll see to the announcement, while you two let Maggie's sisters know your good news."

She did not welcome him to the family. She wanted to, but Maggie was standing beside her, tense and silent. A mother could do only so much. An unacknowledged stepmother even less.

Seven

BESIDE BEN, HER HAND BARELY RESTING ON HIS ARM, Maggie radiated tension as they headed back toward the conservatory.

"Was she unkind to you?" He kept his voice down. There were footmen posted at each end of the corridor, tall serious fellows who put him in mind of Lady Dandridge's matched set.

"Her Grace is never unkind. Never."

He decided not to pry. Whatever Her Grace had said, he was now an engaged man, which had become his objective at some point in the recent past. The relief was fading, leaving a fierce determination to get the woman beside him to the altar, from which position he would be able to keep her safe.

Maggie paused outside the door to the conservatory. "We are not going to set a date." She glanced around and dropped her voice to a whisper. "I do not want to marry you, Benjamin."

"You've been crying." He brushed the pad of his thumb over her cheek, her skin silky soft to his touch. "We don't need to set a date if you're not ready to."

"You aren't listening to me." She wrapped her fingers around his wrist and removed his hand from her face. "I cannot marry you, and this is all moving too quickly. I don't want to shame my family—that's the last thing I want, but I don't want…" She raised troubled eyes to his. "I don't want to make a laughingstock of you when I jilt you."

"Portmaines are not strangers to broken engagements."

"Port…?"

He saw when she recollected his family name. "Were we to marry, you'd become Maggie Portmaine."

"But we're not going to marry."

She was appallingly convinced of this, and it irritated him more—*worried* him more—each time she emphasized her position. "You said things were moving too quickly, Maggie, but if you've conceived, they can't move quickly enough."

Her gaze became haunted, and her hand went to her belly.

"You listen to me," he said, dropping his voice and covering her hand with his own. "Just for today, we are engaged. We need make no other decisions than that. You can jilt me, and I'll step aside, or we can marry, or we can remain engaged for a time and make further decisions later." She was listening; she was even watching his mouth as he spoke. He kissed her on the lips for no other reason than he didn't want her arguing with him.

"I want you for my countess, Maggie. I'd made up my mind before we found ourselves in this contretemps, but I wanted to woo you, to squire you about and give you the attention and courting you deserve. Give me a few weeks. We'll know better what we're dealing with, and we'll placate the Lady Dandridges of Society in the meanwhile."

"I can do that," she said slowly, "but, Benjamin, that's all I can do. You must not take a notion that we will be wed."

"And if there's a baby?"

She shook her head, but when he took her in his arms, she went unresisting into his embrace. He hoped there was a baby, which surprised him. He understood the necessity for an heir but hadn't felt any urgency as long as Archer enjoyed good health. With Maggie, though... He kissed her again, bussed her cheek and her temple.

"Why were you crying, Maggie mine?"

"This is such a tangle." She heaved a sigh but stayed where she was. "My sisters will be happy for me. His Grace will strut and preen. My brothers will be relieved."

She didn't mention the duchess, but she raised her head to peer at him. "May we not tell your sisters just yet?"

He wanted to tell them, wanted to be married at Blessings, with both sisters—as well as their doting husbands—on hand for the nuptials. "We'll wait if you prefer. Neither Avis nor Alex read the social pages, and they both live very retiring lives. Unless I tell them, there's little likelihood they'll get wind of it. Shall we tell your sisters, though? Her Grace seemed to expect it."

She drew back and physically squared her shoulders. "They'll make a lot of noise."

"For today, we're going to let them." He winged his arm at her and led her into the conservatory. The humid air was almost pleasant, with soft late-afternoon sunshine pouring down through glass panes.

"We're over here!" A petite blonde waved at them from one corner of the room. "Jenny and I are losing at whist, and the tea has long since gone cold."

"Ladies." Ben addressed three of the prettiest women he'd ever seen in one location. "Your sister has some news."

"Do tell, Mags." The little blonde dragged Maggie away from Ben's side. "You never have any news, except for when your dog died."

Ben remained standing while Maggie was ensconced on a wicker settee, a sister on each side. The blonde took a chair at an angle to the couch and waved a hand at Ben. "You must sit, Mr. Hazlit. We seldom have Maggie to ourselves, as only Mama's summons can pry Mags loose from her ledgers. Give us your news, my dear. I am literally sitting on the edge of my seat." She scooted a little forward and grinned at her sister.

"Mr. Hazlit has asked... that is, I've agreed... we are engaged."

The squealing was deafening, and the hugging went on for an eternity. Ben had never, not in any role or in his own life, been subjected to so many fragrant female embraces or kisses to his cheek, or teary good wishes.

It was... daunting, and made him realize something as he watched Maggie being swarmed by her sisters again and again *These people loved her.* She was not an awkward relation recognized out of grudging decency;

she wasn't an embarrassment to her family. She was treasured and held dear. Her happiness concerned these people mightily.

And if she did jilt him, she would be disappointing them mightily, as well.

As Ben escorted Maggie to his coach more than an hour and two bottles of champagne later, he had to wonder what would motivate her to risk disappointing people who seemed only to care for her happiness and well-being.

~

"Tired?"

As he asked the question, Benjamin's arm came around Maggie's shoulders. In the space of a few hours, he'd created a bodily sort of intimacy that had little to do with what had happened on that blanket earlier in the day.

Nothing, and everything, in fact.

"A little tired." As if they were really engaged, Maggie let her head rest on his shoulder when the coachman gave the horses the signal to walk on. The illusion that they were a couple was painful and sweet, but it was only an illusion.

"I realized something about you today."

He'd seen her cry, or nearly cry. Maybe he was realizing she wasn't countess material.

"I realized you are shy." He kissed her temple, and Maggie hadn't the fortitude to make him stop. Now that they were engaged—what a peculiar word, *engaged*—he was forever getting his lips on her—her cheek, her forehead, her hair, her hands.

She liked it, which was only going to add to her eventual sorrow. "How does one hide shyness?"

"One gathers great quantities of dignity and propriety about one, until one's true nature is disguised. Your sisters love you."

"Isn't that what sisters do?" She wanted to raise her head to peer at him in the waning light, but she was comfortable tucked under his arm, and this wasn't like any conversation she'd had with him before.

"I suspect they do. Do you suppose my sisters have been waiting for me to get married?"

He sounded unhappy with the possibility.

"One hopes sisters wouldn't be so foolish." Except... hers were being that foolish. Amid all their congratulations and teasing, Maggie had detected a current of relief swirling between them, too, relief that perhaps more sisters were going to follow brothers into holy matrimony, as if she and Sophie were the bellwethers... bell ewes?

"I realized something else today, too."

"You were quite busy with all these realizations, Mr. Hazlit."

"Benjamin." She felt his hand sweeping her hair back from her face, a lovely, soothing caress with nothing of the erotic about it. "When you were upset today, you called me Benjamin. It's nice to hear you say my name."

She'd called him Benjamin when she'd been flat on her back with him on that blanket, too, but he wasn't referring to that. Her intended—her temporary intended—was a gentleman.

Maggie nuzzled the soft wool of his coat, which

bore a trace of his spicy, masculine scent. "We are to comport ourselves as if we are affianced. Your name is not that hard to remember."

"Good." He kissed her hair. "You're rattling your swords, maneuvering your cannon into position. I was worried about you, Maggie mine."

"I am not your Maggie. What was your other great insight today?"

He hitched her a little closer. "I saw the four of you carrying on and laughing and having great good fun together—and it only got worse when Westhaven showed up—and I realized I have allowed someone to steal that from my family. All the while I've been climbing in windows and lurking in doorways to retrieve billets-doux and errant fiancées for others, I've allowed my own family to be robbed of joy and even simple togetherness by something that happened more than a decade ago."

That he was perceptive was not news. Maggie had hired him because he was perceptive and intelligent and observant. That he'd share his insight with her like this, and about something so personal to his history… It had her turning her face into the warmth of his shoulder, hurting for him, and even for these sisters of his in their obscure and lonely lives.

"You should write to your sisters. Tell them what you just told me."

"Believe I shall. Go to sleep. I told John to take us home through the park, and the horses are too tired to do more than walk."

She did not go to sleep, but she closed her eyes and let him think she might be dozing off. Instead she thought about what he'd said, about allowing someone to steal all the joy and companionship from her life, and not even questioning their right to do so.

꩜

After less than two hours as an engaged man, Ben decided it was an improvement in his dealings with his intended. She would be back on her mettle soon, a day, two at most, but for the space of one slow carriage ride, she was willing to allow him all manner of proximity.

It… soothed him to hold her, to breathe in her floral and spice scent, to feel the silky warmth of her hair sliding beneath his palm.

"When will you know?"

She'd been feigning sleep against his side but opened her eyes at his question.

"Two weeks, though this time of year, I sometimes have reprieves."

He mentally translated: She didn't bleed regularly in spring.

"Then I'm going to ask for at least six weeks of an engagement, Maggie. The longer we wait, the more certain you'll be of the necessity of marriage, if you're carrying."

"Women miscarry. Her Grace miscarried several times after Evie arrived."

A cold skein of dread slithered through his vitals. "You aren't planning to *miscarry*, are you?"

"I am not."

"That's… good. I would not want harm to befall you on my account, Maggie. Not on any account."

She sat up and frowned at him. "This is a sham engagement, Benjamin. You needn't affect all manner of protectiveness. I manage quite nicely on my own."

"For the space of a few weeks, my dear, *we* will manage quite nicely on *our* own."

She regarded him in the gathering gloom of the carriage as she started rummaging in her reticule. "I was considering a two-week engagement. I ought to know in two weeks."

"If you know for a certainty you are not pregnant, I can't stop you from crying off at any time, but you must promise me something." He took her hand in his before she could put her gloves on. "You will not cry off until you do know for certain. We would only have to become engaged again, and that will create a great deal of talk indeed."

"But I told you…"

He put a finger to her lips. "We're both exhausted; the day has been trying. We can argue as enthusiastically as you like tomorrow, for I will be calling on you regularly, Maggie, and escorting you to Her Grace's teas and comporting myself in every fashion like a man both besotted and engaged."

"That isn't necessary."

"Yes, my dear, it is."

He escorted her to her own front door to emphasize his point, bowed very properly over her hand, and lingered for a moment on the stoop with her, giving all and sundry a glimpse of Benjamin Hazlit wooing his intended. She tolerated it, probably because she was too tired to remonstrate with him further, then squared her shoulders and disappeared into her house.

Ben waved the coach on and decided to use the last of the light to walk home. Realizations—revelations, more like—such as those he'd had today required further thought. When he got home it was full dark, and the thought of a hot bath and a cold drink loomed like paradise.

He'd just shucked out of his riding attire when Archer came sauntering into his dressing room in evening formal wear.

"I'm getting tired of chasing Abby Norcross." Archer subsided onto a dressing stool. "When they say women have more stamina than men, they aren't just talking about copulation."

"When do you ever speak of anything else?"

"When I actually am copulating, I speak of the lady's eyes, her hair, her gorgeous—"

"Hand me the soap." Ben lowered himself into the steaming tub, grateful in his bones for the luxury of a hot bath. "Where are you off to tonight?"

"Some damned musicale, then a soiree, then the Peasedicks' ball in time for the supper buffet. I have it on good authority Lady Abby will grace at least one of those gatherings with her adulterous presence."

Ben began to scrub at himself, feet, then arms, chest, and armpits. "What if she's not committing adultery?"

"She as good as told his lordship any damned body was more capable of giving her pleasure than he was, and she felt sorry for his mistress."

"Ouch. No wonder he wants her in the country. I have some news you need to be aware of, though I doubt it's making the rounds yet." He dunked, came up, and started lathering his hair.

Archer shot his cuffs. "Gossip is always juiciest when it's fresh, rather like—"

"Are those emerald cuff links, Cousin?"

"Poor quality emeralds, but yes. They bring out the soulful luminosity of my eyes." He batted his eyes then rose and went to poke at the fire. "What is this news you have? I've likely already come across it, because I wasn't avoiding work all day like some people."

Ben watched as Archer managed to look elegant performing a task usually undertaken by the servants. "I'm engaged to marry Lady Maggie Windham."

Archer rose, iron poker still in his hand. "You're what? I'm not sure I heard you correctly, as I tend not to pay attention when you're in the mood to lecture and pontificate. Did I hear you aright? You're engaged?"

"To Maggie Windham."

Ben dunked his head again. When he came up, Archer was very carefully putting the poker back with the matching set of implements to the side of the hearth. It appeared his heir wasn't going to comment, so Ben ducked to rinse again, then came up.

Archer passed him a dry flannel. "You're engaged to marry Lady Maggie. Well, well, well."

Ben glanced over a little warily. Archer could be a merciless tease, but there was no humor in his eyes.

"The engagement might not last. We were not observing the proprieties as closely as we ought when Lady Dandridge came stumping along. I expect the announcement will show up the day after tomorrow, but Maggie is not convinced we'll suit."

Archer resumed his seat on the dressing stool, his expression hard to read. "Maggie Windham is a woman with troubles, Benjamin. You don't need to marry her to resolve those troubles."

"I'm thinking I do. Her reticule has been returned to her, and she said no money had been taken."

"Which leaves you wondering what *was* stolen that meant more to Maggie than money?"

"Precisely, and by whom, and how are they exploiting it? If it was letters, they weren't from one of Maggie's former lovers."

Archer crossed his arms. "They weren't?"

Ben pitched the damp flannel at him. "They were not, though for Maggie's sake I almost wish they were. I could just call the blighter out, wing him, and leave him to convalesce for a few decades on the Continent."

"Oh, of course. Scandal always makes a lady see her intended in the most favorable light. You're marrying a Windham, Benjamin. Do you know how much fun the gossips would have with any excuse to bruit that family's business about?"

"Yes, Archer, I do. Rinse me off, would you?"

Archer obliged by dumping two large ewers of tepid water over Ben's head, then passing him a bath sheet. "When is the wedding?"

"We have not set a date."

Silence while Ben extricated himself from the tub and dried off. Archer waited until Ben was in a dressing gown and dragging a brush through his hair, before he ambled over to stare at the fire.

"You ought to set a date."

"It is usually the lady's prerogative. Did you steal my best wool socks again?"

"Me, steal? From my own cousin? Under our very roof?" He turned and rested one elbow on the mantel. "They are ever so warm, and a man gets chilly running around Town all night. Why isn't the lady setting a date?"

Ben eyed him in the full-length mirror. "She isn't convinced the union will be necessary."

Archer blinked once. "You naughty boy, you. Anticipated the vows *and* the proposal, did you?"

"That is none of your concern, but for your information, I had already proposed. Lady Dandridge will have it we were choosing names for our firstborn, though that was hardly the case. Keep your ears open, please, and don't linger too long with your little lady's maid. I'd like the Norcross situation wrapped up directly."

Archer didn't *even* blink. "You expect our custom to disappear when it becomes known you're the Earl of Hazelton, don't you? You can't get engaged as plain Ben Hazlit, because that miserable, sodding bugger is legally nonexistent. This is famous… just famous."

Archer stalked out of the dressing room and into Ben's sitting room, heading directly for the decanter on the sideboard. "You might be ready to retire, Benjamin, but I am not."

"Then don't. I expect I'll be vacating this house, and you're welcome to the use of it. You're still my heir; you have the courtesy title to protect your entrée into the proper functions. If I do marry Maggie Windham, I'll be repairing North for at least an extended trip."

Archer paused with a tumbler halfway to his mouth. "You're just *handing* me the business?"

"I have never enjoyed sneaking about, Archer,

though I comforted myself we served a useful function from time to time."

"What about the money?"

"I've amply dowered my sisters with some to spare as a nest egg for my own children, though I'm beginning to think distance and coin were not what my sisters needed from me most."

Archer took a swallow of his drink. "This is disconcerting, but not... unexpected, exactly. I've watched you over the past year, getting quieter and quieter, the ladies becoming invisible to you; the pigeons going North more and more frequently. Is this about your sisters?"

"In a way, yes, and in another way, not at all. Do you like children, Archer?"

"What kind of question is that?" Archer turned as he spoke, ostensibly to pour Ben a drink.

"If I fail to produce sons, you're still the only means of securing the succession." Ben sidled over to stand beside his cousin, because something about this conversation was rattling Archer, and nothing ever rattled Archer Portmaine.

"You'll produce sons, you and Lady Maggie, if you haven't made progress in that direction already."

"I want children with her, though both of us are getting a late start at it," Ben said, speaking slowly. "But for her sake, I hope we haven't gotten a start on it already, not like this."

Archer passed him a drink. "She's really reluctant?"

"She'll say we don't suit, but I think that's likely her way of saying I can do better. Either that or she's trying to protect me from whatever trouble she's in."

"In which case..." Archer fell silent for one

frowning moment. "Solve her problems, and she'll fall into your arms?"

"She's fallen into my arms. Perhaps what I'm hoping is that if I solve her problems, she'll become my countess."

Archer looked like he'd say something but downed the rest of his drink instead. Ben waited until Archer was at the door, one hand on the latch.

"Archer?"

He turned slowly, expression guarded.

"Your little lady's maid? I've watched you get quieter and quieter, too, the ladies becoming invisible to you ever since we put Anita Delacourt on a boat for Ireland."

"What are you saying?"

"Della Martin would be starving in the gutter by now if you hadn't forged a few characters for her. I've always thought it one of your more inspired improvisations."

Archer turned to face the door, his voice quiet, devoid of insouciance. "She's passing for French now, and she put up with that pestilential woman and her drunken admirers for three years, just so her employer could grab every jewel that wasn't nailed down and disappear like a thief in the night."

"And a year later, you're still making sure Della is safe. If I didn't know better, I'd say you're smitten."

"And you're not?"

He tossed the question over his shoulder then quietly departed, leaving Ben to ponder the answer.

"Forgive me my concern for you."

Westhaven's tone was grave, as grave as Benjamin's had been in the carriage just the previous evening.

"You are a duke in training," Maggie said. "You must fret over your family. Have some lemonade. Anna says you favor it with great quantities of sugar."

She took a seat at the wrought iron grouping on her terrace, and her brother did likewise. It was a beautiful day, and there were fewer ears to overhear outside the house.

Westhaven crossed his feet at the ankle, leaned back in his chair, and studied Maggie while she tried to busy herself with the tray of refreshments.

Devoted brothers were the most mixed of blessings. Maggie had been up late trying to deal with just this problem: Their Graces might contain damage socially, but it was Maggie's brothers who would poke and pry in the name of *concern*, and with the best of intentions, provoke a far worse scandal than a precipitous engagement.

Westhaven slowly stirred some sugar into his drink. "My countess is ever devoted to my proper care and feeding." Even the mention of his wife had Gayle's normally austere features lightening.

"And how is my nephew?"

He smiled, his entire countenance beaming a sort of quiet joy Maggie found hard to behold. "His little lordship thrives shamelessly. His Grace has finally expressed unstinting approval of something I've undertaken." The smile faded, and Maggie bore the brunt of her brother's piercing green-eyed stare. "And now that you've diverted me from my intended agenda, Mags, you will answer my questions."

"You are my younger brother, Gayle Windham. I need not put up with your interrogation."

"But you will, because much of your property is in my hands, and I'm not above threats to gain the truth from you."

Maggie snorted. "You are incapable of mishandling a business transaction, so your threats are idle. I might answer a few questions out of simple sororal devotion."

He set his lemonade down while resuming his study of the glass. Beads of condensation trickled down the sides, and a wet ring formed on the tray beneath.

"Do you love him, Maggie?"

As broadsides went, that one would do nicely. "I am fond of him."

"You are fond of your old footmen, fond of my horse, fond of chocolates. One doesn't marry out of fondness, not after turning away more suitors than I can count. If Hazlit is in any way coercing you, Mags, I'll meet him, and that will be an end to it."

Strategy being everything, she did not roll her eyes or stand up and start stomping about. "And what would Anna think of your gallantry when it got you injured or killed?"

"What would Anna think of my gallantry if it was so paltry as to get my wealthy sister leg-shackled to an unworthy, deceptive—?"

She held up a hand. "I know about the title, and I don't think Benjamin will be doing much more skulking about if we marry."

"Did *he* tell you about the title, or did His Grace let it slip?"

"He told me, and well before we became engaged. I thought you liked Benjamin."

"I like him, but liking and trust are two very

different things where a sister's happiness is concerned." He picked up his drink then set it down untasted. "You worry me, Mags, so self-contained and quiet. Hazlit—Hazelton—would not have been my choice for you."

"Why not?"

"He's a man who dwells in the shadows and appears to like it there. You have enough shadows of your own."

"Maybe he sees me as I really am because shadows don't deter him." It was an inadvertent approximation of truth and had her brother frowning at her for a long moment.

"So you do care for him." Not a question. "Then why do I still feel as if this union is not well advised?"

Damn him—damn all prying, well-meaning brothers.

She took a dilatory sip of her lemonade. "If it's any comfort to you, I am fairly certain the engagement is temporary. Almost certain."

"Oh, Mags…" His expression turned to rueful humor. "Not you, too."

"Me, too?"

"Anna and I… You can consult the calendar. I'm sure everybody else has. His Grace found great glee in telling me Bart had come early, as if Anna and I were following in some great Moreland family tradition."

"I got the same bit of history from Her Grace. They mean well."

"I mean well, too." He rose, but bent and placed a kiss on Maggie's crown before she could get to her feet. She reached up and circled his wrist with her fingers where his hand rested on her shoulder. He was a good brother—they were all good brothers—and the urge to confide in him was nigh overwhelming.

"It will work out," he said quietly. "And if it doesn't, I can have you on your way to the Continent with an hour's notice. Or Ireland or Scotland. You'll not forget that?"

"Shame on you."

"Yes, on me, but never on you, Mags. Never on you." Then he was gone, disappearing through the garden's back gate.

Maggie managed to wait until she heard the clip-clop of his horse's hooves fading down the cobbled alley before she started to cry.

⁓

"Get the damned ring on her finger before another sun has set." His Grace lowered his voice, even though he and Benjamin were in a private dining room at His Grace's club. "All the tabbies will be looking for it, and you can get a big, flashy piece without spending a great deal. Has to do with the quality of the gem."

"We'll be selecting a ring tomorrow." *Now* they would be. A ring wasn't a detail, but Ben had over-looked the need for one. He took another sip of excellent wine and contemplated the oversight.

"If you want my advice, don't spend a great deal. Made that mistake when I was a young husband. Wanted to shower my duchess with jewels, but she loses 'em. Damnedest thing."

"Esther Windham doesn't strike me as the sort of woman to misplace anything of value."

His Grace stopped ingesting rare beefsteak long

enough to spear Ben with a look reflecting both exasperation and affection. "She isn't that sort of woman at all, which makes it all the more befuddling. I have since concluded she took to 'losing' her jewelry to discourage me from spending so much. When you think the ladies are empty-headed henwits, that's when they're being brilliant. Mark me on this, Hazelton. I have daughters, daughters-in-law, granddaughters, and one duchess. I have made a study of the fairer sex out of sheer self-preservation, as any wise man will."

His Grace prattled on, charming and blustering by turns, showing a side of himself Benjamin hadn't seen previously.

Percy Windham was a duke, and he wore that role like a second skin. He'd wine and dine, bully and bluster, and otherwise pursue his machinations in the Lords with all the enthusiasm of a hound on a hot scent. Beneath the title, however, lurked a man devoted—in his own way—to *family*. His affection for his duchess was legendary, and while he'd pressured his sons to marry, no suitor had thus far been good enough for his daughters, save Ben's own half brother, Wilhelm Charpentier. Ben knew his half brother well enough to be able to vouch for both his title and his considerable wealth.

A daunting thought.

"Have some more wine, my boy. Her Grace counsels me to moderation in all things, and I disregard her wisdom under my own roof at my peril."

Ben obligingly drained his glass and let His Grace refill it. "Have you any advice for me as Lady Maggie's prospective husband?"

The older man's expression sobered, becoming almost wistful. "There's a challenge—advice to a prospective husband when it's your daughter he's taking to wife. I had almost reconciled myself that spinsterhood was what Maggie sought, though it set a wretched example for the other girls. It seems I do not know my daughter as well as I thought I did."

He set his glass down and narrowed ducal blue eyes on Ben. "You break her heart, and you'll have to deal with me and her three brothers, and if you survive that, Her Grace will ensure your social ruin unto the nineteenth generation. I remind you, all of my boys are crack shots and more than competent with a sword."

"It is not my intention to break her heart."

"Oh, it's never our intention." His Grace's brows drew down in thought, and he was once again the affable paterfamilias. "Maggie is different. I hope that's from being the oldest daughter, but her unfortunate origins are too obvious a factor to be dismissed. She's in want of... dreams, I think. My other girls have dreams. Sophie dreamed of her own family, Jenny loves to paint, Louisa has her literary scribbling, and Evie must racket about the property as her brothers used to, but Maggie has never been a dreamer. Not about her first pony nor her first waltz nor her first... beau."

Nor her first lover. The words hung unspoken in the air while the fire crackled and hissed and a log fell amid a shower of sparks.

It wasn't what Ben would have expected any papa to say of his daughter, but then, marrying into a family meant details like this would be shared—Esther

Windham misplaced her everyday jewels, and Percy thought his daughters should be entitled to dream.

In a different way, it felt as if Ben were still lurking in doorways and climbing through windows, but this window was called marriage, and Maggie was trying to lock it shut with Ben on the outside.

"I'm not sure Maggie wants to marry me." It was as close as he'd come to touching on the circumstances of the betrothal. His Grace regarded him for a long moment.

"I'm her papa, but I was a young man once, Hazelton. Maggie is only a bit younger than Devlin and a few months older than Bart would have been. When I married, I had no idea either of my two oldest progeny existed. I'd no sooner started filling my nursery when—before my heir was out of dresses—both women came forward, hurling accusations and threats. If my marriage can survive that onslaught, surely you can overcome a little stubbornness in my daughter?"

It was, again, an insight into the Windham family Ben gained only because he was engaged to marry Maggie. Such confidences prompted a rare inclination toward direct speech. "I think Maggie's dream is to be left alone. If she jilts me, she'll have one more excuse to retire from life, to hide and tell herself she's content."

"Content." His Grace spat the word. "Bother *content*. Content is milk toast and pap when life is supposed to be a banquet. Make Maggie's dreams come true, young Hazelton, and show her contentment is shoddy goods compared to happiness."

"You make it sound simple."

"We're speaking of women and that particular subspecies of the genre referred to as wives. It is simple—devote yourself to her happiness, and you will be rewarded tenfold. I do not, however, say the undertaking will ever be easy. Now, shall we open just one more bottle?"

∾

Dinner with His Grace had not been at all what Benjamin had expected. The man was charming, wily, and surprisingly down to earth in matters close to his heart. If nothing else was made apparent, Ben became aware that in Their Graces' marriage, Maggie had seen an unusual example of true love in high places—an example she did not seem at all inclined to follow.

Questions of dreams, happiness versus contentment, secrets, and family expectations all swirled through Benjamin's brain with a goodly quantity of excellent libation, until he realized he was not walking home, but rather in the direction of a quiet little corner property inhabited by his intended.

Who at this hour ought to be fast asleep.

Though she might not be. Ben made a half-hearted, unsuccessful attempt to persuade himself to leave her in peace. In a note of two whole sentences arriving before the morning post, she'd claimed to have awoken with a headache and begged him not to bother calling on her when she'd be "such poor company."

She'd had twelve hours to get over her headache, if she'd been suffering a headache in more than the metaphorical sense. Ben let himself into her back garden, shinnied up a spreading oak, and dropped onto her balcony.

Only to find her, in her nightgown and wrapper, reclining on a chaise, regarding him with an expression unreadable in the moon shadows.

"Greetings, affianced wife."

She crossed her arms. "Greetings, *my lord.* I suppose I should be grateful you didn't stand amid the roses and serenade me."

"Now that's interesting." He took a wicker chair and tried not to notice how pretty her bare feet were by moonlight. "You don't sound grateful. I was in the glee club for three straight years at university and always chosen for solos. Shall I demonstrate?"

As he filled his lungs with air, she put a hand over his mouth, her fingers bearing the fragrance of cinnamon and flowers. "You are daft, Benjamin Portmaine."

He covered her hand with his own and brought it to his thigh, linking their fingers. "I'm engaged, which might qualify as daft, but my lady seems bent on avoiding me. Be warned, Maggie mine: I gave you today to rally your nerves and even suffered through dinner tête-à-tête with His Grace. Tomorrow we shop for a ring—His Grace's orders, or Her Grace's, carried by her most trusted emissary."

Maggie was quiet for a moment, but she allowed him to keep possession of her hand. "When Papa and Her Grace get to scheming, there is no telling them apart. They work as a seasoned pack, as a team that's been pulling together for years. You can't separate their motives, because their devotion to one another becomes a motive all its own. Westhaven has a touch of the same thing with Anna already, and if his letters are any indication, Devlin with his Emmie. Valentine and Ellen are already exchanging the same fraught looks, and they've been married only a short while."

"And do you suppose we'll exchange those same looks, too, one day?" He brought her hand to his mouth, the better to kiss her fingers and the better to inhale the particular scent that was Maggie.

"Why do you want to marry me, Benjamin? The real reason."

"Honor is a real reason." It was not *the* real reason. He wasn't quite sure he could admit the real reason, even to himself, even in the darkness, but if he said he wanted to keep her safe and make her troubles go away, she'd likely be on a packet to France by morning. "Why don't you want to marry me?"

"I don't want to marry anybody."

"We're back to your glorious independence?"

She remained silent, which was a good tactic. It made him feel petty and a trifle bullying, though no less determined.

"Is it so hard to believe a man could esteem you greatly enough to want to share his fortune, his title, and his life with you?"

She withdrew her hand and rose, shifting to stand at the railing so she looked out over the garden—and could keep her expression from Ben's gaze, no doubt. "I believe a man could want to share his body with me."

Oh-ho. Except her words were anything but an invitation.

"You are cranky, my love. Let me tuck you in. Finding a ring worthy of gracing your elegant hand might take us all day tomorrow, and that would be fatiguing indeed."

"We're not going to take an entire day wasting coin…"

He came up behind her and wrapped both arms around her middle. "Guns down, Maggie. Even the Corsican didn't expect to make war all winter—and see what his march to Moscow cost him when he made the attempt."

She sighed softly, her shoulders dropping. "You should not be here."

"Now there you are wrong. There is no place I would rather be. You, however, should not be alone, night after night, year after year, when any man with eyes and a brain can see what a treasure you are."

"Flattery ill becomes you, Benjamin. You should be blushing to speak such arrant flummery aloud. I hired you to find my reticule, and you end up with a scandal on your hands." She shifted so they were face-to-face, slipped her arms around his waist, and tucked her cheek against his chest. Something in Ben's vitals settled while he drew her closer and rested his chin against her hair.

"This hint of scandal truly displeases you." It should not surprise him to find it did, but it disappointed him. "And it makes no difference that His Grace and Westhaven both were engaged under more scandalous circumstances than we are?"

"Their mothers were duchesses; their fathers were dukes."

And dukes have no dirty linen.

The flat misery in her voice bothered him. It made

him want to put out the lights of any who would insult her or whisper behind her back. It made him really, truly want to marry her and lead her out for the bridal dance for all to see—Maggie Windham bagged an earl, and one damned near besotted—

"Come along." He bent and caught her behind the knees, hoisting her into his arms.

"Benjamin!" She looped her arms around his neck. "You'll do yourself an injury."

She was substantial, but in the best possible, most womanly way. "I will not—because you so religiously forgo your sweets."

"Only when anybody is looking." She let him carry her into the bedroom and lay her down on the bed. Someone had turned down the covers, and a half-dozen pillows were piled on a chair near the window.

Ben started throwing more pillows on the floor.

"What are you about, my lord?"

"You can have done with my lording, or I'll start in with my ladying. I'm making room. You disguise it well, but that bed is big enough for the both of us. Where is the dog?"

"He sleeps in my office. There's a bed for him there. Perhaps he might share it with you, because I have no interest in sharing mine."

"Not much of a watchdog if he didn't realize I was climbing to your balcony." He started shucking his clothes, wondering when he'd decided not simply to patrol her perimeters, not simply to bid her good night, but to impose himself on her in her very bed.

"You can't blame the dog if you're a better sneak thief than he is a watchdog."

Ben paused to put his handkerchief on the night table before he sat to tug off his boots. "Protective of him already? I bet you wouldn't let me have the dog back now if I asked. That's fast work for a mere aging dog. Suppose I'll have to bribe his secrets from him."

"Benjamin, you cannot stay with me. We've caused scandal enough as it is, and if I'm not carrying—"

"Hush." He rose to step out of his breeches, leaving him as naked as the day he came into the world. This had not been in his plans either. Not until she'd forbidden him to stay with her.

He stepped behind her privacy screen long enough to appropriate her tooth powder while he heard her rustling around in the bed. Building a barricade of pillows, no doubt.

When he emerged, her robe was lying across the foot of the bed, leaving Maggie clad only in a summer nightgown. She sat to one side on the mattress, her knees drawn up, her arms linked around them. "You should not do this, Benjamin."

No, he should not, but she sounded forlorn rather than truly upset. He climbed on the bed and scooted under the covers to sit beside her. Lovely cool sheets she had—probably cotton—and her scent was all around him. "Not do what?"

"You will start kissing me, and I'll get all muddled, and if I haven't conceived already, you'll see that I do by morning. I can't think…" She huffed out a breath. "*No* woman could think when you exert yourself to be seductive."

"My dear, you are quite overwrought, though under the circumstances, one can expect no less." He arranged himself on his back amid her pillows. "Come here." He drew her gently down against him and wrapped an arm around her. "It isn't my intention to muddle you."

Though it was gratifying in the extreme to think he could.

"Then what are you doing here?"

She shifted a little, restlessly, as if she'd never cuddled with anybody in a bed before—another gratifying thought.

"Get comfy, my love." He hiked one of her legs against his thighs, taking care that she did not touch his half-aroused cock in the process. "I am going to make an admission which will cause me to blush."

"As long as you don't burst out in song." She moved again, bringing her arm up to curl against his chest. "Should I light a candle to better appreciate your blush?"

"You must please yourself, though I am naked. One would hope you'd appreciate more than just my blush."

She might have chuckled a little at that, and she might have stirred around just a little more to hide it, the minx. She did not light a candle.

"This muddling business, Maggie. It goes both ways." He brought his hand to her nape and started to gently knead the tension there. "I don't want you trapped into marrying me, any more than you think I'm trapped into marrying you. I'd already proposed before Lady Dandridge intruded, if you'll recall."

She went still but said nothing.

"Lost sight of that detail, hadn't you? It has been a

very trying two days." He paused to kiss her crown. "My apologies for that. I haven't had a chance to say that—that I'm sorry for the situation we're in. I'm happy to marry you but sorry the circumstances are trying for you."

"When did you take to chattering, Benjamin Portmaine?"

He liked hearing her say his real, true name, particularly in the dark. And she'd accepted his apology. That meant something, too.

"It's your turn to chatter. Whatever made you consider becoming a swine nabob, Maggie Windham? It's clever of you in the extreme."

"A swine nabob?" She... giggled. He was almost certain she giggled. "If you ever let my brothers hear that term, you are doomed, sir."

"Very well, I'm doomed, but how did you think to invest in pork?"

"Pork wasn't my first profitable venture." She said it quietly, shyly. "When I was twelve, I started reading the financial pages because His Grace always read them, except I realized he wasn't reading them. He was holding them in front of his face while the rest of us piled around the breakfast table, and he was eavesdropping without having to enter into the conversation."

"So you stole his disguise."

"I did. My brothers got away with a deal less teasing thereafter, and I found something I truly enjoyed."

She babbled about this and that project, about some losses she'd taken early on, and about her brother Gayle's collusion in her investment schemes. She kept some investments with no less than Worth Kettering, generally regarded to be a wizard of the funds, for all the man was a scamp with the ladies.

When she dozed off an hour later, Ben felt he'd made progress getting to know his intended and perhaps in winning her trust, as well.

And while he still had not the first clue regarding her dreams, he'd gained considerable insight into his own.

❧

Maggie rose to awareness on the strength of two physical sensations. The first was one of pure animal comfort, which was made up of equal parts warmth from Benjamin's body spooned so closely around hers, and relaxation. The relaxation she attributed to a sense of safety. With Benjamin Hazlit on the premises, Cecily's skulking sneak thieves would regret any further attempts at larceny.

The second sensation was harder to identify and slightly at variance with the first: sexual arousal. Maggie lay on her side, mentally investigating her own impressions.

Benjamin gave off a nice toasty heat, the warmth of his chest along her back a novel sensory pleasure. His legs tangled with hers, his arm around her waist, and his hand…

"Benjamin, what are you doing?" She didn't dare breathe, lest he move his fingers again on her breast.

"I'm going to leave you with something pleasant to dream of." His voice had taken on some of the darkness, insinuating itself into Maggie's ear like a tactile caress. "I'll leave soon, long before it's light enough for anybody to see me climbing down from your balcony."

She hadn't been worried—not about that. If she believed one thing about her temporary fiancé, it was that her welfare was important to him.

"Unhand me, Benjamin."

He applied the slightest, most glorious pressure to her nipple. "Is that what you truly want?" The question was casual, not quite mocking, and after another slight, pulsing caress, Maggie felt his lips on her shoulder.

How was she supposed to *think*—?

When he slid his hand slowly, slowly over her naked hip, Maggie understood that thinking was the last activity he was trying to inspire.

"Benjamin, I will not—"

He didn't move quickly; he moved more like a large cat, shifting with languid grace that did nothing to mask his strength. Without Maggie doing a thing, she was on her back, her intended lying on his side against her.

"Trust me, Maggie Windham."

He rasped this imperative against her shoulder then grazed his nose along her collarbone. Maggie told herself she'd stop him if he tried to join with her again. She'd stop him, no matter how badly she longed for more of the intimacy and oblivion he offered.

He rose up and covered her mouth with his, and Maggie gave up trying to tell herself anything. In the darkness, in the shadows and comfort of her own bed, she kissed him back. She could be more honest in the dark, could give herself permission to run her hand over the smooth, muscular contours of his chest, down the odd angles of his ribs to the flat expanse of his belly.

She could even allow herself to touch him *there*, where a man was both virile and vulnerable. Ben lifted his mouth away from hers and went still while Maggie drew her fingers up the hard length of his arousal.

"You want me." She tried to keep the wonder out of her voice. Two minutes ago, she'd been asleep in his arms, and yet his body was ready to join with hers.

"Always."

He made no move to interfere with her explorations, just stayed where he was, ranged on his side, while Maggie traced the velvety skin crowning his cock, then slipped her fingertips over the little ridge below that.

He drew in his breath, the tenor of the inhalation suggesting these slow, curious caresses were pleasurable for him.

"Shall I stop, Benjamin?" She scored her nails lightly down his shaft then cupped the soft sacs beneath. A hunger radiated up from her middle for more of these scandalously intimate touches.

"Never stop." He settled his mouth on hers, tracing her bottom lip with his tongue. Maggie forgot about teasing him, forgot about learning the intimate shape and feel of him, forgot about her own name as she felt his hand on her throat. She arched up into him as that hand made a slow sweep down her torso, leaving a trail of heat and wanting.

And he did not stop but let his fingers drift down until his palm rested low on Maggie's belly.

"Kiss me, Maggie. I certainly intend to kiss you."

He was threatening something. She complied nonetheless, sinking her hands into his hair and fusing her mouth to his. Somewhere in the back of her mind, common sense was clamoring about bad judgments made in the heat of passion, but those frantic noises were reduced to soft whimpers when Benjamin's hand traveled back up her body to palm her breast.

And then he was gone. Maggie resisted the urge to wail out loud as she felt the mattress dip and shift when Benjamin sat back on his heels, his rampant erection arrowing up his belly.

"You've put me in quite a state, Maggie mine."

She blinked at him. "*I've* put *you* in a state?" She'd meant to sound indignant, but the words to her own ears came out bewildered.

"You are adorable when you're befuddled." He started moving pillows around, while Maggie tried to figure out if she'd been insulted or complimented.

"I am not befuddled."

"Right, my love. Lie back, and we'll remedy that oversight." He crouched over her like a lion guarding his next juicy meal.

"And shall you be befuddled, too, Benjamin?" There was light in his eyes Maggie hadn't seen before—a little wild, a lot intriguing.

"My dear woman"—he dipped his head and swiped his tongue over her nipple—"I am the picture of befuddlement, and you are entirely to blame."

When Maggie thought he'd commence with the kissing again, he instead shoved a pillow under her hips. The result was awkward, leaving Maggie feeling off balance even as she lay on her back in her own bed.

"You can stop me, Maggie, if you really must, but I wish with all my heart you wouldn't. I will not spend. You have my promise I will not spend inside your body."

She might have stopped him if she'd been able to speak at all over the clamor rising from deep in her body. The promise he'd made her was both shocking and reassuring, yet Maggie still felt a hint of worry.

He settled over her slowly, allowing her to feel each inch of skin-to-skin contact—bellies, ribs, chests, then the luscious pressure of his pelvis against hers. She sighed into his shoulder, longing laced with surrender.

For a long moment, he remained merely resting against her, his hand cradling the back of her head, his breathing matched to hers. She closed her eyes and treasured both the peace and intimacy of the moment, treasured him a little for showing it to her.

Still, he did nothing, until Maggie realized he was waiting for her to make an overture. She turned her head and nuzzled his throat.

And yet he did not move.

She kissed him, brought her hand up to cradle his jaw then turned his head to receive her kiss. It was lovely, to be given the latitude to learn his mouth anew at her leisure, to savor the taste and feel of him. She became enraptured with the sensation of her lips on his, her tongue stroking over his, until another sensation intruded ever so gently.

Him, nudging at her sex. The hot, blunt head of

his erection seeking her heat in slow, searching pulses. The pillow beneath her tilted Maggie's hips the better to receive him, and as he began the luscious, tender process of joining their bodies, Maggie went still.

To feel this, with him… She breathed through him, let the pleasure suffuse her until she could no longer stand to remain unmoving. In languid, almost lazy undulations, she moved with him.

Pleasure welled up from nowhere, insisting that she turn frantic and demanding; though from somewhere, Maggie found the resolve to keep to Benjamin's rhythm.

And yet, he knew.

He thrust deep and pushed hard against her while Maggie endured paroxysms of bodily pleasure so intense they left her digging her nails into Benjamin's smooth, muscular buttocks and keening softly against his shoulder. When passion finally ebbed, she slumped back against the mattress, wrung out and dazed.

"Benjamin?"

"Love?" He stroked a hand over her forehead, pushing her hair back in a gesture so redolent with tenderness Maggie had to close her eyes.

Tears welled then seeped down from her eyes into her hair. He held her gently, the hot, full length of him hilted in her body, while Maggie tried to find words of gratitude and regret.

There were none. After several minutes of silence, Maggie realized she could pet his hair, slowly, repeatedly, and it seemed important to stroke her hands over him in some fashion lest he think her… unaware of him.

He turned his head and planted a kiss on her palm then snuggled back down against her. For long moments they remained in that embrace, until Maggie began to move her hips again.

Perhaps he'd intended this as a gift to her, an experience of pleasure to make her think twice about crying off. Had it been merely pleasure, Maggie would not have found fault with Ben's scheme. But this went beyond pleasure to intimacy and generosity of such magnitude, the impending loss of it made Maggie weep all the more even as pleasure rose up once again to claim her.

✻

"You have a terrible megrim." Adele whipped curtains closed as she spoke, shutting out the first beams of morning sunshine. "The worst megrim you've ever suffered. You couldn't keep down even your morning chocolate."

Bridget sat up in bed and watched as more curtains were whisked shut. "Another megrim? Didn't I just have the worst megrim of my life at Christmas?"

"This one is worse yet." Adele poured steaming hot chocolate into a cup and passed it to Bridget, who drank it down greedily—chocolate was sometimes the only good thing about waking up, after all.

Adele poured the second cup directly into the chamber pot.

"So why am I brought low again?" Bridget fluffed the covers over herself. "And what could be worse than when Mama found out Lady Sophia Windham had wed some wealthy baron?"

"This is worse." Adele hefted the breakfast tray

and set it outside Bridget's door. "Even the scent of buttered toast is making you queasy."

Bridget cast a longing glance toward the door separating her from two thick slices of warm, golden, perfectly buttered toast. "My heavens, as bad as all that?"

From down the corridor, Mama's voice rose in a shriek, followed by the sound of some heavy crockery smashing to bits.

"I told that idiot not to let her see the paper for at least another hour," Adele muttered. "Your hair is too tidy for you to have tossed and turned all night."

Bridget obligingly mussed up her auburn braid, while the sound of more breaking china pierced the morning air. "You'd best tell me what's afoot, Adele. That was a new service."

"Their Graces, the Duke and Duchess of Windham, are pleased to announce the betrothal of their daughter, Lady Magdalene Windham, to Benjamin, the Earl of Hazelton, that's what's afoot. In the paper this morning, plain as day."

"I am very ill indeed." Bridget flopped down to the mattress, dread of her mother's temper warring with another, unprecedented emotion. "But I'm happy for Maggie, assuming this earl fellow is acceptable to her. I suppose he'd have to be, if she's marrying him, but this will be much worse than when Lady Sophia's wedding was announced."

Adele met Bridget's gaze for just an instant. "That was bad enough." She went back to tossing pillows on the floor and tearing the bedclothes loose from where they'd been tucked under the mattress. "I'd never seen a woman in such a sustained rage."

"Mama likes to think Her Grace's daughters are too homely to find good matches, or too poorly dowered. I think they're pretty, though not as pretty as Maggie."

"For God's sake, child, keep that sentiment to yourself."

Rapid footsteps sounded in the corridor. Bridget lay back, closed her eyes, and brought the back of one wrist to her forehead.

"Bridget Mary O'Donnell, you will get up this instant!" Cecily slammed the door behind her hard enough to make the French door to Bridget's balcony rattle on its hinges. "This is an infamous day! Infamous! When that woman becomes engaged to an earl, all of creation must take umbrage."

"Mama." Bridget managed a weak croak, though Mama in such a rage was enough to make any sane creature tremble. "Please, not so loud."

"What is wrong with you? Get out of that bed this instant!"

"*Please*, Mama…" Bridget covered her ears with her hands.

"She's been poorly all night, ma'am," Adele ventured. "Poor thing couldn't even keep down her chocolate."

Cecily inhaled audibly through her nose. "This is *most* inconvenient. Dose her with the poppy, and then, Martin, you will attend me in my sitting room. I have plans to make, and they will not countenance this one malingering."

"*Oui, madame.*"

Cecily flounced out, banging the door loudly yet again. Bridget sat up, feeling a headache start in earnest. "Is there any more chocolate?"

"Half a cup. I don't like this, Miss Bridget. When madam gets to scheming, it isn't good at all."

Bridget pushed to the edge of the bed. "I ought to write and congratulate Maggie." Though if Maggie were marrying an earl, it meant the letters would likely be futile, as futile as the vapid, fluttering drivel Bridget had been able to get past Cecily in the past few weeks— drivel intended to let Maggie know exactly what was afoot without alerting Cecily to Bridget's misgivings.

Adele passed her the last half cup of chocolate. "You ought to write and warn her."

Adele had kept her voice very low, almost as if she were confiding in Bridget, and Bridget felt something odd turn over inside her. Being almost fifteen and Cecily's daughter meant a girl had to be very careful, very discerning about who her friends were.

No, not just friends, but allies.

"Yes, warn her." Bridget kept her voice just as low. "And perhaps you could find a way to get the letter to Maggie without going through the post?"

"I'll make sure of it."

⸎

"Maggie, I can afford it." Ben kept his voice down and kept his smile indulgent, but his intended's mouth flattened nonetheless.

"You should be buying me paste." She kept her voice down, too, because every jeweler in Ludgate had been at his shop door this morning, smiling and bowing as Ben led Maggie from one establishment to another, their clerks hovering just far enough away to avoid Ben's ire.

"I will be buying you an emerald, at least, to go

with your eyes. Maybe rubies to go with your hair, diamonds for your flawless skin." That much extravagance might strain his exchequer, not that she'd permit him to indulge such whims.

"I have freckles." And still her expression did not betray her exasperation. Ben was left to note the ramrod straight posture of her spine and the slight narrowing of her eyes. A less courageous man might have taken warning.

"Where the angels have kissed you and where I fully intend to." He spoke just loudly enough for the nearest clerk to overhear, which had the intended effect of spiking Maggie's guns.

"This one is very nice." She aimed a saccharine smile at the clerk as she fingered a very small emerald. "Perhaps we might discuss settings?"

In the end, she won more than she gave up. She chose a different emerald, even smaller but of excellent quality. The setting was plain gold as was the wedding band. When Ben tried to push matching earrings on her, she went into outright rebellion.

"I am both peckish and fatigued," she announced, sounding quite like Her Grace. "Perhaps you'd take me for an ice?"

If Ben hadn't been in her bed just hours previously, if he wasn't still savoring the memory of her passion and pleasure, he might have believed all those airs and graces were the full measure of the woman.

He had her measure, though, knew her passion and determination first hand, so he capitulated gracefully. He handed her up into his curricle and took his seat immediately beside her.

"Can you really afford this?" Maggie asked, fluffing her skirts as Ben signaled the horse to walk on.

The very quiet, almost anxious tone of her question gave Ben an inspiration. "I've been meaning to ask you about that."

She stopped fussing and glanced at him. "What would I know of your finances?"

"Not my finances, but finances in general. I have a great deal of my wealth tied up in the funds, maybe more than is prudent. I was hoping we might discuss it."

He'd never realized how hard it was to be coy, to cast a shiny lure and just let it lie winking silently in the spring sunshine.

A vertical line appeared between Maggie's brows. "How much is a great deal?"

Two hours and two ices later, Ben was the one dazed by the brilliance before him. Maggie Windham understood money better than Ben had ever understood anything in his life. Better than he understood his sisters, better than he understood himself.

And he learned something else, too: the way to court Maggie Windham had something to do with making love to her luscious body, but it had more to do with alleviating the burden of a loneliness so vast and airless she'd been nigh suffocating under the weight of it.

Whatever her secret, whomever she was protecting, money was part of it. As they turned into the park and Maggie's tone grew animated on the topic of trade with the Americas, Ben became determined to free her from that weight, no matter the cost.

Eight

"IT ISN'T VERY FEMININE OF ME TO GO ON THIS WAY."
Maggie made the observation on a belated spurt of
self-consciousness as the curricle turned into Hyde Park.
"Louisa will hear me out, but Westhaven reaches his limit
very quickly when I start in on my economic theories."

"They're sound theories," Benjamin replied. "And
they let me both steal a bite from your ices and feed
you a few spoonfuls of my own."

She had to glance away lest he see her smile. "I
was distracted, else you should not have gotten away
with such outrageous behavior. I know what you're
doing, though."

"I'm glad somebody knows what I'm about,
because I seem to have lost my own grasp of it
entirely." He smiled at her, an open, charming smile
that had Maggie's insides fluttering around like the
birds flitting from branch to branch above them.

"You're making it seem as if we're enamored
of one another." She kept her eyes on the horses
before them, because an honest smile from Benjamin
Portmaine was enough to steal her few remaining wits.

"I *am* enamored of you." He slowed the horses to let a landau lumber on ahead of them. "You're gorgeous, passionate, intelligent, and independent—also a financial genius. I'm the man who proposed to you earlier this week, if you'll recall."

"Must you remind me?"

"Frequently, until you comprehend that I did not ask out of anything other than an honest desire to make you my countess."

She took in a breath, intent on remonstrating him with a list, a long, well-thought-out list of reasons why marriage to her was not in his best interests and marriage to him was not in hers, but her breath froze in her chest.

"Would you like a turn with the ribbons?" Benjamin cocked his wrists so she might have taken the reins from him, except Maggie had all she could do to remain sitting upright on the bench.

"Maggie?"

She averted her face from the sight before her and made herself take the reins from Benjamin's hands. Speech was beyond her.

"Would you like my driving gloves, my dear? And who is that woman, and why did she send you a positively venomous glare?"

"What woman?"

His smile was nowhere in evidence as he studied Maggie's face. "The woman who just drove past us, the one with the pretty child seated beside her whose face was painted in the most atrocious manner and whose bosom was indecently on display."

"Atrocious…" She hadn't meant to repeat the word

aloud, but gracious God, Bridget had been wearing enough paint for a Haymarket whore at midnight. And Cecily hadn't looked venomous, she'd looked smug and evil.

"You just drove past our turn, my dear."

"I'm not quite ready to go home."

He was still inspecting her, and Maggie didn't think for one moment he was fooled. "Then far be it from me to cut short an outing with my affianced wife on such a pleasant day." He lounged back against the seat, and the density of his silence was nearly as disturbing as the sight of Bridget tricked out like a soiled dove twice her age.

"You'll want this." Archer passed Benjamin two fingers of whiskey. "And if I had time, I'd beat about the bush and break what I have to say to you gently, but it's more fun to clobber you over the head with it."

Ben took the drink but did not put it to his lips. "Fun for whom?"

"Me, of course. While you were out swilling claret with old Moreland last night, those two brawny footmen went calling on your ladylove again. They stayed more than an hour, and I heard voices raised in the kitchen even from my spot in the mews."

"You're sure?"

Archer merely lifted one blond eyebrow.

"The same two?"

"Yes, the same two. Drink up, your lordship. It was your own Lady Maggie who let them into her kitchen, and she hugged them, first the one, then the other."

This was not good news. The idea that Maggie was keeping secrets from him rankled, of course. The idea that she was on hugging terms with not one man but two was equally troubling.

"How quickly did the yelling start?"

"Almost as soon as the door was closed behind them. It didn't last long."

Ben paced around the sitting room with his drink. "Did Lady Maggie raise her voice?"

"I am not sufficiently familiar with her voice to identify it," Archer said, sprawling on Ben's sofa. "I made out only one word."

Ben glared at him and resisted the temptation to hurl his drink at his cousin.

"Dandridge," Archer said. "Or it might have been Cambridge or Bainbridge. Would you like a suggestion?"

"No."

"Ask your fiancée who her callers are."

Ben set his drink down very carefully on the mantel. "And if she asks how I know she's been hugging strange men by the pair after dark in her kitchen, what should I tell her, Archer?"

Archer heaved a sigh and directed his guileless blue eyes toward the ceiling. "You tell her you're worried about her, and you wish she'd trust you, but you're too damned stubborn and uncertain of her affections to ask her to confide in you. The sheer novelty of your directness ought to wring confidences from her by the hogshead."

Ben tossed himself down on the sofa beside Archer. "I'm trying to inspire her trust. I think I made a start today, and then you tell me this."

"And how did you go about inspiring her trust?" Archer's tone was level—not at all mocking, which suggested he might live to see the next sunrise.

"I asked for her help."

"With?"

"My bloody finances." Ben grabbed the drink from Archer's hand and took a hefty swallow. "She's a prodigy with figures. She's read that Scot, the one who talks about supply and demand and division of labor, and she's brilliant at it. She sees patterns in finances the way I can parse a scent with my nose or sniff out a straying wife by the way she's dressing too modestly."

Archer frowned at the remains of his drink. "I was under the impression your finances were enjoying reasonable health. You're not going to bequeath me a pile of debt to go with that damned title, are you?"

And why hadn't they ever had this discussion? Archer was his heir, his only paternal adult male family member, his business partner, and the closest thing he had to a friend.

"My finances enjoy modest good health. I've worked like a fiend these past years so I might someday generously dower my sisters, and that objective has been accomplished."

"And this leaves you with a problem, doesn't it?" Archer surrendered the last of his drink without being asked.

"Precisely. For what reason am I to work like a fiend now, when both sisters are happily ensconced in the arms of their swains, and I'm still skulking about

Mayfair, peeking in windows and hating every bloody minute of it?"

Archer rose, glanced at the clock, and brought Ben the decanter.

"Given the state of things with your Lady Maggie, I don't think it's quite time to retire from the sneak-thief lists just yet, old son."

Ben poured himself another drink while Archer appropriated the glass still sitting on the mantel. "Not just yet," Ben said, "but soon, by God. Very, very soon."

❧

"Have you delivered my note to Maggie yet?" Bridget kept her voice casual and spoke in French.

"Not yet." Adele stepped back and surveyed Bridget's hair in the vanity mirror. "With madam determined we must move again this very week, there hasn't been time to slip out." She spoke in French, as well, dousing her hands with scent then fluffing her fingers through Bridget's hair. Even to Bridget's eye, the style was too sophisticated for somebody who'd not yet turned fifteen, but Adele—being similarly cursed herself—understood the dubious challenges of possessing red hair. There was no hiding it, no pretending it would look any less red for being in a tidy bun.

"Mama insists we need more elegant quarters," Bridget said, glancing around at her perfectly lovely room. "She says fifteen is not too young to socialize, and she's made me drive out with her every day this week."

Bridget's gaze fell on the cosmetics scattered around her vanity. They were an early birthday present from Cecily, though even the sight of them made Bridget's flesh crawl. "When we're in the park, the ladies won't look at me, and the gentlemen don't stop looking at me."

"And you hate the way they gawp at you," Adele said, "as if you were on the block at Tattersall's."

In the mirror, Bridget studied Adele's pretty features. Recent weeks had seen a change in the way Bridget and Adele went on with each other. Bridget liked the shift but not the reasons for it.

"When they look at me that way, I feel dirty."

"Oh, child."

Adele put down the bottle of scent, one of Maggie's gifts. Bridget bit her lip, wondering why a bottle of Maggie's perfume should make her feel grown-up in a good way, but all this other—the low-cut bodices, the paint, the new hair styles—should be so terribly disturbing.

Rapid footsteps sounded in the hallway. "Here she comes."

And while Bridget watched, Adele's face became a mask of polite stupidity, a bovine façade of patient, servile endurance. Bridget wished she might copy the expression when in the park, and maybe those men would stop looking at her.

Mama swept into the room, her gaze going to Bridget's face. "Bridget Mary O'Donnell, have you learned nothing from all my painstaking instruction? You need to start putting on your own cosmetics, my girl. I can't be bothered to do everything for you."

Adele melted back into the dressing room—Adele spent a great deal of time there—and Mama picked up a rouge pot. "Hold still and watch."

With her gaze on the mirror, Bridget saw Adele mouth one word before she left Bridget to contend with Mama and her infernal paint and powder.

"Today."

❧

For thirteen years, Maggie Windham had lived a life split in twain. Part of her was the adopted daughter of the Duke and Duchess of Moreland. This side of her had a courtesy title, considerable precedence, loving family, and a daily existence most people would envy.

But in the shadows of that life dwelled another Maggie, one who lived with fear as her constant companion, one who dreaded each morning's post, one who could never gather up enough coin to appease the terrible anxiety that tore at her vitals like the raptors that plagued the mythical Prometheus.

Each spring, she anticipated a demand for money, and each spring she met the demand. For a time, she'd tell herself by next year, she'd have found a way out of the trap her life had become.

She'd be more clever.

She'd bring her situation to her brothers or her solicitors, and they'd be smart enough to see the way out—Gayle had read law, after all, and he was a quietly brilliant man.

As the years went on and the demands grew larger, Maggie decided she'd fake her own death, depositing her fortune in a trust of such complexity even Cecily O'Donnell couldn't pervert its proper use.

And in recent years, she'd thought not to fake her death but to effect her own end in truth. The idea had a sick, dishonorable allure, a seductive, peaceful simplicity to it.

"Mail, Miss Maggie." Millie bobbed a curtsy and withdrew. Maggie hadn't even heard her come in, hadn't heard her knock on the office door.

Maggie glanced at the salver full of mail.

She sorted through the letters—still nothing from Cecily. It was tempting to track down the woman and just ask how much she wanted this year, but Cecily was careful not to give Maggie a clue about where she and Bridget dwelled. Even Thomas and Teddy had lost track of her, and Lady Dandridge left them little time to search.

The post brought no demand, no letter from Bridget—nothing but reports from the stewards, a letter from Sophie down in Kent, and a bill from the milliner. Maggie made herself tend to the reports, and by the time she finished, the afternoon was well advanced.

Benjamin had asked her to go walking with him in Regent's Park, and she'd been unable to come up with an excuse that wasn't insultingly transparent.

And she wanted to go. Even while it felt like the tangled skeins of her life were winding more tightly around her very throat, she wanted what little time with Benjamin she could have.

"Good afternoon, affianced wife." As if she'd conjured him with her thoughts, Benjamin stood in the door to the office, hat in hand.

"Must you call me that?"

He sauntered around her desk and leaned down to buss her cheek. "Yes, until I can call you wife in truth. You look tired, Maggie mine. Has some wretched bounder been keeping you up all night?"

"Not lately." And she'd missed him. Since the night more than a week ago when she'd found him on her balcony, he'd heeded her request to be left in peace. Oh, they were seen in the proper places, billing and cooing by day, but by night, she was again alone—at her request.

Her *stupid* request, except Maggie could not have kept her hands off him, and then a sham engagement would soon turn into the real thing.

"That is not the expression of a damsel pining for her swain, Maggie Windham. I suppose one of your stud pigs has gone into a decline?"

"The farms are thriving. Why on earth are you dressed like that?"

He sidled away and took one of the guest chairs on the other side of her desk. "It took you long enough to notice."

He was in a working man's attire, not shabby, but well worn and meticulously neat. His boot heels were scuffed, his cuffs frayed, and his unstarched cravat tied in the simplest of knots. He didn't look exactly seedy, but neither was he the picture of a prosperous earl.

"Am I to walk out with you when you're dressed like some clerk?"

"You may, or we can take tea in the garden. I had a purpose for my modest attire."

Maggie glanced out the window, where a lovely,

sunny spring day had been completely passing her by. "Tea, then, and if you keep to your pattern, enough sandwiches to fortify a regiment."

"And if you keep to your pattern, some chocolates to sweeten your disposition."

He was an intuitive man, Maggie thought, because he didn't offer a smile to go with his observation.

"I am my father's daughter in some things," she said, going to the door and signaling a footman. "Let's take some air, shall we?"

He held the door for her but didn't take her arm, something Maggie attributed to more of his overactive intuition. Perhaps he sensed her determination to set him free before Cecily's poison spread any further.

"You really are looking a trifle fatigued, my dear," Benjamin observed while they ambled away from the house. "Are these prewedding jitters? If it would help, I can come sing you lullabies."

And she *wanted* him singing those lullabies to her, which was just the worst, most abominable injustice imaginable.

"You are being nonsensical, Benjamin. Why are you wearing those clothes?"

"Because I did not want my pocket picked, today of all days."

His tone was sober enough that she glanced over at him in puzzlement. "I don't understand."

"I'm carrying valuables for my lady." He withdrew a little box from an inside pocket, and Maggie's heart started trotting around nervously in her rib cage.

"Benjamin, what are you about?"

"Come." He took her by the wrist and led her to a low stone wall circling a fountain. "I want to do this properly."

Foreboding mixed with an odd, sentimental thrill as Maggie seated herself on the stone wall. Benjamin took the place beside her, his expression still somber. He flipped open the box, withdrew a gorgeous emerald ring, and tucked the box out of sight again.

"With this ring, I plight thee my troth, Maggie Windham."

She watched, dumbstruck, while he took her hand and slid the ring onto the appropriate finger. It was the stone she had picked out—she was almost sure of it—but the setting was nothing she recognized.

"You should not be doing this." She stared at the golden love knot crafted into the setting, stared at it until a teardrop splattered onto the back of her hand. "Oh, Benjamin, this is foolishness. We are not engaged, not truly."

He folded her into his embrace, resting his cheek against her temple. "It has been two weeks, Maggie, or nearly so. I think we are truly engaged."

She shook her head and tried to draw back, but he did not let her go. "I am not with child."

"Your menses have started then?" And still he did not let her go, but damn him, he understood her well enough to make a direct inquiry.

"Not yet, but they will. I can feel it." She would will it to happen, of that she was certain. No woman could conceive a child with this much tension and anxiety swirling in her vitals.

"Then we're still engaged."

"Must you be so stubborn?"

He let her go and pulled back far enough to aim a look at her that asked silent, pointed questions about who was being stubborn with whom.

"I got a ring for myself, too," he said. "It's not fashionable, but my parents observed this custom, and I noted yours do, as well."

"You don't miss much of anything, do you?"

He passed her a gold band that would have been plain, except it was chased with a swirling, inter-locking pattern reminiscent of the love knot. "You don't have to say the words, Maggie, but if you'd oblige me?" He held out his hand, and Maggie felt her heart—already fractured into a hundred sharp, miser-able pieces—splinter further.

Wordlessly, she took the ring from him and slid it onto the fourth finger of his left hand.

"This is not a real engagement, Benjamin Portmaine. I wish it could be, but it cannot."

He kissed her, a sweet, gentle, heartrendingly tender pressing of his lips over hers. "It's real to me, Maggie Windham. In this moment, sitting here with you, I am betrothed to the only woman I've ever wanted for my countess, my wife, and my love."

She put her fingers over his mouth lest he speak more words of such terrible beauty, but he did anyway.

"I want to make love with you, Maggie Windham. If you're carrying my child, it won't make any differ-ence, save to give us both pleasure. If you're not carrying my child and your menses are imminent, then it will not change your circumstances one whit."

"You will not befuddle me with your kisses and

whatnot," she said, though his particular brand of *whatnot* was a formidable consideration. "I will end this betrothal."

"Most betrothals end," he said, rising and taking her by the hand. "Most of them end in marriage."

She suspected he was going to try to change her mind with his passionate lovemaking, with touches more tender and seductive than words. He would not succeed, but she would let him try.

Just this one, last time, she would allow him to try.

❧

Ben studied his intended while they took very civilized tea in the garden and decided she truly was working herself up to jilt him.

The idea was insupportable. He'd swive it right out of her pretty, befuddled head. No—not swive. Swiving was for randy boys. He'd *love* it right out of her head. She wanted to marry him—he was sure of that—and he needed to marry her.

He was equally certain of that.

"I've moved some of my funds," he said, setting down his empty teacup long minutes later. "Kettering detected your deft hand in my decisions."

"He detected our betrothal announcement in the newspaper, you mean." She did not sound pleased by this.

"Did you know your man of business is protective of you?" That got her attention, for she looked up from the teacup she'd been peering into. "He threatened to meet me if I broke your heart. I don't think he was joking."

"He was. Worth Kettering has a fondness for damsels in distress, though it's a rather questionable sort of fondness. More tea?"

He'd forced himself to swill two cups, mostly to wash down the sandwich he'd eaten without tasting. Anticipation lent a pleasant spice to lovemaking, one best appreciated in moderation. "No more tea, thank you. May I escort you inside?"

May I tear the clothes off your body and fall upon you like a rutting beast?

She nodded, her complexion so pale she might have heard what Ben's brain had almost let come tripping out of his mouth. They made their way upstairs with all the decorum of a lady tolerating a gentleman caller who'd lost track of the time, but when Ben closed the door to Maggie's private sitting room, she was the one who kept right on moving into her bedroom.

He locked the door, followed her into her boudoir, then locked that door, too.

"Are we in a hurry, my dear?"

"You made me dither over tea, as if you'd changed your mind about…" She turned away from him so she faced out toward the balcony.

"About making love with you?" He started to disrobe, purposely keeping her great, fluffy confection of a bed between them. Something like anger began to build in his chest, or possibly worry, because he could not read her in her present mood.

"Yes. Making love."

If removing his clothing piece by piece didn't assure her he'd remained true to his intent, words would hardly convince her. "Do you need assistance with your dress?"

"I do not."

She shifted, and Ben heard her draw in her breath at the sight of him peeled down to his breeches and boots. He sat on the bed, giving her his back so he could tug off his footwear.

Maggie came around the bed and sat beside him. "This doesn't feel right."

When he wanted to hurl his boots hard against the bedroom wall, Ben instead set them tidily beside the bed. "What doesn't feel right about it?"

"It's broad daylight and we're not married and we're not marrying, either."

"This marriage business troubles you exceedingly," he observed. "What is about to happen between us has happened before, Maggie, and at your instigation in even broader daylight than this. I believe you enjoyed yourself, and I most assuredly know I did. Do we need to complicate matters beyond that?"

She turned green eyes on him, luminous with some emotion he could not name.

"I suppose not."

Her busy, brilliant mind wanted to complicate it—he could see that much in her troubled expression—but his not-very-brilliant, lust-clouded mind was determined on simplicity. He took her hand and put it over the fall of his trousers. "It isn't complicated at all. You want me, and I'm happy to oblige you. Take the dress off, Maggie, or I will tear it from your body."

And this—this sincere threat of sartorial violence—was what finally won him a small, impish smile.

"You would not tear it off me, but you might ruck it up and wrinkle it beyond salvation." She drew the dress up and over her head, leaving her sitting on the bed in her shifts, stays, stockings, and boots—though no drawers. Today she wore no drawers.

Ben's breath about stopped in his throat. His fiancée in dishabille was the most arousing sight he'd ever beheld. Her hair coiled primly at her nape was an erotic contrast to her lacy undergarments, silk stockings, elaborately embroidered stays, and all the abundant feminine curves contained therein.

He knelt at her feet and began unlacing her boots. "You have a secret passion for pretty underthings. I intend to be scandalously indulgent about it when we're married."

"Benjamin." She brushed her hand back through his hair, causing him to glance up from the elegant, narrow feet he'd been intent on cradling in his hands. "Please, no more talk of marriage. Not now."

"Right." In a few moments he'd be challenged to form coherent sentences on any subject at all. "Talk later. Kiss now."

He shifted up over her so she was lying on her back with her legs over the side of the bed, and commenced kissing her. He'd been starving for these kisses—for days, for years. She tasted of sweetened tea and chocolates and of every lustful fantasy he'd taken to bed with him each night for the past two weeks.

"God, I have missed you." Her stays dug into his bare midriff, but at least he'd had the presence of mind to keep his breeches on. He climbed on the bed, bracing himself above her on his elbows and knees.

"I have missed you, too, Benjamin Portmaine." She wrapped her hand around his nape and guided him back down to her mouth.

He wanted to ravish; she merely nibbled.

He wanted to plunder her senses; she let one hand drift through his hair.

"Oh, for God's sake." He raised himself up on his arms and glared down at her. "Stop thinking, Maggie Windham, and stop worrying or I'll *make* you stop."

Her brows knit. "It isn't something I can— Benjamin? Where are you going?"

He hiked himself off the bed, flipped up the hem of her chemise, and knelt between her spread legs.

She braced herself on her elbows, peering at him. "Benjamin?"

"Hush. I'm busy." He ran the backs of his fingers up and down the silken skin of her inner thighs. When she slumped back on the bed, he let himself lean in and nuzzle curls slightly darker than the magnificent mane on her head. "Not thinking now, are you?"

"You are *so* naughty." There was resignation and affection in her voice, maybe even something more.

The moment he touched his mouth to her sex, he felt her mighty, surging brain come to a halt. Her body went still, as well, her hand falling away from his hair, a sigh easing from her.

She tasted sweet and flowery—and just a bit foxy, like a fastidious woman becoming aroused. He shifted his attentions up, to the little bud of flesh at the top of her sex, and her sigh became a groan.

"*Move.*" He growled against her damp flesh, not a suggestion to her mind but a command to her body.

She twitched under his mouth then went still, so he rested one hand low on her belly and applied just a slight pressure.

She moved, little seeking undulations of her hips that brought her more snugly against his mouth. He resented her fetching undergarments now, wanted the stays gone, wanted her breasts freed for his touch.

"Benjamin." Her hand landed on his hair and grabbed a fistful. "I can't…"

She could, too. He gave no quarter but harried her endlessly with his lips and teeth and tongue until she was thrashing against his mouth. When she was whimpering and keening on the bed, he sank two fingers into her heat, and she came apart.

Her body seized up, the sexy little sounds caught in her throat, and her grip on Ben's hair became desperate. For a long progression of silent instants, her body fisted around his fingers, and she gave herself up to the passion he built for her.

And then… more silence while Ben lapped soothingly at her folds and then rested his cheek on her curls. When he felt her breathing return to normal, he rose up on his knees and examined her. Above her chemise, she sported a rosy flush, and her eyes were closed.

He crouched over her and kissed her not at all chastely. "That's what you taste like." Her eyes flew open, and her fingers went to her lips. "You were curious, but you weren't going to ask me."

This provoked another of those slight shy smiles. "I wasn't—going to, ask, that is."

"I love how you taste." He announced this, unlacing her stays while she obligingly rested on her side. "I could get drunk on your taste and the sounds you make and the way you go quiet when you're coming."

"When I'm what?" She was up on her elbows again, watching him attack her clothing.

"Your bun is coming loose. Why don't you finish the job?" And why in the name of all that was worthy did women wear so much clothing? "Coming, over-come with pleasure. The French call it *le petit mort*."

She went boneless against the mattress. "One can see why. Is it the same for a man?"

"Hard to say." He tugged the stays away from her body. "Very likely, though we haven't the stamina you ladies can boast." He untied her garters and rolled down her stockings, leaving Maggie amid the bedclothes, her stays undone, her chemise soft and wrinkled around her middle. "Stay right where you are, Maggie mine."

The sight of her sprawled and replete like that did things to what remained of his ability to think. It made him notice, for example, that the bed was the perfect height for a man bent on pleasuring his lady and himself in the next several seconds.

He unfastened his trousers, freed his engorged cock from his clothing, and leaned over Maggie where she drowsed on the bed. "You are mine, Maggie Windham. And I am yours. Never doubt it."

Her eyes came open only to slam shut again as he entered her in one fierce, sweet thrust. He'd barely started to withdraw for the next thrust when she bowed up against him, her sex convulsing with plea-sure around his cock. He cradled her close and bore it, his body on that knife-edge between arousal and release, while she dug her heels into the small of his back and clutched him hard.

And when she went soft and sweet beneath him again, he had all he could do to remain still, hilted in her heat.

"I need a moment," she said, eyes closed. "Kiss me."

That she would give orders pleased him inordinately, and it was a sound plan, to leaven his screaming arousal with some kisses and tenderness. Maggie sighed into his mouth, and while he soothed them both with sweet, easy kisses, she ran her hands over his torso.

If by petting him thus she'd intended to ease his lust, she failed miserably. Everywhere she touched, Ben felt as if his skin had been panting for the feel of her hands. She dallied a little with his nipples, and a groan escaped him.

"You like that." She sounded so smug.

He eased a hand over one full breast and secured her nipple between his thumb and forefinger. "We both like it."

"Uhn." She arched into his hand, which he took for permission to allow his throbbing cock the pleasure of moving inside her, as well. He went slowly at first, easy little movements that might have gone unnoticed amid kisses and sighs and caresses.

But then, bless her, bless her, she started moving with him.

He resisted mightily the pleasure beckoning then demanding that he capitulate. He kept the movement of his hips slow, he tormented Maggie's breasts with his hands, and he kissed her in an unbridled effort to tip her over into satisfaction before he gave in himself.

"Benjamin Portmaine." She spoke through gritted teeth, and Ben realized she was holding back, too, waiting for him, striving to share this most intimate pleasure right down to the moment.

He got a hand under her bottom and anchored her against his thrusts. "Now, Maggie. *Let go.*"

"You… you let go."

He *obeyed*. He obeyed her, he obeyed his body, he obeyed his heart, and as longing coalesced into intense satisfaction, he felt Maggie yielding, as well. His mind went dark, his body filled with pleasure, and his soul was suffused with light.

∾

Gracious, merciful God, she'd been a fool. Maggie lay still, her body spooned into the curve of Benjamin's larger frame, and tried to hide her tears. More damned tears.

He'd notice them. He'd notice the smallest shift in her breathing, the least tension in her body. She adored him for the intensity of his attentiveness, even as she realized this very astuteness on his part made proximity to him an untenable threat to her peace of mind.

"You're going to need a soaking bath." He sounded more smug than contrite. His hand squeezed her buttock, which was perhaps a male gesture of apology—or possessiveness.

"Why will I need a soaking bath?"

"I was too ardent when I used my mouth and my hands, and the first time."

He'd been perfect—passionate when what Maggie

had craved was passion. And then the second time, he'd been lingeringly tender, reminding Maggie that the most devastating intimacies need not be tempestuous.

She'd wanted one last taste of him, one last memory, and yet, the idea of casting him aside remained beyond her ability. Somehow she had to find a way to deal with Cecily, to protect Bridget, to protect her ducal family, *to protect Benjamin*, and all without embroiling the dear, ardent, very perceptive man himself any more deeply in her troubles.

The scandal Cecily could detonate in the middle of their lives was more than any decent man should have to bear, much less one who'd already weathered scandal at his sisters' behest.

"You're too quiet, Maggie my love."

She closed her eyes for an instant, felt the warmth and strength of him at her back, inhaled the scent of his skin, felt the texture of his muscular legs entangled with hers.

"I haven't been sleeping well." It was all she could think of, but she made herself shift away from him and move as if to leave the bed.

"Not so fast." He caught her wrist in a gentle, implacable grip. "Do you like the ring?" He tugged her down against his side, and Maggie allowed it.

"The ring is very pretty, but you should not have gone to so much trouble."

"It's a tiny gem, Maggie. The least I could do was put it in a decent setting. I think it suits you."

And he was going to wear a ring, as well, though most aristocratic men did not. Why should they? Marriage did not make them their wives' possessions, not the way it legally put a woman and her children into her husband's hands.

She would love to be held in Benjamin Portmaine's hands—legally, physically, emotionally.

"I have a question for you, Maggie." His hand came up to cradle her head against his shoulder. Maggie closed her eyes and savored the sheer animal pleasure of lingering with him in bed this way.

"I am not in the mood to offer financial advice, Benjamin. I need at least a dressing gown if we're to talk about the funds."

"This is not about money, I hope. I am attempting to inspire more of your trust."

"Oh?" When she would have peered up at him— the better to determine what that little note of misgiving in his voice was about—he palmed her cheek to hold her in his embrace.

"I am taking a risk, here, Maggie, so please bear that in mind when you answer my question."

"You are adorning this risk with a great deal of anticipation." She considered biting his nipple, because his voice was ominously serious.

"Maggie, who are the two men who come around your kitchen of an evening, and why were they shouting at you the night I last graced your bed?"

"*What?*" She did raise her head, shrugging off the hand that had been offering such tender caresses.

He held her gaze with his own, his eyes so dark Maggie could not discern his pupils. "Who are the two men who come around to your back door after dark, Maggie, cadging hugs even as they raise their voices to you?"

"*You have spied on me.*"

She was out of the bed in an instant, rage and heart-break swirling through her to create a sense of betrayal so profound she understood the urge to do violence to another person. "You lurked in the garden, spying on me and mine, and then you came to my bed, spouting inanities and tender kisses. Get out of my house."

He sat up and tossed her a dressing gown, though Maggie was so angry she didn't even care that she'd been naked.

"Maggie, I'm not castigating you, and I know you value your privacy."

The reasoning tone made her nearly shriek. "Get. Out. Of. My. Bed. This *instant.*"

He eyed her warily as she pitched his breeches at his bare chest. "The degree of your upset tells me something is troubling you, and you never did tell me what was in that missing reticule."

"Letters, Benjamin." She crossed her arms over her chest, nigh hating his tenacity and insight. "Letters from a child who has not one friend in this entire, mean, stupid world." She fired his balled-up shirt at him where he stood beside the bed. "And the men who come around my kitchen? They are my maternal half brothers. I hope you are pleased with your spying, for it has gained you the truth and cost you this idiotic engagement."

"Maggie, you can't cry off the engagement."

She tossed his ring at him, which he caught neatly in one hand. "I just did."

Her voice broke, which enraged her all the more. He took a step toward her, but she waved him away.

"I want you to go. I mean it. I won't say anything; you can nip off to Cumbria, and everybody will forget we're engaged as soon as the next nine-days wonder comes along."

"Maggie, jilt me if you must, but let me help you."

Oh, damn him. Despite his spying, he'd graduated from decent to *noble*. "It isn't your place to help, and it's nothing I can't handle myself."

By the narrowing of his eyes, she realized she'd made an admission, likely confirming what had been only suspicion before. He busied himself with his clothing while he no doubt mentally rearranged arguments and emotional artillery.

"I did not spy on you, Maggie. I did have dinner with your father, but I also set someone to ensure your safety. Guarding and spying are two different things."

"Maybe they are, but this engagement was never supposed to do more than scotch a budding scandal. You have to understand that I'm done with the pretense of it, and we will not marry, not ever."

He sat on the bed to tug on his boots but then regarded her where she stood.

"I love you, Maggie Windham. More than I want to marry you, more than I want to swive you silly three times an hour, I want you to be safe."

"I'm in no danger." Except the danger that her heart would fail utterly, so ruthlessly did he wield three small words. She fisted her hands at her sides lest she give those words back to him, fling herself at his chest, and beg him to take up her problems.

When he rose, he seemed to stand very tall. "You might not be in danger, but you are in trouble. I

LADY MAGGIE'S SECRET SCANDAL

specialize in making trouble go away." He shrugged into his worn coat and whipped his cravat into a limp knot. "I beg you to recall this."

"I beg *you* to go away," Maggie said, but the fight had gone out of her, and she sank to the bed while he remained standing. He loved her, and she was sending him away. The injustice of it—to her and to him— robbed her of all other emotion, despite the fact that this was the only course that would keep him and her family safe from her problems. "I need you to leave me in peace."

"And if you're breeding?"

She shook her head. Not even a God as indifferent and perverse as the one presiding over her life would be so cruel.

"Here." A little white epistle was shoved into her line of sight. He took it back, passed it under his nose, then held it out to her again.

"What's that?"

He didn't glare at her, but his nostrils flared with some male emotion. "I don't know what it is. An old woman gave it to me to put into your hand when she saw me coming in from the mews. I did not recognize her, but I assured her I'd deliver the letter. If I were going to *spy* on you, I might have read it. Remiss of me, to be preoccupied with putting my ring on your finger, when I might have been reading your personal correspondence."

He took the little box out of his pocket and put the ring back in it. Watching him, Maggie felt like every hope, dream, or pleasure she'd known in life had just been neatly tucked away, never to see the light of day again.

"I am not going north to Cumbria, not for some weeks. If you need me, Maggie, you have only to send for me."

"You'll not set any more strangers to guarding me?"

He looked torn, but in the end, the tears threatening to spill from her eyes must have convinced him. "I will not. I wish you'd open that letter."

She shook her head, wanting him gone and wanting desperately for him to stay.

"Are your brothers decent to you?" He'd put the question quietly, one hand on the door latch, as if he couldn't bear to see her face if she were going to lie.

"They're very dear. They're in service to Lady Dandridge, who dotes on them. They keep an eye on me, but not in any manner that would create awkwardness for my father's family."

He seemed satisfied with that but turned again to study her.

"Benjamin, I need you to leave now."

He approached her swiftly where she sat on the bed, kissed her cheek, and only when she'd had one last chance to inhale his scent and his warmth did he do as she asked.

∾

"Will you be needing the coach today?"

Ben looked up from staring at the financial pages—the same pages he hoped Maggie Windham was staring at in her tidy little corner house—to see Archer sauntering into the breakfast parlor. "Good morning, Cousin. I won't need the coach. I'm going around to Lady Dandridge's but can do that on foot."

"Is this business or an attempt to placate an old tabby who's in a position to spread scandal?" Archer took the seat at Ben's elbow, topped up Ben's cup of tea, and then poured one for himself.

"Neither. It seems the matched pair of footmen she's so proud of are Maggie's half brothers."

Archer stirred his tea, frowning at the pattern created by the cream swirling in his cup. "Do you suppose Lady Dandridge knows that?"

"Not likely, and I don't intend to tell her. Maggie is trying to cry off, and I'm hoping her brothers can provide me some insights into what is so bloody objectionable about being my countess."

Archer stared at him for a moment then went back to studying his tea. "I don't suppose you told the woman you're arse over teakettle in love with her?"

"I did." Ben picked up the financial pages and began to carefully refold the paper. "I went about it all wrong."

"There's a wrong way to tell a woman you love her?"

"Nearly shouting it at her when she's angry and frightened and looking for excuses to throw your ring at you might qualify."

A little silence formed—What reply could even a good friend make to such a pronouncement?

"I think I'm going to propose to Della. I'm telling you because it's theoretically possible she'll be the mother of the next Earl of Hazelton, but don't try to change my mind just because her upbringing was humble."

As replies went, that one served. It also explained a great deal, most notably the desultory fashion in which

Archer had undertaken his work recently, and the abundance of late nights likely spent mooning under the window of a mere lady's maid.

"Will she accept your suit?" Ben put the question carefully, because Archer was routinely smitten with the very women who did not reciprocate his sentiments. It was a kind of pleasant sentimental game to him, not one Ben understood.

"I believe she will. Her present employer is a wretched old witch of a fading courtesan who Della will only refer to as Madam. Della's usually free only when her employer goes driving at the fashionable hour."

"Which, given the often rainy weather, is but a few hours a week. Will you and Della continue with the business, or will you whisk your viscountess off to Scotland when you get a ring on her finger?"

"You're being very reasonable about this."

A stalling tactic. Archer hadn't discussed future enterprises with his intended.

"Besides a maternal half brother smitten with his recently acquired baroness, you are my only adult male family, Archer Portmaine." Ben spoke gently, realizing for the first time he'd miss his cousin were their paths to part. In many ways he was closer to Archer than to his own half brother. "Marry where you will, but be sure she loves you."

"Well, as to that…"

Ben shifted back in his chair. "Tell me you haven't cast your heart to an indifferent lady, Archer. Not again."

"She's kept busy. I was going to propose yesterday, but she had some damned letter she had to see delivered and nobody to deliver it. Then the old besom arrived in high dudgeon because it started to sprinkle before she'd even reached the park, and I went over the garden wall like a poaching lad."

"The course of true love and so forth."

Ben poured them each more tea but tried to fathom what in this recitation was making that tickling start up at the back of his mind, one so intense as to feel almost like a prickling of the hairs on his nape.

Something to do with letters and garden walls. Or perhaps with a lady who had no care for the heart of the man who loved her.

"I won't be home until quite late tonight," Ben said, pushing the tray of scones over to Archer's elbow.

"You're on a case?"

"No, I am not, but I promised Maggie I wouldn't set any strangers to spying on her."

Archer paused with a scone in one hand and the butter knife in the other. "You did not promise her you yourself would abstain from spying, though. Do you think the distinction will be any comfort when she discovers you lurking in her mews?"

"She won't discover me, and I'm not spying. I'm protecting."

Archer smiled, shrugged, and went back to buttering his scone.

❧

The letter from Bridget was a litany of horrors, and it still said the same awful things when Maggie read it for the hundredth time the next morning. Not only was Cecily forcing the girl to use face paints, but Adele must alter all Bridget's dresses to fit more tightly through the bust. Bridget was to read lurid texts pressed on her by her mother, things unfit for any young girl, much less one still innocent. Bridget was to forego wearing drawers even on chilly days, and when Cecily drove her in the Park, Bridget was to flirt with the gentlemen who stared at her half-exposed breasts.

And Cecily was muttering dark things about revenge and scandal and people who forgot their humble beginnings.

Worse, Bridget reported that they were preparing to move once again, but Cecily hadn't revealed their next address, and the letter was at least several days old.

The present address, however, was provided plain as day at the bottom of the letter, right below Bridget's final sentence: *Please, Maggie, you have to help me—she's planning something dire.*

This was not adolescent dramatics. Cecily had recounted to Maggie often enough that she'd had her first protector at the age of fifteen, a wealthy cit who'd lavished attention and jewels on her. His Grace had been a passing conquest, one undertaken between other longer engagements—a younger son on leave from his regiment, but a ducal younger son and hand-some enough to turn a seventeen-year-old's head.

To Cecily's way of thinking, Harriette Wilson had allowed herself to be seduced by Lord Craven when she'd been but fifteen, and thus fifteen was a fine age to undertake the life of a courtesan. The younger Wilson sister, now sporting the title of Lady Berwick, had undertaken her trade at the age of *thirteen* and married Berwick while still a minor.

Something drastic was called for, or Bridget would be condemned to the very life Cecily had led, and all of Maggie's sacrifice and saving would have been for naught.

Maggie looked out at the dreary day. The weather meant fewer people would be abroad. It would also mean Lady Dandridge would likely be at home, and thus both Teddy and Thomas would be easily found. They might know where Cecily was removing to, or at least have some ideas how to go on in the midst of such an awful mess.

Maggie got up, donned a cloak, bonnet, and gloves, stashed Bridget's letter in her reticule, and headed off into the rain.

❧

Ben stood on Lady Dandridge's stoop, feeling frustration like a live thing roiling in his gut. It was early afternoon—the proper time to make a morning call—but he was at a point-non-plus.

No Lady Dandridge, no footmen, and the deaf fixture serving as her butler had no idea when her ladyship might return. Rather than head for his club, Ben sidled around the block until he came to the alley running back to the mews.

It was a private mews from the looks of it, serving only the houses in the immediate vicinity.

"We've none to hire today, guv," one of the lads reported when Ben ducked into the stables. "Not that we ever have for hire. Her ladyship says it brings in the riffraff."

The man was well under five feet tall, likely a

former jockey and thus acquainted with the ability of ready cash to facilitate many a transaction.

"It's Hazelton," Ben said. "Earl of, but you're to forget that."

The gnome smiled, revealing a fine set of teeth. "Me memory ain't what it used to be."

Ben flipped him a sovereign. "Perhaps you can still recall where Lady Dandridge has gone off to?"

Bushy white eyebrows lowered. "I am right fond of 'er ladyship. She pays proper and dotes on the cattle. Why do you want to know?"

"I have no interest whatsoever in her ladyship's whereabouts, and wish in fact The Almighty would keep her far from me and mine, but I need to speak with her footmen."

The little man's look brightened. "She dotes on them, too, and a pair of big buggers like 'em can look after theirselves, but they've gone off."

"I beg your pardon?" A second sovereign was neatly caught.

"'Er ladyship took the traveling coach, which means she's away on her annual trip to Bath. Wouldn't think of going nowheres without the twins, though."

"And when will they return?"

"No telling. 'Er ladyship do enjoy takin' the waters."

"Who would have her direction in Bath?"

It was a mistake to indicate how desperately Ben wanted to track the woman down, but the stable lad was an honest snitch.

"Keep yer coin, guv. She always stays at the same 'otel." Ben got the particulars, including the roads Lady Dandridge would take, the inns she favored, and a description of her traveling coach. By the time he was ready to depart, the rain had started down in earnest, not a downpour, but a steady, cold drizzle that might not let up for hours.

Archer would kill him for taking the team clear to Bath, but the alternative was riding through this mess.

He'd do it—ride the whole damned way to Bath—if it was the only way to track down Maggie's brothers and gain a clue into what in the ever-loving hell was troubling her.

❧

As she slogged her way to Lady Dandridge's town house, Maggie tried to think up a credible reason to be making a call in such rotten weather, much less a call on somebody even Her Grace would consider only an acquaintance.

Too late, Maggie realized she hadn't brought along a maid or a footman, nothing to lend credence to the idea that she was out and about for any sane or social reason.

A cold, wet deluge sloshed up onto her cloak.

"Careful there, ma'am." A passing stranger caught her elbow and hauled her back from the street. "Best watch your step."

As a brewer's wagon rumbled past, Maggie felt the dampness seeping up from her boots into her bones. The man who'd stopped her from marching right out in front of an enormous team tipped his hat and hurried off.

Gracious God. She looked around, getting her bearings, trying to slow the pounding of her heart. "Steady on," she muttered. "Bridget is depending on you."

And still, she got lost on familiar streets twice, until she was as sodden as the lanes she was wandering. By the time she arrived shivering at Lady Dandridge's town house, she probably resembled a drowned rat, and her cloak, at least, smelled just as noisome.

She was thumping the knocker hard for the third time, ready to pound on the door with her fists, when she sensed a presence behind her.

"She's not here, and neither are your brothers." Benjamin's voice, raised just enough to be heard over the passing traffic and the miserable rain.

She turned to find him standing right there on the stoop, bareheaded and barehanded. "They're gone?"

He nodded. "To Bath for an indefinite stay."

The last shred of warmth evaporated from Maggie's insides, leaving behind only despair and desolation. An airless darkness denser than description threatened to engulf her.

"Maggie?"

Benjamin's voice came from far away, and yet Maggie could see him clearly right in the center of her vision. Even dripping wet, he looked solid and warm, impervious to wind, rain, and weather.

"Maggie, please let me help you."

She thought maybe he was taking off his greatcoat to wrap around her shoulders, but then she thought nothing—nothing at all.

Nine

"SLEEPING BEAUTY AWAKENS."

Maggie blinked open her eyes to see two men peering down at her. "Benjamin?"

"Here."

The other man, the handsome blond who'd called her Sleeping Beauty, moved off to let Ben perch at her hip.

"Where is here?"

"My town house, which is less than two blocks from Lady Dandridge's establishment. Archer, fetch the tea."

"I want to sit up."

She thought he'd argue with her, but instead he helped her into a sitting position and rearranged the afghans draped over her body. By the time she was decently covered and comfortable, Archer was backing through the door with an enormous tray in his hands.

"This is your cousin?" She watched Archer as he fussed with the tea tray.

"Lady Maggie Windham, may I make known to you my cousin, Archer Portmaine, Viscount Blessings—of all things. Archer, Lady Maggie."

"You stopped me from stepping out in front of that beer wagon." She recognized eyes of a cerulean blue, and the lean, almost ascetic cast of his features. "Were you following me?"

"I was, ah…" Archer looked from Benjamin, whose expression was severe indeed, to Maggie. "I was merely out for a stroll."

"He was following you, though without my permission. Tea, Maggie, or chocolate?"

"Chocolate, please. Why were you following me?"

Archer took a seat across from her in a cushioned chair while Benjamin remained at her side.

"Ben gave you his word not to set strangers to watching you, which suggested to me he'd taken leave of his senses. Since I care for him, and he cares for you, it seemed prudent to make a few decisions on my own. I'll be having tea if you're pouring, Cousin."

Maggie watched as Benjamin fixed Archer a cup of tea, adding cream and sugar. There was an odd intimacy to one man serving another tea, but it reassured her that Benjamin and his cousin did indeed care for each other—that they would respect one another's confidences.

She took a considering sip of her chocolate, feeling as if both men were politely giving her time to marshal her scattered wits. "I suppose I should be grateful you made those decisions, else I might be suffering more than just a chill and some light-headedness."

A look passed between the two men, such as Maggie's brothers might have shared when a naughty topic was to be discussed only after the ladies had left the room.

Or a delicate subject.

"You're safe and sound now," Archer declared with a bit too much cheer. "I daresay that's all that matters, isn't it, Ben?"

"No, Archer, that is not all that matters."

"Well, don't start interrogating the lady just yet. She hasn't even finished her chocolate."

"I like your cousin," Maggie said. "But you won't have to interrogate me."

"I won't?" Ben's expression—truculent when he glared at Archer—was simply concerned when he gazed at Maggie. "I mean, I wouldn't. I might gently inquire, but I wouldn't—Archer, shut up."

"Just drinking my tea." He lifted his cup in a small salute.

"You will not have to interrogate me. I am out of options, and the situation is quite dire, to use another's word."

Ben took her cup of chocolate from her hand, and Maggie felt a lump lodging in her throat.

She was going to do this—to reveal secrets she'd kept for most of her life—and she was going to trust Benjamin Portmaine to take those secrets with him to his grave. She turned to bury her face against his shoulder and spoke quickly, before she could swallow back the words that had been choking her for her entire adult life.

"I have a sister—a full sister."

⁂

Maggie's hand in Ben's was ice cold, and her complexion was so pale the freckles across her nose were clearly visible.

Ben was cataloguing other indicators of her situation when her words sunk in. "A *full* sister?" Across from them, Archer's casual tea sipping had been exchanged for a watchful stillness.

"Her name is Bridget, and she's just a few days shy of her fifteenth birthday." Maggie closed her eyes as if some pang gripped her from the inside.

"Does His Grace know?" Archer winced at Ben's question, but Maggie opened her eyes, her gaze holding a world of misery.

"I'm not sure. Cecily claims he doesn't—not yet."

"Cecily is your mother?"

She nodded then pressed her face to his shoulder. Archer passed Ben a handkerchief and quietly withdrew.

"She is my m-mother," Maggie whispered, "and the devil incarnate."

He had to bend close to hear her last words, but then she was clinging to him, great silent shudders wracking her, and all Ben could do was hold her and hold her and hold her.

While he stroked her hair and murmured useless platitudes, he had the sense Maggie Windham had been overdue for some crying, maybe years—maybe an entire lifetime—overdue.

Then, too, there was her situation to consider. "Your chocolate will get cold, my dear."

"H-hang my chocolate."

He cuddled her closer, pressing his cheek to her crown. "I take it you are concerned for this sister?"

"I am concerned. I'm worried sick." Maggie let go a huge sigh and relaxed into his embrace. "I am furious and entirely out of patience with the whole situation.

Cecily is dropping hints she means to launch Bridget as a courtesan and have her revenge on me, Their Graces, my family, and probably God Almighty."

"And how long has this Cecily been plaguing you?" Against his side, Maggie went still then huffed out another sigh, which suggested Ben's hunch had been accurate. "The truth, Maggie Windham."

"Since my come out. She figured I'd have my own pin money then, and she was right."

"She's been pestering you for *money*?"

Maggie nodded and brushed her cheek against Ben's chest. "Pots of it. Every year, without fail, and all along she led me to believe I was buying a proper education for my brothers, a decent finishing governess for my sister when the time comes, and above all, peace of mind for Their Graces and my other siblings. And now this."

He did interrogate her then, asked her all manner of questions about Cecily, their dealings over the years, the letters Bridget sent, and any memories Maggie had of her mother from years ago.

And all the while, he held her and rubbed her back and let her pour out a tale of misery and exploitation that made his fingers itch to take out his dueling pistols.

"And you're sure Their Graces know nothing of this?" he asked when he'd convinced her to eat something and the pot of chocolate was empty.

"I am not sure. I did not know how to approach my father and ask, oh, just in passing, just how many by-blows did he have lurking in the bushes besides me and Devlin? Or should I have asked Her Grace, since there's a very great difference between tolerating a young cavalry officer's premarital indiscretions and knowing, fifteen years later, he was still sporting about with loose women."

She fell silent while Ben stroked her hair and considered what he knew of Percival Windham. The man was an arrogant, overbearing ass on his worst days, an able politician with a keen eye for strategic compromise most days, and every day—best, worst, and in between—he was a devoted husband and doting father.

And Maggie Windham was every inch His Grace's daughter.

"Maggie love, you're going to sleep on me."

"I haven't been sleeping well."

"So you've said." More than once, in fact. "I'm having the coach brought around, and then I'm taking you home. You will go directly to bed and not awaken until you are thoroughly rested. You will eat a proper breakfast—do you hear me?—and then you will not go haring about in a cold rain without my escort."

She gave him an odd look, and then the corners of her mouth turned up in that dear, unexpected smile. "You sound exactly like His Grace."

"The man has five daughters. My sympathy for him grows by the day."

Her smile died a quick and miserable death. "Six daughters. I won't have him bothered, you know, by Cecily. And this mustn't reach Her Grace. They've weathered scandal and heartache both on account of their children."

"If His Grace is Bridget's father, then he will take responsibility for his actions."

"*I* took responsibility for his actions," Maggie

said, chin coming up. "She's my sister, and after all Their Graces have done for me, it's my duty to provide—"

He stopped this righteous little tirade by the simple expedient of kissing her.

"She's your sister, but she's *his* daughter— perhaps—and if you knew your father better, you'd understand that Bridget is her father's responsibility."

"I do understand him, and I understand that his primary motivation in this life is to treasure his duchess. By-blows bookending his legitimate offspring would cost Her Grace all of her consequence, and more to the point, it would *break her heart* to think her Percy had been untrue. I cannot have that on my conscience, Benjamin. Papa doesn't deserve to support his daughter if he was so selfish and stupid as to sneak about with the likes of Cecily."

"He doesn't deserve—?"

Ben did not account himself brilliant by any lights, but he was bright enough to comprehend that tangling with Maggie's female logic would curdle his wits. Nothing and no one relieved a man of the right and duty to support his offspring, much less a man with a title and means to do so. That Maggie had been raised in the ducal household was proof that His Grace understood this basic tenet of honor even if Maggie did not.

"Have another crème cake, my dear. I'm going to fetch the coach."

She looked like she wanted to argue further, but Ben's grasp of tactics was sufficient that he knew when to get up, leave the room to scare up a footman, and

stay away from Maggie long enough that she was
dozing on the sofa when he returned.

❧

"I haven't more than a few pounds saved," Adele said,
drawing the brush through Bridget's hair. "You're
welcome to them."

More French—they almost always spoke French
when they were alone these days. "Where would I go?"

Adele gave Bridget a despairing look, and Bridget
knew what wasn't being said. In two days, Bridget
would be fifteen, and her sole accomplishment in
life—besides an increasing command of French—was
that she was pretty. Alarmingly so.

When her body had started bulging and curving in
odd places, Bridget had consoled herself that she was
going to look like Maggie, who was beautiful indeed.

Except she wasn't quite as tall as Maggie, she hadn't
Maggie's gorgeous green eyes, and while Maggie's
height looked stately on her, on Bridget it still looked
gangly and ungainly.

And now this awkward, inconvenient beauty was
going to mean Mama could get money for allowing
strange men to do shocking, intimate things to
Bridget. From her reading, from the things Mama
muttered to the dregs of the dinner wine, from the
way the men leered in the park, Bridget had deduced
her looming fate.

She had also figured out her own mother had
gone willingly to the same fate when she was the age
Bridget now approached.

"You could go to Maggie."

"I've asked Maggie for help, and she hasn't replied." To say such a thing aloud made the anxiety gnawing at Bridget's insides coil more tightly.

"She'll help. I had your letter delivered directly to her hand. Maggie has always helped in the past."

"Maggie is *good*. She's no match for Mama." Maggie was generous. She slipped Bridget pin money on those rare occasions when they visited, and she sent along little gifts—the bottle of scent, an inlaid comb, pretty hair ribbons. Bridget liked the scent best, because it bore Maggie's own, comforting fragrance.

But in hurried whispers just a few months past, Maggie had explained that Cecily had legal and physical custody of her minor children, unlike a married woman whose children were in her husband's keeping. If Maggie were to take Bridget under her own roof, Cecily would be able to summon the authorities to snatch Bridget away from her sister's care.

And Cecily would do it, too, on the merest whim.

"Maggie loves you. She'll not stand by while your mother ruins your life." Adele spoke bravely, but Bridget looked at the painted, powdered, barely decent creature in her vanity mirror.

"If Maggie is going to do something, she'd better do it soon."

❦

Maggie decided the lassitude dogging her ever since she'd collapsed into Benjamin's arms on Lady Dandridge's stoop had to be relief at having confided her situation to someone who would keep her secrets—or sheer emotional exhaustion.

"I should be doing something," she muttered as Benjamin ran a warmer over her sheets. "I should be snatching Bridget away from Cecily's clutches and whisking my sister onto a packet bound for some foreign shore. I should at least be finding out where Cecily is biding these days. I should be notifying Tom and Ted, because they might know something—"

Benjamin put a finger to her lips. "*We* will manage all of that. *You* will go to bed."

Maggie stood by the bed and folded her arms across her middle. "How does *my* going to bed accomplish anything?"

"It lets *me* be about the business of gathering information without having to worry that *you're* out wandering around in a pouring rain, ruining your bonnet, your health, and *my* nerves. Get in bed."

He thrived on giving orders, did the Earl of Hazelton. What was harder to admit was that Maggie was almost glad he did.

"You are not to go climbing into any windows but mine, Benjamin." She spoke just as sternly as he had, lest he get ideas about who was fit to give orders to whom.

"I'm going to my club, if you must know. I'm going to bury my nose in a newspaper and listen for all the latest gossip while appearing to be the soul of indifference. I'm going to send notes to Bath and a few other places, and I am *not* going to book passage for anybody thinking to skulk off to foreign shores."

And amid all their other differences, that was the one Maggie was least willing to brace him on.

"We can deal with that when Bridget is safe from Cecily's schemes."

He loomed over her, his eyes dark, his expression implacable. "You are wearing *my* ring, Maggie Windham."

"I am wearing your ring because you were hen-witted enough to sneak it onto my night table when I was too overset to notice, and I did not want to lose it, and leaving expensive jewelry around where any maid might misplace—"

But now the handsome wretch was smiling down at her. "Hen-witted, Maggie? I kiss your cheek in parting, slip a ring onto your night table, and you say I'm the one who's rendered hen-witted?"

"It's one of Her Grace's words. When she uses it on the boys, they positively reel with abused dignity."

"Reel into bed, Maggie, and expect me to call on you quite early tomorrow."

It was a concession, that he'd let her know to expect him in the morning. It both relieved her worry that he might climb into her window that very night and assured her he wasn't going to call anybody out, or worse—drag His Grace into a mess Maggie had spent half her life trying to keep her father and his family free of.

She sank onto the bed, fatigue abruptly weighing on her in body, mind, and spirit.

"I'm scared, Benjamin." She hadn't meant to say that. Hadn't meant to say anything except "Good night." When he sat beside her, his presence—his patience with her—was a genuine comfort. He put an arm around her waist.

"You have been scared for some time, I think."

That was a hard, miserable truth, so Maggie didn't argue. "What does it make me, that I hate my own mother?"

"A mother worth the name would never court your hatred, much less exploit her own children for purely selfish ends."

He stayed there for a moment while Maggie tried to come up with a reply, but her mind would not put words together into sentences. That Benjamin was taking on this difficulty of hers justified her faith in him, even as it rendered any dreams of being his countess into so many ashes.

"Just sitting here in a corner, perusing the papers in all innocence, you have the ability to render an entire room of otherwise brave fellows nervous." Deene took the chair beside Ben's and lowered his lanky frame to the cushion. "One envies you this."

Ben put aside the paper, grateful that somebody had taken the bait after only twenty minutes of staring at the society pages. "Are you hiding from the debutantes, Deene, or studying my methods?"

"Perhaps both." Deene helped himself to a glass of wine and took a leisurely sip. "Haven't seen you out and about with Lady Maggie since your much-vaunted engagement."

"We've been too busy gazing longingly into each other's eyes, billing and cooing."

"Oh, quite." Deene took another sip of wine, giving Ben the impression the marquis had something specific on his mind. "When did you take to reading the society pages?"

"I'm marrying into a ducal family, and thus the society pages become relevant."

"You're keeping informed regarding the beau monde because that's what you do." The bantering note in Deene's voice vanished with this observation. "And because you do remain informed, and you are supposedly marrying a Windham, there's something you should know."

Down to business, and thank Christ it hadn't taken half the damned bottle. "I'm listening, Deene."

And while Ben listened, he made a convincing show of boredom—shooting his cuffs, examining the crease of his trousers, even taking out his watch and flipping it open.

"A rumor has reached me," Deene said very softly. "It's generally known my mistresses have all been red-haired, and so at first I didn't think much of it when somebody mentioned a new offering coming available, a young Venus with red hair and innocent airs."

Ben's insides went still as Deene set down his wine glass. "Coming available when?"

"There's to be a soiree two nights hence. The girl's proprietress is firing her off and has gone so far as to invite a dozen titled, single young fellows with plenty of blunt to come look over the goods."

"And why are you telling me this when I am soon to partake of wedded bliss?" He hoped.

"Because the girl is said to bear a close resemblance to Lady Maggie Windham. Make of that what you will, but the speculation is that Lady Maggie, like her sire before her, began her parenting ventures with a by-blow of her own."

"She has not." Ben's jaw clenched as he spoke, and he realized he'd balled up the paper in his hand.

"Thought not." Deene poured Ben another half glass of wine and did not even glance at the ruined newspaper. "I couldn't exactly approach old Moreland with this tale but felt somebody ought to pass it along."

"Because?"

"Because Moreland, bless his cussed, autocratic hide, takes the welfare of his womenfolk very seriously, and if somebody dishonored Lady Maggie when she was not even out of the schoolroom, then that somebody had best be deciding between pistols and swords, hadn't he?"

Deene's blue-eyed gaze settled on Ben for just a moment, the intensity therein taking Ben just a bit aback.

"Are you pining for my intended, Deene?"

"I am not. I served with her brothers; I stand up with her sisters. Moreland has been more than helpful sorting out my late father's tangled affairs. I consider myself a friend of the family and thus a friend to Maggie Windham's interests—and perhaps to yours, if a friend would be useful."

It wasn't at all what Ben had been expecting. "That's good to know."

Deene crossed his arms and slouched down into his chair. "And now I am going to doze in peace. Be a good fellow and have the waiter bring me a fresh bottle before you go."

Ben made a pretense of studying the paper for a few

more minutes, then got up and ordered Deene the best vintage the cellar had to offer.

෴

Benjamin Portmaine had a decent nature lurking beneath all his high-handedness, passionate kisses, and subtle maneuvers. It was the part of him that meant he carried half of Mayfair's dirty little secrets without ever breathing a word of what he knew.

It was the part of him Maggie found the most trustworthy, also the part of him that had allowed her a passably good night's sleep before he engaged her in an out-and-out donnybrook at breakfast.

"What do you propose, then?" He sat back in his chair and glared at her over buttered toast and Spanish oranges. "We simply whisk your sister off to Halifax, not a word to His Grace, no one the wiser?"

"I propose that *I* whisk her off to Rome, at least—my brother Valentine has connections there. I've sent a note around to Mr. Kettering to gather my ready coin to make sure we travel swiftly and in comfort."

He glanced at the ceiling; he glanced at the window. He stared at the rack of toast cooling near Maggie's plate. When he spoke, it was with lethal quiet. "And what is to stop Cecily from producing some other red-haired lovely and claiming that she is His Grace's daughter, as well?"

"Gracious God."

Maggie rose, this possibility making the half slice of toast she'd eaten abruptly threaten to reappear.

"She'd do it, Maggie. She'd do it with a smile. She'd blackmail Westhaven for a time, wait until the girl was old enough to take up whoring, then set about Their Graces' ruination with great good cheer."

Outside, in the gardens beyond the breakfast parlor's window, Millie was playing fetch with the hound, a pretty and happy picture of what life ought to be like.

"Maggie, we need to tell your parents what's afoot. For one thing, your father deserves to know if he has another daughter, and for another, you need their help."

He'd come up on her side, and she hadn't heard him leave the table. She shook her head. She did not need her family's help. She'd managed thus far without them, and that was how she'd carry on. She just didn't know quite yet how she was going to go about it. "Sending me running to Their Graces is not the sort of help I expected of you, Benjamin."

He heaved out a sigh of such proportions his shoulders lifted and dropped with it. "You should have gone running to Their Graces when Cecily first threatened you, and why you didn't remains a mystery to me."

His tone was honestly puzzled and a little weary.

"Were you up late listening at keyholes, Benjamin?"

"I was up late thinking. Will you walk with me in the garden?"

The same patience that had so comforted Maggie the previous evening was now a greater source of alarm than all his imperiousness or even the kisses intended to distract her. It suggested he was as determined on his course as she was on hers.

When they gained the garden, Millie bobbed her curtsy at them, but it was a pretty day, so Maggie bade her leave the dog outside.

Benjamin took Maggie's arm and steered her

toward the fountain, while the dog chased a butterfly in the opposite direction. "You like him, then?"

"He's a good fellow," she said, wondering what the dog had to do with anything. "He has sense and doesn't get excited over nothing, as a puppy is wont to do."

"Good." More silence, until Benjamin gestured for Maggie to take a seat on a shaded bench. He came down beside her, and Maggie resigned herself to waiting.

"I wrote to both of my sisters last night." He spoke quietly, while Maggie resisted the urge to peer at him. "I realized I owed them both apologies."

"Whatever made you realize that?"

"You. You made a decision when you were just a girl, and you've abided by that decision ever since. You've gone to great lengths to maintain your position, to appease Cecily without bothering anybody, but Maggie, it's time to reevaluate your options."

"What do you mean?"

"Years ago, just about the time you were making your come out, my sisters suffered terribly at the hands of men without honor. I was too young, too unwise, to know what to do about it. My sisters made me promise not to spread the stink of scandal by calling out their malefactor, and the bastard left hot foot for the Continent."

The very quiet of his voice told her this recitation was costing him. "Benjamin, I am so sorry. For you, for your sisters." She linked her fingers with his and squeezed, then made no move to withdraw her hand.

It felt good to touch him, to offer comfort to him for a change, no matter how small the gesture.

"I was sorry for them, too." He brought their joined hands to his lips and kissed Maggie's knuckles. "So sorry that when they said they needed privacy and peace, I left them alone at Blessings and went off to spend time polishing my Town bronze. When Alex declared she was going for a governess, I felt sorry enough for her not to make a fuss, though she's an earl's daughter, a lady in her own right, and entitled to so much more than drafty schoolrooms and other people's children."

Maggie was almost distracted by the pleasure of watching his mouth form words, but he was leading up to a point she sensed would not sit easily with her.

"For years I did as my sisters had requested: I left them more or less alone, I left them in peace, but, Maggie, *it solved nothing*. What might have been a decision made out of consideration for them became an unwillingness to admit I hadn't known what to do. I realized I acted to avoid my guilt at failing to protect them."

He fell silent while Maggie's heart tripped: *my guilt at failing to protect them...*

"That is low, Benjamin."

"It is honest. You deserve the truth from me, even if it scares the hell out of you to be truthful with your parents. They won't hold you accountable for Cecily's schemes, Maggie. You will not lose your family over this."

The dog came trotting up then took a seat at Maggie's feet, his head resting on her thigh. She smoothed her hand over his silky head and tried to breathe.

"They will hate me. If it wasn't for me, Cecily would have no hold over them."

"They love you. If it wasn't for them, Cecily would have no hold over you."

Benjamin had put his finger on an essential, miserable truth: It was very likely that instead of protecting her parents, Maggie's unwillingness to turn to them was in some fashion a way to protect *herself*.

Her pride, her ducal connections, her heart—which in some particulars remained that of a child, even in the body of a mature woman.

"There's something you should know, Maggie."

She nodded but didn't meet his gaze. The forbearance in his tone was burden enough.

"Your mother intends to consign Bridget to the protection of the highest bidder tomorrow night." If he had plunged a dagger into her heart, his words could not have wounded Maggie more deeply. "Cecily has assembled a dozen or so of the randiest, wealthiest bachelors and invited them to a gathering, the express purpose of which is to determine who among them will be Bridget's first protector."

Well, of course. And then, when Bridget was ruined beyond all repair, Cecily would reveal to His Grace what had befallen his youngest, most innocent, and most blameless daughter.

"Take me to His Grace, Benjamin." She scooted off the bench and wrapped her arms around the dog. "Before I lose my nerve, please send for the closed carriage and take me to Their Graces."

❧

A woman gone quiet with her troubles was enough to unnerve most men. Benjamin Portmaine was not just any man—he was the one fellow in the land who did not believe that the competent, independent, pragmatic appearance Maggie Windham showed the entire world was the sum total of the woman. He was the man who wanted not only to know Maggie's dreams but to make them come true.

"It will be all right." He offered words of comfort, the same words he'd offered her on another coach ride just a few short weeks in their past. Then, as now, she let herself lean into him, if only physically.

"You can't know that."

"I can. I wish you knew it, too."

He based his sanguine prognostication on what he knew of Percy Windham, what he suspected about Esther Windham, and what he simply hoped was true about Maggie Windham.

She was still wearing his ring, for example, and he did not for one moment believe she was simply preserving a piece of jewelry from an absentminded maid.

And despite Maggie's muttering about packet schedules and foreign shores, he would not entertain the idea of her departing with her sister, *and without him*. In any case, he did not believe such an outcome was consistent with Maggie's dreams.

He also did not believe Cecily was going to back down unless faced with a veritable ducal armada of opposition to her scheme—because arranging an accident for the woman wouldn't serve. She was Maggie's mother, and Maggie was capable of prodigious feats of guilt.

Maggie frowned out the coach window. "Westhaven must be calling. I don't recognize that other carriage."

"It's Deene's."

"You arranged for them to be here?"

He considered—for one instant—not lying, but prevaricating. "I did, both of them. If St. Just and Lord Valentine had been in Town, I would have summoned them as well. Sindal, too, since he's my half brother and married to your sister Sophie."

She closed her eyes and let out a sigh. "This is a private business, Benjamin. You had no right to go rousing the entire regiment. Their Graces will not thank you, and I do not thank you."

"You will, but before we go in there, I've a little more gossip to impart."

She opened her eyes, and Ben had never seen such a combination of despair and beauty. "What?"

"Some people are concluding that Bridget is your daughter. Deene suggested if that were the case, somebody ought to be calling the girl's father out."

She cocked her head. "*Lucas* said that?"

"To my face. And we need Westhaven's legal training, because no matter how much you trust Kettering, I'll not bring the lawyers into this situation unless you demand it."

She shuddered. "No lawyers."

"We are agreed on at least that much."

Before he climbed out of the coach, he paused to kiss his intended. "For courage, Maggie Windham, which you have in glorious abundance."

She searched his gaze, her eyes luminous with trepidation. "You have a plan."

"I have several, depending on what we learn from your parents. All that's required of you is that you trust me to see the best one implemented."

When she might have argued, he ducked out of the coach and handed her down. She emerged from her carriage with all the grace and dignity of a lady raised under the ducal roof, while Ben offered his arm and prepared to make good on promises he had no clear idea how he'd keep.

❧

"You say Hazelton summoned you here?" Percival, Duke of Moreland, perused first his heir and then the Marquis of Deene. "Both of you?"

"Yes, Your Grace," Deene answered. Westhaven merely nodded, and to his papa's expert eye, looked a trifle worried.

"For a man who has only recently acquired Maggie's consent to marriage, that's a bit high-handed. My love, do you know what this is about?"

When his duchess might have answered, the butler appeared at the drawing-room door. "Lady Maggie and Lord Hazelton, Your Graces, my lords."

While Her Grace handled the introductions and discreetly signaled for tea, His Grace regarded his oldest daughter and the way Ben Portmaine hovered around the girl, clucking and fussing like a mother hen—or a particularly smitten rooster. His Grace passed on tea—never could abide the stuff unless crème cakes were in evidence, as well—and waited for Hazelton to get down to business.

Though a man could wait only so long.

"Hazelton, if you're here to inform us that we're to be grandparents ere a few months are gone, I hardly see what Deene's presence adds to the gathering."

That earned him a slight frown from his duchess, but he'd weathered many of her frowns—most in good cause.

"Deene has information that will be relevant to the discussion, Your Grace." Hazelton's tone was just deferential enough for politesse. "I believe Lady Maggie can trust Lord Deene's discretion."

"She can." That from Deene where the handsome dog lounged against the mantel. "The Windham family can trust my discretion, and that should be beyond doubt."

Oh, it was. Deene had been the one to convey the sorry circumstances of Bartholomew's passing in a Portuguese tavern, the details of which had never once become the subject of gossip.

"Stand down, Deene. I'm too old even to serve as a second anymore."

Another frown from Her Grace, this one more pronounced.

"Your Graces," Maggie spoke very quietly, "I have some things to tell you, and I'm not sure how to start."

"Best state it plain, my girl. Her Grace and I are made of stern stuff, and whatever it is, we'll sort it out." But for all his bluff tone, His Grace felt a frisson of tension in his chest. Maggie had never given them one spot of trouble—not one—and yet, Her Grace's expression had become a deceptively polite mask.

Maggie's gaze went to Hazelton's, and something seemed to pass between them.

"I don't know quite how else to tell you, but my mother—Cecily—claims I have a sister." Maggie was watching Her Grace now. "A full sister."

"Oh, for the love of God." Her Grace rose from

before the tea service and began to pace. "When did she reveal this supposed sister to you?"

Maggie watched the duchess cross to the window. "I've known since shortly after Bridget was born. She'll be fifteen years old tomorrow."

Between trying to do the math, keeping an eye on his daughter, and watching his wife's usually serene countenance fill with ire, His Grace—for one of the few times in his life—did not know what to say.

"My love, perhaps you'd like a moment—"

Hazelton interrupted. "If Your Graces would let Lady Maggie finish, please."

Maggie looked grateful for this intervention, so His Grace held his tongue and sent his wife a visual plea for patience. Her Grace went one better, crossed the room, and slipped her hand into his.

"Bridget is very pretty," Maggie said, "and her mother intends to launch her on a career of… vice, and I don't know how to stop her. I'm sorry… I'm just so sorry. I didn't want to bring this to you, but Cecily is shrewd and she knows the law and I just…"

Hazelton tucked an arm around Maggie, and the room went silent. Westhaven was trying to look anywhere but at his parents, Deene was frowning, and His Grace could feel the duchess holding back a boiling vat of indignation.

"Esther." His Grace spoke very quietly, and he most assuredly did not wheedle. "It isn't what you think."

"More to the point," said Her Grace through clenched teeth, "it isn't what Maggie thinks."

He turned to peer at his wife, but his duchess had aimed a green-eyed glare on dear Maggie.

"Maggie Windham, you are exceptionally bright, probably brighter than all your brothers put together. When was the Peace of Amiens?"

Maggie turned a puzzled gaze on Her Grace. "For the most part, the summer and fall of 1802."

"And when was this Bridget born?"

"Spring of…" Maggie's brows knit in a ferocious scowl. "1803. But you and Papa went to Paris during the Peace, along with the rest of Polite Society. You were gone for months."

"This girl, this Bridget, she is very likely your sister—your half sister," said Her Grace in a terribly stern voice. "His Grace is not her father."

Maggie's brows drew down. "Cecily will claim she followed Papa to France. It's possible she did follow him."

"The woman speaks not a word of French," His Grace retorted. "And I assure you, I can produce all manner of witnesses who will report she remained in London. One hears things in the clubs, and that creature cannot bear to stir far from her preferred hunting grounds."

Maggie's gaze swiveled from the duchess to His Grace, her expression uncertain. "You're sure, Papa? Sure of these witnesses?"

She wasn't asking about the witnesses, not just the witnesses. It broke a father's heart to see the doubt in her eyes, but it warmed his soul to see the hope.

"Daughter, I am certain."

The doubt ebbed, replaced by profound, visible relief. His Grace let out a breath he'd been holding for quite some time. "I gather you are concerned for the girl nonetheless, which does you credit, Maggie."

"And with the child in the hands of that viper," Her Grace spat, "Maggie should be concerned. I cannot believe the woman had the temerity to approach you."

Hazelton got to his feet just when His Grace would have served up a soothing platitude.

"At the risk of differing with my future mother-in-law, I believe Your Grace well knows the temerity Cecily is capable of."

Before His Grace's eyes, his lovely duchess transformed from a woman seized with indignation to a lady with haunted green eyes.

"Lord Hazelton." Her Grace drew herself up to her considerable height. "You will choose your words carefully in this house."

Hazelton glanced down at Maggie, whose hand he held before her own parents. Then he looked up and speared his future mother-in-law with a look of ominous compassion. "I'm sorry, Your Grace, but how long has Cecily been blackmailing you?"

❧

Oh, the hurt in Percy's beautiful blue eyes, the confusion. Esther dreaded to see it.

"It isn't blackmail, exactly." As she spoke, Esther saw Westhaven watching her from across the room, or perhaps watching both his parents, his expression unreadable.

And Maggie... dear, precious Maggie appeared torn between relief and consternation, while Deene looked bored and Hazelton looked worried for his fiancée.

"Duchess," said His Grace. "You owe no explanations. None."

How she loved Percy Windham. His gaze held steadfast understanding, and perhaps some worry—for her—but no reproach, not a hint of reproach.

"I think perhaps I've been silent too long," Esther said. "And if I don't owe explanations, I certainly owe apologies."

"Not to me—" began His Grace stoutly, but Esther quieted him with a look.

"Yes, to you, and to Maggie, at least. Cecily approached me very soon after Maggie came to live with us."

"But we paid the blasted woman off! We adopted Maggie, and that should have been an end to it."

"Should have been," Esther said. "Shall we sit?"

"Of course, my dear." He seated her then glared at their son. "Westhaven, stop lurking at the window like the family duenna. Deene, fetch a man a drink, and you, Hazelton, pour Maggie a spot of tea before the girl faints into your waiting arms."

While the younger men complied with the duke's orders—issued to give her time to compose herself, Esther was sure—Her Grace arranged her skirts and tried to find a way to explain a poor decision turned disastrous.

"Cecily crossed her path with mine a few weeks after the adoption was final and seemed genuinely interested in Maggie's welfare. In the course of the conversation, she also conveyed that she'd like to see Maggie herself, to spend time with her daughter."

Esther made herself meet Maggie's gaze, hoping to find at least tolerance there. Forgiveness might come someday—Maggie was that good-hearted—but for now, the truth was the least she owed her adopted daughter. "I did not trust Cecily's intent, and it soon became clear if I wanted her to keep her distance from me and my family, then I'd have to make it worth Cecily's while."

"My God…" His Grace, perched on the arm of her chair, scowled mightily. "This is why you lost all that jewelry, isn't it?"

Westhaven addressed himself to the tea service. "And why my mother, who is as intelligent as a woman can be, had such trouble keeping track of her pin money."

"You're both right, and I do apologize, but I considered Cecily to be my responsibility. I became Maggie's mother when we adopted her, and that gave me the right to protect her."

"Oh, my love…" His Grace raised her fingers to his lips and kissed her knuckles. "My dear, I wish you'd told me. I want to throttle the damned woman or perhaps throttle myself for not managing her more astutely."

"Papa, what could you have done?" Maggie spoke up, and her defense left Esther pleased and surprised. "Cecily is even now claiming Bridget is yours. Any dealings you had with Cecily would have only given her more ammunition to use against you, and if she thought Her Grace could produce impressive sums of money, only think how deeply she might have stuck her fingers into a duke's pockets."

"Those are valid points." His Grace patted Esther's hand, his expression troubled. "But I rather think we must inquire now of you, daughter, regarding the dealings you've had with this—I blush to descend to cliché—scheming Jezebel, and your reasons for doing so."

"You don't have to answer us, Maggie," Esther said, knowing full well she'd come very close to contradicting her beloved spouse before others. "Tending to Bridget's situation is of greater import than rehashing old news."

Maggie's hand remained in Hazelton's, and Esther saw the earl squeeze Maggie's fingers, and yet the man remained silent.

"I need to explain," Maggie said, "because Bridget's situation is entangled with my own. Cecily has been demanding money from me since my come out, and I've produced it." She named a figure that had His Grace swearing softly under his breath and Westhaven's jaw clenching. Deene—clever lad—topped off His Grace's drink and passed the decanter to Westhaven, while Maggie's knuckles were white where she clasped Hazelton's hand.

"Go on," said Her Grace. "What was all that money in aid of?"

"It was in aid of my brothers' education—I have twin half brothers younger than me—and Bridget's comfort. Cecily is forever moving, I suspect to avoid her duns. Her quarters must be beautifully finished and her dresses in the latest fashion. Occasionally she would allow me to spend time with Bridget, and she let us correspond. I assumed Bridget would eventually come live with me. I just never quite figured out how I was going to bring that about."

His Grace stared at his drink. "This is quite a coil, but Hazelton, you're the one who convened this assemblage, I assume you have some ideas as to how to foil Cecily's schemes? Throttling is too good for such a... creature."

Esther hurt for him, hurt for his inability to show disappointment in his duchess, and hurt for the paternal heartache he'd just been dealt—and by the daughter about whom they tried the hardest not to worry.

"Benjamin has plans," Maggie said, rising, "but I need some air. Your Grace, will you walk with me?"

Esther was on her feet in an instant. "Of course. Percy, my love, no shouting. A cool head is what's called for now."

She kissed his cheek, murmured a heartfelt apology, then left the room with all the tattered dignity of a mother expecting a royal set down from her adult daughter.

❧

"How did you do it?" Maggie linked her arm through Her Grace's as they passed along a walk lined with bright red tulips. The temptation to walk too quickly, to run forever and forever, galloped around in Maggie's brain despite her mild tone.

"How did I pay Cecily?"

"No, how did you deceive Papa? How could you stand to do it?"

The duchess frowned. "Is this really what you brought me out here to ask, Maggie? I expect you want to ring a peal over my head, to put it politely."

"Why would I want to do that?"

They walked along, arm in arm, a picture of serene feminine repose, but inside Maggie's chest, her heart would not stop pounding.

"I had to find a way to protect you both," Her Grace said. "I know you think I kept you from your mother, the woman who carried you and cared for you as an infant, but in my bones—in my heart—I knew if I let her see you, let her have you for an afternoon, then *I* might never see you again. Even if she didn't keep you in the physical sense, she would… contaminate you. With self-doubt, with confusion, or something worse. I don't expect you to agree with me, but please believe that I'm being honest."

This woman strolling along beside Maggie looked like the Duchess of Moreland. She had the same green eyes, the same patrician beauty, the same faultless bearing, but she was more human than the duchess had ever been, and she radiated a particularly dignified and believable form of sadness.

"I don't disagree with you," Maggie said slowly. "Cecily has no honor."

Her Grace passed an unreadable glance over Maggie's features. "Your dear papa, whom I love more than life itself, would say women are exempt from the demands of honor. Between you and me, Maggie, I beg leave to disagree with him. You were right when you said I could not turn this matter over to him."

"Did you think Cecily would entangle herself with him again?"

The question would have been unthinkable only an hour before.

"Not in the sense you mean." Her Grace bent to sniff at a late daffodil. "But you put it accurately: Any dealings he had with her, she would have somehow perverted for her own ends. Your father is not always subtle."

He was *never* subtle. "He would have dealt with her directly, you mean?"

"Very likely, and she would have arranged to be discovered in his arms or with her hands in inappropriate places on the ducal person the very same week you were making your come out."

Maggie walked along beside the duchess, feeling as if her very world was spinning off its axis. "You were trying to protect me from her, and all along I thought I was the one protecting you and His Grace." And still, Maggie's heart was thudding dully in her chest, some nameless tension coiling tighter and tighter. "I don't know what to think, but I do know Cecily cannot be allowed to send my sister, my *half* sister, into a life of debauchery, and yet, she cannot be given the means to further abuse this family, either."

"Maggie." Her Grace blinked at the lone daffodil. "Would it not be enough if Cecily were prohibited from ever again abusing *you*?"

"I have plenty of money," Maggie said, something she'd never admitted to either of Their Graces. "Pots of it, in fact. Taking my money was not abusing me."

"My dear girl." Her Grace shifted her gaze to meet Maggie's, and Maggie was horrified to see tears in the duchess's eyes. "It makes sense to me now: You would not entertain any offers because Cecily's blackmail would follow you into marriage. You do not socialize as befits your station because the threat of that woman using any associations against you haunts all you do. You even left your father's house, the better to deal with her scheming. I see this, Maggie, and I see that you could not trust me or your father to protect you from it, and, my dear, I am so very exceedingly sorry."

The ache in Maggie's chest was threatening to choke her, and still Her Grace was not finished. "You must allow your earl to deal with Cecily, Maggie. He needs to, and he was right to bring this to His Grace. Men such as ours need to protect the women they love, and we need to allow them this."

"But Cecily cannot be trusted," Maggie said, swallowing hard against the lump in her throat. "They don't know her as we do, and they won't be alert to her underhanded ways."

"Your mother has met her match in Hazelton," Her Grace said, and she sounded very, very certain. "He will outwit her; see if he doesn't."

Maggie closed her eyes and barely managed a whisper. "She gave birth to me, but she is not my mother. *That awful, scheming, selfish, unnatural woman is not my mother.*"

Maggie stood there amid the crimson tulips, tears coursing down her face, until she felt strong, slender arms encircle her and a graceful hand stroke over her hair.

"Of course not, my dear," the duchess said, her tone fierce and proud. "*I* am your mother, His Grace is your papa, and you are *our* daughter."

Ten

Ben stood at the parlor window, glancing neither to the right nor to the left of him lest he see three grown men looking as worried as he felt.

Westhaven found the courage to speak first. "Either we've all developed a fascination with red tulips, or somebody had better go out there and fetch the ladies in. They've neither of them likely thought to bring a handkerchief."

Deene screwed up his mouth. "Declarations of love—that's what red tulips stand for."

His Grace cracked a small smile. "You young fellows. Quaking in your boots over a few female sentimentalities. Believe I'll go make some declarations of my own."

He set down his empty glass and left the room.

"Marriage," said Westhaven, "calls for a particular variety of courage. I'm thinking His Grace's experience in the cavalry is likely serving him well right now."

"Come away." Ben took each man by the arm, but neither of them moved. "Let him make his charge in private. I have some ideas for you both to consider, and if you're with me, His Grace will fall in line that much more easily."

Westhaven smiled, looking very like his father. "Don't bet on it. Windhams can be contrary for the sheer hell of it."

This was a joke or a warning. Ben wasn't sure which. "The Portmaine family motto is 'We thrive on impossible challenges.'"

Deene arched a blond eyebrow. "You just manufactured that for present purposes. You're from the North, and your family motto is probably something like 'Thank God for friendly sheep.'"

Which almost had Ben smiling, despite the impossible circumstances. "Westhaven, can you procure something more substantial than tea cakes? Maggie needs to keep up her strength; and Deene, if you want to call me out when you hear my proposition, please recall it's the honor of a lady—or several ladies—we're attempting to uphold."

Deene's lips quirked. "This grows intriguing. Shall we sit?"

Westhaven sent one more glance out the window to where His Grace was strolling amid the tulips, hand in hand with his duchess, one arm around his daughter's shoulders. Maggie looked sweet and shy and about eleven years old.

"Come away." Deene hooked Ben's arm with his own. "You can ogle her to your heart's content for your entire remaining life, but there's the small matter of a damsel in distress to impress her with first."

Westhaven appropriated Ben's other arm, and they led him to the sofa, each taking a chair opposite.

"Now," said Westhaven. "What are we dealing with?"

◦◦◦

To Maggie, the day had grown luminously beautiful.
The ducal gardens, scene of some of her happiest
childhood memories, were an appropriate setting for
the enormous relief singing through her veins.

"You were ever a curious child," His Grace was
saying. "Drove your brothers nigh to distraction with
it and goaded them to excel in their studies. Your
mother was the one who pointed this out to me."

Her mother. Hand-in-hand with His Grace, the
duchess was looking radiantly lovely despite having
dried her tears—and Maggie's—just moments before.

"They goaded me," Maggie said. "I could not have
a pack of boys shorter than me strutting about reciting
Latin all wrong."

"Of course not." His Grace kissed her temple, a
gesture Maggie could not recall him offering to her
since she'd been a little girl. "You are a Windham.
If Westhaven becomes half the duke his mama
expects him to be, it will be in large part because
his sisters trained him up for it." He turned to his
wife but kept his arm around Maggie. "My love,
your gardens grow more beautiful each year, but do
you suppose we should allow those young fellows to
hatch up their plots without some supervision from
their elders?"

Her Grace peeked over at Maggie. "Your father
is concerned for his share of the crème cakes, never
doubt it. But let's go in. Maggie's earl will worry if we
keep her out here too long."

Her parents brought her back to the house at a
leisurely pace, while Maggie reflected that it wasn't

just relief filling her soul, making the world a lovely, safe place for the first time in ages. Relief was there, oceans of it, along with some regret, some worry for her half sister—she could know that now, know that Bridget was not a Windham—and not a little sorrow for years wasted in loneliness.

But what filled her heart, crowding in on the joy, the gratitude, and the relief, was recognition of a love from Their Graces so vast, so magnanimous, it filled up her entire being and illuminated her entire soul.

∾

"Deene is ideally situated to manage this." Ben sat back and did not glance at Maggie. She was seated beside him, her hand locked in his, and while he could feel tension in her, he could also feel her trust.

"I suppose I am." Deene sounded aristocratically diffident, though Ben detected a gleam in the man's blue eyes. "I have an acknowledged fondness for red-haired ladies, begging the pardon of present company for such an admission. I am unwed, newly titled, and known to be self-indulgent in certain regards."

"In most regards," Westhaven corrected him. "Which will serve nicely. When is this gathering to be held?"

"Tomorrow night." Ben said. "What we don't know is where, because Deene was not given an invitation."

His Grace shot a glance at Her Grace. "I have an idea, not regarding the location of this disgraceful event but regarding bait that might simplify its conclusion."

"Bait?" Ben liked the sound of that—Moreland was known for the devious turn of his mind, though in a duke this was more euphemistically described as "wiliness."

"Percival, are you sure?" Her Grace apparently enjoyed the ability to deduce her husband's thoughts, which spoke volumes about the wiliness of a certain duchess.

"I'm quite certain, my love. Give me a moment." His Grace left the room, only to return a moment later sporting several elaborately carved boxes, each about a foot square and several inches high. "The Moreland jewels." He opened the top box to reveal an emerald and gold parure—tiara, necklace, earbobs, bracelets, and rings—sparkling on a bed of dark brown velvet. "Or the appearance of the Moreland jewels."

Maggie peered into the box. "Are they real?"

Ben eyed the gems, his respect for the duke growing as he did. "My guess is they are not. When Her Grace showed a penchant for losing jewelry, His Grace had this set very discreetly made for her to wear in public. It's paste, the lot of it."

Westhaven took the box from his father's hands. "It's a very good imitation."

"And"—His Grace wiggled white eyebrows—"we've plenty of it. Enough to dazzle one greedy woman right into giving up the innocent girl she seeks to ruin."

"I still have some questions about the document," Deene said. "Westhaven, are you certain it will be binding?"

"Absolutely certain. A woman's illegitimate children are entirely in her custody, and their father has no legal obligation to support them or any claim upon them. Cecily's signature will be binding, but we're best advised to see it properly witnessed, which means adult males, sane and sober and willing to testify that they saw her sign it of her own free will. And if I'm to have this thing ready in several copies by tomorrow evening, I'd best be on my way."

"I'll take my leave, as well." Deene rose, bowing to the ladies. "I'll spend the evening trying to determine the location of the party I'm supposed to join without benefit of an invitation, and bruiting about my salacious interest in the young lady."

Which would be no challenge for a man of Deene's reputation. Ben didn't make this observation aloud, but a hint of a smile in Maggie's eyes suggested she could deduce what he was thinking.

"Then I'll take Lady Maggie home," Ben said. "I've some inquiries of my own to make."

When he got his fiancée settled into her coach, Ben tucked an arm around her, and she snuggled docilely against his side.

"You're suspiciously quiet, Maggie Windham."

She remained so until the horses had moved from the walk to the trot. "I'm trying to find the flaw in your plan."

"I'll tell you the flaw." He laced their fingers, threw caution to the wind, and decided to be completely honest. "The flaw in the plan is that we're having to rely on others to execute it. Had your mother not seen us driving in the park, I could pose as one of those randy beggars considering your half sister's charms, but as it is, Cecily would find it too much of a coincidence—not to mention the outside of too much—for your devoted fiancé to be procuring your half sibling."

"Yes." Maggie kissed his cheek, a surprisingly

comforting gesture. "*We* are having to rely on others. This must be bothering you as much as it bothers me."

"Maybe it's good for us. Their Graces and Westhaven seemed to think Deene could be trusted."

"He can. I don't think he's the flaw in your plan."

He kissed her temple, which also imparted some comfort. "When you've concluded where I've gone wrong, you'll please inform me?"

"Maybe I'm just worried."

"Your mother is a formidable opponent. Did you know His Grace suspected the duchess was doing something sly with her everyday jewelry?"

"Supporting one of Sophie's charities, perhaps?"

"Possibly. Cecily had tried approaching His Grace, and he'd threatened her with jail. When she slunk away, it didn't occur to him she'd approach his womenfolk."

Maggie sighed and cuddled closer. "Papa will torment himself over this."

"He's likely been tormenting himself since the day he succumbed to your mother's charms."

"He said not." She sounded sleepy, which was probably to be expected, given her situation. "Papa said the blessing that resulted from his misstep was far greater than any passing burden it might have caused, and he assured me Her Grace felt the same way."

It humbled him to be allowed this glimpse into the man and woman behind the ducal titles—the family. It made a quiet little earldom in the North seem trifling in comparison, not much of a challenge at all, provided he chose the right countess.

"Are you content, Maggie, that we'll foil your mother's schemes and rescue Bridget?"

She stirred a little against him, her weight and warmth feeling so exquisitely *right*, Ben almost signaled the driver to slow the horses.

"I am not content, but I am hopeful—for the first time in years, Benjamin, I am hopeful. Though she gave birth to me, Cecily is *not* my mother, and I'm not sure she ever deserved to be called such, regardless of any relationship she once had to me."

He smiled against her hair, kissed her temple, and held her close. This, then, was what accounted for Maggie's sense of peace, her ability to trust and her ability to finally, and at long last, *hope*. God willing, it would also contribute to her ability to thrive as his countess and as the mother of their children.

⤜⤚

A shift in the air had Ben looking up from his desk to see Archer standing in the door to the sitting room. Ben set his list aside and posed the obvious question: "I take it your lady did not accept your suit?"

"How can you tell?" Archer slouched into the room and threw himself onto the sofa.

"Your posture, the lack of a gleeful gleam in your eye, the fact that your cravat has the exact same creases and seams it sported when you left here at sunset. Was she at least kind about it?"

Though Ben hardly had time for Archer's petty dramas. He'd still not determined exactly where Cecily was holding her soiree, and dawn would soon be upon them.

"I never had the chance to plight the lady my troth. The house is empty; the horses are gone; the place actually echoes. She left me a letter, but I haven't read it yet. I didn't want to be seen crying in public."

"Feel free to cry here—I can use the entertainment. I don't suppose you crossed paths with Deene tonight?"

"I saw him at some hell or other. How the man looks so impeccably noble when he's sporting a doxy on each knee and rouge on his linen defies reason."

Ben tossed his pen down and considered his cousin. "You were so despondent over your lady's departure that you took yourself to a series of gaming hells, likely a cockfight or two, and perhaps an opium den for good measure?"

"Libation is in order when a man's heart is broken."

He sounded as dejected as a university boy upon finding that his favorite barmaid was not exclusively devoted to him and the magic wonder behind the falls of his breeches.

"Archer, why not read the damned letter? The household might simply have gone off to Bath—God knows everybody else I need to talk to has."

This penetrated the dejection Archer was so enthusiastically wallowing in. "Still no word from Lady Maggie's footmen?"

"It's too soon, and in some ways too late. We still don't know where Cecily plans to hold this debacle. The person who whispered about it in Deene's ear has taken off for a curricle race to Brighton, and no one is saying who got the invitations."

"It ought to be fairly easy to make a list of the likely candidates." Archer sat up and eyed the bellpull.

"I've already made a list, and Deene is doing what he can to track down the most likely possibilities.

Take a look." Ben got up and passed over a sheet of foolscap. "Your ear has been to the ground more than my own lately."

Archer studied the list. "Ring for some tea, would you?"

"It's five in the bloody morning, Archer."

Ben's cousin glanced up, dejection nowhere in evidence. "Cook has long since been up to start the bread and churn the butter. Domestics thrive on being useful, so ring the damned bellpull. You've left out a couple of the obvious choices here, and I saw at least two of these scapegraces in the past few hours."

He crossed to the desk, appropriated Ben's chair, and set out a pen, inkwell, and clean sheet of paper.

Ben rang the bellpull.

❧

"I can't drink that." Bridget pushed the tray away gently, even the scent of her morning chocolate disagreeing with her. "I'm sorry, Adele, but my nerves are honestly overset. Mama says I'm to be given my birthday present tonight."

Adele's eyes held all manner of banked emotion. "You comprehend her intentions?"

Bridget nodded and drew her dressing gown more snugly around her. "The caterers are already making a racket in the kitchen. Mama came by last night to see if my rooms were adequate, and she told me—"

Bridget fell silent, wondering how she'd ever been such a fool as to believe her mother loved her.

"She told you to let the man—whoever he is—do whatever he pleases with you, and it won't be so very

painful. She told you to act as if you enjoy it, and he'll
shower you with jewels. She told you to toss your life
away so she might have security in her old age because
she's been too greedy to plan for it adequately herself."

Adele did not speak in French, but no matter. Some
truths would be ugly and scary in any language. "Is it
so awful, Adele?"

The maid set the tray aside and studied Bridget
where she sat on the bed. "It can be wonderful, and all
that talk about the first time being painful is for Gothic
novels. The first time is usually more disappointing
than anything else. Very disappointing and undignified. I laughed—which I do not advise you to do, if
you can help it. Perhaps you'll find a man who takes
care with you because he knows it's your first time."

This little speech did not reassure in the least.
Perhaps the man would take no care with her at
all, because sobriety and spoiled young men were
only nodding acquaintances. Perhaps he'd hurt and
humiliate her and make her do all manner of unnatural
and perverted things for his pleasure, things described
in those awful books Bridget had been given to read.

"Maybe Maggie is ashamed of me." Bridget hated
the uncertainty in her voice. "Maybe she knows what
Cecily is up to and thinks it's what I want."

"I made sure the letter you wrote was delivered by a
very reliable messenger, one who assured me it would be
put into Maggie's own hand. You must not lose hope."

Bridget's gaze went to the dress hanging on her
wardrobe. It was white velvet edged with pink
lace—a horrible combination given Bridget's pale
complexion—and the colors were the only innocent

things about it. "Maybe I'll run off. You said you'd give me a few pounds."

Adele heaved a sigh and started laying out clothes for daytime wear, but even those had become scandalously low cut in recent weeks. "You will not run off. Your mama would find you and snatch you back, and what's awaiting an innocent girl on the streets of London makes the attentions of one wealthy protector seem entirely bearable. You don't believe me, but I know of what I speak."

Bridget did not give in to the urge to cry. She got off the bed, poured herself a cup of chocolate, and then tossed the chocolate directly onto the bodice of the indecent white dress.

❧

"What if Cecily wants to read the entire document?" Archer was down to his shirtsleeves and waistcoat, his cuffs rolled back, and his blond hair slightly disheveled. Ben suspected, by comparison, his own appearance was disgraceful.

"Deene will have to prevent that, else the old harridan will see that she's transferring guardianship of the girl."

Archer frowned and crossed his arms where he once again lounged at Ben's desk. "Is that what you want?"

"It's what Maggie wants, though she didn't say as much."

"Hadn't you better be calling upon your intended?" Archer covered a yawn with one hand.

Ben glanced at the clock and winced. "I don't want to go to her empty-handed. We still don't have an address, and the morning's half-gone." And Deene hadn't had any better luck, nor had the various spies and informants Ben had sent out throughout the night.

Archer stood and folded his evening coat over his arm. "I'm for bed, and I suggest you send a note around to Lady Maggie, telling her to expect you after you've gotten some sleep, shaved, and bathed." He shook out his wrinkled coat and frowned.

"Your letter of emancipation," Ben said, hearing the sound of paper rustling in a pocket of Archer's coat. "You never did read it."

"Here." Archer extracted a folded missive from the depth of the coat. "You read it."

This was more schoolboy dramatics, but Ben was too tired and too frustrated to tease his cousin. He accepted the letter, drew it under his nose, then unfolded it.

Fatigue was making his brain foggy, because he'd swear the exact scent of the letter was familiar to him.

"It's in French."

"It's a love letter; of course it's in French." Archer turned to face the window. "It's only one page, though. A woman needs more than one page to make love to a man. A paragraph will do for his congé."

Ben rolled his eyes and translated as he read. "My dearest friend, I am desolated to disappoint you, but if you're reading this, then the household has moved to our next address, not two blocks over. I will leave my window open of a night and hope your ardor is sufficient to find me again soon. Yours, etc… and the postscript says something about longing for the thrust of your fierce—"

"Bugger off, Benjamin. Does she give an address?"

Ben made a pretense of sniffing the letter again just for the pleasure of aggravating a man besotted, but Archer snatched the paper from his hand.

"I know where this is," Archer said. "Laugh all you want, but she hasn't thrown me over after all. Gloat if you will, envy me the dimensions of my fierce blade, cackle with glee, but never—" He fell silent and stared at Ben. "You have that look on your face, the one you get when you're cracking a case without any evidence obvious to the mortal eye."

"Give me that letter."

Archer passed it over, and Ben held it again under his nose. "For whom did you say Della works now?"

"I'm not sure I have said, but she's an awful old harridan. Della refers to her as Madam, but I think the name is Irish. O'Doule, or O'Dea. I suppose back in the day—I say, Benjamin!"

Benjamin kissed him on the forehead out of sheer gratitude and passed him back the letter. "That letter bears the exact scent of the letter sent from Bridget to Maggie, and Maggie has told me the girl's maid, one Adele, is fluent in French. Send word to Deene and Their Graces. We have the location, and when you again impale the fair Adele on your fierce blade, be sure and tell her she could be the mother of the next Earl of Hazelton. She might consider your suit despite the dimensions of your blade."

"But—?" Archer stared at the letter. "This is the address, isn't it? You sniffed it out. The harridan is Lady Maggie's mother."

"She might have been once," Ben said, yanking on the bellpull. "No longer. Get some rest, Archer, you're going with Deene tonight, and I'm off to see my intended."

❦

"Would you like more tea, Miss Maggie?" Mrs. Danforth encroached two steps into Maggie's office then stopped and frowned at the tidy stacks of correspondence on Maggie's desk.

"No, thank you."

The housekeeper looked like she might be working up to a lecture, so Maggie returned to perusing a column of figures. Tea and scones for breakfast had not sat at all well, which Maggie took as a sign of how nervous she was, how scared for Bridget. The column of figures continued to make no sense whatsoever, when Maggie heard voices in the hallway—Mrs. Danforth and... *Benjamin*.

And then he was there, crossing the little room in two strides, wrapping his arms around Maggie where she stood shakily on her feet.

"You got my note?"

She nodded against his shoulder, reveling in the solid warmth and strength of him.

"I'm sorry it took me so long to get here, but I hadn't changed and Archer needed to locate Deene, and I had notes to send..."

She kissed him, lest he start reporting how long it had taken to heat up his water for shaving. The scent of him was marvelous, all spice and soap, and he gave off an electric energy that caused Maggie's nervousness to coalesce into something much closer to determination.

"I've thought of the flaw in your plan."

At her words, he drew back, expression hooded. "We have the location, my dear. Deene will be accompanied by Archer, who will make sure to witness Cecily's signature, and the jewels have already been secreted in Deene's coach. We also have an ally inside the household, for it seems Archer has been wooing none other than Bridget's personal maid."

"Then tell Deene to speak French to Bridget, for Cecily has no French, though the maid understands it well. But this will not fix the flaw in the plan."

He dropped his arms, went to the door, and bellowed for a damned tray, then took Maggie by the hand and led her to a little settee under the windows. "What is this flaw? From what I can see, unless Cecily reads the documents very carefully first—which Deene will be too arrogant to permit—Bridget should soon be safely free of Cecily's clutches."

"Oh, dear. Such a lot that might go wrong."

"You're not to worry." He glowered at her as he issued this command, though his grip on her hand remained warm and gentle. "You are to leave the worrying to me, and you are to eat something. Mrs. Danforth reports that you are neglecting your tucker, and this is no time to turn up missish."

"Mrs. Danforth had best recall who pays her wages."

The dog rose from his bed and put his head on Maggie's knee.

"You're alarming that good beast," Benjamin scolded. "And he's done nothing to deserve such poor treatment. What is this supposed flaw in an otherwise reasonably sound plan?"

"Benjamin, they'll see her."

"Who will see——?" His thumb paused in the act of brushing over Maggie's knuckles. "Bloody, perishing hell. You're right. Cecily is assembling men to inspect Bridget. They aren't very likely to content themselves with tea and crumpets when it's Bridget they've come to ogle."

"And if they *see* her, she's ruined."

He rose and went to the door, accepting a tray from Mrs. Danforth and then closing the door with his hip. "Perhaps not. Perhaps Their Graces can scotch that talk when it arises."

"Twelve spoiled, wealthy young men with titles and fortunes to waste, Benjamin? His Grace might be able to persuade one or two into silence, but twelve?" Maggie huffed out a sigh. "I wish I could endure this in Bridget's place. Half the titled families of the realm have been holding their breath for years, just waiting for me to revert to my maternal antecedents."

"You are overset." He placed the tray on the low table before them and resumed his place beside her, his expression one of resolute determination.

He passed her a cup of tea, from which she ventured one sip, while a peculiar, distracted expression came over Benjamin's face. A little patient silence stretched until he blinked and aimed a frown at her.

"You will eat something, Maggie Windham. If I have to feed it to you in small bites, you will eat."

The idea of him feeding her with his own hands... It had inordinate appeal, and now that he was here, Maggie's dyspepsia seemed to be abating.

He fed her a bite of sandwich sporting butter, mustard, thinly sliced ham, and a tangy yellow cheddar.

"I don't think the ham is agreeing with me. Something about the smokiness."

He removed the ham from the sandwich and popped the meat into his mouth. "Did you get any rest at all last night?"

"Some."

"Maggie…" He took her empty teacup and set it aside, then studied her for a long moment. "Come here."

She scooted over the few inches necessary to accept his embrace, all of her upset and misgivings going quiet at the feel of his arms around her. She would miss his embrace—miss it sorely, for all her remaining days and nights.

"It will be all right, my love. I have a plan. Shall I tell it to you?"

"Please."

When he told her *this* plan, she couldn't find a flaw in it—though she still managed to worry, right up until darkness fell and Deene took them up in his town coach.

❧

"For the love of God, hurry." Adele was flustered, and that more than anything penetrated the thick haze of anxiety clouding Bridget's mind. "Some marquis fellow has shown up nearly an hour before madam was expecting her guests—not that Polite Society ever shows up on time—and he's got some viscount in tow, and they aren't to be kept waiting."

"A marquis?" Bridget had seen a few marquises in the park or escorting their ladies about on The Strand. They were invariably old and overweight. "I hadn't realized Cecily was aiming so high."

Adele took her by the hand and pulled her over to the vanity. "We haven't time to use those awful paints, thank God, and your hair can't be too elaborate."

Bridget sat, feeling as if she were watching some nervous adolescent play a particularly ill-timed game of dress up. "Adele, I don't want to do this."

"Yes, you do. These two are both handsome as gods, my girl, and I've some acquaintance with the viscount fellow. If you can snabble the marquis, you won't have to simper and smile your way through the evening while your mother does business over the champagne punch. Be nice to the marquis—it's what your mother will expect you to do."

"Handsome has little to do with kind."

"Hold still. Listen to me, Bridget." She switched to French, shooting a particular look at the chambermaid giving Bridget's replacement gown a final pressing. "You want to meet these two lords as soon as may be, and you want to be on your best manners when you do. Your sister would want you to trust them."

Bridget blinked and studied Adele's reflection in the mirror, but Adele's eyes gave nothing away. All too soon, Bridget was standing before her mirror, her hair artfully tumbling from her crown, her powdered and scented bosom far too evident above her bodice, and her nerves as tight as fiddle strings.

"Adele, I can't do this. I don't care if Cecily does beat me. One of those men could take me home with him tonight, and the thought… I think I'm going to be sick."

Adele seized her by the shoulders and gave her a small shake. "You are going to be strong. Your mother has her guests in the small parlor, so the caterers can finish in the salon. But if you don't go down now, then Cecily will come up here. I need you to keep her down there."

Adele was trying to communicate something Bridget simply could not grasp. Tears were threatening, which would aggravate Cecily no end.

"*My sister* would expect me to trust these men?"

Adele nodded slowly once, up and down.

"Then I must trust them."

Bridget turned and left the room, seeing no alternatives—none whatsoever. She had no memory of descending the steps, but all too soon she was standing outside the door to the small parlor, her hand shaking on the latch. She tapped on the door three times—a little death knell for her virtue—then pasted a smile onto her face and swept into the room the way her mother had taught her to.

Only to stop abruptly after two strides. Adele had not lied. Two exceptionally handsome men lounged near the window, their virile, blond beauty making Cecily look exactly like what she was: an aging strumpet far past her prime, trading on nothing more than venal motives and expensive tastes.

"Miss O'Donnell." The taller of the two set his drink aside and crossed the room. "Deene, most assuredly at your service." He bowed over Bridget's hand, his expression gravely attentive. When he straightened, he paused for a moment and perused Bridget's features with a kind of mesmerizing intensity.

"Your sister will see you safe." When he spoke French, it was so beautiful to the ear. Bridget had to concentrate to extract the meaning of his words. He must have seen her befuddlement, because the blasted man did not drop her hand until he'd aimed a very solemn wink at her, as well.

Her sister... Bridget curtsied and replied in French, as well. "I'm sure that is so, my lord."

"Bridget!" Cecily's voice was shrill with false cheer. "Come meet Viscount Blessings. He is also very partial to ladies of your coloring."

Even in her innocence, Bridget had to stifle a wince. Would her mother be suggesting the gentlemen examine Bridget's teeth next?

"Madam." Lord Deene's tone was glacial. "Perhaps I was not clear, or perhaps the toll of long years in your profession has limited your understanding, so I will endeavor to speak more slowly. I came here prepared to reach an agreement with you"—he turned to Bridget—"assuming the young lady is willing?"

Bridget nodded, her heart thumping in her chest while Deene went on in insufferably condescending tones. "I will not dicker and squabble while you comport yourself like a whoremonger before such a delicate flower. Blessings, show Madam the jewels."

❧

"I used to tell Bridget to be glad her mother didn't sell her." Maggie stared out the window of Deene's elegant coach, watching the front stoop of the house Archer and Deene had disappeared into a lifetime and twenty minutes ago. "I was such an idiot."

Benjamin shifted on the bench beside her but kept hold of her hand. "When you took Cecily on, you were not much older than Bridget is now, Maggie. Bear that in mind when you're flagellating yourself for managing the best you could."

"But to think I would be more capable of dealing with Cecily than His Grace would be…" She shook her head, worry and regret trying to erode the calm she felt emanating from Benjamin.

"Her Grace made the same mistake—thought she was better situated than Moreland to deal with Cecily—if a mistake it was, and she was no match for Cecily either."

His arm came around her shoulders, and she let herself rest against him. "I hate this waiting, but I tell myself that this time next week, Bridget and I can be on our way to Italy or Portugal."

She hadn't meant to say that, but fatigue, anxiety, and the warmth and comfort of Benjamin's solid male presence had loosened her tongue.

"Hush." She felt his lips graze her temple, suggesting he was too preoccupied to heed her words. "You think Cecily will wreak revenge on you for stealing her ticket to a well-heeled old age, but I won't allow it, and Their Graces won't allow it."

"You are such a good man, Benjamin." She nuzzled the wool of his coat then turned her head to stare again at the well-lit terrace of the town house Cecily had selected for her current venture. Maggie was tempted to close her eyes, but some superstitious corner of her soul suggested if she stared hard enough, then soon she'd see Deene escorting Bridget out of that awful woman's house and into the safety of Maggie's waiting and anxious arms.

❧

Maggie was growing heavy against his side, paying the toll for sleepless nights, unrelenting anxiety, and more worry than any lady ought to have shouldered on her own, much less when she had loving family—and a devoted fiancé—to aid her.

Now was not the time to argue with her regarding her plan to whisk Bridget off to the Continent, though Ben had no intention of allowing such folly. A coach trotted past slowly enough that Ben caught a glimpse of a lacquered crest on the door, and Maggie struggled upright beside him.

"Are the vultures gathering?"

He let her ease from his side but kept her hand in his. "Not yet. No one with any sense of fashionable manners wants to be the first to arrive, so young Lord Venable will circle the block for a bit before he alights. If Cecily's guests do start to gather, we have a contingency in place."

"A plan?" She turned her head to peer at him in the dim glow of the nearby streetlight. "Even for this you had a plan?"

"You were right: no one can be allowed to see Bridget. She deserves as much chance at a decent match as any other innocent girl, so Archer sent over an evening gown sized for Adele Martin's figure. Adele is young, has red hair, and knows how to deal with amorous men."

"Adele..." Maggie smiled at him, a great, toothy benediction that warmed a man of shadows in all the best places, and then she finished the job: "Oh, Benjamin, I do love you." She cuddled into him, to every appearance unaware that she'd just uttered words to send a man's heart thundering all over inside his ribs.

She sighed mightily, and before Ben could think of a way to point out to her the enormity of her admission, the door to the town house swung open. Deene came down the steps, Bridget on his arm, Archer trailing obsequiously behind.

"Maggie, my love?"

"Hmm?"

"We've got her." He kissed her soundly on the mouth and climbed out of the coach to watch as Deene—with an unhurried casualness for which Ben would make him pay—led Bridget to the coach and handed the girl up. Subdued squeals of feminine glee issued forth, while a footman emerged from the house and, one by one, blew out every lamp on the front terrace.

"You have the documents?"

Deene handed over a ribboned sheaf of papers. "A bit of a tight moment locating another adult male of sound mind, but the butler you sent over from the employment agency eventually served in addition to Blessings. That woman is probably in there still ogling all that paste."

"And Bridget's things?"

"When you're out of sight, I'll have my footmen nip around back and fetch the trunk Adele packed."

"Have them fetch it now." Ben started off in the direction of the town house. "As soon as you have Bridget's things secure in the boot, take the women to Moreland."

"And just where the hell do you think you're going?"

"To finish a case."

When he got to the door of Cecily's town house, he didn't knock. He barged in, located the woman who'd created such mayhem in Maggie's life, and gave himself permission—just this one last time—to deal in shadows and darkness.

❧

"I don't understand." Bridget studied her older half sister, a woman she didn't know very well, for all she did love her. "You are engaged to the very man who's responsible for extricating me from Cecily's schemes, and yet you want to go to Italy?"

"I don't want to go, exactly, but I think a change of scene would do us both good." Maggie was finding something fascinating outside the window, for she surely did not meet Bridget's gaze as she offered this balderdash.

"A change of scene." Bridget glanced around at the elegant comfort of the first ducal residence she'd ever been inside. They were in some sort of small family parlor overlooking sprawling back gardens riotous with spring flowers. "I rather think this scenery quite nice."

"We're not staying here." Maggie rose from her rocking chair and started pacing. "It has only been a week, but Cecily might find us out—she will find us out, eventually—and then she'll come seeking all manner of vengeance. I don't want you here when she does."

"But you said Their Graces have custody of me. Cecily signed papers, and her signature was witnessed. I watched her sign them, too."

"Papers can be stolen or lost; Cecily can claim fraud; she can bribe one of the witnesses."

"Maggie, when did you become such a pessimist?"

This got her older sister's attention, because Maggie turned her head and peered at Bridget. "I'm not a pessimist, dear heart, but I know what Cecily is capable of."

"And is this why you won't marry your earl? Because you think she'll go after him if you do?"

Maggie, pretty, brave, competent Maggie subsided back into her chair and bowed her head. "She will. She'll stop at nothing once she understands exactly what has happened. I know this, and I've tried to tell Benjamin, but he's proud, and he's too good-hearted himself to understand what she's capable of. He doesn't listen."

"Sister?" When Maggie looked up, Bridget pointed to the large, dark, unsmiling man looming in the doorway. "I think he's listening now."

❧

Ben's intended looked so pretty sitting in a sunbeam by the window, the light picking out all the fiery highlights in her hair and bringing out the freckles dusting her cheeks.

"Miss Bridget, you are in error regarding one detail." He advanced into the room and left the door open behind him. "Their Graces are not your guardians, I am. As your legal custodian, I am ordering you to scat."

The girl blinked at him, her eyes brown instead of green, but otherwise much like Maggie's. "Scat, my lord?"

"Begone, shoo, be off with you. Your sister and I need privacy."

Bridget's lips curved up in a smile that presaged heart-stopping beauty, and then—Ben was hard put not to smile right back—she winked at him and flounced out of the room.

"I didn't know you were her guardian." Maggie's tone was considering, which was better than accusatory. Ben appropriated a seat on the end of the sofa closest to her and chose his words carefully.

In an effort not to rush his fences, he did not take her hand.

"I am hoping such an arrangement is more consistent with your wishes."

She turned to gaze out the damned window. "It will spare Their Graces a legal connection with yet another person of dubious origins, and this one not even related to His Grace."

"How are you feeling, Maggie?"

She offered him a small smile. "A little fatigued, to be honest. Events lately have been exciting."

And she hadn't gotten her courses. Ben had conferred with both Mrs. Danforth and Her Grace, and while he wanted to simply announce his impending paternity to the mother of his child—the drowsy, sometimes light-headed, occasionally queasy mother of his child—he suspected Maggie herself might not yet understand her condition.

"Will you walk with me, my dear?"

"I thought you wanted privacy."

"I do want privacy, but with you, I also want to walk in the sunshine, Maggie." She'd given him that—gotten him over the damned shadows, given him the sun.

He assisted her to her feet and did not inspect her too closely when she paused for a minute as if testing her balance. She remained silent while they wended their way through the house, past unsmiling footmen and enormous bouquets of flowers, through silent hallways scented with beeswax and lemon oil.

The silence struck Ben as peaceful, though he suspected it weighed on Maggie. He waited until they were outside, where the air was redolent of the gardens and full of the sounds of a pretty day—the distant clip-clop of traffic passing by, the warbling of birds, the hum of insects.

"You were thinking of going to Italy with Bridget?"

She nodded but had the grace to look chagrined. "You heard us. I do not trust Cecily to leave you in peace."

"Hmm. And if Cecily were not a factor?"

"May I at least suffer this interrogation sitting down?" A spark of her old spirit crackled through her words.

"Of course." He led her to a bench behind a convenient privet hedge and resisted mightily the urge to plead his case with kisses and caresses. He'd spoken the truth earlier—between him and Maggie, the truth in all its forms was going to have to serve. The kisses were honest, but they weren't enough to build a marriage on such as Maggie's parents enjoyed.

And he wanted nothing less for himself, *or for her.*

When they were side-by-side on a bench in a quiet little scent garden, Ben did allow himself to take Maggie's hand. "Italy, Maggie?"

She did not withdraw her hand—and she still sported his ring.

"Italy or even France, given Bridget's facility with the language. I want peace, Benjamin, for myself, for her, but also for you and Their Graces. There has been drama enough, and I know Cecily. I get some of my determination from her, my preoccupation with money, my unwillingness to trust."

"And if I told you she's right now on a ship headed for Baltimore, would you say you'd gotten this sudden need to travel from her?"

She frowned as if trying to place it on the map. "Baltimore?"

"I have a proposal for you to consider, Maggie Windham, not a proposal of marriage—that offer is still quite valid—but one regarding your future."

"I suppose I must listen."

She smoothed her skirts with one hand, the picture of a lady at her leisure. But the other hand, the one wearing Ben's ring, was clutching his fingers more tightly than she likely realized.

"You can be like Cecily—independent, insecure all your days, leaning on nothing and nobody, seeing all in your path as either people out to exploit you or people you can exploit. She gave birth to you, and it's reasonable to think you might share some of her characteristics."

This did not sit well with Maggie. Ben knew it in the way her luscious mouth flattened and her gorgeous eyes filled with distaste. "Go on."

"Or you can decide that your heritage comes far more from your ducal family. You are as closely related to Moreland as you are to Cecily, and he and his duchess had the raising of you. For the past quarter century you've been a Windham, Maggie, and I think that a far more convincing legacy."

She blinked and stared hard at a bed of lily of the valley just starting to bloom across from them. "I kept secrets from my family, from both of my families. Sometimes it felt like nobody knew me—really knew me—at all, as if I were a living shade. It was the best I could do, though."

The tension inside Ben relaxed just a fraction to hear her admit this. She'd done the best she could, alone, with the very few weapons and only the assets a single lady could wield, and without allies to speak of.

He withdrew a sheaf of papers from an inside pocket. "These are yours."

She frowned and took them from his hand. "What are they?"

"Letters from Bridget to you. I haven't read them, but I assume they are what Cecily had stolen from your reticule, and I'm all but certain she directed Bridget to sign them 'your loving little sister' or something equally inconvenient."

Maggie bent over the letters a little, just a small shift in her spine and a downward tipping of her chin, as if absorbing a blow. "Thank you for these, but how did you acquire them?"

"I parlayed with Cecily, and we reached an agreement."

"Oh, Benjamin. You cannot trust that woman. She'll slink away for a time—she left me in peace for a time—and then she'll strike when you least expect it. She's devious, she's underhanded, she's—"

He put two fingers over her lips. "She's gone. I understand devious and underhanded behavior, Maggie. I very nearly consigned myself to a purgatory filled with it until you gave me a choice."

"Cecily will take those choices away." Her grip on Ben's hand was nearly painful, and in her voice he heard a wealth of unshed tears.

"Cecily will never set foot on British soil again, my love. If she does, I will have her committed for the unfortunate loss of reason often resulting from a life dedicated too entirely to vice for too long."

He did not want to speak the word "syphilis" aloud, but with a mad king on the throne and many suspecting the affliction had a venereal origin, Maggie would easily make the connection.

She frowned at their joined hands. "I suspect she was losing her reason. Bridget has confirmed the same. She was obsessed and getting worse. All the moving about, the dresses appropriate only to a coquette." She fell silent.

"You are not to pity her. She left with a bank draft adequate to sustain a modest lifestyle for years to come. Moreover, a few of the jewels in that cache of paste were real. If she's smart, she can attach herself to some aging Colonial of means and live comfortably all the rest of her days."

"Why some real jewels?"

"To ensure the contract was binding, but Westhaven wrote much of the description of the financial consideration in French. It lists jewelry, both genuine and for costume purposes. I did explain this to her."

Maggie was staring hard at the lily of the valley again. "You should not have undertaken all of this,

Benjamin. I love you for rescuing Bridget. I hate that you had to deal with Cecily so directly."

This was a delicate moment, an important moment, and while Ben wanted to get down on his knees before his intended—the way he should have weeks ago—there was more he needed to say, more Maggie needed to hear.

"And yet you dealt with Cecily for years. Without any to aid you and for the sake of a girl you might have turned your back on, you took on that viper and did all that was necessary to protect Bridget, Their Graces, your siblings—some of whom were decorated cavalry, another was skilled in law, and yet *you protected them*. This is not how the daughter of a scheming courtesan acts, Maggie."

She hunched over again, more tightly this time, and made a sound, a wretched, undignified sound, but Ben wasn't finished. "It is the behavior of a woman who holds herself to ducal standards. The dukes of old led armies, Maggie, but you had only yourself, and yet you prevailed."

She was shaking now, her eyes closed, her hand cutting off the circulation to Ben's fingers, but he could not stop.

"I love you, Maggie *Windham*. I love your courage, I love your independence, I love your determination, and I want it for my own." He paused and gathered his own courage. "I want—I pray—that our children take after their mother."

The words took an instant to penetrate the emotion wracking the woman beside him, a silent, fraught moment during which Ben's hopes and dreams, his very heart and soul hung suspended between the light of hope and the shadow of despair.

"Benjamin." She pitched into him, right there in the sunshine, sobbing and clinging and bawling for all the world to see. "Hold me, please. Hold me and never let me go, not ever. Not for anything."

He held her, but he did shift so he was on his knees before her, his arms wrapped around her while she shed more tears and clung for more long, lovely minutes as Ben fished for his handkerchief and thanked a merciful God for a woman brave enough to know when she was loved.

"I wanted to tell you." Maggie was smiling now, and when he pulled back enough to appreciate that fact, she started toying with the hair at his nape.

"Tell me what?"

Her fingers went still. "You never miss a detail, Benjamin. Surely you knew when I nearly fainted at Lady Dandridge's…?"

He rose and dusted off his knees, then resumed his place beside her—right smack beside her. "You'd been wandering in the rain for God knows how long, missing sleep, and likely doing without proper sustenance. If every woman who laced her stays too tightly were carrying, the population would shortly double."

"Benjamin, we are going to have a baby. I should have told you this sooner, but I did not want you to feel trapped."

She was back to smoothing her skirts and gripping his hand, suggesting she hadn't composed herself quite as quickly as appearances might indicate.

"Maggie, do you feel trapped?" It was a sincere

question, the sort of sincere question that kept a sincere man up late of a night and might cause him more than one pang in years to come.

"By the child? Of course not."

Or it might not. "You want this child?"

"Gracious God, Benjamin. I spent years dealing with Cecily because Bridget was mine to love. I've protected my ducal family because they were mine to love. This child is mine to love, and you are mine to love. How could you think I'd feel otherwise?"

"We are going to have to watch this tendency of yours to protect all whom you love."

She smiled a little sheepishly. "I want a big family, but we're getting a rather late start on things."

"Then we'll just have to be diligent about it."

His Maggie—his brave, independent, determined, and very loving Maggie—blushed.

And then he *had* to kiss her. He scooped her across his lap, planted his mouth on hers, and there before God, the birds, and probably the duke, the duchess, assorted siblings, and a few dozen servants spying from various windows, he kissed his future countess in the bright sunshine for all to see.

Lady Louisa's Christmas Knight

COMING OCTOBER 2012
FROM SOURCEBOOKS CASABLANCA

SIR JOSEPH CARRINGTON ACQUIRED TWO BOON COMPAN-ions after doing his part to rout the Corsican. Carrington was accounted by no one to be a stupid man, and he understood the comfort of the flask—his first source of consolation—to be a dubious variety of friendship.

His second more sanguine source of company was the Lady Ophelia, whose acquaintance Carrington had made shortly after mustering out. She, of the kind eyes and patient silences, had provided him much wise counsel and comfort, and that she consistently had litters of at least ten piglets both spring and autumn could only endear her to him further.

"I don't see why you should be the one moping." Sir Joseph scratched the place behind Lady Opie's left ear that made her go calm and quiet beneath his hand. "You may remain here in the country, leading poor Roland on the mating dance while I must away to London."

Where Sir Joseph would be the one being led on that same blighted dance. Thank God for the enthu-siasm of local hunt. It preserved a man from at least a few weeks of the collective lunacy that was Polite Society as the Yuletide holidays approached.

"I'll be back by Christmas, and perhaps this year Father Christmas will leave me a wife to take my own little dears in hand."

He took a nip of his flask—a small nip. Unless he spent hours in the saddle or hours tramping the woods with his fowling piece, or a snow storm was approaching, or a cold snap, his leg did not pain him too awfully much—usually.

⁂

"The little season is a great pain in my backside."

Lady Louisa Windham didn't bother keeping her voice down. She was riding in at the back of the third flight along with her sister Genevieve, to whom it was always safe to grumble.

"We've missed all but the last two weeks of it," Jenny pointed out. "Thank God for Papa and his hunt madness."

From Jenny, that was an admission that she too did not look forward to the impending, though blessedly brief, remove back to Town.

"It's like hunting grouse," Louisa said, letting her mount drop back farther from the other riders ambling toward the hunt breakfast. "Lent ends, and the husband hunting begins, the mamas beating their charges forward into the waiting guns virtually until Town empties out for the holidays. I don't know how many more years of this I can take, Jenny."

"I don't relish two weeks in Town either," Jenny said at length. "We sit about in the same parlors we sat about in all spring, trying to pretend we're only a little envious of the ladies now married or engaged who were not spoken for in the spring. And yet, in some way, we *are* only a little envious when we're supposed to be torn up with it."

"I am torn up with the entire pretense."

"You've been at it a little longer than Evie or I. You're entitled."

Jenny could be counted on for such kindness. She was truly good, truly kind, things Louisa had long since stopped aspiring to. Jenny had willowy blond good looks to go with her sunny disposition, while Louisa, appropriately enough, had throw-back dark hair to go with eyes closer to agate than green.

"Ladies."

Sir Joseph Carrington came up on Louisa's left mounted on a raw-boned black gelding, one suited to the rider's own dark coloring and somber turnout.

Louisa and Jenny greeted him civilly. He was a neighbor, after all and he'd served on the Peninsula with their brothers Devlin St. Just and the late Lord Bartholomew Windham. Just because the man sported a mere knighthood and raised pigs was no excuse to be rude.

"Louisa, Sir Joseph, if you'll excuse me, I promised to help with the breakfast."

Lady Jenny smiled at Sir Joseph and cantered off, abandoning her sister to the pig farmer's company without a backward glance.

Even the truly good had limits to their generosity.

"I've a question for you, Lady Louisa."

Acknowledgments

Writing is usually a solitary activity. Not only does an author spend months drafting material while sitting alone before the computer, but she also spends long hours walking the countryside, driving from coast to coast, and making burnt offerings to the gods of external conflict, all without much companionship.

And while I have a great capacity for enjoying solitude, I am never lonely as a writer, because the team at Sourcebooks, from our publisher Dominique Raccah, to my editor Deb Werksman, to all the "book people"—Skye, Susie, Cat, Danielle, Madam Copy Editor, Madam Proofreader, my fellow Casablanca authors, and countless others—is just a phone call or email away and sometimes closer than that.

These are not *my* books, and the Windham siblings' stories are not *my* stories. These stories belong to you, as the reader, and they belong to the Sourcebooks publishing team members, without whom these tales would never see the light of day. I think this sense of cooperative endeavor informs the mutual regard my characters feel toward each other and is reflected in the writing in intangible ways.

In any case, I'm grateful to be part of such a team. Writing is a pleasure. Writing with that much capable support is a pleasure and a privilege.

About the Author

New York Times and *USA Today* bestselling author Grace Burrowes hit the bestseller lists with both her debut, *The Heir*, and her second book in The Duke's Obsession trilogy, *The Soldier*. Both books received extensive praise and glowing reviews from *Publishers Weekly* and *Booklist*. *The Heir* was also named a Publishers Weekly Best Book of 2010, and *The Soldier* was named a Publishers Weekly Best Spring Romance of 2011. She is hard at work on stories for the five Windham sisters, the first of which, *Lady Sophie's Christmas Wish*, is already on the shelves, along with *The Virtuoso*, the story of Valentine, the third Windham brother. Grace is a practicing attorney specializing in family law and lives in rural Maryland.

Grace loves to hear from her readers and can be reached through her website at www.graceburrowes.com.